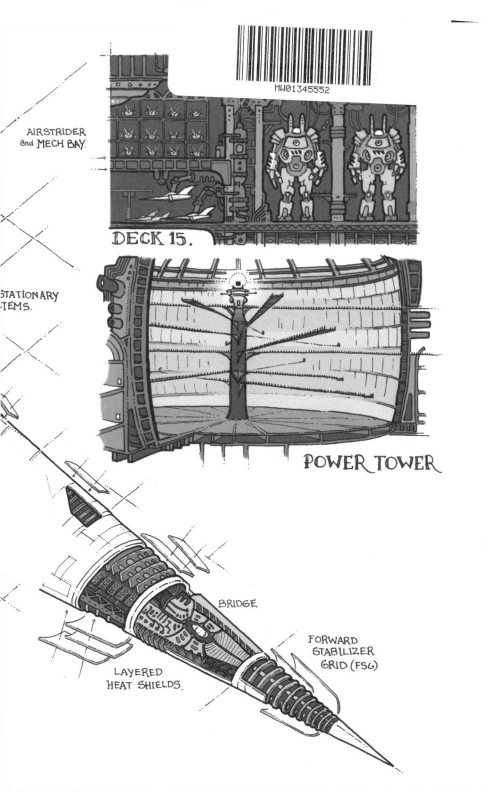

THE INCREDIBLE ORIGINS
OF THE
ONYX SUN

Kalamazoo!

THE INCREDIBLE ORIGINS OF THE
ONYX SUN

CHRISTOPHER MAHONEY

PARIAH
PUBLISHING

Use the Launch Code found at the back of this book to access special features at *www.onyxsun.com,* including games, upcoming book previews, and an editable version of the text!

Text copyright © 2009 by Christopher Mahoney
Illustrations by Rudy Hall copyright © 2009 Pariah Publishing
All rights reserved. Published by Pariah Publishing.
Empowering authors through new media
PARIAH PUBLISHING and the I LOGO are trademarks
and/or registered trademarks of Pariah Publishing LLC.

The ONYX SUN and all related characters and elements
are trademarks of Christopher Mahoney.

No part of this publication may be reproduced or transmitted in any form or by any means, electronic or mechanical, including photocopying, recording, or by any information storage and retrieval system, without written permission from the publisher. For information contact Pariah Publishing
info@pariahpublishing.com

Educators and librarians, for a variety of teaching tools and in-class activities, visit www.onyxsun.com/teachers

This book is set in 12-point Adobe Garamond.
ISBN 978-0-9795202-5-9
Printed in the United States of America.

Kalamazoo!

For my son and illuminating inspiration, Aiden James.

CONTENTS

Prologue:	**The Origin of Unlimited Power**	xi
Chapter 1:	**How Strange Things Started**	1
Chapter 2:	**The Secrets of the Labradory**	14
Chapter 3:	**A Girl Called Max**	25
Chapter 4:	**Grandfather Disappears**	29
Chapter 5:	**Angelina's Secret**	36
Chapter 6:	**The Red Button**	41
Chapter 7:	**The Spinning Shaft**	49
Chapter 8:	**The Burning Beams**	52
Chapter 9:	**The Shuttle of Great Distance**	58
Chapter 10:	**The Dastardly Death**	63
Chapter 11:	**The Clarion Spacedock**	71
Chapter 12:	**An Unlikely Adventure**	73
Chapter 13:	**The Great Hall**	81
Chapter 14:	**Firelight of the Onyx Pioneer**	91
Chapter 15:	**The Onyx Swordfish**	98

Chapter 16:	**To Points Unknown**	105
Chapter 17:	**The Citadel Spire**	114
Chapter 18:	**The Aitken Basin**	120
Chapter 19:	**Machvel's Ambitions**	126
Chapter 20:	**Explosion on the Onyx Pioneer**	134
Chapter 21:	**The Battle for the Onyx Sun**	145
Chapter 22:	**The Miracle Mechs**	149
Chapter 23:	**Strange Properties of the Onyx Sun**	161
Chapter 24:	**The Desperate Plan**	173
Chapter 25:	**Explorations**	186
Chapter 26:	**Moon Walk**	203
Chapter 27:	**Mech Battle**	210
Chapter 28:	**Spy Games**	223
Chapter 29:	**Following the Trail**	237
Chapter 30:	**The Academy**	245
Chapter 31:	**Unspoken Hints**	251
Chapter 32:	**Machvel's Pyramid**	268
Chapter 33:	**Goodbyes**	279
Chapter 34:	**Homecoming**	296
Epilogue:	**The Dawn of War**	305

THE INCREDIBLE ORIGINS
── OF THE ──
ONYX SUN

PROLOGUE

The Origin of Unlimited Power

Fyodor Confucius Goodspeed had always been rather unusual. Even as a child, he had been a ridiculously lanky lad with pale skin, like tissue paper. His head had produced a wild tuft of hair that sprouted from his scalp like a weed. Otherwise, he was completely bald from the moment he was born, all through his life. It was like his cranium generated so much heat it singed the hair from his head. Fyodor had always dressed entirely in white, claiming he had neither the time nor the patience to match what he wore any other way.

Fyodor's most notable difference though was his genius, a word that literally means "unusual intelligence." He used his overwhelming mental capacity to build machines from a young age. Sources of energy were his specialty and, around age seven, he built his first nuclear reactor. Over his parents' gasps at the glowing monstrosity on his bedspread, he commented, "Well, that was easy."

So, as his parents scoured the phonebook for a company specializing in residential atomic reactor removal, Fyodor took out a blank piece of paper and started fresh. He had entirely new ideas how to power things.

Fyodor unveiled his new thinking at the Fourth Grade Science Fair. While other young scientists in the school's gymnasium displayed erupting volcanoes, model rockets, and gyroscopes, Fyodor unveiled a five-inch-wide, by five-inch-tall, by five-inch-long cube. The cube was dark and featureless. It looked like a perfectly cut square of black onyx. Black onyx is a type of stone so dark staring into it is like staring into a void. That was how Fyodor's cube looked: it was a small, perfectly square, infinite void.

Mr. Burton, the school's fourth grade science teacher, stretched his plump cheeks to smile at Fyodor's project.

"Well Fy," said Mr. Burton, using Fyodor's nickname. "It seems that you have entered a rock into the Science Fair. Are you presenting geology?"

"It's not a rock. It's an energy source," Fyodor said plainly.

Mr. Burton laughed, "An energy source! How could that be? It's clearly a rock — a very interesting rock — but a rock regardless. Did you shape it yourself? Do you have a rock chisel around here?"

"No, I don't. Rock cutting is for bozos. This is an energy source. It provides unlimited power."

"Fy," said Mr. Burton, his fat cheeks flattening, "This is a Science Fair, not an Imagination Fair. I'll enter your submission as 'The Onyx Rock: a Rock Cutting Example by Fy Goodspeed.' I'm sure you will do quite well in the fair, although rock cutting certainly won't win first place." He wrote something on the tablet he carried.

PROLOGUE: THE ORIGIN OF UNLIMITED POWER

"It's not a rock," Fyodor insisted. "It is the single smallest, but most powerful, source of energy on Earth. It can power a jet by itself, no fuel needed. It can provide renewable power to a large city. It can even run in a vacuum, like space, without any oxygen. It never runs out of energy yet it produces no pollution! I call it the Onyx Sun." A small smile of pride crossed Fyodor's lips.

Mr. Burton squinted down at Fyodor through fleshy eye slits. His eyes flashed with frustration. "Fy, keep this up and I'll have to give you a zero," he said. "Now, is it a rock or is it a source of unlimited power?"

Fyodor held his teacher's gaze. After a long moment, he plucked the cube from the table and strode down the aisles of exhibits. He approached Tim Cleatus, who was demonstrating to a large crowd how a gas-powered go-kart works.

"This is the fuel tank," Tim was saying, using a metal pointer to identify the object. "It's currently empty since they wouldn't let me bring gasoline to school."

Fyodor pushed Tim aside, cut through the crowd, and ripped a wire from the go-kart's engine.

"Hey! What are you doing?" Tim cried, trying futilely to push people aside.

Fyodor turned to face Mr. Burton at the far end of the gymnasium. Everyone watched. Fyodor held the wire up in the air in one hand and the Onyx Sun in the other. As he brought his hands together, a blue bolt of electricity arced from the cube to the wire. The wire leapt toward the cube like it was a magnet and stuck to its side. Fyodor reached down and pressed the ignition button.

The go-kart engine roared to life. People stepped back. Tim Cleatus stopped in his tracks. Mr. Burton let the tablet fall to his side, his mouth wide open.

"It *is* a source of unlimited power," Fyodor said. He stared at the crowd staring back at him. Then, he shrugged. Fyodor hopped into the go-kart, revved the engine, and raced toward the back of the gymnasium. Students and teachers leapt out of the way. He burst through the emergency exit doors leaving behind a sea of open mouths under a fog of blue tire smoke.

That was the last day Fyodor Confucius Goodspeed attended normal school.

CHAPTER 1

How Strange Things Started

Eleven-year-old Zack Goodspeed curled a baseball in his hand behind his back. He loved this moment at the end of close games. The score was seven-seven. Runners on first and third. Bottom of the ninth. And he was pitching.

Zack looked at the boy at home plate. Tommy Johnson. Tommy was one of those boys kids called "runt" on the playground. It should be easy to sneak a slider by him, Zack thought. Between his unusual height for his age and his position atop the pitcher's mound, Zack had gained a lot of confidence as the team's starting pitcher. He had won so many Little League games that by now he usually threw the entire game and, more often than not, won.

Zack checked the runners on the corners. They glanced back at him, both leading well off their bases. No matter, Zack thought. This game will be over in three pitches. Zack pulled off his cap, ran a hand through his mess of blond hair, and wiped his brow. Then, he pulled the cap back on, positioning the brim just above his eyes.

Zack kicked his leg in the air as his grandfather had shown him. He wound back. But the moment before he released the ball, a bright flash blinded him.

Zack twisted as he threw, trying awkwardly to shield his eyes with his glove-hand. He stumbled on the mound. The ball slipped from his hand. Zack gasped.

He squinted at home plate as the ball arced toward Tommy. The pitch was too slow and right over the plate. Tommy pulled the bat back and walloped the ball. Zack shot upright as the baseball spun into the heavens. For a second, it looked like it might touch the midday moon just on the horizon. But the ball descended and landed — just beyond the fences.

"Home run!" shouted the away team's coach. His squad leapt from the benches. Several of them threw their hats in the air.

Zack was furious. He whipped around to home plate to search for the source of the flash and saw something flicker in the sky. Zack looked to see if anyone else saw it. The away team was too busy watching their runners round the bases. Most of Zack's team had their heads hung in shame.

Zack looked back. It was gone. There was nothing in the sky but blue.

Zack's close friend Andy Lee strode by him.

"You see that flash?" Zack asked.

"What flash?"

"The one in the sky. Just now."

"Is that your excuse? Zack, that pitch was awful."

"It's not an excuse."

CHAPTER 1: HOW STRANGE THINGS STARTED

"Sure. Hey, don't worry about it. It was only a semi-final. I didn't really want to go to the finals anyway. Now, there's more time for my kid brother to annoy me all summer. Yippee."

Andy strode off. Zack's coach walked up to him and gave him a pep talk about the difference between winners and losers. Zack half-listened. He wanted to be home. Finally, his coach walked away. Zack packed his glove into his backpack and grabbed his bike. A couple of his teammates shot him accusatory glances as he rode away. Zack was embarrassed. He rode faster.

The baseball field was only a few blocks from home. So, before long, he was outside his house. Zack's house was a two-story brick building similar to all the other houses on the street. Well, similar to every one, that was, except his grandfather Fyodor's house next door.

Professor Goodspeed's house stood out like a sore thumb that had been hammered on several times. In fact, many neighbors would have nodded if you referred to it as a "sore house." Although its structure was similar to the other houses on the street, Grandfather's domicile had an unusual amount of gizmos attached to it.

A gigantic wind turbine stood in the front yard mounted on a towering white pillar. Grandfather had once told Zack this powered the entire house and detached garage. Large trenches extended from the roof and funneled into an intricate system of drainage pipes. These pipes wound around the house, like multi-colored party streamers, until they ended in a yellow silo on the front lawn. A series of black lights surrounded the silo and beamed ultraviolet light into the yellow basin. Zack had helped his grandfather design this system. So, he knew it could capture rainwater and sterilize it for use in bathing, dishwashing, gargling — anything. The roof of Fyodor's house was also quite a sight. It had an exaggerated sloping shape with gigantic flanges sweeping in all directions. Professor Goodspeed told Zack this roof saved him considerable energy by shading his house all day long. Zack thought it looked like a gigantic pancake had fallen out of the sky.

To the Zoning Board of the town, Grandfather Goodspeed's house was simultaneously something to be marveled at and feared, like a dinosaur trapped in a glassware convention. And with equal caution, they avoided it, despite the complaints.

Zack however was used to the house. It almost seemed normal to him. Besides baseball, inventing was Zack's favorite pastime, and he looked at his grandfather's house as most kids might look at a waterslide park: an opportunity for fun and adventure.

Zack dismounted his bike and walked toward his garage. His father was outside watering his prized rose bushes. He waved as Zack stepped onto the driveway.

As Zack passed the fence separating his yard from his grandfather's, he noticed something strange. The Professor's garbage bins peeked around the side of the fence. Zack thought this was unusual given it was Saturday. Since one of his chores was taking out the trash, Zack knew the garbage trucks only came on Tuesday.

Zack strode around the fence with his bike. Suddenly, it was like the sun had slipped behind a cloud, even though it was a cloudless day. Zack found himself dwarfed by a massive airplane wing shooting into the sky, like a skyscraper, yet jammed into Professor Goodspeed's crushed garbage can.

Zack stepped back. What was his grandfather up to now? A bloom of curiosity sprouted in his chest. Zack leaned his bike against the fence. He had to go next door and find out. Before he could leave though, his father called him.

"Don't bother, Zack. He's not home."

"Really?" Zack called back. "Again?"

"Yep," his father sighed. "I just knocked. Haven't seen him for about a week. Must be off 'inventing' something again."

CHAPTER 1: HOW STRANGE THINGS STARTED

The way Zack's father said 'inventing' it sounded like a sin. Zack had long known his father and grandfather didn't get along. Professor Goodspeed was a wild train-wreck of emotion and energy, while Zack's father was just…dad. Mr. Goodspeed stood about five-foot eleven, had fair skin, and possessed a well-maintained mat of brown hair. Each weekday, he worked at McKinley Bank & Trust downtown, at the corner of Main Street and First Avenue. He had no time for inventions or flights of fantasy. He was focused on things like profit margins, stock options, and compound annual interest — none of which Zack understood. Not because he couldn't, but because no matter how many times Mr. Goodspeed explained these concepts, Zack fell asleep.

Mr. Goodspeed grunted to himself. He pulled a handkerchief from his pocket and cleaned his wire-framed glasses, which already looked meticulously clean to Zack.

Zack plucked his bike from the fence and walked it toward the garage. A rumbling boom sounded overhead.

"Sounds like thunder," Mr. Goodspeed said.

Zack looked up. There wasn't a cloud in the sky still. How could it be thunder?

Just then, Zack heard a loud whistling noise. It grew louder. Mr. Goodspeed looked up from his roses.

"What the heck is that-"

Before Mr. Goodspeed could finish his sentence, a gigantic jet engine slammed onto his rosebushes, inches away from his toes. For a second, Mr. Goodspeed stood there, mouth open, sprinkling the smoking motor with the water hose. Then, he stumbled back, grunting several times nervously. He dropped the hose and called for Zack's mother.

"Jen! Something incredible just happened!"

When she didn't appear, Mr. Goodspeed leapt up the front steps and into the house.

"Jen, you'll never believe this! I think an airliner just crashed. Turn on the TV. Call the police!"

Zack stepped up to the engine. He had never seen one like this before. While most engines Zack had seen on planes were round, this one was wide and flat. It had a grill on the front and a tapered exhaust in the back. It looked much more…modern…to Zack.

"Zack Goodspeed, get inside," yelled his mother. "There's no telling what else might fall from the sky. Up to your room young man, until we figure out what's going on."

Zack thought about arguing with his mother but knew when she used that tone of voice there was no negotiation. He dropped his bike in the front yard and walked up to his room. He showered and changed, then lay on his bed tossing a baseball in the air. Zack left his door open so he could hear his parents downstairs. They called the police, the fire department, the hospital, even the National Guard.

After twenty minutes, Zack heard sirens approaching. He stood up and went to his door. The downstairs was bathed in flickering red and blue light. Zack snuck down a few stairs so he could see what was going on. Someone knocked on the front door. He saw his mother scurry to open it.

"Yeah, someone called in a plane crash?" the policeman at the door said.

"Yes, sir, we did," his mother replied.

Zack's father emerged from the kitchen looking a little pale.

"I saw it myself, officer. Part of a plane fell straight out of the sky."

The police officer looked back and forth at Mr. and Mrs. Goodspeed. He looked doubtful and a little perturbed.

"Sir, where did it land?"

"Right in my front yard!" Mr. Goodspeed said. "Didn't you see it?"

"No sir."

CHAPTER 1: HOW STRANGE THINGS STARTED

"What? That's not possible," Mr. Goodspeed said. He pushed the officer and Mrs. Goodspeed aside as he darted from the house. The policeman and Mrs. Goodspeed followed him into the front yard. Zack slipped down the stairs and leaned out the front door. The front yard was full of police cars, fire trucks, and ambulances but no jet engine. Where the engine had landed nothing seemed out of the ordinary. Mr. Goodspeed's rosebushes stood there, as if nothing had happened.

"I don't believe it," Mr. Goodspeed said. "I can't believe it."

"Jack, are you all right?" Mrs. Goodspeed asked.

"Jen, it was right here. Right here!"

"There's nothing there now, hon."

"But I'm not lying."

Mr. Goodspeed glanced up at Zack and squealed, "Zack saw it too!"

"Honey, did you see a plane crash?" Mrs. Goodspeed asked.

Zack felt conflicted. He had clearly seen an engine fall from the sky and almost crush his father. But now, there was no evidence that had happened. Everything looked as it had before the event, except for the dozen or so police and firemen scratching their heads on his front lawn. Some were laughing at his father. Zack felt embarrassed.

"I'm not sure what I saw," Zack said. Mr. Goodspeed looked crestfallen so Zack hastily added, "But there was something there."

"I don't believe it," Mr. Goodspeed whispered, staring at his bushes. Then, he cocked his head to the side.

"Wait a second," he said. He walked up to the bushes. He grabbed one bud and rolled it around in his hand. He smelled it. Then, his eyes shot open.

"Wait. These aren't my roses!"

"All right. I've had enough of this," the policeman said.

"No, really. I'd know my roses anywhere. They got top prize at the Rose Parade last year."

"Do you know misreporting an emergency is a crime?" the policeman said. "They can put you away for something like this."

"But I didn't do anything. An engine fell out of the sky and landed-"

"I know, on your bushes," the policeman said, pulling a tablet from his shirt pocket. He started writing on it. He tore off a sheet and handed it to Mrs. Goodspeed.

"What's this?" she asked.

"A ticket for disturbing the peace. You can show up to contest it in court or pay it. Trust me. Pay it. I'm being easy on you. Night."

The policeman strode off the porch and signaled for the fire trucks and police cars in the yard to back out.

Mr. Goodspeed looked thunderstruck. Mrs. Goodspeed gently put her arm around him and guided him into the house.

"Jen, I swear. I saw it."

"I know honey. Let's just go inside."

"Zack saw it too."

"Jack, the neighbors are watching," Mrs. Goodspeed said, her voice strained. She forced a smile and waved to Mrs. Cavendish next door who did not wave back. Mrs. Goodspeed led her husband inside.

Zack let them pass then stepped onto the yard. He watched the emergency vehicles leave and the neighbors head back into their houses. Once things were relatively calm, he walked up to the rosebushes. They looked just like Mr. Goodspeed's bushes, but Zack thought all roses looked the same.

Zack felt something cold and wet touch his bare feet. He squatted down and looked at the sidewalk bordering the bushes. A dark, wet liquid seeped from the ground. Zack touched it and rolled it around in his fingers. It felt slippery, like oil. Zack leaned in closer to the bushes. Even though night was falling, Zack thought the mulch around the rosebushes looked newer than the mulch around the rest of the plants.

CHAPTER 1: HOW STRANGE THINGS STARTED

Zack grabbed a handful under the roses. It was damp. He touched the mulch under another bush. Bone-dry.

Zack caught a flicker out of the corner of his eye. He turned to his right and for the briefest second thought he saw something in the top story window of his grandfather's house.

"Zack, come inside. It's getting late," called his mother.

Zack stood and brushed his hands off. Something wasn't right here. He looked at his grandfather's house, but he saw nothing else. The house looked derelict, as it usually did. Zack thought his father was right. His grandfather was probably off on one of his inventing adventures again. Maybe he had imagined the movement in Grandfather's house, Zack thought, but the mulch was real.

"Zack. Inside. Now," his mother said coming to the door.

Zack opened his mouth to tell his mother about what he'd found, but he could instantly tell she was still in no mood for discussions. He walked up the stairs. Zack looked around one last time before he went inside. Everything looked normal. It felt anything but.

The next morning, Zack sat at the kitchen table observing his family.

Zack's mother was busy pan-frying eggs, which she did every Sunday. Zack's father reclined in a chair opposite Zack, reading the local newspaper which he also did every Sunday. Mr. Goodspeed grunted to himself.

"Strange. No articles on nearby airplane crashes," he mumbled between page turns.

Zack huffed as he slumped over the kitchen table, brushing his hands in wide wipes across its surface. Boring, he thought. Would things ever change around here? Zack wondered. He knew if his grandfather were around he would be entertained by Fyodor's strange inventions and wild imagination. Grandfather Goodspeed was a rollercoaster of energy and emotion. Zack seldom found his company boring as he concocted daring plans to build bigger and better inventions. Zack was sure his grandfather would have all kinds of abstract theories about last night's events.

The only problem, Zack thought, huffing again, was that Grandfather often left him for long periods of time. One moment, Zack and Grandfather would be inventing crazy machines in Grandfather's garage laboratory; the next, Zack would be knocking on his front door for hours to no response. It was a mystery to Zack how Grandfather could so easily whisk himself in and out of his life. Zack found himself increasingly baffled and frustrated each time Grandfather vanished.

Zack was about to go to his room when the kitchen door burst open and a ridiculously tall man, dressed entirely in white, stumbled inside. Zack shot upright in his seat. The familiar sensations of joy and frustration welled in his stomach, as he realized his grandfather was back.

Fyodor Confucius Goodspeed, as an adult, looked like a stork that had been stretched and, five minutes later, stretched again. He towered over most people at six feet, six inches tall. He was a stringy man built "thin as a rail," as they say. The abnormality of his figure was emphasized by the fact Fyodor Goodspeed wore only white. He wore white trousers and white shoes. He had white socks and a white button-down shirt. Over this, he donned a white vest and matching white sport coat. He still had a single tuft of white hair that clung to his scalp like a wild bush to a cliff. He resembled a stork that had been washed in bleach and then, five minutes later, bleached again. People often commented on Grandfather Goodspeed during the rare occasion when he ambled through town. They pointed and laughed, while looking for a pair of sunglasses to put on. He was a bright alabaster pillar, but he moved like a man who had just learned to walk.

CHAPTER 1: HOW STRANGE THINGS STARTED

Grandfather Goodspeed slammed into the door, as he tried to shut it. Stumbling backwards, he caught his balance long enough to throw it closed and whirl around to face his family.

Neither Mr. Goodspeed nor Mrs. Goodspeed looked up. Mr. Goodspeed grunted and slowly turned the page of his newspaper. Mrs. Goodspeed continued frying eggs. Zack, however, smiled at his grandfather, suppressing his momentary frustrations.

"Well Kalamazoo," Grandfather Goodspeed said, adjusting his rectangular spectacles, which held two cracked lenses. "Glad to see nothing's changed around here."

Fyodor winked at Zack and ruffled his wild, blond hair. Zack had to cover his mouth to avoid laughing aloud. Grandfather's joke eased some of Zack's tension. Fyodor jittered over to a chair at the breakfast table.

"What's news son?" he said slapping Mr. Goodspeed on the back.

Mr. Goodspeed looked stunned at being addressed in this manner. The back slap had caused a strand of hair to fall across his forehead, and he used a slow gesture to return it to its proper place.

"Father," Mr. Goodspeed said. "Was there something wrong with the door, or is it still a convention you have not mastered?"

"Ah," Grandfather Goodspeed said, leaning back in his chair and crossing his long twig legs. "See, a door is built with two purposes: to open and to close. As long as my efforts achieve one of those two results, then I believe I have successfully operated the door." He pointed at the closed door. "Exhibit A."

"Intriguing," Mr. Goodspeed replied, wrinkling his lips and pushing his glasses up the bridge of his nose. "Some people think a certain form should be maintained in the process."

Grandfather Goodspeed rolled his eyes, spun a finger around his ear, and then pointed at Mr. Goodspeed. Zack laughed. Mr. Goodspeed, catching this motion out of the corner of his eye, scowled. He turned a page in his paper with a crinkle and a grunt. Grandfather shot out of his chair, crossed the kitchen in one giant step, and gave Mrs. Goodspeed a big kiss on her cheek.

"And how is my favorite daughter-in-law?" he said.

Mrs. Goodspeed squirmed away from him, smiling weakly. She scurried to the table, dumping two undercooked eggs on Mr. Goodspeed's plate.

"Fine, thank you," she said.

Grandfather beamed at her. Then, sensing her indifference, he threw his hands in the air and shook his head at Zack.

Mr. Goodspeed neatly folded his paper and set it aside. Picking up a fork, he pushed his undercooked eggs around his plate. He frowned at them. Looking up and putting down his fork, he said, "What brings you over this morning, Father?"

"As opposed to any other morning? Why, to see my family of course."

Both Mr. and Mrs. Goodspeed shot him doubtful glances.

"All right," Grandfather said. "I came over to see if my grandson would like to play a game of baseball."

"Yes! Can I Dad?" Zack exclaimed.

"You just played ball yesterday, Zack. Maybe you should sit with your Mom and me and enjoy breakfast."

"Come on, Dad," Zack said. He didn't know what else to say, but sitting around for another Sunday breakfast sounded like torture.

"Look son," Fyodor said to Mr. Goodspeed. "Young boys love baseball. They simply can't get enough. Remember how much you used to enjoy playing with me?"

Mr. Goodspeed shot him another doubtful glance over the rim of his glasses.

"Ok. Maybe not," Grandfather said. "But Zack loves it. He's got quite an arm. Come on, son. It's the summer."

CHAPTER 1: HOW STRANGE THINGS STARTED

Mr. Goodspeed looked at his wife. She frowned back clearly indicating she thought this was an abnormal occurrence for a Sunday morning, even during the summer.

"All right," Mr. Goodspeed said finally. "But bring him to the shopping mall in an hour. We'll meet you there. We have to run some errands."

Zack jumped up, opened the door, and raced outside. Grandfather followed him, ricocheting off the doorframe.

CHAPTER 2

The Secrets of the Labradory

"Where should we play?" Zack asked.

Grandfather glanced behind them and between his wide strides said, "Zack, I've got a better idea. Let's go to my house for a bit."

"Are we going to do some experiments?" Zack asked.

"Kind of. I think it's time I showed you something special," Grandfather said, now glancing the opposite direction.

"OK."

"All right. That's my boy," Grandfather said, a wide smile splitting his face.

They strode to the Professor's house next door. As they approached the white picket fence around Grandfather's yard, Zack saw a light blinking on a nearby motion sensor. The gate opened. The sprinklers

CHAPTER 2: THE SECRETS OF THE LABRADORY

modified their spray so it didn't hit them as they walked past. A perfect halo of air broke the mist as they strode down the footpath.

Grandfather Goodspeed took a sharp left and paced towards the detached garage. The garage began to growl at him viciously. A camera attached to the roof of the garage and shaped like a giant eyeball followed them as they approached.

"Down boy. Down!" said Grandfather.

"Voice recognized," said a pleasant voice from a speaker mounted on the garage. The growling stopped and the sound of a dog panting replaced it.

"What the heck is that?" Zack asked.

"Oh, that's my new security system."

"That's an angry-sounding dog."

"Actually, it's a recording of my neighbor's black Labrador. That's why I now call this place my 'Labradory.'"

Zack smiled at Fyodor. Many of the people in town, especially Zack's parents, found Fyodor Goodspeed simply wacky. Zack enjoyed his grandfather's quirks though. He found them refreshing.

"Door opening," said the garage speaker. "Welcome home, Fyodor Confucius Goodspeed."

The garage door squealed open. The interior of the garage was pitch black, like a large, gaping mouth. Zack stepped inside. Even the memory of the time Grandfather had almost burned his hair off didn't deter him. Zack could see something special twinkling in Grandfather's eyes today. The door squealed closed behind them.

"Kalamazoo!" Fyodor Goodspeed cried. The lights flickered on and the garage came to life.

The Labradory was a cornucopia of instruments, engine parts, gadgets, books, tools, computers, monitors, and gauges. The computers flipped on. The gadgets started whirring. A monitor blinked to life, displaying reams of text and images. A radio turned on, playing up-tempo jazz music. In the center of the gizmo jungle, on a high steel table, sat a large black cube, five feet wide, by five feet tall, by five feet long. The cube twinkled under a spotlight but seemed to capture more light than it reflected.

"I am so glad your parents let you come over to play 'baseball,'" Grandfather said with a wink. Zack stood still, admiring the chaos of the Labradory and the black cube that stood in the center like a monolith.

Grandfather strode through the mechanical mess to the cube, knocking over quite a few gizmos as he did so. Zack followed, picking his way carefully past several large contraptions that looked precariously balanced.

They came to the steel table and Grandfather Goodspeed pressed a nearby switch. The table lowered a few feet. Zack could see better now. The cube seemed to both capture and radiate energy. Zack could almost feel the energetic waves it gave off. His fingers and toes tingled when he stood this close to it. Zack reached out a hand and touched the cube. A sensation like a million angry bees shot through his arm, into his head, and down his spine. A crashing sound, like a wave, roared in his ears. Zack flew back and fell to the floor.

Grandfather rushed over to him. "My boy, my boy! Are you ok?"

"Yes, I think so."

"Are you sure?" Grandfather said, looking at him with concern.

"Yes. What is that?"

"That, my boy, is the reason I asked you over today. That is my new Onyx Sun."

"What is an Onyx Sun?"

"It is a source of unlimited power."

Zack stared at the cube. Although he could still feel waves of electrical energy pulsating from the cube and had felt its power firsthand,

CHAPTER 2: THE SECRETS OF THE LABRADORY

he had a hard time believing this simple shape could house any kind of power.

"I don't believe it. It's not possible."

"Oh, it is quite possible, my boy. It's just that no one outside yourself has ever seen something like this."

"Is this what you've been working on? Is this why you've been gone?"

"Yes."

"But how did you build it?"

"Ah, that's actually quite complicated."

"But why didn't you show me this before?" Zack asked.

"Because there was nothing to show," Grandfather said. "I created a smaller prototype Onyx Sun years ago, when I was about your age. I thought at the time I'd solved the world's energy problems. But as I tested my device, I realized although it could produce unlimited power — theoretically — it couldn't do so safely. The prototype became dangerous at high power levels. It was too small. I realized I had to develop another one, much larger than the first, to contain the power it generated. Zack, I have done it! I completed this Onyx Sun only last month, and have brought you here for its final test."

Zack shook his head. He was having a hard time believing what Grandfather was saying. Could he really be telling the truth? Was something like this possible? Even if it was, would this be one of his grandfather's experiments that went horribly awry? Questions flooded Zack's head, but one rose to the surface.

"Why show *me?*"

Grandfather stared at Zack and said, "Because you're the only one who understands me. I see genius growing inside you already, as it did in me when I was your age. I think you are going to find it will separate you — separate us — from people like your father and mother. Even if I tried to explain this to them, they could never appreciate what I've done here. But you can, Zack. You do already. Don't you?"

Zack thought about the moments he had been home and felt out of place. He longed desperately to understand his parents, but sometimes they completely baffled him. Grandfather though made sense. It was like his grandfather's weird motivations and mannerisms were a code only he could understand.

Zack nodded and said, "Yes. I get it."

Grandfather smiled and rubbed his hands through Zack's wild hair. Then, he helped Zack up.

"All right, shall we begin, my boy?"

Grandfather strode across the lab and started attaching different instruments to the cube. He attached spectrometers, radiometers, omniometers, bigometers, and smallometers. All kinds of "ometers" were attached to the cube, until Zack could barely make out the object underneath.

"All right," Fyodor said. "We're going to pulse test the cube. Let's see how stable this baby is at its highest energy level. Um, take cover… just in case."

Grandfather led Zack behind a large lead plate on one side of the room. It had a slit in it they peered through.

"If my calculations are correct, this test should give us enough energy to power an aircraft carrier," Grandfather said. He removed a black, rectangular remote from his pocket with a red button on it. The button was labeled "Kalamazoo!"

"Would you like to do the honors, my boy?" asked Grandfather Goodspeed.

"Sure," said Zack, taking the remote.

Grandfather Goodspeed began counting down. Zack joined in.

"…5…4…3…2…1…Kalamazoo!" said Grandfather, as Zack pressed the button.

CHAPTER 2: THE SECRETS OF THE LABRADORY

Nothing happened.

Grandfather peered around the side of the plate.

More of nothing happened.

Then, a sound, like a revving turbine, emerged from the cube. It escalated, until Zack could barely hear his grandfather, who was screaming something excitedly. His lips looked like he was yelling, "It's working!"

The ground began to vibrate. The overhead spotlight shook on the wire that held it to the ceiling. Reams of text flew across the computer monitors. All the "ometer" gauges spiked past the red line. Random objects fell from their shelves. Blue lightning bolts arced from the cube. They streamed up and down the walls lighting papers on fire and blowing up the computer monitors.

Zack looked at his grandfather, who was no longer smiling. Fyodor snatched the remote from Zack and frantically pressed the button. He looked at Zack desperately and his lips made shapes that remarkably resembled, "I forgot to build an 'Off' button!"

Zack covered his ears to protect them against the whine the cube was making. Just when he thought the garage would collapse, a magnetic pulse burst from the cube.

The lights went out.

The noise stopped.

Total blackness overtook the garage again.

When he awoke, Zack had a headache that felt like his skull was imploding. It was still completely dark in the garage, except for a small pool of light. Zack stood and, through the slit in the barrier, saw his grandfather standing over the cube, a penlight in his mouth. He was scraping the surface of the cube with different electronic devices and then comparing the readouts. A swell of frustration rose in Zack.

Had Grandfather even checked on him before he went to examine his invention? Zack doubted Fyodor had even noticed him unconscious on the floor. Zack stepped out from behind the plate.

The clutter that had once been evenly spread around the garage was now piled against the far walls. A perfect circle of empty floor lay around the cube.

Hearing Zack approach, Grandfather Goodspeed said, "Come here, my boy."

Zack shimmied around the circular pile of instruments. Grandfather never once glanced away from the Onyx Sun, offered help, or asked Zack if he was okay. Zack was baffled at how his grandfather could seem so sincere earlier yet care so little now.

"Well, I'd say that was a success!" Grandfather said.

Zack looked around the garage and said, "Um, it sure doesn't look that way."

"Nonsense!" Grandfather Goodspeed said, waving a hand in the air, as if to shoo a fly. "That was a significantly stable high-energy reaction. Instruments can be fixed. It's the Onyx Sun that we care about. The smaller prototype would have destroyed the whole block at that energy level."

"I'm not sure my parents would like that," Zack said, but his grandfather ignored him.

"So, it seems that the Onyx Sun's stability increases exponentially, as its size grows," Grandfather said, checking a device in his hand. "Excellent! This is even better than I expected!"

"Yeah, but you didn't notice it knocked me out," Zack said.

Grandfather scanned him and said, "Poppycock, you look fine. You can stand. You're eyes aren't crossed. And you're not drooling, which is a considerable benefit in social situations."

"Well, it ruined your lab, at least."

CHAPTER 2: THE SECRETS OF THE LABRADORY

Grandfather shrugged and said, "Ah, I have other labs. This was just a tinkering lab anyway—" He caught himself mid-sentence. Zack noticed something shifty in his eyes.

"Other labs?" said Zack. "What do you mean—"

"Kalamazoo!" Grandfather exclaimed suddenly, looking at his watch. "I promised to have you to the mall by 11:00. It's 10:59!"

Grandfather Goodspeed shot panicked looks around the garage. Then, he stopped, turned to Zack, and said, "Zack, my boy, if I show you something secret, will you promise not to tell anyone?"

"Grandfather I don't—"

"Promise, Zack!"

"Ok. I promise."

"Great! I knew I could count on you."

Grandfather dove towards the back of the garage. He threw aside mangled metal devices until he exposed the back wall. He shot one more cautious look at Zack, then clapped his hands together and placed them on the wall.

"Fyodor Confucius Goodspeed…recognized," said a computer voice.

The garage floor rumbled. Zack looked at the Onyx Sun, but this sound was coming from elsewhere. Suddenly, the rear wall split open to reveal a hidden chamber. Bright light shined into the garage. As the door spread wide, Zack could see a white chamber. The walls were cast in white blocks. The floor was a solid sheet of white. The ceiling was covered in white lights.

What caught Zack's attention though was the object inside the room. Hovering in mid-air, unsupported, was a streamlined wedge of an airplane with two cylindrical jets running down its sides. The ship had an open-air cockpit and two leather seats in the back third of the ship. Gold streaks started at the flat nose and ran down the sides, toward the back, where the engine exhausts tapered to ovals. The hull was mostly white except the underbelly, which shone like a glimmering gold plate.

"What is that?" Zack stammered.

Grandfather smiled at Zack, his face as bright in this light as his attire. Zack could see the excitement of a young boy inside him.

"That, my boy, is the world's first Onyx Sun-powered airplane. I call it the Onyx Airstrider. It can go faster and farther than any aircraft in the world, and it never needs refueling," Grandfather said, smiling at the ship like a proud father.

Zack took a closer look at the ship and noticed the engines looked familiar.

"Wait a second. The jets on this thing look just like the one that landed on my dad's bushes!"

Grandfather looked taken aback and said "Ah yes. Quite sorry about that. I'm afraid an engine fell off during my first supersonic flight test yesterday. I know he loved those roses. Pity."

The boy inside Grandfather disappeared, as a crinkle crossed his forehead, and he looked at his watch.

"Quickly Zack! We're late. Into the ship."

Zack leapt forward, as his grandfather bumbled into the cockpit. Zack climbed up the short triangular wings, as the engines whirred to life. Grandfather took a black remote from his pocket with a red button on it. The button was labeled "Kalamazoo!" He pressed it. Nothing happened.

"Ah!" Fyodor Goodspeed said in frustration and flung the remote out of the ship. "Wrong one."

He produced an identical remote from his suit. He pressed the button, and the ceiling over the ship split open. Sunlight, treetops, and blue sky appeared above. Grandfather grabbed the controls, and the white-gold ship rose from the garage. The roof closed behind them.

CHAPTER 2: THE SECRETS OF THE LABRADORY

Zack was now eye-level with the pancake roof of Grandfather's house. To his right, he could see a neighbor mowing his lawn, oblivious to the rising airship just fifty yards away. The man mowed along, back and forth, whistling as he went. To him, it was just another normal day.

"Here, put these on," said Grandfather, handing Zack a pair of goggles. Zack put them on.

"One little Onyx Sun, my first one, powers this entire ship," said Grandfather. "With its power alone I can produce enough stable energy to levitate the ship, using atomic repulsion. The engines on the side are for back and forward motion, like this!"

The ship shot forward. They accelerated so quickly Zack felt like a gigantic hand was pressing him back in his seat. Wind ripped through his hair and his eyes watered even with the goggles on. The airship blistered past neighborhood houses and climbed into the sky. The experience was soundless except for the rush of air. There was no jet engine noise though, like Zack remembered from his trips on airplanes.

Fyodor dodged a flock of geese and the ship veered sharply left. Zack could see his school fly by and his team's baseball field. They ripped by the town hall and several churches. People entering a church looked up as they sensed something streak by, but the ship was already gone. They crossed themselves and stepped inside the church.

"Wow!" Zack shouted over the wind.

"Not a bad way to travel, huh?" Grandfather said, winking at him.

"What about the engines? Are they going to fall off again?"

"Probably not," Grandfather shouted over the wind. "But who knows? Won't it be exciting to find out!"

Zack swallowed hard. He felt torn between excitement and sheer terror. Suddenly, breakfast with his parents sounded more appealing than spiraling out of control in a one-engine experimental plane.

The distant horizon quickly became the ground under the ship. Zack could make out the flat mass of the shopping mall butting against dense neighborhoods ahead. Grandfather slowed the ship. The parking lot was packed with cars, but Zack couldn't see any people. They must all be inside, he thought.

Grandfather found an empty parking space between two SUVs. As the airship hovered to a landing, both car alarms went off.

"Whoops! Not too subtle," Grandfather laughed. "Now, remember Zack: not a word to anyone. Our secret."

"Can I ride in the Airstrider again?"

"As long as the secret stays ours, you can get a ride anytime you want."

"Deal!" said Zack. He jumped out of the cockpit, slid down the wings, and ran toward the mall.

"Zack!" shouted Grandfather, as the airship took off. "Catch!"

A white baseball fell to earth. Zack caught it mid-stride. He noticed it had "Goodspeed" written on the side in marker. Grandfather smiled and said, "So your parents don't get suspicious!" He waved to Zack and the Onyx Airstrider shot off.

Mrs. Goodspeed waited outside the mall's main entrance.

"And where have you been? Your father is already inside," she said.

"Playing baseball," said Zack showing the baseball to his mother as he ran past. "With Grandfather."

"With no glove?"

"Ah, well, we don't throw very hard."

Mrs. Goodspeed looked around the parking lot and saw nothing but parked cars and a white-gold streak racing through the sky. She blinked and looked again. The streak was gone.

She shook her head and went inside the mall. Seconds later, she had already forgotten what she had almost seen.

CHAPTER 3

A Girl Called Max

After being forced, pressed, and prodded into several school outfits, Zack asked his parents if he could explore the mall on his own. "All right," said Mrs. Goodspeed. "But meet back here in one hour. We have to buy you a book bag."

"But Mom, the summer just began. We still have three months until school starts."

"Well, maybe we should shop for it right now instead?"

"Never mind," Zack said, dashing out of the store.

The mall was abuzz with activity. Families and couples milled around in a steady stream of traffic. People shot into stores. People moseyed. People talked. The whole scene was a dull roar of energy and movement.

Then, Zack saw her.

Even through the crowds, Zack could pick out Angelina Maximillian. She walked alone two stores down from Zack. She slowly studied each window she passed, a faint smile on her mouth, as if she could see something amusing others could not. Angelina was a few months older than Zack and went to the same school. She was a strikingly beautiful brunette, with olive skin and eyes like pale blue crystal. She was tall and thin, yet often hid herself under baggy jeans and a beaten-up gray hoody.

For all her good looks, she had few, if any, friends. Zack remembered her moving to his town about a year ago. She was an orphan and had been adopted by Mr. and Mrs. Jones, who lived on the other side of Grandfather's house. Although Angelina was nice to her foster parents, Zack noticed she never seemed to warm to them or anyone for that matter. She often kept her distance from everyone and when addressed by adults, listened but said little in return.

At school, the few friends she did have were all boys, and they were the toughest, rowdiest ones at that. They called her "Max" and even though she rarely hung out with them, they respected her and were careful to keep a quiet alliance with Angelina.

Zack had never talked to her, because she seemed unapproachable. But as he walked through the mall, and she walked toward him, alone, he decided this was the time.

They were within feet of each other when someone bumped into Zack.

"Watch it, Goodspeed!" said Tom Riley, a thick, tall boy from school with a thick, tall attitude. "You should watch where you're going, punk."

For emphasis, Riley bumped into Zack again. His two companions, Jeff and Peter Otis, freckly, straw-haired boys with ten teeth between

CHAPTER 3: A GIRL CALLED MAX

them, laughed. Tom glared down at Zack then slid by him. The Otis brothers followed.

"*You* bumped into *me!*" Zack shouted, realizing almost instantly the mistake he had made.

Tom turned around. "I what?" he said.

"You bumped into me," said Zack, more meekly this time. Out of the corner of his eye, he could see Angelina watching the boys. She slowly walked over.

"That's right. I did," said Tom. "But you should watch where I'm walking too."

Tom noticed the baseball Zack was holding and tore it from him. Tom tossed it in the air a few times and then ground it into Zack's forehead.

"Just watch it Goodspeed. Or you'll find yourself in a brawl," said Tom.

"Really?" said a raspy girl's voice behind them. "Now, why would you want to fight him?"

Tom and the Otis brothers turned to look at the voice. Around Tom's hulking body, Zack noticed Angelina. She was shorter than Tom, but stood confidently close to him, staring straight into his eyes.

"This doesn't involve you, Max," said Jeff Otis.

"No, I'm sure it doesn't," Angelina said not taking her eyes from Tom. "But when has that ever stopped me?" She stepped closer to Tom. "Take off Tom. He's with me."

Zack's heart skipped a beat.

"With you?" Tom said. "You're kidding me, right? This little punk?"

"Yeah," she replied. "That little punk. That a problem?"

Tom's eyes blazed at Angelina. He looked at the Otises, then back at her with a scowl. He turned to Zack, pointing a finger into his face, "This is not over."

Zack just stared back, his heart racing in his chest. The Otis brothers and Tom Riley stalked off.

"That was incredible," Zack said with a long exhale, but Angelina Maximillian was gone.

CHAPTER 4

Grandfather Disappears

Dinner that night was fairly uneventful. Zack finished his meal in record time so he could go visit Grandfather again. There was so much he wanted to ask him. How did he build the Onyx Sun? How did it work? Did Grandfather really have other labs? Where were they? When could he ride in the Onyx Airstrider again? What else was Grandfather hiding?

Zack thought if he got over to Grandfather's house before sunset, he might get to take another ride in the Airstrider. Maybe Grandfather would let him invite Angelina. Zack thought a ride in the Airstrider might impress even her.

"Don't eat so fast, Zack," said Mrs. Goodspeed. "Jack, tell Zack not to eat so fast."

Mr. Goodspeed turned the page of the *Evening Post*. "Don't eat so fast, Zack," he said with a grunt.

"Done," said Zack pushing his plate back. "Can I go see Grandfather now?"

"You already spent time with him today," Mrs. Goodspeed said, picking up his plate. "Why would you go over again? It's too late for baseball."

"I just like spending time with him."

Mrs. Goodspeed looked worried. She glanced at Mr. Goodspeed, who had put down the paper and was staring at Zack.

"Zack, let me tell you something," he said. "My father, your grandfather, is not…normal. He lacks a certain…composure other people have."

Zack felt a sting. What was his father saying?

"No one doubts his intelligence, son. But his brilliance means nothing if other people don't understand him. He's an enigma. Do you know what an enigma is, Zack?"

"Yes, I do, Dad. It means he's a puzzle. But I understand him," said Zack.

"No, you don't. You may *think* you do, but you see only what he shows you. There has always been a side to him he keeps hidden from the rest of the world."

"I get that. It is hard for some people to understand him, but not me! He doesn't hide things from me."

Even as the words left his mouth, Zack knew they were wrong. Hadn't he just today learned what Grandfather had been working on the past few months? Hadn't he today seen the Onyx Airstrider for the first time, even though it was probably in the Labradory for years before that? Zack was confused. He shot looks at his father and mother. "It's like you don't like him."

"That's not it, son," said Mr. Goodspeed. "It's just that we've learned what to expect from him. See Zack, when I was growing

CHAPTER 4: GRANDFATHER DISAPPEARS

up, I was a lot like you. I thought my father was the world's smartest person. Our house provided its own energy and water. Our car drove itself. Our pets were all robots. I had a dog, named 'Tin Tin', until I accidentally left him outside and he rusted. The point is, Zack, as I grew up I started to realize I didn't know my father. He was always off somewhere working on something. He brought great things into our house, but ultimately, he kept much more to himself."

Zack looked down at the floor.

"Even worse," Mr. Goodspeed continued. "People began to pick on me. They teased me about our house, and how a robot — not my mom — made me breakfast every morning."

"Well, people already tease me!" said Zack.

"Who does? How could anyone tease you, Zack? You're perfectly normal," Mrs. Goodspeed said.

"Look, son," Mr. Goodspeed continued. "Your Grandfather may be a special person, but the world will never know this, because he will never share himself with others. It's best to just stay away from people like that. If you get too close, you'll just be disappointed. Eventually, you'll want to know something more about him and he won't share it. Just go on with your life. Do something, anything, but leave your grandfather to his secret life and his mysterious inventions."

Zack was a firestorm of emotions. He loved his grandfather. How could he ever dismiss him as his father was suggesting? Even after all the times Grandfather had disappeared, Zack still looked forward to each time he reemerged. Grandfather always brought something new with him and an energy Zack had never known from anyone else.

Zack excused himself and went to his bedroom. Dusk was settling in and his room was dark. Only the dim light of a streetlamp illuminated his room. Zack left the lights off, closed his door, and fell into his bed. He buried his head in his pillow. His heart was beating fast and his head hurt. He flipped over and threw his pillow to the floor.

From this position, Zack could see the dark outlines of his plastic models hanging from the ceiling. Grandfather had helped him build many of them. These were Zack's favorite things in his room. Late at night, he tried to stay awake as he imagined all the places these planes, and rockets, and spaceships could go. There were fighter jets and commercial airplanes. There was a NASA Space Shuttle with its large rust-colored fuel tank. A space station hung nearby, a fan of solar panels stretching from it like the foils of a kite. There was also an exotic-looking ship Grandfather had custom-designed for Zack.

Zack stood up and walked over to this model. It was a long, white-and-gold ship that looked like a cross between a needle and a wedge. The nose of the craft was pointy but the fuselage tapered into a flat triangle as it progressed. A flat bank of rockets emerged from its tail, capped by two stabilizer fins that shot out like a "V." A low glass dome perched on the fuselage, where the pointy nose began to flatten into a wedge. This was where Grandfather had said the bridge was, but given the tiny size of the glass bubble, the ship would have to be enormous if everything was to scale.

Grandfather had given Zack the model three Christmases ago. Zack and his family had been opening presents all day in their house. Zack had gotten everything he wanted: a new baseball glove, some video games, and a ski jacket. Grandfather had helped Zack carry his treasures up to his room. Once there, Grandfather had presented Zack with a wedge-shaped roll of newspaper.

"What's this?" Zack had asked.

"Open it."

Zack had opened it and inside was the model plane.

"To add to your collection. This one I made myself. It's not from a kit."

"What is it?"

CHAPTER 4: GRANDFATHER DISAPPEARS

"It's an airplane of sorts. Designed to skip along the outer atmosphere so we can travel from one city to another faster. It levitates using atomic repulsion. Atom particles are captured through microscopic holes in the fuselage and then shot from the nozzles in the back."

"It looks like a spaceship."

"Well, it's not really a spaceship," Grandfather had laughed, "but it's close. It travels at high altitudes just below space. Although I guess there is no reason why it couldn't fly in space."

Grandfather's gaze had wandered out the window as he started whispering to himself, "A spaceship. Boy, wouldn't that be a kick? I would just need a cube big enough to stabilize the energy. Hmmm."

Zack had kept talking and asking questions about the model spaceship, but Grandfather had seemed to drift away, like he was no longer there. He had wandered over to Zack's desk, pulled a wrinkled piece of paper from his suit and started madly scribbling down notes. After a few minutes, he had left the room without a word, bumping into the doorframe on his way out. No one saw Grandfather for nine months after that. Zack had frequently knocked on his front door, but nobody had answered. His house had looked deserted.

When Grandfather finally had emerged, he had looked exhausted, but full of a wild energy. He had said nothing of where he'd been only, "Zack gave me an inspiration."

Zack walked back over to his bed and collapsed into it. He enjoyed his grandfather's company, but maybe his father was right. He shook the thought from his head, and before he drifted off to sleep, Zack said out loud, "I believe in you, Grandfather."

Zack woke in the middle of night to the clangor of garbage cans falling over. He sat up in bed, but everything was silent. He wondered if he had just dreamed he heard something. Zack climbed out of bed and walked to his window. Everything looked normal. Through the light of the streetlamp, Zack could see the narrow strip of grass between his and his grandfather's house. There was a long fence dividing the two yards and crushed metal trashcans were stacked against Grandfather's side. From this vantage point, Zack could just barely make out Grandfather's back yard. Since the house and its gigantic sloping roof blocked out most of the streetlight, Grandfather's back yard was almost completely dark. Zack could barely see anything back there but did catch a glimpse of a tall silhouette creeping through the blackness.

Zack pressed his face to the window. Even in the dark, he was sure he could see a man creeping along the lawn from Grandfather's house to the woods at the back of his property. Zack opened his window and leaned out. The shape had just made it to the woods when a thin sliver of light from the street caught the figure in its glow. Zack saw a tuft of white hair shooting off the figure's scalp like a wisp of smoke.

Grandfather!

Zack almost fell out the window. Grandfather Goodspeed paused at the line between the yard and the woods and looked back at Zack's house. Then, before Zack could do anything, Grandfather leapt into the forest and disappeared.

Zack turned back into his room. He looked at the clock on his bedside table. What was Grandfather doing in the woods at 3:48 AM? Zack grabbed some shorts from his floor and slid them on as he shimmied into a t-shirt. He opened his door and crept past his parents' room. He could hear his father grunting in his sleep. Zack tiptoed downstairs.

Once outside, Zack raced next door. The gate to Grandfather's yard, which normally opened automatically when Zack approached with Grandfather, did not move. Zack tried to push it open, but it refused to budge. Zack climbed over it. The moment Zack's feet touched

CHAPTER 4: GRANDFATHER DISAPPEARS

Grandfather's lawn the sprinkler system whisked to life, and instead of spraying away from Zack, it focused right at him. High-pressure water shot into his face and stung his eyes. He stumbled wildly across the lawn, but the streams followed him. Zack almost tripped over a water jet that sprang from the ground in front of him. He ran erratically until he lurched onto the path between Grandfather's house and the detached garage. The garage began to growl at him.

"Shhhh!" Zack whispered. "I'm going to find my grandfather."

The garage growled louder.

"Oh shut up!" Zack hissed.

The garage erupted into barking. Spotlights flashed to life around Grandfather's house, all focused on Zack. The loud barking echoed throughout the neighborhood. Lights flicked on in houses up and down the street. The lights in Zack's house came on, and Zack could hear his father's muffled shouting. A window flew open. The spotlights on Grandfather's house went dark. The barking stopped. Mrs. Goodspeed leaned out her bedroom window.

"What the — Zack?" Mrs. Goodspeed said. "What are you doing out there? And why are you all wet?"

Zack felt small.

"Uh…sleepwalking?" he said.

Mrs. Goodspeed looked around the neighborhood. People were peering out their windows and standing in open doorways in their night robes.

"Get inside," hissed Mrs. Goodspeed. "Now!"

CHAPTER 5

Angelina's Secret

"This is decidedly not normal, Zack. Decidedly *not* normal!" Mrs. Goodspeed said. They were huddled around the breakfast table at 4:00 AM. Mr. Goodspeed, attired in a plaid robe, swayed silently in his chair, slowly trying to press his hair back into its daytime orderliness. Mrs. Goodspeed stood before both of them, pointing a clenched fist at Zack. Her knuckles were white and Zack could see the veins in her fingers.

"Sleepwalking? Whatever! Goodspeeds do not sleepwalk. I've never even heard of a Goodspeed doing something so absurd."

She paused for a second and squinted at Zack.

"Well, except for your grandfather," she said.

The phone rang.

CHAPTER 5: ANGELINA'S SECRET

"You're lying," Mrs. Goodspeed said, as she stepped toward the phone. "You were trying to see your grandfather again. Zack, why? Your father warned you about this. And in the middle of the night! This behavior has got to stop."

She picked up the phone and her voice became flowery, as if she was talking to a kitten, "Hello? Oh hi, Betty. No, Zack's fine. Just sleepwalking. Sorry to wake you. How's Dennis?"

Mrs. Goodspeed pointed toward the stairs without looking at Zack. Zack stood up and trudged upstairs, followed by a half-awake Mr. Goodspeed.

It was 7:30 the next night before Zack was allowed to come downstairs. He silently ate his dinner then was ordered straight back to his room by Mrs. Goodspeed. Zack was lying on his bed when someone knocked on his door.

"Zack?" said Mrs. Goodspeed as the door opened. "You have a visitor."

Mrs. Goodspeed grimaced at him. Zack didn't understand why until he saw who walked in: Angelina Maximillian. She wore a dark hooded sweatshirt and baggy jeans.

"Ten minutes, Angelina," Mrs. Goodspeed said. "Zack is being punished."

"You can call me Max."

"Excuse me dear?"

"You can call me Max. Everyone does."

"I see," Mrs. Goodspeed said. She nodded curtly and closed the door, wincing at Angelina's attire as she left.

"Hey," said Angelina to Zack.

"Hey," Zack replied. There was a long silence between them, and then he said "Hey, thanks for that thing at the mall."

"Forget it," said Angelina in her raspy, but feminine voice. "Tom Riley's a loser. He just wants to tick people off."

"Well, he does a good job."

"Yeah, no kiddin'."

Angelina walked around Zack's room with her hands thrust in her hoody pockets. She looked at his model spaceships.

"You build those?"

"Uh, yeah, some of them. Some my grandfather helped me with. He built that one."

"Wicked," said Angelina flatly. Clearly, she did not think the model was that cool. She walked over to Zack's baseball collection on his bookshelf. Picking one up, she said, "You woke the entire neighborhood up last night. What were you doing? Your mom said you were sleepwalking."

"Um, no," said Zack. "That's not really true. I was looking for my grandfather, actually."

"Is he lost?"

"No. I mean, I haven't seen him *today*, but sometimes he disappears without telling anyone. I kind of think that's what happened this time."

"How do you know?"

Zack looked at Angelina, as she cautiously eyed him. Although she seemed tough on the outside, Zack sensed something vulnerable about her, like she wanted to believe what he said but was afraid to trust him. Zack decided to tell her anyway.

"Well...I saw him disappear into the woods last night."

Angelina looked away. She paced around his room. She tossed the baseball in her hand.

"Do you know where he goes?" she asked.

"No. He just leaves. No one knows where he goes. My parents don't really care. I think they actually feel relieved when he disappears.

CHAPTER 5: ANGELINA'S SECRET

They don't like me hanging out with him. I think they're afraid he'll rub off on me or something."

Zack paused, sighed, and said, "All I know is he goes somewhere. I don't know where."

"What if I knew?"

"How could you?"

"I don't. Well, not entirely. But I do know roughly."

"How?"

"Maybe I followed him."

"You what? How? Why?"

"Shhh," Angelina whispered, pointing at his bedroom door. "Your parents might hear. I don't know. Maybe I was curious. Maybe I was bored. Man, I don't know. I just wanted out of my foster home. I wanted to do something. This neighborhood is so dull."

Zack looked at her. Angelina fiddled with the baseball she held. She seemed unsure she should be in his room.

"Well," Zack said at last. "Where is he?"

"Not far," she said. "Actually, he's in the woods."

"Still? You're lying," Zack said.

"Look, maybe I shouldn't have come," Angelina said, walking toward the door.

Zack stepped in front of her.

"No. Wait," he said. "Hey, I'm sorry. That just sounds strange, that's all."

Angelina stepped back a little. Her expression softened.

"You have no idea," she said.

"Look, why are you telling me this?" Zack asked.

Angelina glanced away and said, "I don't know. Maybe because I know you two are close. I see a lot of stuff from my house. I see you two spending a lot of time together when he is around, and…I know what it is like to miss people."

Zack was shocked at this admission. For the first time since he had known her, Angelina Maximillian looked exposed. She wasn't making eye contact and she shifted back and forth on her feet. Zack had heard the stories in school about Angelina. He had heard that no one knew who her real parents were, not even her. Her father apparently had left shortly after she was born and her mother had disappeared after that. The kids at school said Angelina had been through eight foster homes, ending only recently with the Joneses.

"Ok. I get it," Zack said.

"You do?" Angelina said. She looked doubtful.

"Yeah. I do actually. I know you just want to help."

"Yeah," Angelina said, straightening. She regained composure. "Yeah, I do. Plus, hey, I'm curious about where the old geezer got to."

"I thought you said you knew."

"No," she replied. "I said what if I knew? I don't actually know where he is. But relax. I do know where to start, and that alone is going to shock you."

CHAPTER 6

The Red Button

Zack and Angelina left the bedroom and crept toward the stairs. "We have to get into your grandfather's backyard," she whispered.

"Didn't you hear what happened when I tried to do that last night?"

"I have that part covered," Angelina said. "The first thing we have to worry about is how to sneak you past your parents. It's late, and I doubt they'll let you outside right now, after last night."

They both listened to the noises coming from downstairs. They could hear the TV in the living room. Mrs. Goodspeed was probably watching the evening news. Mr. Goodspeed punctuated the drone of the TV with a grunt and the sound of a newspaper page turning.

"There's no way we're walking right by them," Angelina whispered.

"Any ideas?" Zack asked.

"No. What about you? You're supposed to be the smart one, from what Tom Riley says. I think that's half the reason he hates you."

"And the other half?"

"Bad luck maybe?" Angelina said. "Forget Tom. He hates everyone. Right now, we need an idea to get by your parents."

"Come on. Back into my room," Zack whispered.

Zack and Angelina slinked back to Zack's room and closed the door behind them. Zack walked to his window and looked out. The ground was too far away to jump and there were no ledges or nearby trees for them to climb down.

"All right," said Zack. "So, we're not walking right by them and we're not going out that window. We need another solution."

Zack looked around his room and tapped his forehead. What would Grandfather do, he thought.

"We should see what we have in the room," Zack said. "Grab some stuff and put it on the floor."

Zack and Angelina gathered supplies from Zack's room and laid them on the floor. They found books, clothes, a spool of fishing line, a ream of photo paper, baseballs, a roll of duct tape, a digital camera, a multitool, and several bed sheets.

Zack huffed at the mess on his floor. "Somehow, I thought looking at this would give me an idea."

"Well no rush," Angelina said sarcastically, as she bit a fingernail. "We have all night."

Zack tapped his forehead and paced up and down his floor. He considered tying his bed sheets together and hanging them out the window, but that would drop them right outside the living room window. Zack's parents would surely see them. Zack briefly considered making a parachute out of the fishing line and bed sheet, although they'd need to climb onto the roof to get enough air to jump off and

CHAPTER 6: THE RED BUTTON

this thought deterred Zack somewhat. With the luck that ran in his family, the chute would not open in time, and he would end up in Mr. Goodspeed's rose bushes.

Zack stopped pacing and looked at the photo paper. About fifty sheets of shiny paper lay on the floor. Ten feet away sat Zack's color laser printer. Zack looked back at the digital camera lying on the floor. Wheels started turning in his head. Zack felt the familiar sensation of ideas coming together. Dark, fuzzy shapes started to float around in his head. As ideas came together, his plan became clearer. Zack felt a little like his grandfather, turning idea after idea over in his head until he could almost see the finished product in his mind like it was real.

Zack turned to Angelina and said, "Grab the camera. I have a plan."

"This is never going to work," Angelina whispered as she walked downstairs.

"Shhh. Yes it will. Just focus," Zack hissed back from the top of the stairs. He pointed toward the living room.

Angelina huffed and continued down the stairs. She walked with her hands behind her back, where she held Zack's digital camera. The lens was facing away from her. Angelina reached the bottom of the stairs and turned into the living room.

"Well, goodnight!" she said to the Goodspeeds. Zack heard the rustling of newspapers. Mr. Goodspeed must have jolted awake on the couch.

"Well, goodnight dear," Zack heard his mom say.

From his vantage point at the top of the stairs, Zack could see a light sweat break out on Angelina's brow. My mom must be watching Max carefully, Zack thought. Zack could see Angelina fumbling with the camera behind her back. She seemed to be trying to reach for the shutter button, but couldn't find it.

"Is everything all right dear?"

"Oh yes. Fine," Angelina said. Zack saw Angelina straighten, as she gained control of herself. Angelina forced a smile, found the shutter button, and pressed it. A flash splashed in the hallway behind Angelina as the camera took a picture.

Zack could hear his father jump up from the couch and a torrent of newspapers fall to the floor.

"Lightning," Mr. Goodspeed said. "Did you see that Jen? A little early in the season for that don't you think?"

Zack could hear his father shuffle around the living room and could see his feet moving toward the window.

"Strange," Mr. Goodspeed said.

"Oh, I forgot to tell Zack something," Angelina said. "Do you mind if I run upstairs for a sec?"

"It is getting late dear," Mrs. Goodspeed said.

"I promise I'll make it quick."

There was a pause and Zack thought he heard his mother huff. "Very well dear. But be quick."

Angelina half-bowed as she walked backwards out of the living room. Zack noticed she was careful to hide the camera from sight as she turned and ran upstairs.

"Got it," she said, reaching Zack and handing him the camera.

Ten minutes later, Zack and Angelina stood in Zack room's admiring an eight-foot-tall by twelve-foot-wide photograph of the Goodspeed's hallway. Zack had downloaded the picture Angelina had taken onto his computer. He had blown the picture up and split it into sections that fit onto single pieces of paper. Then, Zack had printed each of

CHAPTER 6: THE RED BUTTON

these sections, taping them together with Angelina's help. He taped the final mural so it hung from his ceiling.

What they saw in front of them now was a perfect replica of what Mr. and Mrs. Goodspeed could see from the living room: a yellow hallway, potted flowers sitting on a small table in the middle, the end of the stairway railing to the left, and the edge of the front door to the right.

"I'm sorry I doubted you. It's perfect," Angelina said.

"The lighting is off," Zack said, "But I think it will do. Let's go."

Zack and Angelina peeled the photo from the ceiling and shuffled toward the stairs, each holding a side. The photo rippled as they walked, but hung together. They tiptoed downstairs until Zack could peer around the corner into the living room. Mr. Goodspeed was asleep on the couch again, and Mrs. Goodspeed was turned away from the hallway, as she watched TV from her armchair.

Zack motioned for Angelina to follow him and they slid the photo into place and taped it to the ceiling. They taped it so there was a passageway on one side of the hall for Angelina to walk through and a hidden corridor behind the photo for Zack to sneak by, undetected.

After attaching the photo, Zack ran quietly upstairs, grabbed his backpack, threw the baseballs, bed sheets, and multitool into it, and ran back downstairs.

Meeting Angelina on the ground floor, Zack said, "Ready?" Angelina nodded back. They both strode down the hallway toward the door, Zack on the hidden side, Angelina on the exposed side.

"Well goodnight again!" Angelina called about halfway down the hall. From his position behind the giant photograph, Zack could hear his father stir again amidst his newspapers and his mother say, "Goodnight dear."

Zack and Angelina reached the door at the same time, opened it, and stepped outside into the starlit night.

✳ ✳ ✳

Once outside, they sprinted next door to Grandfather Goodspeed's house. Zack was about to open Grandfather's front gate, when Angelina grabbed his hand.

"Not that way," she said. "You know what happens if you go that way."

She pointed at the Labradory. Already sensing their presence, the garage let out a low growl.

"Follow me," Angelina said.

They ran down the street, past Grandfather Goodspeed's house and into the Joneses' yard. They raced along the chain-link fence bordering Grandfather's yard and emerged at the rear of the house. Zack could see Grandfather's entire backyard through the fence.

"This is how I could see him," Angelina said. "Since your house is separated from his by that wooden fence, you couldn't see what I see, even from your bedroom window. I bet your grandfather never thought the Joneses, being as boring as they are, would ever pay attention to what he was doing back there."

"And I bet he doesn't know about you," Zack said.

"Exactly," Angelina replied. "He never suspected that I would be over here with nothing to do but spy on him."

"So, this side —"

"Is wide open," Angelina finished. "Come on. Climb over."

Zack and Angelina climbed over the fence and hopped into Grandfather Goodspeed's backyard. Zack half-expected the garage to make a commotion when his feet hit the ground, but all was silent. Angelina led the way to the woods at the back of the property.

"Hold my hand," Angelina said.

"What?" Zack said. He wasn't used to holding anyone's hand anymore, especially a girl's.

CHAPTER 6: THE RED BUTTON

"I said hold my hand," she repeated. "It's dark in the woods and what we're looking for is not easy to find."

"And what are we looking for?"

"A red button," she replied.

"A red button?" he asked.

"Yes," she said. "'Press the red button, down the spinning shaft, past the burning beams, across the shuttle of great distance, through the black box, to the call of the clarion.'"

"What does that mean?" Zack asked.

"It's something your grandfather used to mumble as he walked around in the woods. I'm glad he said something. His voice was the only way I could follow him."

"Follow him where?" Zack said.

"I'll show you," Angelina said, grabbing his hand and plunging into the woods. Zack was surprised that although her grip was firm, her hand was small in his.

Angelina ran forward. She moved left and right. She ducked under branches and vaulted logs and Zack did the same, barely keeping up with her. Occasionally, a limb would catch on his backpack and Angelina would wait for him to get loose. They darted onward. She seemed to know the entire forest like it was her own house.

"How many times did you follow him?" he asked.

Angelina ducked under a branch and said, "Seven."

"Seven? And you never told me?"

"I didn't know you. Plus, I thought I could get further than I did without help."

"What do you mean?"

"I lost sight of your grandfather at a certain point. You might be able to help me. You'll see. Ah! There," Angelina said pointing.

At first, Zack could see only the black silhouettes of trees and the even blacker shapes of leaves in his face. Then, as his eyes adjusted to the darkest part of the dark forest, he saw it. A faint red glow was coming from the base of a tree ten feet ahead. Angelina stepped forward and spread aside the foliage. A button glared back at them, pulsated with a bright red glow and the unmistakable words of Zack's grandfather inscribed on it:

Kalamazoo!

CHAPTER 7

The Spinning Shaft

Angelina reached down to press the button at the base of the tree, but Zack grabbed her hand.

"Are you sure you want to do that?"

"Zack, this is the part I *am* sure of."

"Ok. It's just that bad things seem to happen when people go around pressing red buttons labeled Kalamazoo!"

"Zack, this one is okay."

"All right," he said, letting go.

Angelina pressed the button and a faint whirring sound emanated from the tree. Zack stepped back and half-closed his eyes. A rectangular outline of white light came from the trunk of the tree. Then, suddenly, the whirring stopped. Slowly, the trunk of the tree opened. A white shaft appeared inside the tree as a piece of the trunk slid aside like an elevator door. Zack's eyes watered at the sight.

Inside the tree was a brightly lit shaft, just big enough to accommodate one adult, or two children. Angelina stepped into the tree, as if it were a phone booth. Zack looked at her unsure.

"Come on," she said. "Scared?"

Zack looked at the woods around him. Then, with his heart beating in his throat, he stepped inside. The inside of the tree was bright and had only two features on the wall next to the door: a button labeled "Close" and a button labeled "Kalamazoo!" Angelina pressed the "Close" button and the door to the tree sealed shut with a hiss.

"Now what?" Zack asked. He was sorry to see Angelina reach for the "Kalamazoo!" button.

"Hold on to your socks," she said. "You may not like *this* button."

Zack closed his eyes.

Angelina pressed the button.

Nothing happened.

Slowly, Zack opened his eyes and looked at Angelina. She was smiling back at him.

"Well," he said. "That wasn't so bad."

Zack noticed Angelina's hair was doing something strange, like it had a breeze flowing through it. Although the floor seemed solid under his feet, the walls of the tube were doing something strange too, like they were spinning extremely quickly.

Zack looked up. He could see the top of the shaft disappearing as they rapidly rotated downward.

"Whoa!" said Zack, holding his dizzy head.

"Here," shouted Angelina over the loud whirring. "Stand in the very center of the floor and close your eyes."

CHAPTER 7: THE SPINNING SHAFT

Zack did as he was told. In the center of the floor, the shaft felt like it was barely moving. All he could feel was the wind whipping through his hair as they shot downward. He opened his eyes a little and saw Angelina smiling back at him, her face inches away from his.

"You rode this seven times when you followed my grandfather?" Zack screamed.

"No," she yelled back. "I followed your grandfather about seven times. But I rode this about twenty. No harm in having a little fun."

The spinning increased. Zack looked up. A long white shaft stretched above them into a pinpoint of darkness that seemed a mile away. Zack became dizzy at this sight. His knees felt weak.

Angelina put a hand on his arm and said, "We're almost there."

Zack could barely keep his body steady but then everything stopped.

CHAPTER 8

The Burning Beams

"You still with me, tiger?"

Zack's head was spinning, but he was sure they were no longer moving. Angelina's black hair hung loosely around her shoulders. The door to the chamber opened with a hiss, and they stepped out. Zack slammed into the doorframe, while trying to steady himself.

"You a little motion sensitive, sport?" Angelina said with a smile.

"Nah, I'm fine," Zack lied. His stomach felt like it was in his throat.

"Fun, huh?" Angelina replied, winking at him.

"Sure. Loads. So, where are we?"

Zack looked around. They stood in a white corridor, about a hundred feet long. Behind them was the narrow cylinder of the spinning

CHAPTER 8: THE BURNING BEAMS

shaft. In front of them, across the hallway, was a single, white door that looked like an airlock. Zack stepped towards the door to get a better look.

"Whoa. Easy there," said Angelina pulling him back. "You don't want to rush that way."

"Why not?"

Angelina pointed toward a small gold plate on the wall. She pressed it and the room went dark. Twenty beams of red light shot across the hallway in front of them. The entire room glowed crimson as the beams randomly danced across the hallway.

"That's why," she said.

Angelina pulled a gum wrapper from her pocket and balled it up. She tossed it toward the beams. One sliced through the wrapper and left two burning embers to fall to the floor.

"Ok, so they're lasers. Why don't you just turn them off?" Zack asked.

"Great idea. How?"

"With that gold plate on the wall," he said. "Same way you turned them on."

Angelina pressed the gold plate and the hallway turned white again. No beams were visible. Angelina reached into her pocket, pulled out another gum wrapper, balled it up, and tossed it. Again, the wrapper was sliced into two embers.

"Of course," Zack said. "I forgot lasers are invisible in normal light. So, any ideas how to turn them off?"

"No. This is the part I couldn't figure out. I wasn't able to follow your grandfather to see what he did here. I couldn't ride the elevator with him obviously. So, I waited in the woods while he took the elevator down. But by the time the shaft came up to get me and I rode down, he was gone."

"And how am I supposed to help here?" asked Zack.

"I don't know," said Angelina. "Think of something. You two spent tons of time together in his garage. I heard all the explosions and noises coming from there. Didn't you two ever work on something like this?"

"Never," said Zack. "This is totally new to me. Why would he even build something like this?"

"I don't know, but I am guessing to keep people out. Maybe he's hiding something down there."

Zack remembered his father telling him he would never know the "true" Grandfather because Fyodor would always keep secrets from him. This made Zack frustrated. He was tired of being left in the dark. He was tired of wondering where Grandfather went and what he did. The little glimpses Zack had gotten into Grandfather's secret world showed Zack that Grandfather was inventing incredible things, like the Onyx Sun. Clearly, Grandfather wanted to share some of these inventions with him, Zack thought, even if that meant Zack had to foil the traps designed to keep other people out.

Zack scanned the room. He realized if he had missed seeing the lasers before, he might also have missed some feature that would help him now. The hall looked white and featureless though. The airlock door at the far end just looked like a standard door.

Then, Zack noticed a small red button next to the door on the far side. Maybe more in his mind then anything, he thought he could even see the word "Kalamazoo!" printed on it.

"I bet that does something. You see that button down there?" he asked.

"Yeah," said Angelina. "But how are we going to push it? We're here and it's there."

Zack looked around. He couldn't see anything of use in the hallway. Then, something occurred to him. He took off his backpack and removed two baseballs.

CHAPTER 8: THE BURNING BEAMS

"Maybe these will help."

Angelina frowned and said, "How exactly?"

"Press the gold plate," said Zack.

Angelina did so and the room became dark except for the red beams. Zack studied them. In the dance of lasers, there was a single, recurring hole that hovered for a second over the button.

"Look!" he said. "You see that? There is a small hole in the beams. Maybe I can get a ball through and hit the button on the far side."

"I don't know. It'd have to be a pretty good throw."

"True, but what other options do we have?"

"What if all the button does is open the door?"

"Well, we won't know until we try."

Zack returned one baseball to the backpack, stepped toward the center of the room, and leaned in to study the beams, tossing the ball behind his back. Zack rubbed the baseball in his palm. Depending on where the beams moved, the gap for him to throw the ball got bigger or smaller. He waited and watched. Then, as one beam crossed another, Zack saw a large gap open. Zack leaned back and threw the ball.

The baseball arced through the air. It was a perfect pitch to hit the button, but just as the ball got within ten feet of the far wall, four beams simultaneously converged into the ball's path. The beams sliced the baseball into four embers, which fell to the ground beside the door.

Angelina sighed.

"Dang!" Zack said. "Where did those beams come from? I didn't see them before."

Angelina reached into Zack's backpack and grabbed the other baseball. Handing it to him, she said, "Make this one count or we'll never find out where your grandfather went. And we'll also have to ride back up that spinning elevator."

Zack's heart skipped a beat. He nodded at her and stepped a little closer to the beams. He watched them move. He started to notice that some moved in predictable patterns. He saw the same giant gap appear in the lasers and, just like before, four beams came together to block the hole a second later.

"It's a trap," Zack said to Angelina. "Look. That hole is *supposed* to tempt me. Every time it opens, those four beams come together to block it right after. There has to be another way."

Zack watched and waited. Just as he was about to rethink his plan, he saw it. A narrower gap, barely large enough for a baseball, appeared for a few seconds right in front of the button. Zack waited to see if the pattern repeated itself. It did. He grimaced. He would have only a few seconds to throw the ball and no more than a couple of inches to mis-throw or the ball would be sliced apart again.

"There it is," he said to Angelina pointing at the gap.

"You've got to be kidding me."

Zack shook his head.

"Zack, that's impossible."

Zack looked down and rubbed his eyes. He shook his head to clear his mind. He waited. By now, he was able to feel the moment coming by just watching the laser patterns. He watched the cycle repeat itself, anticipating the exact moment to throw the ball. He saw the gap come and pass. He learned the pattern in the beams preceding the gap. Then, on the next cycle, almost as in a dream, Zack felt himself rear back. He hurled his arm through the air and spun forward to pitch the ball. Angelina gasped when Zack released the ball because, at that moment, there was a solid field of lasers between them and the button. Yet, as the ball arced through the air, the lasers danced out of the way as the ball approached. The ball spun toward the door and right before it got there, the lasers blocking the button spread aside. The small hole opened and the ball passed by, barely grazing one of

CHAPTER 8: THE BURNING BEAMS

the beams. A thin slice of the cover sheered off, but the ball continued on its path and hit the button.

The room went dark. Zack heard Angelina fumbling around and suddenly the room lit up. Angelina was standing by the wall with her hand on the golden plate.

"Are they off?" Zack asked.

"I don't know," Angelina replied. "Only one way to tell."

She picked up Zack's backpack and threw it toward the door. It arced through the air and landed on the floor by the door unharmed.

Angelina squealed in excitement and threw her arms around Zack's neck. She kissed him on the cheek and then raced to the far end of the hallway yelling, "You did it, Zack!"

CHAPTER 9

The Shuttle of Great Distance

Zack and Angelina walked to the end of the hallway and retrieved Zack's backpack. Zack picked up the charred baseball.

"Ready?" Angelina said, stepping toward the airlock door.

With a hiss, the door whisked open. Beyond lay a rectangular room cast entirely in concrete slabs. In the center of the room, stretching from front to back was a narrow trench. The trench disappeared into a dark hole in one side of the room. There were no other features save another gold plate near the entrance.

Zack walked to the center of the room. He hopped into the shallow trench and peered into the hole. He could see a line of lights stretching into the distance, like a subway tunnel.

"So," he said. "What now?"

CHAPTER 9: THE SHUTTLE OF GREAT DISTANCE

"Well, there is this gold plate," said Angelina, pointing to the wall.

"More lasers?"

"I don't think so. But you may want to get out of the trench, just in case."

Zack climbed out and walked over to the gold plate. He hesitated for a second then pressed it.

Nothing happened.

They waited awhile and more of nothing happened.

"Maybe it is broken," said Angelina.

"If my grandfather built it, it works…maybe. It may have quirks, but it will work eventually."

Zack tapped the plate several more times.

"Yeah, well, nothing is happening," Angelina said.

Zack walked back to the trench and climbed down. He looked into the tunnel but saw nothing unusual.

"Well," he said looking back at Angelina. "We might be able to crawl through it. Although I don't know how long it is —"

Just then a faint wind flowed from the tunnel. Zack looked back and saw the same string of lights stretching into the distance. He crouched down further and leaned into the tunnel. Then, he saw it — a solitary light in the center of the trench was moving toward him. Wind began to pour from the tunnel and the floor started vibrating. Zack realized suddenly the object was moving very quickly because when he blinked it jumped significantly closer. Zack felt an overwhelming need to get out of the trench. Fast.

He leapt from the trench but given the speed of the object, his mind wondered, mid-leap, if he would make it in time. Out of the corner of his eye, he saw an object shaped like a large bullet speeding through the tunnel toward him. He felt a hand grab his and pull. His feet whipped from the trench the very moment a bullet train arrived…

…and stopped.

Zack felt himself lying partially on top of Angelina.

"What is that?" she said, pushing Zack off her.

Zack looked at the object sitting in the trench. Up close, it resembled a silver cigar. The craft was long and slender, with two cone-shaped ends. It sat in the trench, steaming. It was covered in a translucent substance. Zack approached the ship and touched it.

"Ouch!" he said, jerking back and waving his hand around.

"What? Is it hot?" Angelina said, approaching him.

"No," he said. "Cold. Really cold. It's covered in ice."

They both studied the object as it warmed. As the ice fell from its sides, they could make out windows on both ends and four rows of seats inside. Zack gingerly touched the craft and found it warmer. He noticed a notch on the side of the craft and pulled on it. A wide gull-wing door rose from the side of the vehicle. Inside, there were four rows of black leather seats facing the direction the bullet had come. Once the door was fully open, the chairs swung around and faced the other direction, toward the dark tunnel mouth.

"Well, we didn't come all this way for nothing," said Angelina, as she jumped inside the craft. "Come on, Zack."

Zack looked at her, then the tunnel. Angelina waved him inside and Zack crawled aboard. He took a seat beside Angelina at the front of the bullet, facing the tunnel. The hatch closed with a whoosh.

"Wait," said Zack. "There are no buttons —"

Two seatbelts leapt into the air and twisted around their laps like serpents, winching them into their seats. The bullet train whirred to life and shot into the tunnel. It whipped forward so fast, Zack felt like his eyes were being pushed into his skull. He wrestled his head to the side enough to see Angelina's face pressed into a smile. This train was faster than anything Zack had ever been in — even the Onyx Airstrider.

CHAPTER 9: THE SHUTTLE OF GREAT DISTANCE

The train shot down the tube, shaking as tunnel lights streaked by like furious lightning bugs. Although the tunnel looked straight from the platform, Zack could feel his body being thrown right and left, as minor turns became rollercoaster corkscrews at this speed. The rush of wind around the craft was deafening.

Then, suddenly, the tube fell away and all was quiet. Zack looked out the side windows. The bullet train hung in midair in the midst of an enormous underground cavern. Large spikes of purple and blue crystal hung all around them and decorated the floor below them. Although Zack could tell they were still racing forward, the immensity of the room made him feel like they were floating across the chamber like a cloud.

"I don't believe it," Angelina said. "We're inside a gigantic geode. I saw one of these in science class, but I had no idea they could get *this* big!"

"I have never seen crystals like that. Have you?" asked Zack.

Angelina shook her head in response.

The bullet arced through the air as the forest of crystals sped by. Zack felt like they hung there forever, but then he noticed the far wall of the chamber approaching them…fast. Angelina grabbed Zack's hand. Zack pulled his seatbelt tighter. Just as Zack thought they were going to be dashed to pieces against the spiky cavern wall, he noticed a tiny hole in its surface.

The craft punched into the gap with a hollow "pha-wump" and continued rocketing along the tube. A torrent of wind again shook the ship. The train whipped around in circles and then arced like a snake left and right. At the far end of the tunnel, they could see a white spot approaching them. It sat in the distance one moment and then was upon them the next. They stopped with a violent jerk that threw Zack forward, squeezing him against his seatbelt.

Zack shook his head. A bright room had replaced the dark tunnel, but Zack couldn't see specifics. All he could see were fuzzy shapes through the translucent frost around the ship.

The seatbelts clicked and slithered off their laps. They stood and walked to the door. Steam rose from the craft, as they forced open the door and climbed out.

"This looks exactly like the last station," Angelina said.

"Yeah. Except we've got to be pretty far away now. At the speed we were traveling, that geode alone was probably a hundred miles across."

A single door led out of the room. They opened it and walked into the blackness beyond.

CHAPTER 10

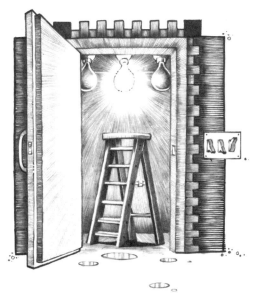

The Dastardly Death

There was only darkness here.

Zack couldn't see a thing but heard Angelina step forward slowly. He followed.

A spotlight flickered on in the center of the room. Something began to shimmer like a bright column in front of them. A 3-D hologram of Grandfather Goodspeed appeared.

"Grandfather!" Zack exclaimed. "We found you! I was afraid you'd left. Angelina, people call her Max, Max helped me —"

"Relax, Zack," Angelina interrupted. "I think it is just a recording or something. It doesn't seem to recognize us."

Zack saw she was right. As they approached the center of the room, the image of Grandfather just smiled at them, its white clothes and hair shimmering in the darkness. Angelina stepped toward the image. It turned to watch her, following her every movement with twinkling eyes and a broad smile. As she neared the other end of the room, another spotlight illuminated three light switches on the far wall.

"Ah! Ah hah!" said the image of Grandfather loudly with a grin. "The Luminous Light Switches!"

Angelina said, "The what?"

"The Luminous Light Switches!"

"What are those?" she asked.

"Why *those* are the Luminous Light Switches, of course," said the Grandfather image, pointing at the wall. "I think I said that. Although I don't really know for sure. I have forgotten already. I'm afraid I wasn't constructed with much memory. I need an upgrade. Can you upgrade me?"

"Uh, no. Sorry," Angelina said. "So, what are the 'Luminous Light Switches' and what do they do?"

"Well, that is the real question isn't it?" said Grandfather's 3-D image, turning to look at Zack with a wink.

"Yes. That's why I asked," Angelina said. "Zack, maybe you can talk to him."

Zack stepped forward. As he approached the switches, he noticed an outline in the wall, like the crease of a door.

"And what is this?" Zack asked. "A door?"

"Ah, you are a smart boy!" the hologram said. "You have discovered the Tall Door of Truth!"

"And that is?" said Angelina.

"Why, *that* is the Tall Door of Truth!" said the hologram pointing at the wall. "I think I said that. Although I don't really know. Sorry. I have forgotten already. I'm afraid I wasn't built with very much memory. I need an upgrade. Can you upgrade me?"

"No, we can't," said Angelina tensely.

"Oh, that's too bad," responded the Grandfather image.

CHAPTER 10: THE DASTARDLY DEATH

"What is behind the Tall Door of Truth?" asked Zack.

"Why, behind the Tall Door of Truth lies the Three Lightbulbs of Logic," said the hologram.

Angelina slapped her forehead. "And what are those?"

"Why they're the Three Lightbulbs of Logic," said the Grandfather image. "I think I said that, although I don't know —"

"They're part of a puzzle," said Zack to Angelina.

"Ah! Why yes they are," said the hologram, chuckling. "Smart boy."

Zack thought about how his father had said earlier that Grandfather was an enigma. Zack was beginning to see how true that was. Why would Grandfather place this riddle here, in a dark room under the Earth, probably hundreds of miles from home, past a room of lethal laser beams? What was he hiding? The opportunity to discover the answer drove Zack mad with curiosity.

As he often did when he was thinking, Zack combed a hand through his unkempt hair, in a vain attempt to pat it down. It quickly popped back up into its traditional spikes and swirls.

"How does the puzzle work?" Zack asked.

"Well, that's the fun part," said the hologram. "See, you have to decide which Luminous Light Switch belongs to which Logical Lightbulb."

"No problem," said Angelina. "We'll just open the door and flip all the switches on and off."

"Ah," said the Grandfather hologram. "See, that is the trick. You may open the door only once, and when you do, you may not touch the light switches again."

"Ok, so we turn two lights on and open the door," said Angelina. "Then, the switch that is off is the dark light bulb and the two switches that we turned on go with the two light bulbs that are bright."

"Yeah, but two lights will be on and two switches will be on. We won't know which goes with which," asked Zack.

"Oh. Right," said Angelina. "I didn't think of that. Well, we have a fifty-fifty chance at that point. We'll guess."

"Highly unadvisable," said the hologram, shaking its head.

"Why?" asked Zack.

The hologram smiled and said, "Because as of two minutes ago, when we started talking, the Terrible Ten-Minute Timer started."

Zack and Angelina looked at each other.

"The Terrible Ten-Minute Timer?" said Angelina skeptically.

"Yes," said the hologram. "The Terrible Ten-Minute Timer. I guess I forgot to mention it. I am not entirely sure. I am sorry. I wasn't installed with much mem—"

"So, what the heck does The Terrible Ten-Minute Timer do?" Zack interrupted.

"It times ten minutes, of course," said the hologram. "Duh."

"And what happens at the end of ten minutes?" Zack asked.

"Ah. Well. I'd rather not go into details," said the hologram. "But basically, you die a Dastardly Death."

"Ah. Ok." said Angelina. "That, you did not mention yet."

"I didn't?" said the hologram. "I'm sorry. I can't remember."

"This is the weirdest thing ever," Angelina whispered to Zack.

Zack put his head in his hands and said, "This whole day has been weird. Spiraling elevators, barking garages, lasers that almost sliced us in two."

"Zack," said Angelina, pulling his hands away from his head. "Focus. I'm going to need your help on this. You're the brainiac. Get a grip."

Zack looked at her, straightened and said, "Sorry. You're right."

"So, any ideas?"

"Yeah, let's go home."

"You can't," said the hologram. "This room is now completely sealed. I'm afraid it has to be to contain the water."

CHAPTER 10: THE DASTARDLY DEATH

"What water?" asked Zack, his eyes wide.

"Ah, well, that's the dastardly part. Unless you solve the puzzle in ten minutes, water will flood this room and kill you," said the hologram with a smile. "I am somewhat certain I mentioned you might die, yes? I'm not sure. Sorry."

Zack moaned.

"Oh darn, did I just give away the secret?" said the hologram. "I am so bad with secrets, you know. I always forget what's a secret and what's not."

"Can't you just tell us the answer?" said Angelina.

"No. Afraid not," said the hologram, shaking its head. "I don't remember what it is."

Zack moaned again.

"Look Zack," said Angelina. "Ignore him. There has to be an answer."

"I don't know," said Zack.

"Look," said Angelina, shaking him. "You're a Goodspeed. Your Grandfather built this puzzle. You can figure it out. Plus, what choice do we have at this point?"

"All right. Ok, you're right."

Zack walked closer to the light switches, waving an index finger at them as if they had been bad, and said, "We can't turn three lights on. That won't help and we can't turn only two on. Turning one on still leaves two off. So, no matter what we do, we have to find a way to guess which individual switch works which individual light bulb."

"Two minutes," said the hologram.

"Look Zack, you can figure it out, I know you can. If we turn two lights on and open the door, we'll only know which off light switch matches the one off light, right? There will still be two switches flipped on and two light bulbs that are lit. So, the question is how we pick between those two," Angelina said as she glared at the hologram, which just smiled back.

Zack worked the problem around in his head. Three on. Two on. One on. None on. No matter which scenario he thought of, they would still only be able to eliminate one light bulb. That still left a fifty-fifty guess between the other two — a chance Zack was not going to take unless he had to.

"One minute," said the hologram, wincing a little at Angelina's scowl. "Sorry, I had to mention it. Dastardly Death sequence initiating."

Sounds of rushing water filled the chamber.

"Zack?" said Angelina, as she looked around.

"I don't know Max!" said Zack. "I can't see the answer. Wait... see. I can't see it. I can't see it! I get it! The answer is about more than just sight."

"What? Zack? What are you talking about?" Angelina asked worriedly. Zack was rushing back and forth across the room.

"Is that it?" he said frantically. "Yes, that's it. It has to be it. We only get one shot at this."

"Thirty seconds," said the hologram.

"How high are they?" Zack asked the hologram.

"Excuse me?"

"The light bulbs! How high up are they?"

"Well, they're on the ceiling," said the hologram. "Where light bulbs usually are, silly boy."

"No!" said Zack in despair. "They can't be."

"Of course, there is a ladder in the center of the room, which can reach them," said the hologram, with a wink. "I have no idea why it's there though."

"That's it! I know!" said Zack. He raced to the far wall and flipped two light switches on the right side on.

"Fifteen seconds," said the hologram.

CHAPTER 10: THE DASTARDLY DEATH

"Zack, if you know the answer why don't you just tell him!" exclaimed Angelina.

"Not yet, Max. We don't know, yet," Zack said.

"Ten seconds," repeated the hologram.

"Zack?" Angelina said. She was shaking.

"Seven seconds."

"Now!" Zack exclaimed. He turned off the middle switch and opened the door. He ran into another square black-walled room. Angelina raced in after him. In the center of the room was a tall ladder and at the top of the ladder were three light bulbs on the ceiling. Only one of the light bulbs was on, and it cast a pale glow on the ladder.

"The light bulb that is lit belongs to the light switch on the far right, which I turned on," he said.

"Correct," said the hologram. "Four seconds."

Bellowing sounds of water crashed through the room. Zack raced up the ladder. He touched the two light bulbs that were off. One was cold, and the other was warm! It *felt* like a light bulb should feel when it has been turned on and then turned off.

"Two seconds."

"The left switch, which I never turned on, belongs to this cold light bulb and the center switch, which I turned on and then off, belongs to this warm one!" exclaimed Zack.

"Zero."

The sound of crashing water roared throughout the room. Zack winced, closed his eyes, and gripped the ladder. The sound of rushing water grew louder like it was about to burst into the room then stopped abruptly.

Angelina gasped.

A single drop of water leaked from the ceiling, cascaded through the air, and splashed to the floor, at the foot of the ladder.

"Puzzle solved," the Grandfather hologram said. "Dastardly Death sequence aborted."

Zack almost collapsed at the top of the ladder. His legs felt weak and his hands were trembling. He could see the hologram smiling at him from the other room. He stepped down the ladder and walked with Angelina into the first room.

The image of Grandfather beamed at him. The image seemed to shimmer even more with emotional energy. His eyes twinkled and a wide smile split his face like a toothy canyon.

"You have solved my riddle, young one," it said. "You are a smart boy indeed. You are worthy of my greatest secret."

The hologram waived its hand at the chamber around him. "Kalamazoo!" it said.

The ground shook like an earthquake. A gigantic outline of a circle appeared at their feet. The circle cracked from the main floor and they began to slowly descend. Below them, beyond the rim of the circular floor in every direction, was the most incredible sight Zack had ever seen.

The hologram smiled at them from the center of the circle and, as it disappeared, said:

"Welcome to the Clarion Spacedock."

CHAPTER 11

The Clarion Spacedock

The circular plate they stood on descended into a vast, white chamber. Zack gasped at the sight. His entire town could fit in this space. In every direction there was immense openness. Zack could barely make out the two walls of the chamber stretching into the distance. Dozens of Onyx Airstriders raced through the air, darting across the cavern. On the walls, Zack could see thin, slivers of windows with large crowds behind them. The people seemed to be checking monitors, eating, talking, and pointing at features in the Spacedock. Zack heard a PA announcement echo throughout the cavern.

"Flight schedule uploaded," it said. "Primary power system ready for installation. Prepare for Onyx Sun installation."

The most incredible thing Zack saw though filled the vast space in the middle of the canyon. An enormous spaceship, just like the model

Grandfather had given him but a million times larger, lay in the hangar like a gigantic white-gold dragon. It seemed to Zack to be almost a mile long. Just like the model, it was a tremendous wedge, pointed at one end into a long needle and tapered flat at the other, where wide jet nozzles shot out. The nose cone and underside were entirely gold, but the top was covered in white. Zack could see two tailfins at the end of the fuselage, rising from the ship like a "V." The streamlined glass orb of the bridge perched on the front of the fuselage. It looked like a translucent teardrop. Zack could see hundreds of people inside, buzzing about like a swarm of bees.

As the circular floor descended, Zack saw people prodding the underside of the ship, putting tubes in, pulling tubes out, and hurrying up long ramps into the fuselage. Caterpillar-like trains of goods were driven into the ship by large trucks. Massive clamps, which emerged from the sidewalls, held the ship in place. From this angle, Zack saw a wide line of text running down each side of the front of the fuselage. It read, "Onyx Pioneer."

Zack looked up. The hole in the ceiling from which they had descended was now just a black speck. He looked at Angelina. Her eyes were wide and glistened at the corners, as she stared up at the spaceship.

"Who could have done this?" she whispered.

Zack knew. Only one man could have accomplished something like this, without anyone knowing. Only one man had the intelligence, creativity, and drive. Only one man was "abnormal" enough to think this big. The one man everyone doubted.

As the circular platform touched down on the hangar floor, Zack looked up at the spaceship, hovering over him like an immovable god, and said a single word:

"Grandfather."

CHAPTER 12

An Unlikely Adventure

Zack and Angelina stepped off the circular plate. The moment their feet left the pad, it whooshed past them and returned to the ceiling.

"Don't worry. We'll find another way out," Zack said.

Angelina nodded back slowly, still looking stupefied by what they had discovered.

Zack and Angelina wandered around the floor under the spaceship. Hundreds of people milled about carrying boxes, driving forklifts, and talking to each other. Trains of vehicles whisked past.

Just then, on the left side of the chamber, a door swooshed open and two people stepped out.

"Duck!" Zack said, grabbing Angelina and pushing her behind a stack of nearby crates.

Two men strode across the bay and paused in front of the crates. Zack could barely see their faces from where he and Angelina hid.

One of the men, who was broad-shouldered and had a cleft chin jutting from his face, pointed a finger at the other man and said, "Listen, Dr. Machvel. These launch interruptions have to stop."

The man to whom this was addressed stared back with a wry smile. He was older and olive-skinned. He had a shock of peppery hair, a pointed black beard, and deep eye sockets like pools of oil. His protruding brow cast a shadow over his face. He spoke in a low, steady voice that was almost a hiss. "Very well, Commander Chase. My intention was to protect the ship and her crew. I will cease my inspections, which were merely…safety precautions."

"Do you think I'm stupid?" said Commander Chase. "You have been delaying our launch for weeks, with no firm evidence of any risk to the ship or crew. Now, Professor Goodspeed has okayed this launch, it is his ship, we are his crew, and that will have to be good enough."

"Very well, Commander," replied Dr. Machvel. Sharp teeth peeked out behind his lips as he added, "Although I must stress that the Onyx Sun is an experimental technology, capable of great power and… great destruction. Should something go wrong, the effects would be disastrous."

Zack noticed Dr. Machvel smiled slightly as he said this, like the Onyx Sun's dangerous aspects excited him.

"Duly noted. Now that's settled, we're launching," said Commander Chase.

Grandfather Goodspeed emerged from a nearby doorway. He strode in his typically haphazard, but confident, way across the bay towards Commander Chase and Dr. Machvel. A group of men in white flight suits followed him, pushing a levitated platform with the Onyx Sun on it. Grandfather skittered to a halt near the men and addressed Commander Chase first.

CHAPTER 12: AN UNLIKELY ADVENTURE

"Robert," he said.

Then, he looked at Dr. Machvel, and said flatly, "Ian."

They both replied, "Professor."

Fyodor Goodspeed looked around the landing bay, took a deep breath, and said, "Well, this is it. So, do we have the cooperation of our Engineering Chief?"

Dr. Machvel looked up and said, "Yes, Professor. I only wish you to consider —"

Commander Chase cleared his throat.

"What Dr. Machvel means to say is, 'Yes. You have the complete support of the Engineering Department.' Final countdown can begin," Commander Chase said.

"Excellent," said Grandfather. "Then, let us begin." Turning to the men behind him he said, "Gentlemen, please load the Onyx Sun onto the Power Tower. Dr. Machvel will make sure it is attached properly to the ship's systems and main atomic engine. Then, all flight staff can be seated, and we can load the final supplies."

Grandfather leaned back to look at the Onyx Pioneer, spreading his arms wide as if he wanted to hug it. Zack thought he might fall over.

"Today, we make history!" Grandfather said.

Fyodor put an arm around Commander Chase's shoulders and walked down the landing bay. Dr. Machvel and the technicians left in another direction with the Onyx Sun.

"Come on," Zack said to Angelina and rushed after his grandfather and the Commander. A long embankment of supply boxes hid Zack and Angelina from view. Thankfully, both the men were tall, so Zack could catch wisps of their conversation over the boxes.

"…final preparations…leave in an hour…colony families on board…" he heard Commander Chase say.

Grandfather's excited voice rose over the boxes louder, "Good. We launch immediately. All systems go."

The men stopped walking as Commander Chase turned to Grandfather. Zack heard whispering. He could tell they were engaged in an intense conversation, but he couldn't hear them.

"Stay here," Zack said to Angelina. He slipped around some boxes to get closer. He crouched behind a crate that was low enough that if Grandfather turned around, he could easily peer over it.

Zack heard Commander Chase say, "…but he'll never understand why you left. You need to tell him soon. We can't delay the launch."

Zack chanced a glance over the box at Grandfather's face. He looked sad. His head hung low, and he rubbed his right thumb inside his left hand.

"I've thought about this, Robert," said Grandfather. "He'll never understand. He is just a boy. He needs to be with his family. I am just — a distraction. An amusement for now. As he grows older, he will lose that boyish innocence and boundless imagination and become like his parents. I've seen it happen before, with my own son. It will happen to Zack."

Zack's heart skipped a beat at the mention of his name.

Commander Chase sighed, "You know your grandson better than I do, Fy. I would never dispute that. But we all know you care about him. You don't want to disappoint him. Let him know you're leaving."

Grandfather shook his head, dropped his hands to his side, and said, "No. I appreciate your thoughts Robert, but my mind is made up. He would never believe me even if I did tell him. And even if he did believe, he would want to come, and he can't. The boy needs to be with his family. As different from me — and maybe him — as they are, they are his mother and father."

Commander Chase studied Grandfather Goodspeed's face then said, "Ok. I'll begin the final countdown then. We launch in thirty minutes."

He strode down the hangar but stopped and turned back.

CHAPTER 12: AN UNLIKELY ADVENTURE

"At least send him an email, Fy. Something. Give him something to help him understand someday."

"No," said Grandfather. "It is better this way. Maybe, someday —" Grandfather glanced at the towering spaceship over him, "— maybe somehow, I can show him all this, and he'll understand."

Commander Chase nodded slowly, then turned and walked toward the ramp leading into the ship. Grandfather stood for a long time, kneading his palms, then finally sighed and walked toward the ship.

Zack jumped up and ran back to Angelina. "I don't believe this," he said, pulling her to her feet. "He is leaving again!"

"What are you talking about?"

Zack pointed at the figure of his grandfather stumbling up the gangway. "My grandfather is going somewhere in that ship. It sounds like he's never coming back!"

Angelina looked at the ship then glanced back at Zack, "Where is he going?"

"I have no idea. But it sounds far away."

"Zack, I'm sorry," Angelina said, putting her hand on his shoulder.

Zack was angry at Grandfather for leaving again. Especially now that Zack had seen what Grandfather had been working on during his long absences, Zack wanted to be included. He didn't care if it took him away from his parents. He just wanted to go.

"I'm not going to let this happen again," he said. "I'm not going to let him just leave."

"Zack, what do you mean?"

"I mean that I am tired of him popping in and out of my life. I am tired of him hiding things from me, and then finding out how cool the things he's been working on are."

Zack turned and looked at the ship.

"I'm not letting him go this time. I'm going with him."

Zack looked at Angelina. She just stared back at him. She squinted at him so intensely, her eyes looked like slits. Her face tightened, as she considered what he was saying. Then, a devilish smile emerged on her face.

"You mean you're going to get on that ship?"

"Yes."

"How?"

"I don't know, but I'll sneak on if I have to."

"Really?"

"Yes."

"Then, I'm in."

"Are you sure?"

"I've never been so sure. Zack, you think I'd miss this? I'd have to be crazy to not see what's on board that thing. It's a freaking *spaceship!*"

Zack laughed. He was thankful to have a person like Angelina with him. He wondered how the kids at school hadn't known that under her cold, tough exterior, Angelina was warm and adventurous.

At that moment, a mechanized voice boomed through the hangar, "Final launch in forty-five minutes. Prepare for countdown."

Swirling orange lights came to life by the ramps leading into the ship. Geysers of steam shot from the bottom of the fuselage. People began rushing around the hangar either disappearing into exits in the side of the Clarion Spacedock or clamoring aboard the ship. A stream of cargo trains cleared the final cargo from the floor, leaving Zack and Angelina on an exposed surface.

"Ok, then," Zack said. "Let's do this! We don't have much time."

They sprang toward the ship. The largest ramp in the center of the fuselage was now clear of traffic. As they approached, they heard metal grinding on metal and the ramp began to rise.

Angelina was ahead of Zack. She held out her hand to him and shouted, "Come on! Hurry!"

CHAPTER 12: AN UNLIKELY ADVENTURE

Zack grabbed her hand and caught up to her. They leapt around the steaming geysers. As they reached the ramp, Angelina tore ahead and sprang for it, as it was already several feet off the floor. She lifted herself onto the ramp then spun around on her stomach and held an arm down for Zack.

"Jump, Zack!" she shouted.

A flicker of doubt shot through Zack's mind, as he vaulted toward the ramp. He flew through the air seemingly weightless, seemingly forever — his arm outstretched — reaching for Angelina. Just as he began to fall, Zack felt her grab him. Their arms met in mid-air and she clasped onto him. For a moment, he dangled beneath her, swinging from the rising ramp.

"Pull!" he exclaimed, as he grasped the ramp edge with his other hand. Zack saw that in another twenty feet, the ramp would meet the fuselage of the ship. He would have to be inside by that point or he would have a very long fall to the floor.

"I can't lift you!" Angelina said. Zack struggled and sweated as he tried to pull himself onto the ramp. Angelina's arm was getting sweaty and Zack's grip slipped.

"I'm losing you!" shouted Angelina.

"Hold on to me!" Zack said. He pulled his other hand from the edge of the ramp and used it to latch onto Angelina's arm. She yelped in pain, as his entire weight dangled from her. Zack rocked his legs back and forth as if Angelina's arm was a rope swing. His body began to sway like a pendulum. Their arms slipped.

"Zack! I can't hold on much longer!"

"Hang on Max! Just a few more seconds!"

He swung back and forth wildly, his body almost lying flat with the ramp at the top of his swings. He threw his leg over the edge of the ramp. His sneaker hit the deck then slid off.

"Hang on!" he shouted.

"Zack!" Angelina grunted, her face red.

Zack wasted no time. He put all his weight into his swing. His grip slipped farther down Angelina's arm each swing, as his body flailed wildly higher. He gave one last attempt and, as his whole left leg cleared the ramp, he lost his grip on Angelina.

For the faintest moment, Zack thought he was falling to the floor far below. He seemed to be floating in mid-air, neither on the ship nor off it. Then, as he caught sight of the ramp passing under him, he realized he had managed to swing his leg and most of his lower body over the ramp. Zack's torso landed on the ramp with a thud. He immediately arched his back, grabbing wildly at floor and rolled completely onto the ramp a second before it slid shut with a hiss.

Zack Goodspeed was thankful for many things in life: his grandfather, his parents, his baseballs. At that moment though, Zack had never been more thankful for anything than he was now for just being alive.

Zack turned to Angelina, who was lying on the floor next to him. She smiled at him and they both began to laugh. Zack rolled around on the floor of the ramp, holding his sides. Their laughter echoed throughout the empty loading bay. Angelina rolled toward Zack, put a hand on his shoulder, smiled at him — those sparks in her eyes brighter than ever — and said, "Let's never do that again."

CHAPTER 13

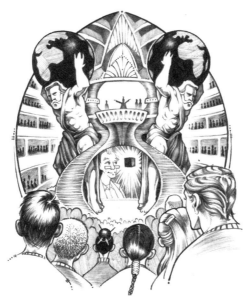

The Great Hall

Zack and Angelina picked themselves up and surveyed their surroundings. They stood in a well-lit room crowded with cargo boxes. There was one exit: a wide door on the far end of the chamber.

Zack and Angelina walked toward the door. It whisked open. Both Zack and Angelina dove for a hiding position behind the boxes. When nothing happened, Zack relaxed.

"Must be an automatic door," he said. Angelina nodded.

"Seems pretty quiet," Zack said, peering out of the room. There was a long white hallway that disappeared in an arc in both directions. There was a large word painted on the far wall that read, "Deck 14."

"Yeah," said Angelina, as she led the way out of the room.

Two adults strode out of a nearby doorway. They wore white flight suits and immediately noticed Zack and Angelina.

"You two!" the taller man said.

Zack and Angelina turned to face him. The man eyed them.

"Where are your flight suits?"

"Um," Zack stammered. "We lost them?"

"You lost them?" the tall man said. "You believe this, José? This is why children shouldn't be allowed on the ship."

The shorter, fatter man named José grumbled in a frog-like voice, "I couldn't agree with you more, Malik."

"Look, you two, there are spare flight suits in the dressing chamber," the man named José said. He motioned to the room from which he and Malik had just emerged. "Get in there, put on some clothes, and meet everyone in the Great Hall."

"Uh, sure," said Zack. "Only, where is the Great Hall again?"

The two men looked at each other. Malik shook his head and said, "Did you sleep through orientation?"

"No. Sorry, we…uh…missed it," Zack said. Angelina cautiously nodded in agreement.

Malik crouched down so he was eye-level with Zack and pointed a finger down the hallway.

"Go to the elevator down that hallway to the right," he said slowly. "Take it to Deck 3. You'll see it as soon as you get off the elevator. Okay? You got it now?"

"Yeah," Zack said.

"Be there in five minutes. Don't be late."

Malik and José trudged off down the hallway, while Angelina and Zack jumped into the changing room and quickly donned two flight suits. Zack liked the uniforms. They were white, loose fitting, and had cargo pockets on the pants and shirt. He felt like a jet fighter pilot.

Once they were dressed, they walked down the hallway toward the elevator. Deck 14 seemed to hold the ship's cargo, since each door

CHAPTER 13: THE GREAT HALL

they passed whooshed open to reveal piles of cargo boxes. Otherwise, Deck 14 looked boringly utilitarian to Zack.

After a longer walk than Zack anticipated, they found the elevator. The doors slid open and they stepped inside.

"This looks like a service elevator," Angelina said.

Zack nodded. The elevator was wide and had several large tarps hanging from the ceiling to protect the walls. There was a panel by the door that had buttons labeled Deck 1 to Deck 15. Zack pressed "Deck 3." The elevator shot up and a few minutes later stopped. The door swooshed open and Zack and Angelina stepped out.

If Zack had had any doubts that the inside of the Onyx Pioneer might be boring, they were dispelled now. As they stepped off the elevator, they saw a massive archway that led into an expansive chamber. The archway was vaulted like a cathedral. At the top of the arch perched a stone etching of the Onyx Sun with beams of energy radiating from the cube.

Zack and Angelina walked through the arch and strode into the Great Hall, trying to act like they belonged there. The congregation inside the Great Hall seemed to represent every nationality, age, and race of Earth. Each person had a small insignia on the left chest pocket of their flight suit. Some people near Zack and Angelina, who spoke like Americans, had badges of heroic eagles on their chest. Others had heraldic shields and seemed to be from European ancestry, as Zack heard from them the lilting tones of languages that sounded like French, Italian, and Spanish. Other people with darker skin wore proud tribal crests that seemed to signify their African descent. Assorted Asian people wore elegant letter-symbols. There were other insignias that matched people of Latin American, Indian, Middle Eastern, Australian, and other ancestries.

The most interesting thing to Zack, though, was that people did not band together based upon their nationality, sex, or ancestry. Instead, people seemed to be grouped together based on markings on wide, gold belts they wore at their waists. Some people had striped gold belts with a powerful amulet stamped onto it that looked like a hand grabbing a lightning bolt. Judging by the wide assortment of tools these people carried, Zack assumed they were probably the engineering crew. Maybe these were the people the man named Machvel commanded, Zack thought. Other people of thicker stature wore plainer belts with stout firearms at their sides. These people looked like police. A third group of people had jagged belts adorned with a solid square of gold at the center decorated with an ornate pattern that looked like fire. From the quick-witted, yet twitchy look of these people and the high incidence of spectacles, Zack thought they might be some kind of intellectual elite. A fourth group wore flowing robes with wide sleeves. They floated around the chamber with placid expressions and slight smiles on their faces. Their arms were crossed so their hands hid in their sleeves. They wore gold belts stamped in the center with a single, watchful eye. They reminded Zack of monks. A fifth group was the most boisterous. They wore belts with enormous gold exclamation points for buckles. Given this group often broke into song, laughter, or fits of juggling, Zack guessed they were here to entertain the crew. The sixth and final group had the stern look of people with deep responsibilities. Several members of the other groups seemed to be watching them, as if waiting for a command. The people of this group wore simple, gold armbands and belts with a thick red stripe in the center.

Zack and Angelina wound their way through the crowd. The hall was vast, and the farther they walked, the more it seemed to go on. It was much longer than it was wide, with thick columns stretching from the floor every fifty feet. It was like an enormous cathedral, with the columns meeting the roof where the vaulted ceiling hovered. The room was five stories tall, and at each stage, Zack could see ornately carved balconies of stone that stretched the

CHAPTER 13: THE GREAT HALL

length of the hall. On these balconies, groups of people crowded together, talking excitedly.

Finally, Zack and Angelina reached the end of the chamber. The wall at this end was decorated like an altar. A series of wide stairs led from the floor, covered in blue and purple rugs edged with gold. Towering stone statues of the titan Atlas rose on either side of the back wall, his muscles straining from the vast globe he carried on his back. In between these statues was a stained glass window that stretched from the floor to the ceiling and glowed with golden light. Unlike other stained glass windows Zack had seen on Earth, this one was composed of frosted glass and edged in a golden frame. The glass formed the figure of a mostly bald man in spectacles holding a cube in one hand, which radiated brilliant light. Zack realized in shock the man was his grandfather.

He was about to say something to Angelina when the balcony above the stained glass window filled with a small crowd. Each of these people wore the red and gold belts that seemed to signify high office, yet each person had different national insignias on their breast pockets.

Angelina put one hand over her mouth and pointed to the balcony with the other. Zack looked up. Commander Chase strode onto the balcony with a straight back, followed by a glowering Dr. Machvel. Grandfather Goodspeed lurched in last, bedecked in his traditional white suit, complete with white vest, tie, jacket, shirt, shoes, socks, and slacks. A new gold watch chain extended from his vest buttons to a pocket in his vest. He stumble-walked onto the balcony with a quizzical, half-smile like he was mildly surprised he could even move from one place to the other. He traipsed to the end of the balcony, stretched his long arms to support himself on the railing and surveyed the people below him.

Silence overtook the chamber and the assembly looked up at the balcony. Grandfather held the silence for a moment, smiling down at everyone. His silver-white tuft of hair seemed to quake with internal energy as he shot glances around the chamber. He waved wildly to a few people in the crowd. Zack and Angelina stepped behind some taller adults, to make sure they weren't seen, but peered out enough to see Grandfather steeple his fingers, look down, and close his eyes.

He stood like that for a long moment, then looked up suddenly and said, "Space. Wow. It's big."

Grandfather beamed at everyone, and continued, "Rumors say it goes on forever, and ever, and ever, and such. But no one knows for sure. That's the sad thing. Not one human on Earth has ever traveled farther than our own Moon. That's like only traveling from your dining room to your kitchen when you live in a castle. In other words, space is *huge* and mostly unexplored, just like old castles."

"Although that doesn't mean one can't know how big space is. In fact, today, here, now, at this very moment, in this very spacecraft, which we have built together, we stand on the frontier of knowing the vastness of our own universe. We have collaborated to build a vessel unlike any other. For the first time in human history, man can visit the stars as easily as pulling up his socks."

Peals of applause rippled throughout the cathedral. Grandfather waited for them to subside, then continued.

"Each of you has committed to this wondrous journey. You've left your countries and your friends. Some of you have even left your family. Many of you have made up alibis; lies to keep your family and friends at ease while you travel. You've said you are moving abroad or going on a long journey. You've told these lies because they wouldn't have understood or believed you if you had told the truth. I applaud you. If you hadn't had the strength to do that, none of us would have been able to take this next great step for mankind."

People applauded again but softer. Zack noticed a couple of people touching the sides of their eyes. One woman pulled her child, standing nearby, closer. Zack wondered if this was how Grandfather had justified

CHAPTER 13: THE GREAT HALL

his departure in his own mind. That he was going to do something incredible. Something Zack would not understand. Something Zack wouldn't have been able to believe if he hadn't been standing here. Zack, scoffed to himself. Even if that was his reason, it didn't make it sting less when he did disappear.

"The Onyx Sun engine that powers this ship," Grandfather continued, "is a source of unlimited energy, which I have tapped for the betterment of mankind. For the first time in our history, man has been given the ability to go anywhere and do anything he wishes. Nothing now stands between us and the apparently limitless universe. This is our manifest destiny!"

The chamber erupted into thunderous waves of clapping and cheering. Grandfather smiled at the audience below him and held up a hand. The clapping continued for a while, then pattered to a stop. Grandfather let his hand fall.

"So, I hear space is limitless," he said. "That is what they tell me. That is the rumor. But maybe I heard wrong amidst the universal vastness. The only way for us to know is to go. Prepare the Onyx Pioneer for launch."

The crowd cheered as Grandfather Goodspeed lurched from the balcony, and Commander Chase stepped forward. "Command crews to your control stations," he said. "Security Team, secure the hatches. SciTech and Engineering Corps, report to your departments on Decks 6 and 7. Entertainment Troupe, store all the elephants. Spiritual Conclave, pray for our safe passage. Godspeed to all."

The room began to clear. People whisked away in all directions. Zack and Angelina, the lone stowaways, had no idea which way to go. Zack started walking in the direction of the main entranceway when he bumped into a thin Indian boy, a little shorter than himself. The boy fell over backwards and dropped the handheld computer he had been holding to his face.

"Sorry," Zack said, helping the boy up. Angelina picked up his computer.

"No problem," the Indian boy said, straightening out his uniform. Zack noticed he wore a badge that was orange, white, and green and had a blue wheel-like circle at its center. "I was just studying the Arabic mythology behind the Orion constellation."

"Okay," said Angelina, drawing out the word and handing back his computer as if she might catch something if she held it too long.

"It's actually quite interesting," the boy continued, not noticing Angelina's reaction. "The constellation can be seen all over the world and is one of the brightest. Many ancient civilizations — Greek, Indian, and Arab — have unique mythologies for the Orion Constellation. It's like the ancient world was obsessed with it."

"That's, uh, interesting," said Angelina and looked at Zack like she wanted to leave.

Zack smiled at her, then turned to the boy and said, "Anyway, sorry for bumping into you again. See you later."

The hall was almost empty. Zack and Angelina started to walk away, when the Indian boy called after them, saying, "Hey! I didn't see you in pre-cadet training."

Zack turned around, but Angelina was quicker to answer. "Actually we were late admissions," she said.

"There are no late admissions," the boy said. He looked at Angelina disappointedly, as if her lie had been too obvious. "Training is required for everyone on the Onyx Pioneer, even the children of the staff. I was there. I did not see you there. Who are your parents?"

Zack was unsure how to answer this, but felt for some reason, like telling him the truth. Something in the Indian boy's eyes seemed honest and trustworthy.

"We're with Professor Goodspeed," Zack said.

CHAPTER 13: THE GREAT HALL

The boy stepped back, mouth open, as if thunder had just boomed through the Great Hall. Then, he leapt forward, grabbing Zack's hand, and shaking it wildly. A smile exposed his pearl white teeth.

"Forgive me. I had no idea," he said. "I am honored to meet the children of the father of our voyage."

"Actually, he's my grandfather," said Zack.

"Ah yes, of course," said the boy, still shaking Zack's hand. "My name is Sanjay Soon. My father is the Vice-Chief of Engineering under Dr. Machvel. Welcome to the Onyx Pioneer."

"Thank you," said Zack retrieving his hand. "Thanks. This is Angelina Maximillian. People call her Max."

Sanjay reached out to ring Angelina's hand, but she stepped back.

"Uh, nice to meet you," she said.

Sanjay looked disappointed but turned his wide, pearly smile back to Zack.

"Say, Sanjay," Zack said. "Since we missed training, we're not sure where we're supposed to go."

"If you are with Professor Goodspeed, you are to come to the Command Deck with me. All officers and their families are to watch the launch from there. It has the best view, after all. The entire room is glass and sits on the very top of the ship. Come, I will show you."

"That's great," said Zack. "Thanks. Just one thing." He reached out to hold Sanjay back. "We'd prefer not to…bother…my grandfather, since he is busy with the launch. Could we sit somewhere else, perhaps?"

Sanjay eyed Angelina and Zack closely. He looked at once inquisitive and conspiratorial. Then, he smiled and said, "Of course. You can sit with me. There are plenty of seats on the command deck. My father and mother would be honored to have the grandson of Fyodor

Goodspeed sitting with us during the launch. My father and your grandfather designed much of this ship together over the Internet for years before they even met. I am sure my father will want to ask you what you think about it."

"Thanks," said Zack as they followed Sanjay out of the Great Hall.

CHAPTER 14

Firelight of the Onyx Pioneer

Sanjay led Zack and Angelina to a bank of elevators. An empty elevator arrived and the trio stepped inside. This elevator was different. It was white and tubular, with a floor-to-ceiling glass wall at the back. All they could see right now through the window was a dark elevator shaft.

As the doors slid closed behind them, Zack was suddenly reminded of the spiral elevator. He glanced at Angelina as Sanjay pressed the "Deck 1" button and the elevator shot upwards. Angelina grinned at Zack as he pressed himself against the rear wall.

Sanjay, still full of wide, white-toothy smiles, turned a questioning look to Angelina, who said, "He doesn't like elevators."

"I'm fine," Zack said.

He forced himself to not think about the elevator. Just then, the dark shaft behind the window shot away, and a new sight presented itself. Angelina gasped and put a hand to her mouth. Sanjay smiled even wider. Zack forgot his queasiness.

Beyond the glass was an oblong cavern crisscrossed with catwalks. Purple-blue light emanated from the center of the cavern, where a dark spire rose from the floor almost to the roof. Mounted upon this tower, standing on one end like a diamond, was the dark shape of the Onyx Sun. It spun rapidly, occasionally firing lightning bolts that arced along the catwalks.

Angelina stepped toward the glass wall and put her fingers on it. Sanjay stepped up too, resting his hands on a nearby railing. Even Zack stood a little straighter.

"What is that?" Angelina asked.

"That is the heart of the Onyx Pioneer," said Sanjay. "That is the Power Tower. It focuses the energy from the Onyx Sun and uses it to power the entire ship. We have learned from experimentation that the Onyx Sun gives off so much energy we had to build these catwalks to absorb the extra power."

"It's amazing," said Angelina.

"Yes," said Sanjay. "This took our research teams over a year to perfect. My father worked many long hours on its design, but it was Professor Goodspeed who finally figured it out."

Sanjay locked eyes with Zack and said, "Your grandfather is a genius. I know people sometimes misunderstand him, but the crew on this ship respect him."

Zack swelled with pride. Sanjay's compliment somehow lessened the sting of Grandfather's long absences. Zack wanted to say something, but nothing seemed equal to Sanjay's comment. Zack just nodded and turned back toward the window.

CHAPTER 14: FIRELIGHT OF THE ONYX PIONEER

The elevator shot through the room. As fast as it was going, it barely seemed to move through the enormous cavern. Finally, Zack could see the ceiling approaching. The ceiling shot by, and they were once again faced with the dark elevator shaft. The elevator slowed. A muffled ding sounded, as it stopped.

"Deck 1. Top floor. Bridge," said a mechanized voice. "Now get out! Shoo! Scram, you young kippers!"

"The elevators here are kinda rude," Angelina said.

Sanjay sighed and said, "Yes, that was an Entertainment Troupe prank. They rewired all of the elevators. My father was very annoyed. He and his team are still working on fixing them."

The doors parted and Zack, Angelina, and Sanjay stepped onto the Onyx Pioneer's bridge. The bridge was an oval room topped with a clear glass dome. It was a streamlined chamber that seemed to fly along the hull of the front of the ship. In the back half of the chamber, where Zack stood with his friends, there were hundreds of seats. The front half of the room was recessed and covered in monitors and gauges. Zack guessed this area was the control center. About thirty people milled about, all wearing the plain gold belts with a red stripe. Several consoles emitted blue 3-D holograms that the command crew studied and discussed. Some of these holograms showed a model of the Onyx Pioneer. Others showed a cratered sphere. Some people darted across the deck, talking out loud as if to themselves.

Zack, pointed to one of the people writing on a computer tablet and talking to himself.

"What is that guy doing?" he asked Sanjay.

"Oh, that is one of our sensor systems engineers," he replied. "He is probably making sure the flight deck is clear of all the cargo we loaded into the ship and double checking the condition of external monitors."

"Yeah, but who is the wacko talking to?" asked Angelina.

"Oh," said Sanjay, nodding. "I see why you are confused. A lot of the Onyx Pioneer's systems are voice activated. Any person can talk directly to the main computer."

"So," said Zack. "That guy can talk to the computer and it talks back?"

"Yes, and the computer is very friendly. Well, at least it was until the Entertainment Troupe rewired it too."

Sanjay sighed and said, "For a while the only response you could from it was 'Go slap yourself with a salami!'"

Sanjay made a face like he had tasted lemons.

"It was quite frustrating. After that, the Engineering Corps voice-firewalled the system so people can now only access information relevant to their jobs. I hear the Entertainment Troupe's system is a mess — as is to be expected — but the rest of the ship's functions are better. The only people who have total system access are your grandfather, Commander Chase, and Dr. Machvel."

"My father can access almost all of the engineering and science functions, since he is Dr. Machvel's backup," Sanjay said with a distinct note of pride. "He is forbidden to interact with the computer on any subject beyond those relating to science and engineering, however."

Just then, the elevator opened behind them and a stream of people poured onto the bridge. Grandfather Goodspeed bumbled about at the head of the line. He walked by Zack without noticing. Zack did note, however, the intense look of concentration on his grandfather's face as he focused on walking somewhat normally past the bridge's general seating area. Professor Goodspeed firmly gripped the stair's railings, as he descended into the command center, pacing himself as he treaded on each stair. Commander Chase and Dr. Machvel were at his sides as he walked. Commander Chase looked poised to grab Grandfather Goodspeed at any moment, should he falter,

CHAPTER 14: FIRELIGHT OF THE ONYX PIONEER

while Dr. Machvel simply leaned away from the lurching man with a grimace.

Upon reaching the front of the bridge, Grandfather Goodspeed turned and faced the crew assembled on the bridge. He smiled like someone who is supremely surprised at the outcome of their recent efforts. Three hundred people peered back. Fyodor said nothing. He simply looked at the faces around him, catching each person's eye and nodding. As his eyes wound their way around to Zack and Angelina, Zack pulled Angelina behind Dr. Soon. Zack waited until he noticed several people down the line nodding and affirming Grandfather Goodspeed's attention. Only then did Zack and Angelina move back into the crowd to stand with the others.

Grandfather Goodspeed concluded his review of the bridge and, for the briefest of moments, glanced at the spot Zack and Angelina occupied. Zack thought he caught the faintest recognition in Grandfather's eyes. But before Zack could do or say anything, Grandfather turned toward the front of the bridge.

"Commander," he said. "Take us out."

The command staff fanned out in front of the consoles. Commander Chase sat down in a golden chair at the prow of the bridge. A cadet approached the Commander and placed a small envelope in his hands, saying, "The launch code, Commander."

Commander Chase nodded and tore open the envelope. He pulled a small strip of paper from the envelope and looked at it. A blue hologram of a numberpad popped up in front of him. He rapidly tapped the image, entering a long string of digits. Finally, he tapped the Enter button and the computer's soft voice said, "Launch Code Accepted. Onyx Sun power ramping to seventy-five percent for launch."

A deep rumbling grew from within the Onyx Pioneer, like the growling of a hungry beast. Zack imagined the arcs of lightning in the

Onyx Sun's core rapidly intensifying. In his mind, he could see a violent electrical storm wilding its way through the center of the craft.

The entire ship shook. The staff on the bridge took their seats. Dr. and Mrs. Soon told Sanjay, Angelina, and Zack to sit down, but the children ignored them and walked to the railing between the seating area and the recessed bridge. Grandfather's back was turned and Zack felt confident he wouldn't turn around, given the activities involved in launching the ship. Zack wanted to see this, and he could tell from the challenging expression on Angelina's face and Sanjay's mirthful smile that his companions did too.

The Onyx Pioneer rumbled. The long hangar outside the cockpit swayed a little. The walls of the Clarion Spacedock floated toward and away from the ship.

"Prepare the final countdown and open the gate," Commander Chase said to the crew.

Zack noticed the far wall of the Spacedock was actually two gigantic doors. The doors split in half as they opened, like two behemoth gods praying to the passage of the Onyx Pioneer. The doors spread wide. A vast, dark passage lay beyond.

"Illuminate the path," said Commander Chase.

A series of lights came on, one after another, along the length of the launching bay, like a path of stars. It seemed to Zack to stretch for miles.

The rumbling intensified. The entire ship shook. Mrs. Soon insisted the children sit down and buckle up, which they did. Even Dr. Machvel and Grandfather Goodspeed took their seats.

"Countdown on my mark," said Commander Chase. The shaking of the ship intensified. "Loose forward stays."

The Onyx Pioneer shuddered as the docking clamps receded. The ship swung to the right of the massive bay.

CHAPTER 14: FIRELIGHT OF THE ONYX PIONEER

"Compensate with starboard atom-thrusters," said Commander Chase. Zack could feel the Onyx Pioneer yaw to the left and then stop, perfectly centered in the line of lights.

"Hold position," Commander Chase ordered.

"Professor Goodspeed, the Onyx Pioneer is ready for launch," Commander Chase said.

Grandfather Goodspeed, from his seat to Commander Chase's right, peered out the line of lights and said, "Launch authorized."

Commander Chase tapped illuminated pads on his chair and the cabin lights dimmed. Now, only the trail of lights was visible stretching into the distance.

The vibrations intensified, the noise reaching a deafening pitch. Angelina grabbed Zack's arm. He looked at her, and she smiled back devilishly. "This is going to be wicked," she said.

Commander Chase rapidly brushed the glowing control panels and shouted over the shaking, "Launch!"

An invisible hand slammed Zack back into his seat as the engine noise hit its crescendo and the Onyx Pioneer shot down the launching tube like a scorching missile.

CHAPTER 15

The Onyx Swordfish

The life of a fisherman is one fraught with long stretches of boredom capped by ten minutes of exhilaration. Fishermen subjected themselves to this for lots of reasons: to earn a living, to be outside, but most of all, so they could have that one great fishing story that none of their friends could beat.

Reginald Flank stood on the deck of his boat, the Alleyah, floating in the Pacific miles from shore, experiencing a boring day.

"Ten hours I have been out here," he thought, shaking his head and squinting at the sun. "Adrift. My lines out, waiting for something to bite. Ten hours."

Of course, Reginald was exaggerating a little. This is also a trait common to fishermen. Usually it comes in the form of "I once caught a fish this big" and then the fisherman exhibits what an exaggerator he

CHAPTER 15: THE ONYX SWORDFISH

is by stretching his arms wider than he can possibly reach and much wider than the fish actually was. In most cases, in fact, the fish in question could be measured on a fisherman's finger. This trait, however, was most likely a result of the life these men led. After all, with all this time to kill, what else was there to do but invent wild stories to tell one's friends when back on shore?

In actuality, Reginald had been sitting on the Alleyah for eight hours: 5:30 AM to now, which was 1:30 PM.

This was the time of day Reginald hated the most, and that was no exaggeration. After this length of time on a ship, in the middle of the ocean, under the glaring midday sun, Reginald was parched, burnt, and generally melancholy. Around noon, he had cracked open a couple of beers, and although they momentarily alleviated his ennui, he was now in that post-beer funk that can only be described as oppressive laziness. He sat in the slight shade the cockpit of his boat offered, staring at the back deck, which people in his trade called the "stern".

The stern was square, empty, and painted a rather unpleasant shade of aquamarine, which contrasted with the brilliant white of the rest of his boat. A set of large fishing poles, seven in all, extended off the stern — two on each side and three directly in the back. Their lines sank into the ocean depths below, beyond sight, but attached to each, Reginald knew, was a nasty-looking hook with a large piece of fish meat. This, combined with the two-hundred-pound, industrial fishing line he used, provided seven deadly lines for large fish to nibble upon. Reginald was counting on catching some big fish, as he had reeled in several large swordfish in roughly this area last week.

Most fishermen, you see, are suspicious as well as big fat exaggerators. So, Reginald had thrown all science aside in his choice of fishing locale, disregarded his mind telling him the swordfish had probably migrated somewhere else, and decided to fish this spot purely because it *felt* right. This was the heartbreak life of a fisherman. Sometimes your suspicions were right and you got yourself a nice, big fish to eat or mount over your mantle and talk about at dinner parties. Sometimes your feelings were vastly wrong and all you got was a nice, pink sunburn.

Reginald huffed. He already had the sunburn. He retreated farther into the cabin and found the captain's chair. He spun it around to face the stern, sat down, and threw his feet onto the hand railing on the back wall of the bridge. He huffed again, this time rubbing his eyes to emphasize his boredom. Reginald stared at the seven fishing lines disappearing into the ocean. His eyes closed even though he fought them. He drifted off to sleep.

As exceptionally boring as fishing can be, this is generally a very bad idea when one is a fisherman.

Sometime later — he had no idea how long — Reginald came to. Immediately he noticed that the air was much cooler, the sunlight was dimmer, and there was a light breeze. Reginald's boat rocked back and forth more wildly. He could hear the fishing rods clanking around in their moorings.

Reginald stepped onto the deck and immediately recognized the signs of an approaching storm. On the horizon, a dark bank of clouds had replaced the sun. The ocean was murkier there, like oil, and was rapidly approaching his small boat.

Reginald sprang into action, grabbing the fishing rod farthest to the right, loosening it from the stirrup that held it upright. He began to reel in the line quickly, while he glanced at the approaching storm. The sky opened and a torrent of rain plummeted down onto the ocean. In moments, Reginald knew, he would be in the midst of that storm.

CHAPTER 15: THE ONYX SWORDFISH

He reeled the line in faster. His hands and shoulders ached with the effort. Thankfully, years on the water had trained Reginald for this. He kept reeling. He had been through things like this before.

But then, something happened that Reginald did not expect. As he was winding the line in, it suddenly stopped, as if grabbed by something enormous. Reginald could immediately tell it was not a swordfish. He knew what the bites of even the largest of swordfish felt like and this was something much, much bigger. Maybe it is a whale, he thought. Maybe a great white shark!

The line started to unreel sporadically, in fits and starts. A few inches would go out, then nothing, then a foot, then nothing, then an inch or two, then nothing. Reginald just stared at the line, debating his circumstances. If it was a small shark, he might be able to land it before the storm hit. What a story that would make! Reginald slowly put both his hands on the rod. With tremulous movements, he lifted one of his hands just enough to grab the flywheel on the reel. He gave it a few, gentle turns.

The fish, or whatever it was, did not like that. The reel spun to life again, this time in faster jerks. It fed out a few feet at a time. It stopped. It fed out ten feet more. It stopped. Finally, the reel spun into action and the line flew out the back. The reel was feeding out hundreds of feet and the line was darting across the face of the water as the fish, or shark, or whale swung too and fro under the surface. The reel began to smoke. Reginald knew he had a thousand feet of line on the reel but already much of that was fed out.

Reginald dove back into his cabin to retrieve his knife. Springing back onto the deck, he leapt toward the rod to cut it loose. As he did so, the reel jerked to a stop. The line was out. The entire boat lurched to the right as the fish pulled them. Reginald crashed into the sideboard of the boat. Water began to pour over the gunwale as the boat was dragged partially under the surface. Reginald threw himself at the rod. Water shot over his body and waves crashed into his face as he swiped at the line with his knife.

But as the knife blade approached the line, the rod quaked in its mooring and broke loose. The rod flew into the air and then dove under the surface of the water.

The boat immediately righted itself and returned to its rhythmic rocking on the waves. Reginald huffed against the backboard of the boat, exhausted, sunburned, and wet.

"What was that?" he whispered aloud as seawater dripped from his face.

As if in answer, the second reel made a quiet "tick." Reginald shot a glance at the reel. It ticked again, this time faster, and before Reginald could get to his feet, the second reel sprang to life and rapidly fed out line. Reginald swooped forward, as the third rod started to click. It too sprang to life. Then, the fourth reel broke into a fury. The fifth, the sixth, and the seventh too started spinning wildly.

Reginald did not hesitate. He immediately unlatched all the reels from their moorings. If this leviathan of the deep wanted to, it could take the reels but not the boat.

All the reels spun out line at an alarming rate. All the reels smoked. The smell of burning cord hung in the air. Reginald stepped back.

The second reel reached the end of its line and was jerked violently off the deck, arced through the air, and then plummeted down into the depths of the water. The third followed suit, as did the fourth, fifth, and sixth reels.

But, the seventh stopped. The rod and reel just sat there smoking.

Reginald stared at it, as he began to sense a deep rumbling in the ocean. Reginald glanced at the storm but it was not close enough yet. This was much more local. Something gigantic was surfacing. Reginald stumbled back into the cabin of his boat. The waves around the ship leapt into the air like angry serpents. The boat rolled back and then

CHAPTER 15: THE ONYX SWORDFISH

shot forward and dipped its nose under the surface. Reginald held on for dear life. The whole surface seemed to quake, and water sprayed into the air in massive jets.

Only a hundred feet in front of the Alleyah, the ocean boiled into a bubble and a colossal metal tube broke through the surface. The tube reached higher and higher into the air until it towered over Reginald's tiny boat, like a skyscraper in the middle of the ocean. Water poured from its sides, but the ocean, for the most part, calmed down. Reginald could see six fishing rods hanging from the side of the tube, hooked on its mouth.

Reginald fell onto the floor of the stern. He held a shaky hand to his head and wiped the mixture of sweat and saltwater from his brow. He felt like crying, more from wonderment than fear.

Then, as he sat there, pondering this event, the final reel ticked. It ticked again, then tick-ticked, then tick-tick-ticked. It zipped to life and shot out line as the ocean again began to rumble, but — this time — the vibrations seemed to be coming from deep inside the tube. The rod and reel shook, the boat rocked again, and at the crescendo of this violent activity, a gigantic white-and-gold craft shot out of the tube. Reginald caught only a glimpse, as the ship — shaped like a streamlined wedge — darted off into the stormy skies. Its sheer velocity punched a hole in the cloudy sky, and for a moment, a halo of sunshine shone down like a yellow spotlight on the launching tube and the little white boat beside it.

Then, as the hole in the clouds closed and darkness once again overtook the stormy sea, the rod vibrated rapidly in its mooring and shot off the deck, escaping into the sky just behind the Onyx Pioneer.

Reginald just stared at the sky for a very long time. Even with the storm growing close, he just sat and watched. After a while, the launching tower receded back into the waves more gently than it had come. The ocean was again quiet and calm.

At last, Reginald stood and looked around at the now featureless ocean that stretched from horizon to horizon. He began to laugh out loud. He held his sides and bent over the stern railing.

His friends were *never* going to believe this. He finally had his fabulous fishing story — the most incredible of all fishing stories — and it was no exaggeration, whether people believed him or not.

CHAPTER 16

To Points Unknown

Of course, the launch experience for Zack, Angelina, and Sanjay was somewhat different. At the launch order from Commander Chase, Zack felt a deep compression on his chest similar to the feeling he had flying in the Onyx Airstrider. His whole body pressed into his seat. His eyes felt like they were scraping the back of his skull. He found it hard to lift his arm, hand, or even his finger from the leather chair he sat in. He couldn't turn his head to look at Angelina, but he could hear her mirthful yelling as the Onyx Pioneer shot down the tube.

The tube flew by in a flurry of motion. The lights along the tube whipped by like stars darting by a ship in hyperspace. Far in the distance, Zack saw a pinpoint of light, but by the time he acknowledged it, they had rocketed past the aperture, into the open air.

Upon the wings of the wind, the rumbling in the Onyx Sun transformed into a voluminous whooshing. Air seemed to be flooding by the craft like a torrent of water. Zack saw his grandfather at the front of the ship, smiling with a look of total exhilaration on his face. His tuft of white hair quaked in the rumble of the wind like it was about to leap off his scalp.

Zack managed to twist his head over to his left just enough to see Sanjay. Sanjay did not look exhilarated, like Angelina. Instead he looked like he was concentrating. Noticing Zack's gaze, he said, "Atmospheric turbulence is expected to last 60 seconds. Then, we will be in the sub-stratosphere."

"And then?" asked Zack.

"Well, then the hardest part of the trip is over. The part with air turbulence," Sanjay said. "The Onyx Pioneer is unlike any other spaceship ever built. It uses hyper-accelerated ions generated by the Onyx Sun to slice through the air in front of the ship by negatively charging it, and positively charging it in back."

"What does that mean?" asked Zack, almost shouting over the noise.

"Simply put," Sanjay yelled back. "It makes the air in front of us easier to pass through than the air behind us. The ship goes forward partly because it is easier than falling back to Earth. Instead of fighting the air, we are using it. We are slipping through it like water. The advantage is a much smoother ride."

"Oh, I can tell," Angelina shouted across Zack. "Smooth as silk."

"Well, the initial launch is rough because air at this velocity always is," said Sanjay. "We're moving so fast it is almost like cutting through a solid mass. The air barely has enough time to move before we are gone. The Onyx Pioneer is streamlined to try to offset some of this effect, but we are still moving very fast. Trust me. If we didn't have

CHAPTER 16: TO POINTS UNKNOWN

the ion effect or this shape of ship, the ride would be significantly more turbulent."

"We're moving that quickly?" asked Zack.

"Mach thirty-five," said Sanjay. "Or thirty-five times the speed of sound."

"So, what happens when we reach the sub-stratosphere?" Angelina asked.

"We don't know," Sanjay said. Zack's pulse quickened as Sanjay continued, "Well, I mean this has all been tested theoretically."

"Theo—" Zack paused as the ship hit an air pocket and dropped suddenly. The ship caught itself and rocketed on, "—retically?"

"Well, we have flown the Onyx Pioneer up and down the coast during night tests, but we couldn't risk radar detection by launching it above a certain level until we knew we were leaving. Don't worry though. Theoretically, there's supposed to be a big bang and then total silence."

"Yeah," said Angelina to Zack. "Because we'll either be in space or dead."

Zack forced his head around so that he could provide her with an unappreciative smirk.

"I wouldn't worry, Zack Goodspeed," said Sanjay. "Your grandfather is an unimaginably wise man. His theories are as good as reality."

Zack nodded at this, but he couldn't help thinking of all the mishaps Grandfather had exposed him to over the years. There was, of course, the lab explosion just the other day when the Onyx Sun had destroyed his garage. But, the history of Grandfather Goodspeed's failed experiments was even longer and more distinguished. Zack thought this was probably the reality of genius inventors. Less wise minds probably found fewer ways to mess everything up. But Zack's grandfather was another story. When he screwed up, he messed up big time.

Zack thought back to examples of this. There was the robotic housemaid Grandfather had developed ten years ago, when Zack was one. Grandfather had programmed the robot to perform household tasks, like emptying the trash, cleaning the carpets, and vacuuming the drapes. Grandfather had brought it over to Zack's house to show his parents. The robotic maid was a sight to behold. Zack was too young to remember it, but his parents' frequent and frantic re-telling of the story had given him a perfectly clear image of the events. The maid was cast in solid metal, shaped like a woman, and gilded. She wore a small jet pack that allowed her to dart from place to place around the house, sweeping and dusting, and optimizing her efficiency in the process, Grandfather had said. The travesty of the maid's jetpack setting Mrs. Goodspeed's drapes on fire was only bested by finding baby Zack in the trash bin an hour later, giggling and sneezing. Apparently, his small size had caused the maid to consider him "debris." Amidst Mr. Goodspeed's red-faced accusations, Grandfather had argued that the robot had performed within its design parameters. Zack was small enough to be considered "waste," if you completely ignored the fact he was human. This only elicited a barrage of grunts from Mr. Goodspeed.

Then, there was the teleportation box. Grandfather had constructed a small, square box that could zap objects around the globe. The only drawback, Grandfather had explained to Zack when he was eight, was if the item rematerialized in a place where another object existed, the atomic code of the two objects mixed and produced an "inter-spatial hybrid", which basically meant an illogical mess. For this reason, Grandfather Goodspeed had decided to teleport his test subject into a stretch of desert in Egypt he knew to be empty from a visit ten years prior. The subject he chose to teleport was an apple.

"One of the world's most harmless fruits," Grandfather had said. "A pineapple is prickly and bananas have those slippery peels. So, this should be much safer."

CHAPTER 16: TO POINTS UNKNOWN

So, Grandfather had teleported an apple clear across the globe in the space of a nanosecond. Unfortunately, ten years is a long time to have last seen a place, even in Egypt where most of the country is empty desert. When the apple had materialized, there was a palm tree in the space, and the two objects combined. When Grandfather had teleported the "apple" back to the lab, a startlingly red palm tree greeted Grandfather and Zack. The tree had a waxy, red skin and tended to rot rather quickly. Zack had urged Grandfather to stop experimenting with teleportation. The fact the tree had shattered the small teleportation box left Grandfather with little choice. It had taken Zack and Grandfather several days to uproot the tree from the garage's floor and grind it up. Mr. and Mrs. Goodspeed had welcomed Grandfather's gift of a bowl of pink and slightly coconut-flavored applesauce with uncomfortable smiles.

It was, however, too late to worry about this, as the Onyx Pioneer was rocketing through the heavens approaching some kind of bang, either euphoric or catastrophic.

Zack held onto the arms of his chair as the whole ship shuddered. He looked at Grandfather Goodspeed who fiddled with the touch screen in front of him.

Then, with a crack that seemed to echo in the center of Zack's skull, the ship burst through the atmosphere and into the sub-stratosphere.

Either Zack's eyes were closed or he was dead.

Was he dead? Was he in space?

As he opened his eyes, he began to hear the sound of loud cheering. The bridge roared with applause and cheers. Zack saw Grandfather Goodspeed standing at the peak of the bridge with his hands clasped together over his head and a wide smile on his face. All around the windows of the bridge Zack could see an endless field of stars, cast against the black night of open space.

They were in space!

Zack noticed how his body now seemed to weigh almost nothing. Angelina rolled by him slowly, head over heels, smiling and laughing. Her jet-black hair hung from her head and almost brushed Zack's knee as her body rolled by.

"Come on, Zack," she said. "Take off your belt and stay a while."

"Welcome to space, Zack Goodspeed," said Sanjay, as he unbuckled his harness and pushed forward to fly out of his seat.

Zack lifted the clasp on his harness and the four straps floated off his chest, like the lazy tentacles of an octopus. Zack knocked against one, and it reacted by dancing slowly away from him. He pushed himself out of his chair and immediately started to drift toward the ceiling a little more quickly then he would have liked.

"Uh, guys," he said, but Angelina and Sanjay were busy pushing each other around the bridge, each trying to win a zero-G wrestling match.

"Guys," Zack said as he coasted up to the glass ceiling twenty feet above the deck. He smacked against it with an "Ooof." As he rubbed his face, he looked out at the stars beyond the oily cheek print he had just left on the window.

Never before had Zack seen so many stars. Instead of the few white ones he saw standing on Earth, he now saw the heavens covered with stars of all colors. They were so closely packed together, it looked like there might be more light in the night sky than dark. There were large stars and small stars, bright stars and dim stars, red stars, yellow stars, and brilliant blue stars. Zack even fancied he saw one or two green stars. There were stars in little pools of black space and there were stars that seemed to touch. There were even clusters of stars huddled around each other like close friends.

CHAPTER 16: TO POINTS UNKNOWN

"Incredible, huh," Angelina said, as she floated up to him, softly stopping in front of the glass ceiling.

"I can't believe it," Zack said. "I had no idea there were so many."

Sanjay flew from across the room and stopped near them. "There are seventy sextillion stars out there," he said. "That is the same as seventy thousand, million, million, million."

"That's incredible," Zack whispered.

Sanjay nodded and said, "Yes. Unfortunately our cities give off so much light pollution on Earth that it is unusual for many of us to see this many stars anymore. Even far away from the cities, our lights outshine the stars."

"Seriously?" Zack said.

"Yes. You have to remember," Sanjay continued pointing out the window. "Many of those little stars are millions of light years away. It is hard to outshine the lights of New York, New Delhi, or London when you are that far away, even if you are a gigantic ball of fire many times larger than our own sun."

"Which star system is the closest?" asked Zack.

"Alpha Centauri," said Sanjay pointing towards the sky at the edge of the bridge where the vast curvature of Earth was just appearing.

Angelina gasped and said, "Look at that."

They floated to the edge of the bridge, where they could make out the blue arc of the Earth. It twinkled like a brilliant sapphire, peacefully floating and slowly turning. Its shape stretched from one corner of the bridge to the other. Zack could make out only about ten percent of its vast diameter yet, in this "little" slice of Earth, he could see swirling storm clouds crossing entire continents, deserts, nations, deep forests, and expansive oceans.

"It's amazing," he said.

Angelina and Sanjay nodded. A thought suddenly occurred to Zack.

"Is there life like this on other planets?" he asked Sanjay.

"Who knows?" Sanjay said, then quickly amended his statement, "The probability is very high when you consider how many stars there are out there and how many planets probably revolve around them. There is even evidence emerging right now that there may have been life on other planets in our solar system, like Mars. If that is true, the statistical probability of life elsewhere is extremely high. Maybe we'll have the chance to explore out there someday. But for now, our priority is founding a permanent colony in space."

"Where?" said Angelina. "Alpha Centauri?"

"No. That is too far away," said Sanjay, looking at Angelina with a frown. "I keep forgetting you missed flight training. If your grandfather only knew…or perhaps that is why you are hiding from him?"

"Sanjay," Angelina interjected, her fist clenched. "If you are thinking of telling his grandfather about us —"

"Relax Max," said Zack, putting his hand on her shoulder. "Sanjay, look, my grandfather doesn't know we're here…at all."

Sanjay looked taken aback and floated a few inches away. "What?" he said pointing a finger at Zack. "You tell me this now, Zack Goodspeed? I could get in trouble for this. You could jeopardize my father's career."

Zack floated closer to Sanjay and looked straight into his eyes. "Sanjay, we didn't want to hide this from you," he said. "We had no idea what my grandfather was up to, and by the time we realized, we were already here. I couldn't just stand by and watch him leave once we found the Onyx Pioneer."

Sanjay frowned again. "And her?" he said nodding at Angelina.

"Max was the one who figured out where Grandfather disappeared to all the time," Zack said. "I couldn't have gotten here without her."

CHAPTER 16: TO POINTS UNKNOWN

"Ok, Zack Goodspeed. I forgive you for not telling me. But you must let your grandfather know you are here soon. I cannot lie for you."

"Don't worry, we'll tell him soon," Zack said.

"Good. It's agreed," Angelina chimed in. "Now where are we going?"

CHAPTER 17

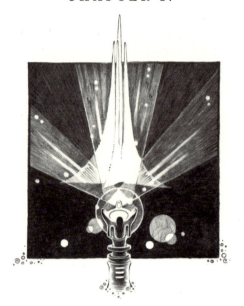

The Citadel Spire

"Well," said Sanjay. "You will see soon."

"Oh, that's a cop out," said Angelina.

"No, believe me," Sanjay replied. "If you think this part of the journey has been amazing, there is more ahead. We will be there very soon."

At that moment, the whine of a PA system reverberated throughout the ship. Zack noticed his grandfather at the head of the bridge, putting a wireless headset on. Five holo-panels near him illuminated 3-D images of five crowds of people from the other parts of the ship — the engineering, security, spiritual, science, and entertainment teams. Grandfather turned to face the crowd assembled on the back half of the bridge.

"Let's go back to the crowd so we're not seen by your grandfather," Angelina said to Zack.

CHAPTER 17: THE CITADEL SPIRE

Zack nodded and they pushed off the dome to float back to Dr. and Mrs. Soon. After landing, Zack and Angelina again carefully peered through the crowd to the front.

Grandfather tapped the mike on his headset and a "thud, thud, thud" sounded throughout the ship. "Can everyone hear me?" he said, almost falling into a console to his left. Commander Chase caught Grandfather about halfway down and righted him.

"Ah. Thank you, Commander," he said. "Poor motor control, I am afraid. Apparently, all my energy went to my higher functions at birth."

Commander Chase looked a little embarrassed and stepped back as Grandfather straightened his back and smiled out at the crowd.

"Welcome to space!" he shouted.

A booming cheer, applause, and whistles sounded throughout the ship. The crowds in the five holograms responded with cheering and clapping that mirrored the activity on the bridge. Waiting for the noise to subside, Grandfather added, "Stage one of our journey is complete. After years of theory, construction, and tests, we now know for sure we have a usable, inexpensive, powerful source of space travel. Never again will humanity be mired to a single planet. Our future now lies out here!"

Fyodor pointed to the star-laden window behind him. Cheers erupted again. Zack and Sanjay joined in. Angelina added several piercing whistles, through fingers pressed to her lips. Mrs. Soon winced at the volume of the whistles coming from such a young girl.

Again, Grandfather Goodspeed — with an unwavering smile — waited for the noise to subside.

"Humanity has been held back in space travel by only two things: its transportation and its habitat. Years ago, when I first developed the Onyx Sun, I realized I had unlocked the secret to the first puzzle. The proof is in what we have all witnessed today. We can launch and land numerous times using the same power plant and it will never fail, pollute, or need to be refueled. With that great riddle solved, the only obstacle to our sustained exploration of the stars now is a permanent space-based habitat. Commander Chase, if you will."

Commander Chase stepped forward, adjusting his headset.

"Thank you, Fy. As all of you know, the plan for the Onyx Pioneer has always been to form a colony on the far side of the Moon."

Zack and Angelina shot surprised looks at each other.

"This part of the Moon is constantly facing away from the Earth as it orbits it. So we can escape visual detection there. Especially if we position our settlement inside one of the numerous craters on the surface, we should avoid any prying eyes from passing satellites as well. The Aitken Basin, near the south pole on the far side of the moon, is the largest lunar crater and the chosen site for our establishment."

Peels of applause sounded through the ship.

"The fifteen hundred members of the Engineering Corps, led by Dr. Machvel, are the linchpin to our success over the coming months. When the Onyx Pioneer settles in the Aitken Basin, it will serve as our temporary living quarters and base of operations while we construct our permanent settlement."

Commander Chase checked his clock, and said, "We will land in approximately four hours. At this time, we will power-down the ship and settle in for the night. At 06:00 Zulu, Earth time, we will rouse the ship. The Spiritual Conclave shall have service at first muster. Following this, the Engineering Corps will commence with the preliminary base construction, which will involve site preparation. The SciTechs will support this by launching several unmanned probes into the surrounding terrain to survey the site and take soil samples. The Security Team will provide logistical backup by loading and unloading the construction equipment and making sure that ship integrity is maintained at all times."

CHAPTER 17: THE CITADEL SPIRE

Commander Chase paused and looked at the hologram of people the farthest to the left. "The Entertainment Troupe is simply asked not to get in the way until construction is complete." Loud whistles came from that hologram, and Zack could see all the people in the crowd jumping, laughing, and jeering.

Commander Chase suppressed a smile, badly, and continued, "The ultimate goal, of course, is the completed construction of our permanent lunar establishment — the Citadel Spire."

The lights in the bridge went dim. A single, larger 3-D hologram appeared in the center of the Command Deck. The hologram was of a large installation with five wings shooting from a central tower, like the five legs of a starfish. As the hologram spun, Zack could see towers shooting toward the sky at the end of each of the five wings. The towers were beveled at their edges and resembled upright airplane wings. At the center of the establishment, where the five wings met, a single spire overshadowed the rest. This tower was perfectly circular, and tapered to a sharp point at its top.

"This base," said Commander Chase "was designed by Fy Goodspeed, using knowledge obtained from experiments with numerous biosphere projects on Earth. The Citadel is capable of sustaining the ten thousand people of our crew, indefinitely. It features five wings and six towers. Fifteen hundred people will live and work in each of the wings, except the Executive Order tower. Twenty-five hundred people work for that branch, which is why they occupy the taller middle tower and command center of the base. Each of the lower towers will contain one of the other five teams: the Spiritual Conclave, the Security Team, the SciTechs, the Engineering Corps, and the Entertainment Troupe. It is *especially* designed to contain the Entertainment Troupe."

Again, loud whistles, moans, and cheers came from the entertainment hologram and this time Commander Chase grinned widely.

"Construction of the Citadel Spire Phase 1 is estimated to take three months. The new vehicles Fyodor Goodspeed has invented should speed construction considerably. In case we run over, which we will not," Commander Chase raised an eyebrow and the Entertainment Troupe's hologram quieted down, "we have enough oxygen and supplies to last us five months. Dr. Machvel will sum up with a preliminary risk analysis."

Commander Chase stepped back as Dr. Machvel slunk into view from the shadows at the side of the crowd. Zack noticed how the doctor's smoldering eyes made his face look more jagged and his black goatee seem pointier. Dr. Machvel eyed the crowd, less like Commander Chase and Grandfather did, and more like a famished wolf might.

"The surface of the Moon has gravity," he said. "And that is about all that will be familiar to you. There is no air. No water. Even the soil is more like dust than dirt. It is a completely barren wasteland that somehow, you think you are going to tame. I don't really know why, but that's not my concern. My concern is only to tell you about what it will be like to build there. I cannot stress enough that you need to complete the construction on time. Make no mistake. You are going to be in a hostile environment that currently does not support life. Should you fail, you must retain enough resources to head home, or you will surely perish."

A silent pall covered the ship. The people in the Entertainment Troupe hologram looked terrified — several of them fainted dramatically — while the Engineering Corps nodded, the Conclave prayed, the SciTechs shook their heads, and the members of the Security Team looked as they always did, stony-faced and prepared.

Grandfather Goodspeed stepped forward and ushered Dr. Machvel away. He said, "Yes, well, thank you for that rousing assessment, Dr. Machvel. Why I dreamed up a settlement for us on barren wastelands is beyond me."

CHAPTER 17: THE CITADEL SPIRE

A forced set of chuckles passed through the crowd.

"Make no mistake," Grandfather Goodspeed said. "We will succeed. We have the technology. We have the resources. We have the power the Onyx Sun provides."

The crew gave Fyodor a round of applause, less lively than before, and then settled back into their seats. The hours passed slowly for Zack. He watched the Earth grow small in the bridge window, as Angelina slept and Sanjay read something on his handheld computer.

At last, Commander Chase whispered something to Grandfather. Grandfather Goodspeed turned back to the crew, smiled, and said, "We have almost arrived!"

CHAPTER 18

The Aitken Basin

People clamored around the bridge to find their seats. Grandfather Goodspeed, Commander Chase, and Dr. Machvel again took their positions. Zack, Angelina, and Sanjay sat down next to Dr. and Mrs. Soon.

As the children watched the orb of the Moon grow in the glass dome, Angelina leaned over to Dr. Soon and asked, "Doctor, do you really think that we'll be able to build an entire moon colony in just three months?"

Dr. Soon smiled and replied, "Yes, I admit that it seems daunting, but Professor Goodspeed has been very clear about the way we are to construct the Citadel to make this happen. See, the building will go up in phases. The first phase is simply to construct the skeleton of the structure and to apply the skin. We will be using a combination of

CHAPTER 18: THE AITKEN BASIN

materials we are bringing from Earth and compounds indigenous to the moon. Once we have done this, we will vacuum seal the compound so that we can begin filling it with air. The Onyx Pioneer carries in its cargo holds vast quantities of compressed air."

"That way we will have the foundation of a livable environment," Sanjay chimed in.

Dr. Soon looked approvingly at his son and continued, "Yes. This is true. But it will not yet be self-sustaining. In order to actually live permanently on the Moon, we will have to build the arboretum very soon after."

"The arboretum? What is that?" asked Zack.

"Arboretums are typically large, contained areas of plant life," Sanjay said. "On Earth, they are used to conserve certain special trees or to protect a forest. The Redwood Forest in California, where 2,000 year old trees still grow, is essentially an arboretum."

"You are correct, son," Dr. Soon said. "Only, our arboretum is not for conservation's sake. It is for survival. See, since humans breathe oxygen and trees provide it, we have constructed a large arboretum — called the Bodi Biodome — to maintain our oxygen levels in the air. It is a very delicate balance, though. If we breathe too much oxygen too quickly, the trees and other plant life will not be able to keep up and we will suffocate. At the same time, if the trees and plants provide too much oxygen to us, this can also endanger our health."

"Too much oxygen can be a bad thing?" Angelina asked.

"Yes," Dr. Soon said. "See, on Earth we have gotten very used to our air being a certain way. Our air is 21 percent oxygen, 78 percent nitrogen, and 1 percent other elements. We can tolerate slight changes in that balance, but extreme variances can be deadly."

"How do you plan to balance it in the moon base?" asked Zack.

Dr. Soon smiled widely as one would when looking at his or her own newborn child and said, "Your Grandfather has provided us with a mechanism that stimulates and represses the oxygen production of the plant life in the Bodi Biodome. Basically, before we water the plants, a computer samples the oxygen content in the Citadel Spire in each of the six towers. If the oxygen levels are low, a stimulating chemical is sprayed on the trees by automatic sprinklers that look just like ones you would see on Earth. If the oxygen is too high, the sprinkler system sprays a repressing compound to stop the trees from producing as much oxygen. The air is measured once every half-hour, and minor adjustments are made in the chemicals. This way a balance is always maintained. You will find, children, much of life is about balance. Sanjay knows this is what our religion, Hinduism, also teaches us. Now, you children will see the balance of nature in practice."

"Where will the arboretum be located?" asked Zack.

"The entire foundation of the Citadel Spire is the Bodi Biodome," Sanjay said. "It needs to be this large since trees do not produce oxygen that quickly. The forests stretch along the first few floors of each wing and in the center, where the command tower stands, the first twenty floors are open space so the largest plants can grow there. The command levels are above this on floors twenty-one and higher."

Zack looked at Angelina and she raised her eyebrows.

"That sounds incredible," Angelina said. "But what about water?"

"If cleaned correctly," Dr. Soon said. "Water can be circulated repeatedly. The floor of the Bodi Biodome is actually semi-permeable, meaning that eventually the water not used by the plants seeps through the floor. There are vast catch basins under the floor that capture the water and clean it before sending it back up to the sprinklers and to other human uses. Water will never run out as long as we are efficient in recapturing it from the soil, the air, and from…uh…other places we use it."

"Like the bathroom," Sanjay said matter-of-factly. Zack and Angelina giggled.

CHAPTER 18: THE AITKEN BASIN

"Sanjay Soon," Dr. Soon said. "There is no reason to mention such things. But, yes. Each place we use water, the Engineering Corps and SciTechs have been careful to design reclamation systems that can efficiently reclaim and decontaminate the water."

"Byproducts," Sanjay said looking carefully at his father, "are also captured, separated, and re-circulated. Certain wastes are captured and used for fertilizer to help the trees grow."

Angelina and Zack couldn't help but smile behind their hands.

Dr. Soon looked like he was done talking about the subject given the direction it was turning. He turned to his wife and said something in Hindi that, even though Zack didn't understand the language, seemed to have the tone of disapproval. Mrs. Soon leaned over and glared at her son. Sanjay slouched down in his chair to avoid her eyes.

"Well, anyway," he said to his friends. "That is the end of the first phase of construction, which we must complete in three months. That and the basic creation of the living quarters."

"What about food?" Zack asked.

"Hydroponics," Sanjay said. "In the SciTech wing, we have a great many laboratories that will grow our food in what are basically tubs of water. This way, we don't need soil. We introduce the nutrients the plants need to grow through the water, just like in the Bodi Biodome."

At that moment, the PA system screeched, as Grandfather fumbled with the headset.

"Sorry about that again," he said. "Ladies and gentlemen, we have begun our descent into the Aitken Basin so put your seat backs and tray tables in their upright position and stow any belongings you have taken out during our flight. We also ask at this time that you discontinue use of any portable electronic devices such as laptops or CD players. We thank you for flying Onyx Air. We will be arriving on the Moon shortly."

Zack laughed and could see, as he lifted himself slightly from his seat, his grandfather chuckling to Commander Chase.

"I always wanted to do that," Zack heard Grandfather say before he turned off the headset.

Now that the Earth was far behind them, Zack could barely tell they were moving. The stars were so far away they didn't shift position as the Onyx Pioneer sped through space. However, Zack could see the pale orb of the Moon directly in front of them. It was growing bigger quickly. He could make out the face of the Man on the Moon clearly, as it smiled benevolently at the approaching craft. What was once a quarter-shaped sphere soon covered most of the dome. Craters, which looked like little bumps at first, became gigantic canyons as the Onyx Pioneer shot over.

"Attention, crew," came Commander Chase's voice over the PA. "You are going to feel a little pull as we land. This is a minor-G landing, but you'll feel it."

Indeed, although it was not like takeoff, Zack could feel the heavy weights again on his arms, legs, chest, and head.

"Begin landing roll," Commander Chase said.

The Onyx Pioneer began a slow roll. The Moon circled the bridge's windows until it covered the entire top of the dome.

"This will bleed off some of the speed," Commander Chase said to the bridge crew. Then, he added, "Visual attained on the Aitken Basin."

Zack could see a wide ridgeline rapidly approaching. The Onyx Sun rolled over again so that the ridgeline now appeared below them. Zack was shocked by the stark difference between the plain black sky and the jagged white horizon of the Moon's surface.

The Onyx Pioneer shot over the ridgeline and into the largest canyon Zack had ever seen. Zack had once visited the Grand Canyon on Earth and this easily beat it. The crater had to be several thousand miles across.

CHAPTER 18: THE AITKEN BASIN

The Onyx Pioneer floated down toward the surface. Undulations in the surface of the Moon flew by under them, like a white sea frozen in time. It was several minutes until Zack could even see the opposite ridge of the crater on the far horizon. The Onyx Pioneer approached a vast crater within the Aitken Basin and slipped over the edge of the bowl. This crater was smaller but still several hundred miles across.

"Engage landing engines," Commander Chase ordered the crew.

The heavy weights pulled at Zack again, as the nose of the Onyx Pioneer lifted into the air. For a moment, all Zack could see out the bridge window was dark space. Then, gently, the nose tipped back down and the craft came to rest on the surface of the Moon. All around him, Zack could see endless tracts of white-gray dust with a craggy ridgeline in the distance.

Zack heard the sharp sound of engines whirring down as Commander Chase stood, turned to the crew, and said, "Welcome to the lunar surface, pioneers of the Onyx Sun."

CHAPTER 19

Machvel's Ambitions

With the sound of the crew's cheers still echoing in their ears, Zack, Angelina, and Sanjay retired for the night as Commander Chase had ordered. His last words were to the bridge staff to turn on the artificial gravity.

Zack, Angelina, and Sanjay took an elevator to Deck 8 and proceeded down an oval corridor interspersed with white doors on both sides every twenty feet.

"The crew quarters are on Decks 8 through 11," said Sanjay pointing a finger to the individual doors. "Each family has a cabin of its own. Individuals are placed in groups of six: one from each of the departments. Even though many of our tasks are separate, your grandfather setup this system so the different teams still talk to each other. It forces us to work together."

CHAPTER 19: MACHVEL'S AMBITIONS

"Where are you staying?" Zack asked.

"Tonight, I will stay with my parents," Sanjay replied. "In a few more years, I will be too old and will have to room with the other members of the crew. At that time, I will choose a discipline."

"Will you follow in your father's footsteps?" asked Angelina.

"Yes," said Sanjay, with a proud smile. "I hope to attain the rank of Junior Engineering Cadet in a few years. It is very tough, though. Every cadet has to review hundreds of hours of memo-files."

"Memo-files?" asked Zack.

"Yes," said Sanjay. "This is another of your grandfather's inventions. Instead of classroom learning we have a library on Deck 4 that contains thousands of memo-files."

Zack shrugged.

Sanjay sighed and said, "This would have been so much easier if you weren't stowaways and had attended basic training."

"Humor us," said Angelina.

"It would be easier to just show you."

"Well, then show us," Zack said.

Sanjay huffed, then said, "All right, but quickly. I have to report to my parents' cabin shortly."

Sanjay led them down a hallway, up an elevator to Deck 4, and down another white, oval hallway, until a slightly larger door appeared on their right. It was labeled "Library." Across the hallway, was a door labeled, "The Academy." Sanjay led them toward the library door, and as they approached, the door whisked open. They stepped inside.

The room beyond looked to Zack like the pictures he had seen of old libraries in England. It was a lengthy, wood-paneled room with rows of bookshelves stretching from the entrance to the end, from the floor to the ceiling. The floor was covered with large Persian rugs. Brown, leather couches were spread around the chamber. An army of oak desks sat in the center of the chamber, huddled around a stone fireplace. The fireplace's chimney rose like a column in the center of the room and disappeared into the wooden panels covering the ceiling.

The only part of the library Zack did not recognize was the books. Instead of the clutter of different-sized books Zack was used to on Earth, the bookshelves here held thousands of translucent panels glowing with blue light.

Zack walked up to one of the bookshelves. It was about six stories tall. Each story was inscribed with one of the golden insignias of the Onyx Pioneer teams. Zack saw the eye from the Spiritual Conclave, the fist holding a lightning bolt from the Engineering Corps, and others. Narrow catwalks clung to the side of each row connected by a spiral staircase in the middle of the library.

Zack removed one of the panels from the shelf. It slid out easily. It was the size of a large book and danced with blue light like it was full of energy. On the spine and front of the panel was inscribed the title "US History until 1865."

"Don't touch that!" said Sanjay racing over and pushing Zack aside. Cupping his sleeve over his hand, Sanjay grabbed the panel from Zack, wiped it down, and gently slid it back onto the shelf. "Memo-files are very delicate and should not be smudged. I once read a memo-file one of my classmates had touched and, to this day, I still have fuzzy memories of Astronomy."

"Sorry," Zack said.

"It's ok. I don't mean to freak out. It's just that I still have a very hard time telling the difference between a nebula cloud and a blurry fingerprint."

"So, these files allow you to memorize things?" Angelina said.

"Well, yes. Sort of," Sanjay said, walking over to one of the leather couches and plucking an object from the seat that looked like a pair of streamlined glasses. "Basically, you sit down and put this electronic visor over your eyes. The visor wirelessly downloads any memo-file you

CHAPTER 19: MACHVEL'S AMBITIONS

select from the library. The headset is voice activated. So, you tell it what subject you want to learn about, and it retrieves the data from the files on the walls. That is why we never need to actually touch them."

He looked at Zack disapprovingly, then continued.

"The visor translates the data in the file into a series of light and electrical impulses that beam straight into your brain. If there is audio with the file, it hyper-accelerates the information and shoots it in through your ears. The file may also contain other sensory data, like what the winds on the seacoast of New England feel like in fall. All information is passed to the visor wearer by stimulating certain areas of the brain."

"So, it is like you are actually there?" asked Zack.

"Well, not really. A memo-file passes so quickly you don't really experience it as it happens. Each file lasts only about fifteen seconds. However, you do have a very strong memory of the event afterwards. Chilly and salty."

"What?" Angelina asked.

"Chilly and salty," Sanjay said, gazing into the distance. "The seacoast of New England in the fall is chilly and salty. I can almost smell the seaweed in the crisp air and taste the salty, wet breeze."

"A memo-file did that?" Zack asked.

"Yes," said Sanjay. "I have never actually been to New England — or America for that matter — but, I have a distinct memory of what the seacoast is like. In my head, I can even see the coast of Newport, Rhode Island."

"That is great!" Angelina said. "I'll *never* have to study again! Ten minutes in this library, and I will have graduated from college."

"Well, not quite," said Sanjay. "See, the memo-file beams the information into your brain, but that is no guarantee that you will actually remember it. Every fifteen-second session, therefore, is followed by a one-hour oral exam, which the headset administers."

"So, it really doesn't save that much time," Zack said, feeling deflated.

"Well, it really depends on how much you can remember," Sanjay said. "I am good at science and math. So, when I took basic Algebra and introductory Geometry, I needed only one try with each of those subjects to get an "A" on both. However, I am not as good at the humanities, like literature. I had to go through the memo-file and test on Huckleberry Finn four times to get a good grade. Still, even a few hours is a lot less time then sitting in class for a few months to study the same thing."

"True," said Zack. "I'd like to see what other subjects the library has. Let's take a look around."

Angelina and Sanjay split off in different directions and wandered around the library. Zack followed Angelina for a bit as she studied the Security Team shelves on the bottom floor, which held titles like "Optimum Riot Suppression" and "A List of the World's Most Suspicious People." Zack left her and met up with Sanjay as he looked at the Engineering Corps titles on the fourth floor. Zack saw one file called "The Power Stability of the Onyx Sun" and noticed his grandfather recorded it.

Zack climbed the stairs and explored the titles on the highest level by himself. The memo files here belonged to the Executive Order. He found files like "The Governing Dynamics of Leadership" and "How Genius Affects Teams", also recorded by his grandfather.

When they met back on the main floor, Sanjay looked at his watch and said, "Well, now I must leave you Zack Goodspeed and Max."

"You're going?" Zack asked.

"Yes, I'm afraid I must. Commander Chase's orders. We have a long day in front of us tomorrow."

"And where are we supposed to sleep?" Angelina said. "Can't we stay with you?"

CHAPTER 19: MACHVEL'S AMBITIONS

"I am afraid not," Sanjay said. "Every crewmember has been assigned a place to sleep. If you were to return with me tonight to my parents' cabin, I am afraid they would realize you don't belong here. However, you can stay in the library. No one comes in here at night."

"And if somebody shows up?" Zack asked.

"You were smart enough to sneak onto the Onyx Pioneer. I am sure you can avoid anyone you run across."

With that, Sanjay stepped through the library door and let it whisk shut behind him.

"No problem," said Angelina. "No one will find us here. This room is huge and even if someone did come, we could hide behind one of those couches or something."

Zack looked at her, feeling not entirely convinced, but eventually nodded.

"All right," said Angelina. "Now, let's try out a few of these memo-files before we go to bed."

"Now, *that's* a good idea," Zack said.

Angelina sat down on a nearby couch and put on a visor. He heard her say, "Tactics of Warfare, Volume One." A tiny voice from the visor said "Loading" and moments later Angelina grabbed onto the couch's arm and sat up stiffly. She clenched her teeth, but before Zack could do anything it was over.

"Are you okay?"

"Yeah. Whoa. That was intense."

"Maybe you should choose something more calm for your next memo-file."

Angelina wiped her eyes, smiled, and said, "No way. That was wicked."

A voice from the visor said, "Test commencing."

Angelina pulled down the visor again. As Zack walked away, he heard the headset voice begin the test.

"What was the most common use of infantry in the American Civil War?"

Zack strode down the aisles. There were so many topics that interested him it was impossible to choose. He was just about to decide on either "Legendary Bandits of the Old West" or "The Top Selling Videogames of All Time" when he heard voices in the hallway outside the library.

He ran to Angelina, but she had already removed her visor and was running toward him.

"We need to find a place to hide. Now!" she whispered.

They darted toward the back of the library and dove behind a couch there. The idea of hiding here now seemed ludicrous. Anyone walking into the room would clearly see their heads peeking out.

"This is not going to work," said Zack.

"Yeah, no kidding," Angelina replied.

Zack noticed a large air vent in the back corner of the room. He pointed to it. Angelina nodded, and they shuffled on their hands and knees to the grate. The voices outside grew louder.

Zack tried to pull at the grating, but it was solidly screwed shut.

"What now?" Angelina asked.

Zack threw off his backpack. He whispered, "Please, please, please" as he rifled through it. At last, he jabbed at something deep in the bag and pulled it out, holding it up to show Angelina.

"A multitool!" she whispered, as Zack held it up. "Quick. Unscrew the grate."

Zack flipped through the many tools until the screwdriver stuck out. He frantically unscrewed the vent grate as the voices got louder. They were just outside the door, but they seemed to have paused momentarily.

"Hurry, Zack!" Angelina whispered.

"I'm trying," he said. "I just hope these screws aren't too long." As if in answer to his question, the first screw fell out.

CHAPTER 19: MACHVEL'S AMBITIONS

"Perfect," said Zack. "They're short screws."

He removed the second and third quickly and was halfway through the fourth when the library door whisked open. Zack and Angelina froze as Dr. Machvel strode into the room with a man wearing a SciTech uniform. While still in the doorway, Machvel stopped and pointed a long, bony index finger at the other man.

"I won't let you back out now," Dr. Machvel said.

"Keep your voice down. The whole crew will hear you."

"I don't care about the crew. Many of them are loyal to me anyway."

Zack quickly removed the last screw. Then, with a careful tug, he pulled the grate free.

"Inside," he whispered at Angelina.

She dove inside the air duct, which was just tall enough for her to crawl into. Zack followed, pulling the grate quietly closed behind them. His pulse raced. He leaned the grate toward the wall just enough so it stayed closed, but anyone who looked would see it was unscrewed. The grate made a scraping noise as Zack let go of it. Dr. Machvel stopped talking suddenly and looked into the room.

"Shhh! Did you hear something?" he said.

Zack and Angelina held their breaths. Then, after a few moments, Machvel grabbed the other man's arm and pulled him toward the end of the library.

He hissed, "Victor, you have seen what the Onyx Sun can do for this ship. But that old fool Fyodor has missed the real point. He has no idea what power like this could do. The real future of this device lies in *other* uses."

The SciTech man looked down at his feet. He shifted his weight back and forth. Finally he looked up and said, "I don't know. Stealing the Onyx Sun is not going to be easy."

CHAPTER 20

Explosion on the Onyx Pioneer

Zack nearly jumped out of the air duct, but Angelina held him back. She put one hand over his mouth and held an index finger to her lips.

Outside the duct the two men stood there staring at each other. Machvel looked perturbed.

"You don't believe me, do you?" he asked.

"It's not that. I'm just not sure this is the best way to do this," Victor said. "Why don't we just talk to Professor Goodspeed instead?"

"Talk to Fy Goodspeed?" Machvel said in a high voice that cracked. "Have you ever tried to reason with him?"

Victor shook his head.

"Well I have. He's a self-righteous, self-absorbed, prevaricating mad man! He sees no other purpose to the Onyx Sun but this little

CHAPTER 20: EXPLOSION ON THE ONYX PIONEER

mission we're on. I bet you don't even know what he did to fund this journey do you?"

"I've heard rumors. I heard some stuff about some government helping him."

"You don't know the half of it," Machvel shouted, backing Victor against the wall. "There are things people would be shocked by. So, don't assume he's so pure or reasonable. He is obsessed with one thing: the colonization of space."

"I…I need to go to bed. My wife's going to wonder where I am," Victor said, heading for the door. "Can I think about it and let you know tomorrow?"

Machvel turned toward Victor so his back was facing the grate. He put his hands behind his back. Zack could see him pull something from his sleeve. It looked like a long silver tube.

"Very well," Machvel said. "You think about it."

Victor turned to walk away. The moment he did, Machvel lunged at him. Zack was shocked that such speed could come from such a decrepit old man. Machvel latched onto Victor's shoulder and raised the metal tube over his head. Victor winced and screamed, trying to break Machvel's vice-like grip. Machvel plunged the tube between Victor's shoulder blades. Victor arched his back like he was about to dive into a pool. Then, he relaxed. A lazy smile spread over his lips, and he blinked slowly.

"Too bad you couldn't be one of my true believers," Machvel said. "I would have rather had your impressive mind at my disposal. Unfortunately, the mind control chip now implanted on your spine will dull your abilities somewhat. But never mind that. You're one more soldier in my army of thousands."

Zack wriggled forward and accidentally pushed the grate. It squeaked across the floor. Zack gasped, but quickly put a hand over his mouth. He sat there for a few seconds. It was very quiet in the library. Zack looked out the grate and was met with the stench of Dr. Machvel's hot breath.

"Well, what do we have here?" Machvel said, tearing the grate away and thrusting his hands into the vent.

Zack and Angelina tried to crawl away, but Zack was too close to the grate. Machvel grabbed his leg.

"You're not getting away that easily!" he shouted, his grip vice-like around Zack's leg. Zack could feel Dr. Machvel's long fingernails digging into his ankle. He was pulling Zack out of the vent.

Machvel managed to wrench Zack halfway out of the vent, as he leaned into Zack's face and said, "And who might you be?" The stench of his breath made Zack's eyes wince. It smelled like sulfur and garlic, or sulfurized garlic, or something just like that.

Angelina pounced on top of Zack and pulled him halfway back. "I've got you, Zack!" she said.

"Zack?" Dr. Machvel said, pulling Zack harder. "Zack Goodspeed? Oh, what a find we have here, Victor. The old fool's grandson!"

Angelina whirled around in the duct so her feet pointed out of it. She began to kick at Dr. Machvel's hands, as she shouted, "You are not taking him!"

"Help me!" Machvel yelled to Victor, as he frantically tried to avoid Angelina's kicks.

Angelina stomped on his hands and Machvel let go, howling in pain. She pulled Zack inside and they scurried down the shaft as fast as possible.

Dr. Machvel called down the shaft, his head pressed as far as he could go inside the vent, "You won't get far! You have to come out eventually." Then, he disappeared back into the library. Zack heard him say, "Hurry! We don't have much time. Those brats could tell Goodspeed everything! We need to act now."

"Go, Max!" said Zack. "We have to get to my grandfather."

CHAPTER 20: EXPLOSION ON THE ONYX PIONEER

"I am, Zack. I am —"

Angelina's sentence abruptly stopped, and Zack saw her slip out of sight. He heard a scream but scarcely had time to register this before the floor dropped out from under him. Too late, Zack realized they had rushed into a drop in the shaft.

Zack shot down the air duct like he was on a waterslide. He slid on his stomach, headfirst, as air rushed up at him. He could hear Angelina ahead of him shouting, "Whooooooa. Wahoo!"

They slid left and then right, the duct evened out for a bit, but they were going so fast, they couldn't stop before it dropped again. At one point, it whirled around in a wild loop.

"I think I am going to be sick," Zack shouted.

"This is the best!" Angelina screamed back.

The shaft shot down at an even steeper angle just then, to the point where Zack momentarily thought he was free falling. Then, it leveled out. Zack could see a rectangular light rapidly approaching them at the end of the tunnel.

"Uh, Zack?"

"Yeah?"

"I think we're coming to the end of the shaft!"

Zack could see the grate at the other end of the vent flying toward them, but before he could think, Angelina hit the grate, blasting it off its hinges, and flew through the opening. Zack followed a split second later.

As he flew out of the vent, Zack's first observation was of a classically decorated captain's chamber. He saw brown leather furniture, model sailboats on bookshelves, and oak paneling covering the walls.

Zack's second observation though was that the oak walls seemed to be flying toward him rather quickly. Zack's impulse was to duck, but of course this is impossible to do when one is flying through thin air toward a wall. So, Zack did the most he could in the split second he had before he hit the wall: he bunched himself into a ball.

Zack hit the wooden paneling with an "Ooof" and fell onto a lumpy mass, which also said "Ooof."

"Get off me," moaned the lumpy mass, which sounded just like Angelina. Zack rolled off her and fell another foot onto the solid ground. Apparently, they had landed on a couch, he now realized.

"Ugh," moaned Zack as he slowly patted himself down. There didn't seem to be any broken bones.

"You okay?" Angelina asked.

"Yeah, you?"

"I think so, but *man* was that a wicked ride!"

"I know. Where are we?"

"Someone's room, I guess."

"*My* room," said a deep voice.

Zack and Angelina whirled around and saw Commander Chase standing near a doorway leading into a bedroom. He was dressed in white pajamas and pointed a gun at them.

"Commander Chase," Angelina said, jumping up.

"Easy!" ordered Commander Chase as he stepped forward and nodded the gun at her. Zack saw this as a clear signal for them to sit down. Zack pulled on Angelina's pants. She sat down.

"Who are you exactly?" he asked. "You're not on the crew. I know every single person on this crew. And how do you know my name?"

"That's a long story, but we need to see Grandfather Goodspeed immediately," exclaimed Zack, sitting up.

Commander Chase stepped forward, "I said easy! Sit on the floor. Put your hands where I can see them."

Zack and Angelina put their hands up. Zack had never done this before and, even after seeing it in countless movies, he felt a little silly holding his hands up in a "Please don't shoot me" gesture.

CHAPTER 20: EXPLOSION ON THE ONYX PIONEER

"Now," said Commander Chase. "I want to know *exactly* who you are and what you are doing here."

"I am Zack Goodspeed and this is my friend Angelina Maximillian or Max for short."

"Zack Goodspeed?" Commander Chase said. His gun tipped away from them. "As in Fy Goodspeed's grandson?"

"Yes."

"I want to see some ID."

"We're eleven years old!" said Angelina, holding her arms out to her sides. "What possible ID could we have? It's not like we have driver's licenses."

"Well, I have my school ID," Zack said.

"Let me see it — slowly," Commander Chase said as Zack reached for his back pocket. He removed a flimsy paper ID.

"All right," Commander Chase said, taking it from Zack. "Where's yours?" He nodded at Angelina.

"I burned it," she said. "I move around a lot. What do I need another school ID for?"

Commander Chase eyed her. He let his gun drop to his side. "All right. Well, IDs can be faked anyway. So, let's pretend for a moment you are who you say you are. What are you doing on my ship and better yet, how did you get into my quarters?"

"*My* ship," a voice boomed through the living room. The door to the hallway stood open and the silhouette of a ridiculously tall man stood in the doorway. Grandfather Goodspeed stepped into the light. His jacket was off and his sleeves were rolled up above his elbows. His gold watch chain twinkled in the hallway light as it swung from his vest pocket. Two guards flanked him, their automatic weapons trained on Zack and Angelina.

"Lower your weapons," he said to the guards. He bumbled into the chamber. He peered at Zack and Angelina over the cracked lenses of his rectangular glasses. Zack had never seen so many wrinkles at the corners of Grandfather's eyes, as he squinted at them.

"After all, Commander Chase," he said. "This *is* my grandson."

Grandfather stepped closer and bumped into the corner of one of the couches as he plopped down into another.

"Although, I haven't the slightest idea what he is doing here," he said.

Zack opened his mouth to speak, but Grandfather held up a finger.

Grandfather glanced at Commander Chase, in his pajamas, and one of Grandfather's bushy eyebrows shot up. Commander Chase, a little embarrassed, stepped back. Then, Grandfather turned his gaze back to Angelina and Zack.

"Nice place, don't you think?"

Zack and Angelina nodded in unison.

Grandfather continued, "You know, I am very proud of *my* ship. It has been the result of a lifetime of work from the time I was about your age. It all started with an atomic reactor I built. I learned then that I had a knack for inventing things. Next came the Onyx Sun. Then, the idea for an Onyx Sun–powered aircraft. Then, an Onyx Sun–powered spaceship. I knew I could do it. I knew I could create an entirely new way to power things and then use that power to help mankind grow beyond our single planet."

Grandfather shot up suddenly, almost toppling over, and exclaimed, "And here we are! Over forty years of tireless work, and today, this day — this one we are talking about right now — we are actually sitting here, on the Moon."

He began to pace around the couches. He tripped on an ottoman and went flying to the ground. Commander Chase leapt forward and helped him up.

CHAPTER 20: EXPLOSION ON THE ONYX PIONEER

"Thank you. Thank you," he said, dusting himself off. "I'm all right. Where was I? Ah yes! And here we are! You can't imagine the pleasure it brings me to be here. There were times when I wondered if it would ever happen. And — you know firsthand, Zack — there were many setbacks. Just the other day, for instance, I destroyed my lab because I forgot to build an 'Off' button! Silly really, but mundane details like that have almost stopped me at every stage. However, I never really gave up hope, and you know why?"

Zack and Angelina shook their heads.

"Because a little boy once gave me a great idea," Grandfather said, loudly. "A little boy once inspired me to dream bigger. It's what children do. Your imaginations are boundless. Zack's simple suggestion gave me all the ideas I needed. He transformed my stratospheric airplane into the Onyx Pioneer, capable of landing on the Moon."

"I did that?" Zack asked.

"Yes," said Grandfather. "Well, obviously I did all the science and inventing. Little stuff like astrophysics and quantum mechanics, but you know what? All that can be learned in books. What you gave me can't be. You gave me your imagination, Zack. So, your contribution was the first and greatest. Plus, you must have passed my little initiation test to get into the Clarion Spacedock."

"Is that what that was?" Zack said.

"Yes," Grandfather said chuckling. "It's a series of intellectual, physical, and emotional tests we gave all new recruits."

"We could have died! Isn't a little harsh?"

"Ah, well, space is harsh my boy," Grandfather said waving a hand dismissively in the air. "If you can't make it past that, you can't make it in the vast vacuum of space. But you did make it. And so you are here."

Grandfather whirled around the corner of the couch and plopped onto the pillows.

"That is why, when I saw you here just now, my first reaction was surprise, but my second — and deeper reaction — was one of gratitude. This ship was your idea. You deserve to be here."

"Now you," Grandfather said, turning to Angelina who was smiling at his kind words. "You, I don't know. So, you, we'll throw out the airlock."

Angelina's jaw dropped and her face became pale. She opened her mouth to protest. This was the first time Zack had seen her scared.

"Right away, sir," said the guards stepping forward to grab Angelina. Zack jumped in front of them, but everyone stopped when they heard a cackle coming from the couch.

Grandfather had tears in his eyes, as he said, waving to the guards, "I'm kidding! Step back. It was just a tasteless joke. No, you I know too. You are my mischievous neighbor. I believe your name is Angelina Maximillian, is it not?"

"Yes. It is. But how do you know that?"

Grandfather looked left and right, like he was about to tell a big secret. "Do you really think I didn't see you following me into the woods all those times? At first, I didn't know, but eventually I became suspicious when it started to seem like I was replacing the pistons in the Spinning Elevator more often than usual."

Zack noticed Angelina was smiling devilishly. Something about her expression sparked a thought in Zack's mind.

"Grandfather! Dr. Machvel is going to steal the Onyx Sun."

"What? Dr. Machvel? Zack, you're joking."

"No, I'm not. We just overheard him talking to another man about it in the library."

The smile faded from Grandfather's face. He looked intently at Zack, then whirled around to face Commander Chase.

"Do we have any reports of something like this?" he asked.

CHAPTER 20: EXPLOSION ON THE ONYX PIONEER

"No sir," said Commander Chase. "Even if someone wanted to steal the Onyx Sun, how could they? It can be removed only during a total power outage. Even at night, the ship still pulls power out from the Onyx Sun for life support. The only time it can be moved is when the ship is off, like this morning when we put it in place before liftoff."

Grandfather swayed around again, like a tree in a violent wind. "There you go. The Onyx Sun cannot be removed. I concur with Commander Chase's assessment, especially since I was the one who designed it this way. We simply couldn't risk a power source of the Onyx Sun's magnitude falling into the wrong hands."

"But Grandfather, we heard Machvel and another man named Victor planning it!" said Zack. "We were hiding in the library and heard them talking about stealing the Onyx Sun to use it for something else. Machvel used some kind of mind-control chip on him."

"Victor Schultz?" said Commander Chase suddenly. "The Head of SciTech?" Commander Chase shot a worried look at Grandfather Goodspeed. "Fy, this man *has* been identified as a minor security risk. We noticed several months ago that parts from the base construction modules were disappearing whenever he was in charge of the shift. We never had any direct evidence to charge him with though."

"Are you sure?" Grandfather said, standing. One of the guards grabbed for his arm to help him up, but Grandfather shooed him away. "Is this a possible threat then?"

"I think at least we should put the ship on alert and double the guard around the Power Tower, sir," said Commander Chase.

"But they could only shut down the entire ship from the bridge," said Grandfather Goodspeed.

"Yes, sir," said Commander Chase. "Which is why I am recommending I order the Security Team to report there immediately."

"But they can't just shut the bridge down!" Grandfather said thrashing his arms around. "They would have to destroy it. Would someone really destroy *my* ship to get the Onyx Sun?"

A violent shudder ripped through the ship. A deafening explosion accompanied this. Zack held his hands to his ears as the lights flickered and then went dark. Zack felt the ship falling. The cushion of air it sat on must have been powered by the Onyx Sun, he realized. The ship crashed to the surface of the Moon. Then, Zack felt weightlessness return as the artificial gravity shut off, and the Moon's low-G environment took over.

CHAPTER 21

The Battle for the Onyx Sun

"Commander!" called Grandfather Goodspeed.

"Yes, sir."

"Get to the Power Tower immediately. Protect the Onyx Sun!"

"On my way!"

A beam of light flickered on from a flashlight Commander Chase held and flew around the room. The Commander pulled three white belts from a nearby closet. He floated around a little as he strapped one on his body then tossed two to the security guards.

"Low-G rocket belt," Grandfather said to Zack, as he reached inside the closet and pulled out three more. He handed two to Zack and Angelina. "Put them on."

Zack strapped on the belt. The moment he did, he felt air bursts shoot from the top of the belt. His feet met the floor. As he walked, it felt a little weird, like he was semi-floating, but he did feel substantially more grounded.

"The belt will adjust to keep you on the floor," Grandfather said. "Unless you want to walk on the ceiling. Then it will let you do that too, if you tell it to. Quickly now! To the Engineering Core!"

Grandfather, Zack, and Angelina ran as fast as they could into the hallway and turned right. The scene was one of complete panic. People in their pajamas were everywhere. Some were screaming. Some were trying to calm others down. A thick cloud of smoke hung in the air and loose wires and tubing hung from ceiling panels.

Commander Chase and the two security guards followed them out and turned left toward the Power Tower. As the Commander went, Zack saw him calming the injured and enlisting the rest to join his force.

Grandfather, Zack, and Angelina rushed toward the Engineering Core. The smoke thickened the farther they walked. They had to stoop to avoid suffocating on the fumes. They ran by people covered in soot who were herding in the opposite direction. Zack tried to keep his mind focused on getting to the Engineering Core as he stumbled along, coughing. Grandfather lurched forward so dangerously, Zack feared he might fall and break something. The person who concerned Zack more though was Angelina. He had never seen her look so angry. Zack could almost feel the heat coming off her. No matter how many times Zack looked at her and tried to get her attention, Angelina just looked straightforward and pressed on. She led the way to the Engineering Core even though she had no idea where it was. Grandfather Goodspeed occasionally stopped her to direct her down another corridor. Then, she would march ahead of them again.

They came to an elevator.

"Let's take the stairs, just in case," Grandfather said. "Go up one level to Deck 7, Max. That's where the Engineering Core is."

CHAPTER 21: THE BATTLE FOR THE ONYX SUN

Zack and Grandfather followed Angelina up the stairs next to the elevator and, at last, they came to a large, white door that read, "Engineering Core" in big, gold letters. One half of the door hung to the side, apparently blown from its hinges. Angelina, Grandfather, and Zack crawled around it and into the engineering headquarters.

The Core was a wide, low room with flat-panel monitors covering every square inch of the walls. A waist-high island stood in the center of the room, and several people huddled over it, tapping different controls. The power was on in here but barely. The lights flickered. Sparks shot out of broken wires hanging from the ceiling. Several of the larger flat-panel monitors were cracked. The scene was one of total chaos. Dr. Soon was already milling around the room barking orders at his team.

Grandfather Goodspeed jumped into the fray, yelling to different crewmembers, "Where did we get hit? What? The bridge! Totally destroyed? What was it? A bomb! Was anyone hurt? Well, thank goodness for that. No, no. Reroute all controls to the Engineering Core. What? We were hit here too? Well, thank goodness you repelled the attackers. Pressure leaks on Deck 2? Evacuate it then seal it off. We have to keep the Engineering Core stable. Yes, I'm sure! This is our only hope!"

As Zack advanced slowly into the chaos of the room, the backside of the Core awed him the most. The Engineering Core's rear wall was entirely glass and looked out onto the Power Tower. Zack noticed the cavern was bathed in the eerie blue light radiating from the Onyx Sun as it whirled atop the tower in the center of the room. Violent bolts of purple-blue lightning arced to strike the numerous catwalks crisscrossing the dark space like a black spider web.

As Angelina and Zack looked out, two teams of people emerged from opposite sides of the cavern on a catwalk perched in the center of the chamber, closest to the tower. Zack could not make out who was who. All he could see were two dark clumps of people silhouetted against the blue glow of the room. Streams of red tracer bullets crisscrossed the chamber, like swarms of angry bees engaged in a fight for life. Yellow explosions flashed on the catwalk as the two forces hurled grenades at each other.

The light inside the Engineering Core started to flicker as the opponents approached the Power Tower. A barrage of explosions hit the tower and the lights died. In total darkness, all Zack could see was the face of Angelina next to him, bathed in the undulating blue glow and bursts of yellow from the explosions. She stood there with her hand on the wall window, totally fixated, her mouth half open.

Grandfather lurched toward the window next to Angelina. The flashes from the firefight danced silently on his white suit, like the reflection of a movie.

"Oh my God," he said.

The blue light turned to a dim purple as the two forces neared each other. There were fewer people as dark bodies fell from the catwalk or slumped into a heap where they were hit. The Onyx Sun's light splashed around the chamber like a purple ocean. It blacked out completely then it shot back to life. The arcs of lightning became wilder and more sporadic. Bullets continued to rain down on both sides of the chamber. One group reached the access-hatch at the base of the Power Tower.

"Who is that?" shouted Grandfather Goodspeed, pounding on the window. "Whose force is that?"

The entire ship began to shake as a low-pitched whirring sound echoed from the chamber. There was a flash of light and a violent explosion from the base of the tower. Sparks flew into the air like stars. Zack winced, but forced himself to watch. The Power Tower tipped towards the Engineering Core, as it plummeted to the floor.

Everything went dark with a gigantic bang.

CHAPTER 22

The Miracle Mechs

"Zack!" shouted Grandfather Goodspeed.

Zack shifted in the pitch darkness. He was lying on the ground. His head throbbed and he rubbed it with an aching hand. Other people bumped into him, but he could not see them. Zack had never known such blackness. No light shone anywhere. Zack could not even make out rough shapes of people as he heard them grunting and moaning around him.

"Yeah?" Zack said coughing. The air was still thick with smoke.

"Oh thank goodness," said Grandfather Goodspeed. Zack could feel hands fumbling on his leg. "Oh thank goodness you are alive, my boy."

"Yeah, I'm alive," Zack said, surprised by Grandfather's uncharacteristic concern. "I can't see anything though."

"I know, I know. Hold on," Grandfather replied. A small pool of light struck Zack. It came from a pin on Grandfather's tie. "I always keep a backup light around. You wouldn't believe how many times I have found myself in the dark."

"I might," Zack heard Angelina say. She sat up next to him. "My foster parents used to think there was a war going on in your garage."

"Exactly," said Grandfather Goodspeed. "You wouldn't believe the predicaments one finds oneself in as an inventor."

"Try me," Angelina said.

"Ah, well, yes, you might be able to understand at this exact moment, yes."

Grandfather stood. His pin-light splashed around the Engineering Core as he wobbled to his feet. Once standing, Grandfather turned around slowly. In the shallow pool of the pin-light, Zack could see people lying around the Core, groaning. Several tried to stand up. Grandfather Goodspeed noticed Dr. Soon lying on the floor and stepped over to help him.

"Rajah," he said to Dr. Soon. "Are you all right?"

"Yes, it would seem so."

"Great. Help the others. Thankfully, it doesn't look like anyone is seriously injured. You two!"

Grandfather pointed at two Security Team members sitting in the back corner of the Engineering Core. As he strode over to them, he left Dr. Soon in darkness. Dr. Soon tripped over someone lying on the floor.

"Oh! Sorry," said Grandfather Goodspeed whirling around. He reached into his trouser pocket and produced several more tiepin lights.

"Distribute these to the crew, Rajah. Thankfully, I always keep a few on hand, but we must work quickly. They don't last long. Start

CHAPTER 22: THE MIRACLE MECHS

assessing the damage. Zack, Max, these two guards, and I are going to the Power Tower."

"Do you think that is wise? The traitors, whomever they are, could still be in there," Dr. Soon said.

"It is quite all right, Rajah. I doubt many stuck around after the tower fell. I have to check to make sure Commander Chase is all right."

"And the Onyx Sun?" Dr. Soon asked.

"Well, yes, that too," Grandfather said. "But the first priority for us is to make sure the crew is safe. And Rajah —"

Fy grabbed Dr. Soon by the upper arm.

"Trust no one. Dr. Machvel has obviously corrupted a significant portion of the crew."

"Dr. Machvel?"

"Yes. Zack and Max alerted me right before this trouble. I will tell you everything later," Grandfather said. "For now, make sure everyone is all right. We'll uncover the culprits later."

Grandfather grabbed Zack and Angelina, strode to the door, and wriggled through the opening in the twisted metal. The two guards followed.

They walked through what seemed like miles of dark corridors. For every one step his grandfather took, Zack found himself taking two. By the time they reached the doors to the Power Tower, Zack was holding his aching sides and huffing.

Angelina smiled at him. She barely looked phased. "Tired?" she said.

Zack shook his head. "No. Why?"

Angelina smiled back. "Sure," she said.

"Children, quiet," Grandfather whispered. He approached the Power Tower entrance. All Zack and Angelina could see in the pin-light was the frame of the door and pure blackness beyond. The doorframe looked like a hungry mouth.

Grandfather edged his toe onto the catwalk. Once his full foot was on it, he jumped up and down on one leg.

"Seems solid enough," he said. "But you two stay here."

Zack opened his mouth to protest, but his grandfather held up a hand that was large enough to cover his entire face.

"You stay here. No debates."

Grandfather reached into his pocket and gave them each a pin-light.

"My last ones."

With that, Grandfather strode into the darkness. Zack commented to himself that for once Grandfather looked normal as he walked. Zack would expect anyone to stumble about in the darkness of the Power Tower, as Grandfather now was. Zack and Angelina attached their pin-lights to their shirts.

"Let's just use mine," Zack said. "Save yours for later."

"All right," Angelina said, attaching the pin to her shirt but leaving it off.

They could see the faint shape of Grandfather for a while, as he shimmied along the catwalk, but eventually he disappeared into the darkness.

They waited for what seemed like an eternity. Occasionally, Zack heard the echoes of something being dropped in the cavern or echoes of voices or coughing. He thought he could make out Grandfather's pin-light far away, but the blackness was so oppressive that it could have been his eyes playing tricks on him.

Finally, they saw the pin-light returning. It was making awkward lurches in the darkness. At first, Zack thought it might be Grandfather's normal, or should one say abnormal, walking style. But when Grandfather got closer, Zack saw he was holding up a badly injured Commander Chase.

CHAPTER 22: THE MIRACLE MECHS

Commander Chase's uniform was ripped and scorched in several sections exposing the taut muscles underneath and, quite often, bloody gashes.

Zack and Angelina raced to their aid.

"No!" Grandfather said. "Only once we are off this catwalk."

Zack and Angelina waited with their toes on the threshold of the doorframe. When the two men were finally close enough, Zack and Angelina reached out and helped pull them into the corridor.

Commander Chase collapsed to the floor, pulling Zack and Angelina down with him.

"Wait here," Grandfather said. "And watch him. He should be all right. I checked his wounds and they are not immediately life threatening. Be careful, though. His arm is broken."

Zack watched his grandfather make over twenty trips into the darkness and back. Every time he returned, he helped one of the crew limp into the corridor. People from other parts of the ship arrived to help, as did Dr. Soon from the Engineering Core.

"Damage report complete," Dr. Soon said, stopping Grandfather in the corridor on one trip back. "The pressure is holding. Now that the fires are out, the oxygen level is holding too. We have lost full power, obviously. I can't tell if the Onyx Sun is just disconnected or —"

"It's gone," interrupted Grandfather. "I have pulled people from every part of the Power Tower. I couldn't see it anywhere. Machvel's got it. I would guess he's gone too."

"You really think that Ian could have done *this?*" Dr. Soon said.

"Yes, I do," said Grandfather. "I have it on the best authority: Zack's word."

Zack nodded at this, but Dr. Soon still looked like he couldn't believe it.

"Rajah," Grandfather said. "You and the rest of the crew go inside and pull the remaining injured out. There are more people in there I couldn't reach on my own."

"Where are you going?" Rajah asked.

"We have pressure. We have oxygen. But we need power," Grandfather said. "Space is an immensely cold place. It won't be long before we start to feel it. I have to salvage the only power source we have left."

"Here," Dr. Soon said. "I will come. You will need me."

"No, you stay here and direct the rescue efforts," Grandfather said. "Zack has assisted me enough times in my Labradory to help. I have the feeling Max is a fast learner, as well."

Dr. Soon nodded and rushed into the Power Tower with the others to help the injured.

"Come," Zack's Grandfather said, striding off down the hallway. They crossed several corridors, entered and left numerous large halls, and climbed down a few ladders since the elevators were out. This last fact Zack considered at least a minor benefit of their present situation. He hated the super-fast elevators of the Onyx Pioneer.

As they descended levels, Zack noticed that the corridors were becoming wider and more utilitarian looking. Eventually, Zack saw "Deck 14" written on the wall in golden paint and recognized the rooms full of cargo.

"The last deck of the Onyx Pioneer — Deck 15, where we are headed — is designed for the construction equipment we carry," Grandfather said when he noticed Zack looking around. "It is the widest in the ship. It's almost as wide as a highway on Earth. It has to be to allow our construction equipment and Mechs to get in and out of the ship. I'm betting you'll like this floor, Zack."

"Mechs?" asked Zack.

CHAPTER 22: THE MIRACLE MECHS

Grandfather smiled at him. Zack could see that boyish spark in his eye again, even under the dirt on his face from the day's events.

"Yes, you'll see," said Grandfather. "In fact, if our predicament were different, I think you would enjoy a lot of stuff on Deck 15."

Grandfather leapt toward a nearby ladder, hobbled down it, through the hole in the floor, slipped, and crashed onto the deck below.

Zack looked down the ladder. Seeing Grandfather's gangly limbs spread across the floor, Zack said, "Are you all right?"

"Fine! Just fine. Just watch that last step."

Angelina huffed at this. "It is a miracle he is still alive," she said.

"Not a miracle," came Grandfather's voice from below. "No such thing as miracles. There's only science."

"Well, then," whispered Angelina to Zack, as she stepped down the ladder. "It's a miracle of science."

Zack followed them down the ladder. When he reached the end, he turned around to find his pin-light did not illuminate the far wall of the hallway. Zack could only see his grandfather before him — white suit, with pale skin, sparkling eyes, and smile in stark contrast to the blackness around him.

"Deck 15!" said Grandfather.

Zack's mouth fell open.

"How wide is it?"

"Like I said: it's wide," Grandfather said. To illustrate his point, he pulled a gadget from his pocket and threw it across the corridor. Zack waited several seconds, and then heard it hit something.

"Whoa. That's far."

"That wasn't the wall it hit. That was the floor. I can't even throw that far."

"Wow," Zack said. "But won't you need that thing you just threw?"

"I have no idea," Grandfather said and to illustrate this point, he pulled a second gizmo from his pocket. This gadget had a red button on it. Grandfather clicked it several times. Nothing happened. He pointed it at the floor, at Zack, and at the open air while he shook it violently. Nothing happened. So, Grandfather shrugged and hurled it into the darkness. The gadget hit something far away.

"See! The floor again," said Grandfather with a dazzled expression. "Awesome. This place is simply huge."

"Well, unless we get some power soon, this is going to be the coldest huge place in the world," said Angelina, her arms crossed and tapping her toe.

"Ah yes, you are right," Grandfather said, whirling around and striding down the corridor. "But technically, this is not the world, you see, since this is the Moon!"

Angelina slapped her forehead. Since Grandfather was ahead of them and already murmuring to himself about something else he saw or thought, he missed this. But Zack saw it and chuckled at Angelina's frustration.

"Ok, so he's a little flakey," he said.

"A little?"

"Well, a lot, but you'll get used to it."

"I hope not."

"Well, it kinda grew on me. But, you know, he's got a point. This *is* a big hallway."

"Well, unless we get some power soon. We're not going to have much longer to be throwing things across it to prove it."

"Ah! Here we are!" exclaimed Grandfather stopping in front of a door that towered over them. Zack removed his pin-light and shone it up at the ceiling. In the shadows, he could barely make out the top of the steel door. Unlike the doors in the hall above them, which were smooth and slightly concave, this door was covered with giant

CHAPTER 22: THE MIRACLE MECHS

crossbeams that formed an "X." Zack almost felt like this was a warning not to open it.

"It looks like you keep something vicious in there," said Angelina.

Grandfather just smiled his boyish smile and strode over to the right side of the door. Zack saw Grandfather kneel down in front of a small control box by the floor. He produced a wrench from his vest and whacked the box several times. Loud clangs echoed through the corridor. The box burst open and a stream of wires flew from it. Grandfather returned the wrench to his vest and pulled a small knife from his back pants pocket. He cut several wires.

"Uh, isn't that dangerous?" Angelina asked.

"No power," Grandfather said. "At least not yet."

He tied several wires together, returned the knife to his pants, and from somewhere — Zack didn't see where — pulled a small five-inch wide, by five-inch thick, by five-inch tall black cube.

"An Onyx Sun!" Zack exclaimed.

"Yup," said Grandfather. "My first one. I took it from the Onyx Airstrider in my Labradory before I left."

"Well, couldn't that power the Onyx Pioneer?" Zack asked.

"Not by itself. It wouldn't be stable enough. Maybe it could activate some individual systems, but we need a much larger Onyx Sun to power the entire ship."

Grandfather held the Onyx Sun up and several exposed wire-ends leapt toward it, fusing to its sides and spraying blue sparks onto the floor.

"But where are we going to get enough power for the entire ship?" Zack asked.

"From them," said Grandfather nodding toward the door.

A screech of metal on metal howled through the corridor as the doors vibrated and split open. The ground shook. Zack took a step back. In his pin-light, he could see a giant metal block appear in front of him, beyond the door. Hydraulic pumps stretched from the block to a wide pillar of metal that disappeared into the darkness above him. Zack stepped further back and looked up, pointing his pin-light toward the ceiling again. He could make out faint shapes in the darkness. There was something big and metal protruding from the dark.

The doors ground further back and stopped with a loud thud. The sound faded. Zack stepped back more. Suddenly a fluorescent light in the ceiling flickered to life and bathed the area beyond the door in an eerie glow.

A giant stood in front of Zack — not the kind you read about in some silly books, but a bright orange, metal leviathan reaching toward the sky. It was shaped like a human, but instead of arms it had wide metal columns. Instead of muscles, it had thick hydraulic cylinders. Each finger on each hand was built from metal beams as large as electricity towers on Earth. The block Zack saw in the dark was really just one pod of one of the robot's tripod feet. Each block was the size of a house. The robot was crowned with hulking shoulders and instead of a head it had a squat, angular geode of golden glass. Two towers of floodlights rose from its shoulders. A white number one was painted on the robot's chest.

The colossus towered over Zack at such a height he could barely see its entire shape. Its form stuck out at him, over him, like it was going to fall on him. Zack shuffled back quickly, tripped, and fell to the floor.

He just sat there, as Angelina sprang forward and exclaimed, "Wicked!"

Grandfather stepped inside the bay, walked up to the giant, put his hand on the block of steel, and patted it affectionately, as one might pat a fluffy dog.

"This is where we will get the power from. This is a Mech Leviathan," he said.

"Can I drive it?" Angelina asked.

CHAPTER 22: THE MIRACLE MECHS

"Well," Grandfather said, stepping back and removing his hand. "I'm not sure about that. We've never had such a young operator before. Then, again, the only person who has really driven one is Commander Chase. Even I haven't driven it. Well, that is not entirely accurate. I did try to drive one once, but it was rather disastrous."

"I can't imagine why," Angelina mumbled to Zack. "One of his stumbles could wipe out half of Los Angeles."

Zack suppressed a laugh and asked his grandfather, "What is it for?"

"The Mech will help us with heavy lifting during the construction of the Citadel Spire. Now, you can see how we plan to build it in just three months. There will be more time for us to talk about this later. Right now, we have to move quickly."

Grandfather flipped a switch on the inside of the door. Lights on the ceiling flickered to life one after the other. Zack could now see about twenty Mechs standing behind the first one. Each had a white number painted on its chest. Both sidewalls had a few Mechs housed under arched bays, facing the center column. Hoses and cables, big enough to hold up a bridge, hung down from each bay.

"The bays on the side are for maintenance and service," Grandfather said. "As you can see, we used them to store several Mech until we got here."

"I'd love to see what an oil change is like," Angelina said.

"Ah, yes," said Grandfather, as he reeled off into the service bay on the left. "Messy. Very messy indeed."

As if to prove a point, as he entered the bay, he slipped and slid several yards before catching himself on a Mech standing nearby.

"Ah, yes, watch your step," he said. "Oil everywhere."

Angelina shook her head and pointed to the ground, which was meticulously clean. Zack chuckled and faked a slip, which made Angelina laugh.

Zack and Angelina walked over to Grandfather, who was standing near a Mech's leg. Zack noticed a platform attached to the side of the leg. The platform had a railing around it about waist high, except for a small gap in the front. Grandfather stepped through the gap and onto the platform. He ushered Zack and Angelina on as well then said, "Hold on."

He pulled a lever on the side of the railing and the platform shot upwards. They flew up the side of the Mech, passing its bright orange calf, knee, and waist. The platform slowed and stopped at the chest, just before they got thrown into the robot's armpit. Zack could see a door in the side of the Mech's chest here. Grandfather put his hand on a black panel next to the door. A scanning light swept his hand, and the door whisked open.

The inside of the Mech was tight but manageable. There was a black leather chair in the center of the room mounted on rails running up the wall into the dome above them. Zack guessed the pilot sat on the chair, and it rode up the rails into the dome.

Grandfather sat in the pilot's chair and pressed several buttons on its side. A small hole opened in the floor in front of the chair and a joystick rose from it. A control panel also swung around from the side of the chair. Grandfather stepped out of the chair and twisted his body under the control panel. He pulled a screwdriver from his suit and began disassembling the panel. A minute later, he held a small Onyx Sun in his hand, just like the original. Grandfather tossed the Onyx Sun to Zack and then reached into his suit to produce two other screwdrivers, which he gave to Zack and Angelina.

"See," he said. "Each Mech is powered by a small Onyx Sun. If we get enough of them, we might have a chance of surviving."

CHAPTER 23

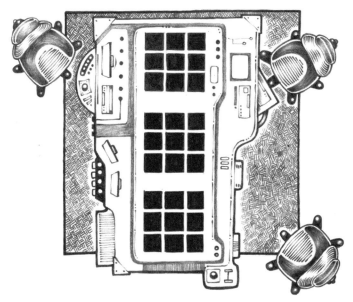

Strange Properties of the Onyx Sun

Zack got used to climbing into the Mechs, as he worked from one to the next. He began to recognize the functions of the joystick that emerged from the floor. He saw buttons on the control panel labeled "rocket boosters," "welding torch," and one especially large one labeled "ion shield." He became familiar with where the harness on the seat was and how it worked. Although he understood the urgency to collect as many Onyx Suns as possible, he took the occasional liberty of inspecting and toying with each Mech, as he moved through the columns of the hulking beasts.

Zack enjoyed stepping around the robots and seeing how they were put together. He started to comprehend the basics of how the Mechs worked, how the hydraulics powered the arms and legs, and how the controls could be used to operate the different tools each

Mech had. The gears started whirring in Zack's head again, and soon he was visualizing in his mind improvements he could make to the robots. What if he replaced the hydraulics with electric motors, which were easier to maintain and could be controlled wirelessly? What if instead of steel, which Zack guessed they were made of because of the spots of rust he saw, the robots were constructed out of a lighter, stronger material, like titanium? What if Zack designed a Mech where all the hoses and wires, which were currently exposed, were moved internally so the robot was less likely to get caught on things? Zack became inspired by all the possibilities and before he knew it half an hour had passed.

Grandfather whistled far down the bay to call them back together. Zack finished collecting the Onyx Sun he was removing and then met his grandfather and Angelina in the center of the Mech bay.

"Well, how many do you guys have?" asked Grandfather. "I have eight."

"I've got four," Angelina said. "I had problems finding the cubes and getting them out."

"I've got ten," Zack said, holding out two cupped hands, which tingled with electricity from holding the cubes. Grandfather's eyebrows jumped up his forehead.

Angelina said, "Nice job, Zack."

"Well, it would seem my grandson also has an affinity for tinkering," said Grandfather Goodspeed, patting him on the back. "Nice work Zack. Here give them to me. All right. So, twenty-two in total. That means we just need five more. We'll leave the last three Mechs alone."

"Don't we need as many as we can get?" asked Zack.

"Yes and no," said Grandfather. "You'll see what I mean soon. Come on."

Grandfather led the way and together they collected the final five.

CHAPTER 23: STRANGE PROPERTIES OF THE ONYX SUN

As they were riding the platform down the leg of the last Mech, Grandfather's pin-light started to flicker. By the time they reached the bottom, it died and Zack's was already starting to dim.

"They have great battery life, given their small size," Grandfather said, "But, unfortunately, they die just like every other battery in the world. Maybe one day I can build an Onyx Sun small enough to power even these."

As they hurried up the stairs to the Engineering Core on Deck 7, Zack's pin-light flickered off as well. They stood in total darkness for a few seconds, until a thin stream of light emerged from Angelina.

"Last one," she said, positioning the pin-light on her flight suit.

"Right," Grandfather said. "Let's be quick. It's already getting cold on the ship."

Grandfather was right, Zack realized. He had been so busy studying the robots, Zack hadn't noticed the chill in the air or the fact he could now see his own breath.

They hurried toward the Engineering Core. As they went, Zack saw most of the crew assembled in the hallways. In the dim beam of Angelina's pin-light, Zack saw people lining the floor of the hall moaning, while others rushed around trying to assist the injured in the faint light of their own dying pin-lights. Other people huddled together for warmth. Zack noticed for the first time he could see his own breath. A shiver passed through him both because he was cold and because he realized what would happen if they didn't restore the power soon.

Zack, Angelina, and Grandfather found the Engineering Core doorless and stepped inside. Two men stood on either side of the center command console holding welding torches up to light the room.

"I had the door removed so I could command the crew better," Dr. Soon said. "Then, as the welders were leaving, our pin-lights died. So, I asked the welders to stick around."

"Good thinking," Grandfather said stepping up. "We had better work fast."

Grandfather produced twenty-seven Onyx Suns from his suit. Dr. Soon seemed equally stunned as Zack and Angelina were at where the cubes where coming from. Grandfather's suit was never lumpy or bulgy, but one after the other, Grandfather produced five-by-five-by-five black cubes from his pockets. Oblivious to their expressions, Grandfather arranged the cubes in three groups of nine. Each group of nine he placed on the table in a square formation — three wide by three long.

Completing this, he said, "You are about to experience some of the electro-magnetic-kinetic properties of the Onyx Sun. I won't say this is *where* the device draws its power from, but more so that *it is an example* of the source of its power."

Grandfather spread his arms wide, ushering the crowd back that had gathered around the center console.

"Please stand back. I have tried this only once before."

"How did that go?" Angelina asked.

"You remember you said your foster parents thought there was a war in my garage."

"Yeah."

"Well, it was probably from this experiment."

"Great."

Everyone stepped back a little, but curiosity kept most of the crowd nearby. Having experienced several of his grandfather's mishaps, Zack stood back farther than most people. Angelina noticed this and joined him.

From the set of nine Onyx Suns on the left, Grandfather plucked the cube at the center of the square. He rubbed it in his hands, slowly at first, then quickly. Then, clenching it in one hand, he raised his fist high over his head and slammed the Onyx Sun onto the console.

"Ba-wow!"

CHAPTER 23: STRANGE PROPERTIES OF THE ONYX SUN

A shockwave burst from the cube and crashed through the crowd. People covered their ears and stepped farther back. Only Zack and Angelina stood anywhere close to Grandfather now.

Zack looked at the table where the Onyx Sun sat. In the flickering lights of the welding torches, Zack could see something stirring in the darkness of the cube, like there was life inside. Faintly glowing blue-black shapes swirled around inside the cube, pressing against its sides. Blue spots of light gleamed from the cube, like eyes, as the storm of glowing shadows inside the cube whirled faster. The Onyx Sun looked like a cube-contained thunderstorm.

Zack watched the cube as the storm inside it began to spin faster. Small arcs of blue lightning leapt from the cube onto the console, causing the monitors there to sporadically spring to life and then shut down, like the lights of a disco floor.

As the sparks grew into a small storm, Grandfather grabbed the cube from the table.

"Ow! Ow! Ow!" he said, handling the cube nimbly, like a hot potato. He dropped it back into the center of the first group of Onyx Suns.

The stormy Onyx Sun landed askew of the other cubes, but the moment it landed, eight bolts of lightning surged from it, striking each of the other cubes. The middle cube centered itself so that it was aligned with its brothers. Then, as the lighting intensified, the other Onyx Suns began to shake. All eight flew from their positions and fused to the sides of the center cube.

The rumbling stopped and in the place of the cubes was a black plate, five inches high, by fifteen inches long, and fifteen inches wide. The storm inside the center cube calmed and faded.

Grandfather tapped the square plate and, seeing it was not sparking, picked it up.

He handed it to Zack and said, "Hold this. You may feel a slight shock."

Zack bent under the weight of the plate, as Grandfather dumped it into his arms. Even though it was only the size of a large book, it weighed as much as a television set. Zack peered at it as he strained to hold it up. Energy radiating from the plate made his hands tingle and his fingers numb, but it was nowhere near as intense as touching the larger Onyx Sun.

"Don't be a wuss," Angelina teased him, when she noticed him straining.

Grandfather performed the same feat with the next group of nine cubes. The second plate, he dropped into Angelina's arms. She immediately folded under the weight and someone in the crowd stepped forward to assist her.

"I got it," she said in a strained voice.

"Not light, huh?" Zack said.

Angelina scowled at him.

Grandfather whacked the last Onyx Sun on the table. The people in the crowd, used to the sequence of events by now, covered their ears, as the sound wave crashed through them. Grandfather fused the last set together and put the plate on end so it was standing up.

"Zack. Max. Bring the other parts here. Put them on the table on each side of mine," Grandfather said.

Zack and Angelina lurched toward Grandfather. Zack scraped the plate across the console as he barely managed to lift it. Grandfather helped him, then Angelina. As Angelina lifted her plate onto the console, the welders' torches sputtered and went out.

The Engineering Core fell into a blanket of darkness, save Angelina's pin-light, which was very dim.

"We haven't much time," Grandfather said, and with a grunt Mr. Goodspeed would have been proud of, Grandfather helped Angelina lift the third plate onto the console.

CHAPTER 23: STRANGE PROPERTIES OF THE ONYX SUN

The three plates were lined up so their flat sides faced each other, like dominoes. Grandfather pulled a hammer from his suit and ushered the children back.

"All right," he said, removing some tissue from his vest and stuffing it into his ears. "Everyone cover your ears. I really hate this part."

The crew did as they were told. Grandfather waited until they were all braced and then with a fast sweeping motion, swung his arm through the air and hammered the center plate.

"Ba-wing!"

The center plate screamed. The people in the crowd moaned as they clenched their ears and leaned as far away from the cube as they could get.

At first, nothing happened.

Then, a blue-black storm, larger and brighter this time, stirred inside the center plate. It rapidly swirled around inside its casing until the plate looked like a tsunami of oil trapped inside a narrow box. The high-pitched scream rose in intensity. The Engineering Core's window wall shattered. People cringed. Larger lightning bolts arced from the plate in the center. They crept along the console, and shot into the air. Grandfather ducked several of these, until the bolts settled on the two plates to the sides of the center one. The bolts shook and flickered like an electrical storm. The three plates shot together with a bang, like a clap of thunder.

For Zack, at least, everything went dark.

* * *

When he came to, the first thing he noticed was that he was on the floor. The second thing he noticed was Angelina standing over him saying something in a funny voice as if from far away. The third thing he noticed was that the entire Engineering Core was lit again.

Zack stood and shook his head. The center console was fully lit. Bright, multi-colored lights flashed across its surface as it displayed the status of the ship. The display monitors on the wall that weren't cracked streamed reams of text and video. The lights overhead poured a dazzling light into the room. People were clapping each other on the back and shaking Grandfather's hand.

Beyond the gaping hole in the back of the Engineering Core, the Power Tower was as dark as ever. Zack pulled on Grandfather's sleeve and pointed at it.

Grandfather turned around, glanced at what Zack was pointing at, and said, "Ah, yes. The power is localized right now. Since we haven't plugged the Onyx Sun into anything, it is only powering the systems within its immediate range."

"Is that why my head is tingling?"

"Well, it could be that or the fact that you fainted."

Angelina snickered at this. Zack looked at her angrily.

"I did not faint."

Grandfather looked down at him, studying him behind the cracked lenses of his copper spectacles. A big smile split his mouth. He put his hand on Zack's head and messed up his already chaotic blond hair. "You're right," he said.

Dr. Soon helped Commander Chase limp over to the console.

"Commander," said Grandfather. "You should be resting."

"He insisted, Fy," said Dr. Soon.

"I can't believe it," said Commander Chase looking around the bridge. "You've saved us all, Fy."

"Well, not yet. Here, sit down and let one of the SciTech physicians look you over while we plug the Onyx Sun in. Dr. Soon? Would you care to assist me?"

Dr. Soon helped Commander Chase sit in a nearby chair, then said, "Yes, Fy. I would be pleased to."

CHAPTER 23: STRANGE PROPERTIES OF THE ONYX SUN

The two men rounded up a small team of people. Zack noticed how strange it looked having people from the Entertainment Troupe and Spiritual Enclave helping the Engineering and SciTech teams. It was apparent the day's events had brought everyone closer.

Grandfather ordered the people assisting him to put on gloves. He also asked several lean looking Security Team members to run to a nearby supply closet and grab an "atom lift."

As they sprinted from the room, Zack asked, "What's an atom lift?"

"It is very similar to the technology we use to levitate the Onyx Pioneer," said Grandfather. "It collects atoms from the air, hyper-accelerates them, and shoots them out the bottom. This creates a field capable of hovering the atom lift in thin air. It also gives us an almost frictionless surface to push the cube across."

Grandfather looked toward the ceiling as if he was pondering something.

"Won't the lift need power?" Zack asked.

Grandfather looked back at him and said, "Precisely what I was thinking, but I think we will be fine. Typically, smaller devices on the Onyx Pioneer, like the lift, are rechargeable. When they aren't being used, they are left in charging stations, which draw energy from the Power Tower. Although the Power Tower has been down for hours and the lift is probably dead, I think the proximity to this Onyx Sun should power it."

The Security Team members returned to the bridge with what looked like a flat, white football. As they stepped into the bridge, the atom lift leapt from their hands, fell to the floor, and hovered there.

Grandfather nodded at Zack and said, "There. See."

"Are your theories always right?" Sanjay asked Grandfather, as he appeared from the crowd.

Grandfather looked at Zack and they both laughed.

"Only when they're not wrong, which can be quite often."

Zack nodded in agreement. "He's not kidding."

"I would believe it," Angelina added.

Grandfather pushed the atom lift along the floor. It floated easily and at one point got away from Grandfather's grasp. He clumsily dashed after it, but Angelina managed to stop it first with her foot. Grandfather positioned the atom lift next to the center console and then turned toward the crew.

"On the count of five, lift the Onyx Sun onto the lift. One. Five!" Grandfather said.

The crewmembers lifted the cube onto the atom lift, which sank a little but continued to float.

"All right everyone," Grandfather said, addressing the crew. "Please stay in the Engineering Core. It will probably get dark in here once we leave. So, stay put. In a few minutes, we will hopefully have the whole ship up and running."

Grandfather patted Zack on the back and bushed up his hair again. Zack and Angelina found a place by Commander Chase's feet and sat down. Grandfather led the small team out of the Engineering Core, pushing the Onyx Sun in front of them with their gloved hands. As they rounded the corner and disappeared into the hallway, some of the monitors in the Engineering Core flickered off. The center console shut down, whirring itself into standby mode. The overhead lights seemed to be the most resilient. But after a few moments, they too became dimmer and eventually blinked off.

Blackness overtook Zack and Angelina again. Zack could hear Commander Chase wheezing to his right and feel Angelina's warm body huddled next to him to his left.

"Don't worry guys," Commander Chase said. "It will be all right. In fact, if you hadn't let us know what was going on when you did, this could have been a lot worse."

CHAPTER 23: STRANGE PROPERTIES OF THE ONYX SUN

After what seemed like an hour, Zack noticed a faint light in the distance. He stood. He felt Angelina stand too and follow him. They stumbled past people in the dark, until Zack could feel the frame of where the window used to be. Across the cavern, he could see the faint outline of the doorway connecting the corridor and the Power Tower. The light in the corridor was growing brighter.

"The Onyx Sun must be turning on the hallway lights," he said to Angelina. In the faint light, he noticed she was just looking back at him. At this close distance, Zack saw for the first time he was taller than Angelina. He remarked how under her tough exterior, she was extremely girlish. She had long black eyelashes, eyes that gleamed at him, and her dark hair hung over her narrow shoulders like a veil. He could see her better, as more light poured from the doorway far away.

The Onyx Sun must be getting close to the Power Tower, he thought. The light from the doorway in the Power Tower became intense, and someone in the Engineering Core said, "Hey! Look!"

Zack felt Angelina pull back, as people rushed to the hole in the wall. They pressed around Zack, and he turned toward the light too. Far in the distance, he could see the perfect outline of the doorway from the main corridor. The silhouettes of a large cube and several people stood on the edge of the catwalk. A very tall shape, which could only be Grandfather, motioned for the others to stay as he darted into the darkness. He returned pulling violently at something that looked like a thick cable. He ushered the others away from the cube and held the cable up. Zack saw a violent bolt of energy arc from the cube-shape to the cable-shape. The cube floated toward the cable and the two fused together in a shower of blue sparks.

Immediately, the ship was awash in light. Zack could feel the inertia of the ship rising in the air, as the atom lifts in the bottom of the hull again put a cushion of air between the fuselage and the surface of the Moon. The Onyx Pioneer's systems whirred to life. The sounds of computers rebooting and beeping competed with the noise of people cheering. The Engineering Core was bright again, but this time, so was the hallway outside, and every other area Zack could see. The Power Tower glowed a brilliant blue again.

Zack looked for Angelina in the crowd. He noticed Sanjay dancing around the center console but did not see her. He pressed through the jubilant mob and found her in the back corner of the room — away from the people who were cheering, and screaming, and crying — and as she smiled at him, he felt new hope.

CHAPTER 24

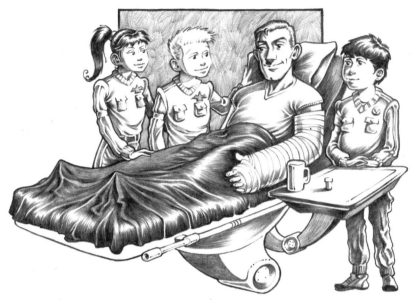

The Desperate Plan

Grandfather and the Engineering Corps spent the next four hours positioning the Onyx Sun the best they could. They managed to affix it to the center of the catwalk and lift it enough that they could remove it from the atom lift and place it on the deck. As the situation in the ship calmed, Dr. Soon sent more of his team to help. They managed to weld foot-high retaining walls on each side of the cube, so it would not move. Grandfather collected the power cables that had once run through the Power Tower, and fused them one by one to the Onyx Sun. As he did so, Zack could see more ship systems coming to life, as indicators on the monitors changed from red to green.

Zack, Angelina, and Sanjay watched all this from the Engineering Core. They had to step aside for a bit when Dr. Soon ordered a small group to fit a new window to the back wall. The rest of his team was busy replacing the cracked monitors, stuffing hoses back into the ceiling, and rewiring the exposed wires. Around the time the window-wall was finally locked in place and the last monitor had been replaced, Grandfather strode through the door of the Engineering Core, sweaty and dirty. His white suit looked like a zebra skin as black stripes crisscrossed his vest, shirt, and pants from where he had clearly wiped his hands.

Zack walked over to his grandfather, who briefly nodded to him before leaping over to talk with Dr. Soon.

"Status?" he asked.

"Well, better then I thought and worse then I thought," Dr. Soon said. The two men congregated around the center console, which had also been fixed. An image of the Onyx Pioneer whirled around on the console. Dr. Soon waved his hand over the panel, and the image on its surface jumped into the air as a 3-D hologram.

Zack, Sanjay, and Angelina stepped over. As the hologram spun around in mid-air, Zack could see most of the ship highlighted in green light, but significant portions of it were red. The bridge glowed entirely red.

"Most of the ship is fine," Dr. Soon said. "We experienced minor pressure leaks throughout the hull, but my team has spot-welded those and our air pressure is holding."

Dr. Soon waved his hand another direction over the console. The 3-D image of the Onyx Pioneer stopped spinning and zoomed in on a view of the Power Tower.

"The Power Tower of course is operating under full power, but thanks to your efforts, we can safely pull 50 percent of normal capacity from the Onyx Sun. We are unsure how much stable power the new Onyx Sun will generate since it is much smaller than the last one."

"It will be less safe at higher power," Grandfather said. "Technically, it is not even a real Onyx Sun, since I cobbled it together from a bunch of smaller ones."

CHAPTER 24: THE DESPERATE PLAN

"Well then, the first order of business should be testing it," Dr. Soon said. "While you were working on it, we used it only to power essential ship systems, like artificial gravity, life support, and lighting."

Grandfather nodded at this and said, "Yes. Now that the Power Tower is clear, we can spin it up and test it at full power."

"Will do."

Dr. Soon bowed his head and waved his hand over the console again. The graphic shifted until a bright red, circular area could be seen on the top of the Onyx Sun's hull.

Dr. Soon said, "The only area of complete loss was the bridge. It could take us a month or more to rebuild it. In the meantime, I have had almost all ship systems transferred to the Engineering Core. Navigation and flight control systems, however, are completely inoperable."

Grandfather lowered his head and said, "Is it too dangerous for us to return to Earth without these systems online?"

"It's not too dangerous. It's impossible."

A cadet wearing an Engineering Corps uniform strode over and gave Dr. Soon a handheld computer. Dr. Soon scrolled through the information on the screen and asked the cadet, "Are you sure this information is correct?"

"Yes, sir," said the cadet. "I triple checked it."

"Very well. Thank you," Dr. Soon said, giving the handheld to Grandfather. "Well, it may not matter if we have full ship systems or not. Preliminary data from the new Onyx Sun says it doesn't have enough power to get us out of here anyway."

Grandfather took the handheld and scrolled through the information on the screen, his eyebrows knitted. He put it down on the console and, in one stride, crossed the room to the wall monitors. He rapidly tapped several panels. Zack saw text stream by as Grandfather tapped the screen with one hand, while working a scientific calculator he produced from his suit with the other. After a minute, he stopped and reviewed his results quietly.

He turned around and said, looking at Dr. Soon and Zack, "The data is correct. I checked it without the computer's help. We're staying here…for now."

In another step, he strode back to the console. Grandfather dismissed several cadets working nearby and pulled Zack, Angelina, Sanjay, and Dr. Soon closer.

"We're not getting out of here without the original Onyx Sun," Grandfather whispered.

"What about the three Onyx Suns from the last three Mechs?" Zack asked. "Would those help?"

Grandfather shook his head and said, "The Onyx Sun does not work like that. The only way it can achieve the power it does is by being in a cube formation. Adding three more won't help. In fact, it will lessen the stability of the others. The cube works only in mathematical cubes. In order to build an Onyx Sun you can have one cube, eight, twenty-seven, sixty-four, and so on."

"What do you mean?" Angelina asked.

"Cubes," Zack said. "Those numbers are the cubes of 1, 2, 3, and 4. One times one times one is one. Two times two times two is eight. Three times three times three is twenty-seven. And so on."

"It is the only way to build an Onyx Sun," added Sanjay. "You have to stack all the blocks together to form a larger cube."

"So, can you build more Onyx Suns?" Zack asked.

"Impossible," said Grandfather, shaking his head as he placed his hands on the console and leaned over it. "First, I don't have the materials. Second, even if I did, it would take too long. The Onyx Sun Machvel stole took me a year to build."

Grandfather's head shot up, as if he just realized something. "Speaking of time, Rajah, how long *do* we have?"

CHAPTER 24: THE DESPERATE PLAN

"Well," Dr. Soon said, looking like they were now coming to a topic he did not want to discuss. "The good news is, thanks to our efforts in the last three hours, we have a lot longer."

"Give us the bad news," Zack said. He was tired of waiting. The whole day had been a series of unknowns and mysteries.

"The bad news is our food will run out in five months. And the worse news is that our air supply, at current consumption levels, will run out in four."

Grandfather stepped back from the console as if he had been shocked. His eyes darted around the room. He stepped back in, lowered his voice and asked, "Four months, Rajah? What can we do in four months?"

Dr. Soon looked down at the handheld on the console. He picked it up and spun it around in his hands. Not looking up, he said, "We have to build the base. The Citadel Spire is our only hope. We need to get the Bodi Biodome and the hydroponics labs online to start producing oxygen and food, as soon as possible."

Grandfather ran a hand through his tuft of hair and nodded.

"This might work," he whispered. "It doesn't leave us much room for error, but our original plan was to build the base anyway. Phase 1 was supposed to take three months."

"Well," Dr. Soon said, putting the console back down and looking Grandfather straight in the eyes. "I'm afraid it's more complex than that. During the last few hours, before we took Commander Chase to the infirmary, he ordered a ship-wide search for Dr. Machvel. They didn't find him, of course."

"Well that's good news," said Zack.

"Not really. There's more. They didn't find a lot of stuff."

"Like what?" Grandfather asked.

"Three thousand members of the crew, some of our food, and a significant portion of our construction supplies."

"Those pirates!" Grandfather shouted, slamming his fist down on the console. Several people in the Engineering Core looked their way.

Dr. Soon stood still, like he was afraid to say anything.

Zack couldn't stand it any longer. Amidst all the talk about survival, one question had been pressing against his skull the most, as if it might leap out on its own.

"But where the heck did Machvel and the rest of the crew go? We're on the Moon! Where could they possibly disappear to?"

"I don't know," Dr. Soon said. "But they're not on this ship. We found the heavy freighter missing from Deck 15."

"What is the freighter for?" Zack asked.

"It's designed to carry construction equipment from the landing zone to the construction site of the Citadel Spire," Dr. Soon said.

"But how could they fly it without power?" Zack asked. The gears began whirring in his head. He considered all the possibilities. He could already see problems and answers to problems appearing in his head. They could have brought their own power. They could have another ship to transfer power. The question he had no answer to though was the one driving him crazy. He had to know what happened to Dr. Machvel.

"All the airships on the Onyx Pioneer are rechargeable, like the atom lift," said Grandfather. "They probably had enough power stored in the freighter to make it anywhere on the Moon they wanted to go. If they were smart, they would have plugged the Onyx Sun they stole into the freighter."

"Could they go back to Earth?" Zack asked.

"No," Dr. Soon answered. "The freighter was not designed for re-entry into Earth's atmosphere. It would break up."

The gears in Zack's mind stopped. He was stumped.

"Pirates!" Grandfather shouted again. "I should have known it. Machvel was always asking me questions about how things worked on

CHAPTER 24: THE DESPERATE PLAN

the ship, especially the Onyx Sun. I took it for intellectual curiosity, at the time. He was my head of engineering, after all."

"What could he want with the Onyx Sun?" Zack asked.

"I don't know. Unlimited power, maybe?" Grandfather said. "There's a lot anyone could do with the Onyx Sun. He could build a base to support space exploration, like us. He could try to take credit for inventing it, since I never made any public announcements. He could even have more dire plans. We have to get it back. Not just because it is ours to begin with, but because power of that magnitude in the wrong hands could be catastrophic."

"But our first task has to be building the base," said Dr. Soon. "We won't be able to look very hard for Machvel if we run out of oxygen."

"No, we have to find Machvel first," Zack said. He couldn't believe anyone could suggest they just let someone who almost killed them go. "If we wait too long we may never find him."

"Zack, that's true," Grandfather said, "but Dr. Soon is right. Survival is our first task. Searching for Machvel is too risky and too uncertain. We may not find him in time for it to make a difference."

"But if we found Machvel, we would find all the extra food and supplies. It would keep us alive."

"If we found Machvel, I doubt he would give up easily, Zack," Grandfather said. "He would fight us. We would have even forces, because even though he has fewer members of our crew, many of our people have been hurt by the explosion and ensuing battle. Wounded and weak is no way for us to beat him."

"But how can you all just let him get away!"

Grandfather crouched down so that he was the same height as Zack.

"Zack, no one wants to let him get away, but right now it is a matter of priorities. Our immediate survival is simply first."

Zack glowered at his grandfather. He suddenly felt like maybe the people on Earth were right. Maybe Grandfather was out of touch with reality. To Zack, letting a man like Machvel go was like letting him win.

Grandfather turned back to Dr. Soon and said, "So, how long will it take you to build the base, Rajah?"

"Me?" said Dr. Soon.

"Why yes," said Grandfather with a smile. "Commander Chase is in the infirmary and you are the second in command of the Engineering Corps under Dr. Machvel."

"What about you?"

"I would do it, Rajah, but as much as I appreciate your analysis of our situation, I have to try to fix the Onyx Pioneer in case you're wrong. If the base construction fails, maybe I can do something to get us home. So, how long?"

Dr. Soon fumbled for words, "Uh, well, I think we could have the basic support systems up in three months —"

"Ah," interrupted Grandfather. "But that is running it awful close. You'll have to do better."

"Yes," Dr. Soon said growing pale. "Well, yes we will. This is going to be a challenge with three thousand crew members missing and so many supplies stolen."

"Not to mention, only three working Mechs," said Zack.

Grandfather smiled at Zack's comment, but did not take his eyes off Dr. Soon. He seemed to enjoy watching Rajah squirm. He whispered out of the side of his mouth to Zack, "Great men rise to challenging occasions."

"Three Mechs. Ah, yes," Dr. Soon said, wiping his brow. "Well, I imagine we can substitute some of the Mech tasks with the other machinery. And we'll have to cross-train the crew. We can have the

CHAPTER 24: THE DESPERATE PLAN

Spiritual Conclave and Security Team do some of the easier tasks for the Engineering Corps and SciTechs."

"Now you're thinking. Although for our sake, keep the Entertainment Troupe away from the delicate projects. Perhaps they can do administrative tasks like cooking and fetching things we need. And don't be afraid to enlist the Executive Board members as well. No one can relax until this is done. We all have to chip in."

"Right," said Dr. Soon, wiping his brow.

"Now that's set and we have a plan," Grandfather said. "I'm going to take my grandson and Max to visit Commander Chase to see how he is doing. Sanjay, you are welcome to join us if you like."

Sanjay looked at his father, who nodded and said, "Go ahead, son. I have to work."

Sanjay sprang around the console and joined Grandfather, Angelina, and Zack as they walked out of the Engineering Core.

✶ ✶ ✶

Commander Chase had seen better days. He was lying in an infirmary bed with a cast over his left arm when Zack, Angelina, Sanjay, and Grandfather walked in. Zack commented how even as banged up as he was, Commander Chase's chiseled jawline and angular face still displayed raw strength. The SciTech medical staff were rushing around the other beds checking on the patients who filled the infirmary to capacity. Every bed was full and some people even lay on the floor.

Commander Chase welcomed his guests and tried to sit up, wincing as he did so.

"Relax," Grandfather said. "We're just here to visit. You don't need to get up."

"Thanks," said Commander Chase, as he let out a sigh.

"How are you?" asked Angelina.

"Well, the doctor says my arm's broken, and I have a few bruised ribs, but I'll be fine."

"Good," said Grandfather Goodspeed. "Because I already have an assignment for you."

"Yes, sir," said Commander Chase.

"I need you to watch Zack and Max here while I fix the Onyx Pioneer," Grandfather said. Zack felt a twinge of disappointment. He had assumed Grandfather and he were going to be able to spend more time together, fixing the ship.

"My team and I are going to be doing a lot of spacewalking, in order to fix the bridge," said Grandfather, looking at Zack. "And your parents would never forgive me if I let you float away."

"But I —"

"No, Zack. We're not discussing this. I haven't forgotten that you stowed away on my ship. When I said I was glad to see you here, I was, but that does not make you being here okay. I didn't have time before the explosion to add that I was planning on taking you straight home. If the Onyx Pioneer were working right now, in fact, you and Max would find yourselves back on Earth."

The twinge of disappointment turned into a surge. Zack felt ashamed and embarrassed at having stowed away on the ship, but also angry that Grandfather wouldn't want him to stay. How often did they get to see each other? Not often, Zack thought. Yet here they were stranded on the Moon. It was the perfect opportunity to spend time together.

"But we're on the Moon! They would understand."

"No, Zack. We have to get you back as soon as possible. Family comes first."

"How can *you* say that? You disappear all the time!"

Zack blurted this before he realized what he was saying. He immediately regretted it. Grandfather looked like he had been slapped. For a moment, he stared at Zack like he couldn't speak.

CHAPTER 24: THE DESPERATE PLAN

Grandfather blinked several times and cleared his throat, "Well, Zack. That's different. I'm an old man. My family is all grown up."

"Yes, but you could spend more time with me," said Zack.

Grandfather cleared his throat and coughed a little.

"Zack," said Commander Chase, wrapping his good hand around Zack's arm. "It's all right, Fy. Go ahead. The crew is going to need you soon. I'll watch Zack and Max."

"Thank you, Commander," Grandfather said looking away. "I trust you'll watch over them well."

Grandfather left. Angelina and Sanjay looked uncomfortably at Zack.

"Guys," said Commander Chase to Angelina and Sanjay. "Give us a moment, ok?"

They both nodded and slipped away to check out some of the weird-looking medical devices in the back of the infirmary.

"Zack, your grandfather wants only what's best. Your place is with your mother and father."

"But I also want to be with him."

"I know. There's a time for that. But that did not give you the right to sneak onto his ship."

"But I had no idea where he was going and when I found out how long he'd be gone, I didn't want him to go without me."

"That's no excuse, Zack."

"Well, how long was the mission originally scheduled to be anyway?" asked Zack. He could see he had hit the mark, as Commander Chase searched for words. "How long?"

Commander Chase finally looked at him, sighed, and said, "One year."

"See!" said Zack, throwing his hands in the air. "He disappears in and out of my life with no warning at all. He's here. He's gone. I can't tell."

"Zack, look. Your grandfather talks about you constantly. You know, when you first fell into my room, I knew you already. I had to make sure you were who you said you were, but he talks about you so much, and shows me pictures of you so often, I recognized you immediately as if you were my own grandson."

"Really?"

"Yes, Zack. He cares about you more than anything else in the universe, even the Onyx Sun."

It was hard for Zack to imagine this. If Grandfather cared so much about him, why did he spend infinitely more time with the Onyx Sun? Still, Zack had to admit to himself that Grandfather did look surprised that Zack thought they should spend more time together. And it did feel good to hear that he talked about Zack all the time.

"Did I tell you I have a son back on Earth?" Commander Chase said.

"You do?" Why didn't you bring him?"

"I wanted to, but my wife didn't want to leave our home and the rest of our family. So, I came up here alone, because I believe in what your grandfather is doing."

"Do you miss him?"

"Are you kidding me? Of course I do. I think about him every day. And the more I think about him, the more I miss him. That's what being away from people you care about is. But I don't love him any less just because I am away from him."

Zack looked at the floor. He shuffled back and forth and finally looked up and nodded. "I get it," he said.

"Good," said Commander Chase. "Because your grandfather cares about you very much. He just has lots of things he needs to do. You have to realize though that one of the main reasons he does this stuff is to share it with you eventually. That is why he was glad to have you aboard. You get that, don't you?"

CHAPTER 24: THE DESPERATE PLAN

"Yeah."

"Ok. Good. I'm glad we talked about this."

At that moment, the sound of metal crashing to the floor interrupted their conversation. Zack saw Sanjay lying on the ground with an expensive-looking medical device splayed across him. Angelina was protesting to the nurses that they hadn't meant to knock it over, while trying to pick Sanjay up.

"Well, looks like I gotta go," said Zack.

"Yeah, I give you about ten seconds until the nurses eject all three of you."

Sure enough, once Angelina managed to collect Sanjay from the floor, half the nurses picked up the device while the other half hurried them out of the room. Angelina, laughing from all the commotion, grabbed Zack as they rushed by. The three of them waved goodbye to Commander Chase as the infirmary door opened for them to leave and slammed shut behind them.

CHAPTER 25

Explorations

"So, I'm guessing we're not sleeping in the library tonight," Zack said as soon as they were outside.

"No. My father told me Professor Goodspeed's quarters have been prepared for you," said Sanjay.

"He didn't give us a key."

"We don't use keys here, Zack Goodspeed. Remember when you asked about that cadet on the Command Deck who you thought was talking to himself before launch? Our central computer is voice activated. Just say anything and the door will open."

"But how will the computer recognize our voices? We stowed away."

"It has been programmed to recognize your voice now, from what my father tells me. See, the central computer is always listening for voices. That way you can access it no matter where you are. The computer has heard your voice many times now and filed it away. My father added to the file that you are a trusted member of the crew."

"Neat," said Angelina.

"Yes, it is," said Sanjay. "It is infinitely practical too. We can use it also to identify intruders, because when they talk, the computer does not recognize them because it does not have their voice on file or their file says they are not welcome. The computer then alerts the Security Team."

"Why didn't it pick us up right away then?" asked Zack.

"We shut down certain functions, like that, for the maiden flight of the Onyx Pioneer, so we could focus the computer on the launch," said Sanjay. "We weren't sure how it would go, and we wanted to make sure the computer was focused."

"I appreciate that," Angelina said.

"No kidding. Me too," Zack agreed.

"We all do," Sanjay said. "So now that it is activated, all you need to do is validate the computer knows who you are. Here, let me show you. Computer, identify."

"Voice is of Sanjay Soon," said a calm female voice all around them. "Son of Dr. Rajah Soon, the new Head of Engineering, and Miriam Soon, Third Acolyte of the Spiritual Enclave. Sanjay Soon is ten years old and three years away from entering the Cadet Training Academy. Preliminary testing indicates an aptitude for math and science, with emphasis on applied materials. Sanjay Soon is single. Sanjay has no documented relations with any other member of the crew, although biometric signs indicate elevated heart rate when near Penelope Tibault, age eleven, and Anna Cruz, age ten."

Sanjay's eyes grew wide. He said, "Computer end report!"

"End of report," said the computer voice.

Angelina and Zack laughed.

"Seems like the computer thinks you should get a girlfriend," Zack said.

"Sometimes the computer is a little too nosy for its own good," said Sanjay, blushing.

"Who are Penelope and Anna?" Angelina chided.

"Who? Uh, I don't know. Some crew members I guess," Sanjay said.

The computer voice sprang to life again and said, "Inaccurate. Sanjay Soon was last with Penelope Tibault Saturday in a storage room on Deck 17. Anna Cruz is currently waiting to have dinner with Sanjay in Dr. and Mrs. Soon's quarters."

"Computer! End report! End report!" Sanjay said, brightly flushed now.

"End of report," said the computer voice placidly.

Zack was leaning against the wall of the hallway he was laughing so hard. Angelina was bent over holding her sides.

"I have to go," said Sanjay.

"Apparently," Zack laughed.

"Say 'hi' to Anna for us," Angelina teased.

Sanjay sneered at them and walked away.

"All right," Angelina said, smiling and drying her eyes. "Let's try."

"Ok," said Zack. "Computer, identify voice!"

The computer voice said, "Voice is that of Zachary Atticus Goodspeed, eleven years old, son of Jack Goodspeed, forty-one, and Jane Goodspeed, thirty-nine. Zack is the grandson of Fyodor Confucius Goodspeed, patriarch of the Onyx Sun. Zack has not yet been tested. Zack has no documented relations, but elevated heart rate has been detected —"

"Computer! End report!" Zack said.

"End of report," said the voice.

Angelina giggled at him. "Gee, I wonder what it was about to say?" she said.

CHAPTER 25: EXPLORATIONS

"No idea," Zack lied.

"And, excuse me, Atticus? Your middle name is Atticus?"

"Yeah, well, my grandfather insisted on helping to name me before I was born. You can imagine my parents' surprise. That was the name he settled on after they nixed 'Einstein' and 'Darwin.' Apparently Atticus was the teacher of the Roman emperor Marcus Aurelius, although I have no idea why they thought that sounds more normal. Never mind that. You go now."

"All right, Atticus," said Angelina, watching Zack out of the corner of her eyes. "Computer! Identify voice and if you add any of that relationship crap, you're going to find yourself floating out an airlock."

"Confirmed," said the voice. "Voice is of Angelina Maximillian, eleven years of age. Preliminary testing data from one memo-file indicates a strong aptitude for military strategy, excellent physical constitution, and quick reflexes."

Angelina looked pleased at this. "All that from one fifteen-second memo-file? I'm impressed."

The computer voice added, "No known relations."

Angelina's smile faded. She said in a half-voice, "That's enough, computer. End report."

"End of report."

Zack watched Angelina carefully. A shadow fell over her face. Finally, she grimaced, as if she had swallowed a bitter pill.

"You okay?" Zack asked.

"Yeah. Fine," she said, but she sounded distant. "Come on. Let's crash for the night."

✳ ✳ ✳

Zack and Angelina had to ask directions several times, but eventually they found their way to the door to Grandfather's suite on Deck 8.

"Well, all we have to do now is say something," Angelina said. "Open!"

The door did not budge.

"I think I might know what the password is," Zack said, but Angelina ignored him.

"Open now!" she guessed. "Fly open. Open thou. Do open! Open says me! Wide open. Spread open. Open this! Open this stupid door!"

Zack waited and watched Max exhaust herself. Finally, she turned toward him breathless and said, "I don't think we're getting in."

"Kalamazoo," said Zack and the doors whisked apart. Angelina looked at him exasperated.

"What kind of word is that?" she asked.

"My Grandfather's kind of word."

"But it makes no sense."

"Exactly," said Zack, stepping inside the room. Angelina joined him.

The room was set at the front of the Deck 8. The walls followed the lines of the bow of the ship to form a curved triangle chamber. The sidewalls came to a point at the front of the chamber. They were transparent so Zack could see the surface of the Moon and the dark ridgeline of the crater in the distance.

Much to Zack's surprise, the room wasn't decorated in Grandfather's traditional white and gold. Quite the opposite. The floor was paved with shiny, black tiles and softly illuminated by halogen spotlights that reflected on the floor like stars. Zack had never been to an art gallery before, but he imagined this was what one looked like. Curved stairways on both sides of the room cascaded down to a lower floor by the front of the ship. Between the stairways, a long platform jutted out over the lower chamber, like a cliff. On this platform was an assortment of black leather couches levitating above the floor, like comfortable-looking atom lifts.

Around the room, on every flat surface including most of the floor, lay an assortment of paper piles, books, and notebook computers.

CHAPTER 25: EXPLORATIONS

Zack stepped onto the platform overlooking the lower floor. From here, he could see the recessed deck beneath him. At the front of this area, where the glass walls met, was a solid golden statue. The statue, at its base, was just a square block, but farther up the shape of a winged man taking flight emerged. His arms stretched for the sky as his eagle's wings spread wide. It looked like the statue of a well-muscled Greek carved straight from a block of gold but left unfinished at the bottom.

"Not bad, huh?" a voice behind Zack said.

Zack swung around to find the benign face of his grandfather beaming down at him. Grandfather reached out a hand and ruffled Zack's hair.

"Nice view, huh?"

"Incredible," Zack said and felt like this word alone had eased the tension between them.

Angelina walked over to them and said, "Professor Goodspeed, I have one question that I have been wondering about since we first found the Clarion Spacedock. And now that I see that statue, I have to ask."

"Yes?"

"How the heck did you afford all this?"

"Yeah, I was kinda wondering that too," Zack said.

"Well, it certainly wasn't cheap," said Grandfather. "But thankfully, I have a number of inventions that I have patented back on Earth. Whenever people use one of my inventions I get a royalty."

Zack looked at his grandfather quizzically, who continued, "Well, it hasn't all been smoke and explosions in my lab, Zack. Once in a while I made something work, usually something much smaller. Fewer risks in building something small. Not as much fun, but less risky. And most of the time, people need more of the small things. So, when you fill up your gas tank, or buy cloth, or pour clean water, I have little inventions that have contributed to making those things work. What my smaller inventions have lacked in grandeur, they have made up for in popular use."

"So, is that why you still live in that dumpy house?" Angelina asked. "You put all your money here?"

Grandfather's eyebrows shot so high they barely seemed able to hold onto his scalp. He began to laugh.

"No, believe it or not," he said, "I live there by choice. It is a totally self-sufficient house. It provides its own water, power, and air conditioning. Perfect!"

Angelina looked skeptical but said nothing more.

"Of course, for an undertaking of this size, I couldn't finance the whole thing myself. So, there are a few outside investors."

"Who are they?" Zack asked.

"For now, that will remain for me to know. Now children, it is time for bed, even though one can never really tell here on the Moon. We get about two weeks of daylight then two weeks of night, as we orbit the Earth. So, we'll have to live by our watches, and mine says 10:30 PM."

Grandfather directed Angelina into one bedroom to the right of the chamber, and Zack into a bedroom next to his own on the left of the chamber. On his way to his room, Zack noticed a number of other doors off the main room on both the first and second floor.

"Where do those go?"

"To other guest rooms. I had my quarters constructed to entertain people."

"Like the different teams?"

"Well, yes. Partially I will use it for ship-wide celebrations. And I also wanted my room big so we can entertain anyone we should meet in space. I guess you could look at this room as an embassy of sorts."

"Who would you meet out here? Wait, you mean aliens?"

CHAPTER 25: EXPLORATIONS

"Yes. Possibly," Grandfather said. "If so, my quarters could house them. Assuming they aren't shaped like enormous Brussels sprouts. If that was the case, they'd have to sleep on Deck 15 due both to their size and the fact that I can't stand the smell of Brussels sprouts. But enough of that for now. It's time for bed."

Zack said goodnight and stepped into his room. His bedroom ran along one side of the ship so the curved window Zack had seen in the main room continued through his room. The other walls and the floor were black marble and — like the main room — reflected their surroundings. On one side of the room was a closet, and on the other a wide bookshelf ran the length of the wall, covered in memo-files. A memo-file visor lay on a bedside table. The bed itself was enormous and covered by a black velvet bedspread. It hovered in the center of the room, its atom lift humming softly. Just looking at it made Zack tired. Suddenly, the weight of the day's events overtook him.

Zack climbed into bed. With a view of the dusty moon, a dark ridgeline, and the twinkling light of seventy sextillion stars, Zack fell into a deep sleep.

✷ ✷ ✷

Zack felt like he was being shaken awake on Christmas morning.

"Come on, Zack. Get up!" he heard Angelina say. "Commander Chase says we get to moonwalk this morning."

Before Zack could respond, Angelina bounded out of the room. Zack opened his eyes. The Moon looked exactly as it had when he went to sleep. There was no indication it was any later or earlier than when he had first gone to bed, beyond the fact his watch now read 6:03 AM.

Zack lumbered into the bathroom attached to his room. If it wasn't for the Moon's surface visible out his window, Zack might have thought he was staying at a trendy hotel on Earth. The bathroom was all black marble and gold fixtures. Zack hopped into the shower, quickly washed, then sprang out, refreshed.

He opened the closet in his bedroom and found a crowd of Executive Board uniforms with red and gold belts, all in his size. A note was pinned to one of the uniforms.

"Kalamazoo! Welcome to the crew," it said in Grandfather's unmistakable handwriting, which was only slightly more legible than an infant's.

Zack jumped into a suit and left his room.

In the main chamber, Angelina and Sanjay sat at a black table near one of the exterior windows. Zack hadn't noticed the table the day before, given the abundance of papers covering all the furniture. Zack wondered what else might be hiding under the mess.

Angelina munched wildly on oranges and cereal, as Zack approached. The table was covered in piles of papers, except for the two places his friends occupied.

"Go ahead," Angelina said, her mouth half-full. "Clear yourself a spot. Your Grandfather said we could. He said he read all these papers months ago."

"Then why doesn't he throw them away?" Sanjay asked, looking around with a frightened expression like the papers might bite him and infect him with Grandfather's messiness disorder.

"He never throws anything away," said Zack, grabbing a stack of papers and laying them on the floor. "Says he might need them later, but he never forgets a single thing he reads. So, I guess 'I really don't know' is the right answer."

Zack sat down as Sanjay nervously flicked a paper away that was encroaching on the little pool of orderliness he had established. Zack noted as he sat with his friends that today they were both wearing crew uniforms. Angelina's was adorned with the plain gold belt of the

CHAPTER 25: EXPLORATIONS

Security Team, while Sanjay's belt had the hand grabbing a lightning bolt of the Engineering Corps. Zack watched his friends eat, happy they were together.

"So, how do I get food around here?" Zack asked eventually.

"Compliance," sounded the computer voice. A hole in the ceiling opened and a set of dishes fell out. Zack thought the dishes were going to smash into the table when, suddenly, they stopped a few inches short and hovered slowly to rest on the area Zack had cleared.

"Wicked, huh?" said Angelina, still stuffing food into her mouth. "So, what do you want?"

"I dunno. Maybe bacon and eggs," Zack said.

"Compliance," came the voice again as three slices of bacon and a handful of scrambled eggs fell out of the hole in the ceiling and plopped into his bowl. Flecks of egg splattered in a small circle around his dishes.

"Charming," said Sanjay scowling at the mess.

"Before your grandfather left for the day, he mentioned the system might have a few quirks," Angelina said through rapid bites of toast. "He said something about how the dishes have mini atom lifts in them, but the food doesn't, since he has not yet developed an edible atom lift. He said something about having not yet invented organic repulsion."

"Well, I think he discovered it, since that is what I feel right now," said Sanjay, staring into the cold bowl of oatmeal he was stirring.

Angelina leaned across the table to Zack and whispered, "He ordered too quickly and the oatmeal arrived before the dishes. He had to scoop the oatmeal off the table and into his bowl."

Zack laughed, until Sanjay looked at him.

"Sorry," Zack said.

"Gross," Sanjay said, poking at his food with his spoon.

Zack shrugged and dove into his meal. The bacon and eggs were perfectly cooked and delicious.

Angelina rushed them through breakfast and before Zack knew it, they were standing on Deck 15 outside the Mech Bay. The bay was open and Zack could see the first three Mechs were missing.

"Commander Chase told us to meet him here," said Angelina.

Zack took the time to look around. He could see now why Grandfather had been unable to throw his gizmos across the width of the hallway. The corridor was vast. Zack guessed it would take him five minutes just to bike across the width of the hall. Its length was even more impressive. The hallway shot into the distance and came to a point far away. The deck looked like it was a mile long. All around the hallway were more massive doors with giant "X" crossbeams on them. The door at the end of the hallway near where they stood though was wider and had two "X" beams on it. It was labeled "Airlock."

As Zack examined the door, four orange lights around the doorframe spun to life and a siren sounded.

"Airlock alert," said the computer voice. "Exterior bulkhead closed. Standby. Interior curtain opening."

The vast door split right in front of Zack, and he felt a sudden rush of air blowing by him into the airlock. Zack and his friends stumbled to the side of the hallway.

The airlock bulkhead slammed open. A gigantic metal foot came into view, and then another. Zack could hear the loud whining of mechanical motors, as a massive orange Mech stomped into the hallway. It moved in sharp, but sure movements. Each step shook the floor with a loud "thud." If Zack thought these machines were impressive standing still, he was even more impressed by them moving. It was like being visited by a giant.

The Mech turned toward the children standing against the wall, and with a whir of motors, it saluted them with one hand. Zack could see the small shape of a man sitting in the angular glass dome that made up

CHAPTER 25: EXPLORATIONS

the Mech's head, but since the glass was semi-reflective, he couldn't tell who it was. The Mech's hand fell back to its side, and the entire robot gave off a sudden hissing noise, as if it were shutting down. The man in the cockpit disappeared into the chest. Zack guessed he was riding the control chair down into the Mech's chest. A second later, his guess was confirmed as Commander Chase emerged from the door in the Mech's chest and slid down its side on the elevator platform.

Commander Chase strode up to the children.

"That was cool!" the children said almost in unison.

"Yeah, Mech Leviathans are a lot of fun to drive. We had to spend some time this morning working on them though. Seems that somebody removed all the Onyx Suns from the front Mechs. We had to get the cubes from the back and move them to the front so we could pull three of these bad boys out."

"Yeah, we were kinda in a hurry to get them when we did that," Zack said.

Commander Chase laughed and said, "I understand. I guess we *were* in a hurry then, huh?"

"How is your arm?" Angelina asked, pointing to the cast on his left arm.

"Fine. It's a little sore and a little hard to drive the Mech, but I'll manage. So, you guys wanna see how I drive this thing?"

"You bet!" Zack said. Angelina and Sanjay were already running toward the Mech.

Commander Chase led them inside the robot.

"Hey Zack. Sit in the Command Chair," said Commander Chase. Zack jumped at the opportunity even though Angelina looked disappointed. He climbed into the seat and was surprised how snug it was. He thought this was what it must feel like in a fighter jet.

"All right, Mech Leviathan basics. You could probably learn this from a memo-tape in fifteen seconds, but I'm a little old fashioned.

I don't think there is a memo-tape in the world that can replace real experience. And that's one thing I *do* have."

Commander Chase pointed to a button under the left side of the seat and said, "Right now the Mech is in standby mode. Once you push that button — push it now Zack — there you go. Now you are on."

The joystick emerged from the hole in the floor, and the panel of buttons and flat-screen monitors swung around from the side of the seat.

"This is drive mode," Commander Chase said. "The Mech won't move while you are down here in the chest, but you can run diagnostics and basic functions. If the command dome above you ever cracks, the driver's seat slides down here too. The portal into the dome then closes to protect you from a loss of cabin pressure."

"Cool," said Zack, as he played with the controls.

"To move a Mech, you basically use the control stick," Commander Chase said. "Left goes left. Right goes right. Press forward and you will walk forward. Pull back and you'll step back. If you ever get too much momentum, you can use the hand brake to your right."

For the first time, Zack noticed a metal bar sticking out of the right side of the seat, like a hand brake on a car.

"On this monitor, you have your basic functions," Commander Chase said, pointing at a screen on the control panel. "The spinning thing here is the radar. Friendly units are green. Enemy units are red."

"Enemy units?" Zack asked. "You mean like Machvel?"

"Exactly," said Commander Chase. "We did some reprogramming this morning. If that heavy freighter Machvel and his followers stole returns, you'll see it here as a red triangle. It is just a safety precaution. I don't think we'll be seeing him again. I don't think he knows we survived. But just in case you do see him, feel free to fire off some shots to thank him for my broken arm."

"What is this?" said Angelina, pointing to a yellow button on the console.

CHAPTER 25: EXPLORATIONS

"Those are your thrusters," Commander Chase said. "If you need to jump, you can use that, but be careful. This drains power quickly, and since we have such small Onyx Suns onboard, it can shut down the rest of the Mech if you overuse it."

"The thrusters can be very tricky to control. I had a hard time with them in the simulator," Sanjay said.

"All right," Commander Chase said. "The last part of your instruction involves moving the arms and legs in movements other than walking."

Commander Chase opened a supply cabinet next to the command chair and removed a series of black straps with small, white domes on them.

"Here," he said, handing half of them to Zack. "Put these on. They will be labeled, left arm, right arm, left ankle, and so on."

Commander Chase helped Zack strap the bands around his uniform. There were bands for seemingly every joint in his body. There were ones that went around Zack's fingers and neck even. After a few minutes they were done. Zack felt like a prison inmate with his white flight suit and black bands.

"The white transponders on these bands track your body's movement," said Commander Chase. "Typically, Mech pilots wear these under their uniform, but you're new so I wanted you to see them first. When you go into the cockpit, lasers on the top of the dome scan you to check the position of your arms and legs. You press this switch on the joystick to engage the scanner and flip over to body movement mode."

"I get it," said Zack. "So, I walk with the joystick, then flip over to move the body of the Mech."

"Exactly," said Commander Chase. "That way you can approach an object with the joystick. Then, stop, switch over, and pick it up. If you bend down and close your hand, the Mech will mimic that movement and do the same. The dome has heads-up displays projected on it that will help you angle your Mech's body to grab things. When you get more advanced you can move and maneuver the Mech's body at the same time by leaving the switch in the center position. Any questions?"

"When do we go outside?" Angelina asked. She looked like she might jump out of her skin.

"Right now, let's go back down to the bay and put on pressure suits so you guys can walk me back out," Commander Chase said.

The Commander led the way out of the Mech, down the platform, and over to the Mech bay. From a metal cabinet there, he pulled three pressure suits that looked like slim, orange versions of astronaut outfits. He gave one to each of the children and said, "Just put them on like pajamas and I'll zip you up."

As easy as this sounded, Zack found himself struggling. Angelina and Sanjay finished suiting up before him, and as Zack squirmed inside his uniform, they came over to help. He was hot with the effort of putting the suit on and the embarrassment of not knowing what he was doing. They helped him put on a headset that included a boom microphone and an earpiece. Through this headset, he heard Angelina ask, "Got it now?"

"Yeah," Zack said. He gave another tug on the suit and slipped into it with a "thunk". Suddenly, he was a lot more comfortable. Commander Chase zipped him up and handed him a helmet. The helmet looked like a cross between an airplane rudder and a motorcycle helmet. It was glass on the front, but metal in back. It was edged with a row of halogen lights on each side. A ridge ran along the top of the helmet and flew off the back, like an orange icicle. As he put it on, it hissed closed and Zack could feel the cool air of the suit's oxygen tanks enter his lungs.

"All right?" said Commander Chase to all three of them.

The Commander's voice sounded robot-like over the headset. Zack, Angelina, and Sanjay gave him the thumbs up. Walking in the suit was

CHAPTER 25: EXPLORATIONS

a little stiff until Sanjay showed Zack where the pneumatic assistors were. Zack turned them up, and the suit moved much more fluidly.

As they stepped into the hallway, Commander Chase pointed to the Mech and said, "Ok. I'm going to go start her up."

The Commander rode the platform back to the top of the Mech. He stepped inside, sealed the robot's chest, and a minute later, Zack saw his silhouette enter the Mech's glass dome. Zack felt the whir of the Mech Leviathan's engines spinning up, as the deck under his feet began vibrating.

"Ok, let's go outside," Commander Chase said.

For the first time, the reality that he was about to walk on the Moon hit Zack. His thoughts over the explosion and Machvel's escape faded from his mind for the first time.

"Do you realize we're about to become the youngest people to walk on the Moon?" Zack said to Angelina and Sanjay.

"Even better, only twelve people in human history have walked on the Moon before us," Commander Chase said over the intercom.

"Well then, let's do it!" Angelina said.

Commander Chase laughed over the intercom.

Zack noticed Sanjay turn on a belt on his suit that looked similar to the gravity belts they had used the previous day. Zack noticed he had one on his suit as well. He found the switch and flipped it. He felt his feet become firmer on the deck. Zack motioned for Angelina to do the same.

"You won't need those until we are outside beyond the artificial gravity of the ship," Commander Chase said, "but good thinking ahead, Sanjay. Now, go into the airlock ahead of me."

The children walked into the gray airlock and then turned back to face Deck 15. Zack was amazed by the sight: a monstrous orange robot stood like a towering god a hundred yards away from him, waiting in the center of a white corridor large enough to build a city upon.

The Mech's knee motor whirred, as it lifted its right leg into the air, leaned forward, and slammed it onto the ground. Zack's whole body shook as the Mech made another similar movement with its left leg. Earthquakes rocked him as the Mech steadily advanced. Ten steps in, the Mech stopped next to them with a slam that almost shook Zack to the floor. From this proximity, all Zack could see in front of him was the massive metal block of the foot and the towering shadow of the behemoth over him.

"All right, I am closing the airlock now," Commander Chase said.

The orange lights at the corners of the inner airlock door again spun to life. The siren sounded and the door ground closed behind the Mech.

"Hey guys, for the best view you should stand in front of me at the center of the airlock. Don't worry, I won't move," Commander Chase said.

"Ok, let's go guys," said Zack.

Angelina and Sanjay followed him to the center of the room. They were now in front of where the two massive exterior doors met. For a brief second, the airlock was dark except for the spiraling orange lights behind them.

Then, a white light split the exterior doors, and Zack was staring at the surface of the Moon.

CHAPTER 26

Moon Walk

One Christmas when Zack was nine, his parents gave him a remote-controlled robot. It quickly became Zack's favorite toy. Zack loved to make the robot walk forward, turn around, and pick up the blocks he had scattered on the floor.

Zack remembered at first Grandfather had been enthralled with the robot too, until — five minutes later — he discovered the robot could not pick up heavy objects, fly, or hold intelligent conversations on interstellar hyper-drive theories. Then, Grandfather had just looked at the robot, down his long nose, through the cracked spectacles perched on the end, and said, "Juvenile. Simply juvenile."

Regardless, Zack loved his robot and spent entire mornings using it to haul blocks and stuffed animals from one end of his bedroom to the other. He became an expert at manipulating the robot to stack and arrange the objects he moved.

It had been the saddest day of his life when his robot broke. Mr. Goodspeed had made an honest attempt to fix the little robot, but, not being mechanically inclined, he only managed to replace its batteries. For a long time, Zack looked in every toy store he visited for another robot like his, but he never found one. He thought about asking his grandfather to help — he would have been able to fix the robot in a minute — but every time Zack brought the toy up Grandfather scowled. Zack thought he would never again find a robot he enjoyed as much.

He realized now he was wrong.

The sight that met Zack as the airlock opened was like his bedroom experiments taken to a colossal level. Two massive robots lumbered across the flat surface of the Moon, carrying armloads of steel beams from a hatch in the side of the Onyx Pioneer. Thirty orange bulldozers, about half as tall as the robots, raced around the surface, like mechanized dogs. One of the Mechs would point in a direction, and a bulldozer would race off to flatten the surface of the Moon. As they stepped from the airlock, Zack could see the cockpit of each bulldozer was shaped like the geometric, gold domes the Mechs had. Through the glass, Zack could see the tiny figures of the drivers inside.

Zack, Angelina, and Sanjay stepped forward. Even with the gravity belt on, Zack felt himself walking a little funny, like he was floating in waist-high water. He couldn't feel his whole weight, like he usually did. The Moon's surface was strange to him as well. Zack had often looked at the Moon and expected it to be solid rock. Now, however, he realized the surface was much more powdery. It had a hard crust under a layer of dust. Each step felt softer than it did on Earth and kicked up plumes of debris as they walked.

"Hey guys, see that platform about three hundred yards ahead? Go there," Commander Chase said.

CHAPTER 26: MOON WALK

Zack saw what the Commander was referring to. A metal platform rose from the Aitken Basin in front of the bulldozers and Mechs. Zack and his friends walked to the platform, found a stairway on the side, and climbed about a hundred feet up to the top.

From this vantage point, Zack could see the bulldozers flattening a vast, circular area at the center of the crater. Inside this, the Mechs dropped armloads of metal beams into six piles: five equally spaced on the edge of the circle, and one larger one in the center.

The platform shuddered as Commander Chase's Mech approached behind them. He stopped next to the platform. All Zack could see to his right now was the Mech's knee joint, like a massive orange wall blocking out any view in that direction. Zack looked back at the ship and noticed wide foot treads indenting the Moon's surface, like a trail of swimming pools leading from the airlock to the platform.

"The dozers are prepping the surface," Commander Chase said, using the Mech's arm to point. "This will give us a flat foundation from which we can build the Citadel Spire. The Mechs are removing the framing materials from the Onyx Pioneer's cargo hold on Deck 14 and putting them in place. Each pile is positioned so that we can build the six towers first. That is why the pile at the center is the largest. The Bodi Biodome and Administration tower at the center is about twice as high as the other towers. It just barely reaches the top of the crater so we can see the surrounding lunar surface without others seeing the location of the base. Once the framing is done, the Mechs will weld on the plating."

"And then we can fill it with air," Sanjay said.

"Correct," said Commander Chase. "And plants, and most importantly, people. We have to pressure check it, but once that is done, we can start living in the Citadel Spire."

"Wicked," Angelina said. "But how do the Mechs and bulldozers know what to do?"

"Good question," said Commander Chase. "I'll come down and show you."

The door in the chest of the Mech opened and Commander Chase rode the elevator down. As he did this, Zack watched the activity in the crater. On the far left side, he could see a Mech putting down another pile of metal beams. As it released the pile, it stood up and looked around. This movement reminded Zack of when he used to position his toy robot before picking up a block. Sure enough, within a few moments, the Mech stopped twisting around, reached down, and grabbed a single beam.

As tall as the Mech was, the thin beam towered over it. With the beam held in its hands, the Mech looked like a metal version of the javelin throwers Zack had seen on TV during the Olympic Games. The Mech lit a torch that emerged from its forearm. It heated the end of the beam until it glowed red-hot. Then, the Mech whirred around, sidestepping away from the pile of beams and, with a massive thrust, stabbed the beam into the ground. A violent shudder shook the ground and a dull, blasting sound hit Zack. The Mech thrust the beam farther into the ground. Each time, it reached high into the air, grabbed the beam towering over it, and forced it downward into the ground. It looked like a vampire-slayer stabbing a stake into the chest of its victim. After several long thrusts, the top of the beam was at eye-level with the Mech. The Mech walked back to the pile and grabbed another beam. It repeated the same stabbing motion a few hundred feet away from the first beam.

Commander Chase walked over to the children.

"How do they know where to put the beams?" Zack asked.

"They have heads-up displays on their domes that show them. Here, check this out. Computer. Enable Mech Command."

"Acknowledged," said the mechanized voice over their headsets.

CHAPTER 26: MOON WALK

A metal pole shot up from the back of the platform. On the end of the pole sat a large spotlight. The spotlight tilted so it pointed toward the front of the platform. A multi-colored beam of light shot from the cylinder.

Glowing squares now hovered in front of Zack, his friends, and Commander Chase. There were thirty images stretching across the platform, like ghostly TV screens. Many of these were blank, but three showed activity. Zack stepped forward and looked closer. On the screen, he could see a robot hand reaching out and picking up a metal beam. The bottom of the screen said "Mech 13." Zack peered through the translucent screens and saw a Mech bending down to grab a beam at the exact same moment.

"They're inside views!" he exclaimed.

"Exactly," Commander Chase said. "This allows the construction commander to observe the progress of the Mech crew, by getting an inside view of each Mech. Watch. Computer. Bring up Mech 13 on the main screen."

The thirty screens dematerialized and one larger screen appeared. Zack felt like he was inside the Mech now, as he could see the entire cockpit of Mech 13. Zack saw the ends of the pilot's legs, the control panel glowing to his left, and the joystick in his right hand. In front of the pilot, Zack saw the golden dome of the Mech's head. On the dome was a mixture of the Moon's surface and a large structure traced in glowing green lines.

"I can't see the whole thing," Zack said.

"Mech 13, step back a little," Commander Chase said into his headset.

Zack saw the Mech turn around and back up. At the same time, the view moved on the glowing screen. Zack could now see the entire crater, from Mech 13's point of view. He saw a wide installation with five bladed towers. At the center, where the ends of the towers met, a much larger center spire stretched into the sky like a needle. The center tower looked like a very narrow pyramid that had been stretched until it was impossibly thin and tall.

"Not bad, huh?" said Commander Chase, smiling as he watched Zack's face. "It's even more incredible when you see it actual size, huh?"

"I've seen models of the Citadel Spire," Sanjay said. "But this is incredible."

"It's so tall. How do the Mechs build the upper floors?" Zack asked.

"Good question," said Commander Chase. "The first Mech is almost done with the ground floor of that tower."

They looked to the left and saw that, indeed, one of the Mechs had finished pile-driving the foundational beams into the ground. The Mech leaned down and grabbed another beam. It shuffled around the base of the wide tower and then stopped. The Mech squatted down. Panels in its back spread open and splayed out to the side like wings. From the space behind the panels emerged two cylindrical jets.

Zack saw one jet fire, then the other. Blue flames shot from the engines. The ground rumbled as the Mech slowly lifted from the surface of the Moon. As it floated above the metal beams, the Mech swung its arms around so that the beam it was holding was sitting on top of one of the foundational beams. A blowtorch emerged from the Mech's other forearm. The end of the tube flickered, and a small jet flame shot from it. The Mech floated backwards a little. The Mech sprayed its torch around the joint where the two beams met. The beams glowed red and fused. The Mech floated back to the surface to grab another beam, leaving the fused beams to cool.

"That can't be easy," Angelina said.

CHAPTER 26: MOON WALK

"Yes, our pilots are highly trained," Commander Chase said. "They have each spent thousands of hours in the simulators. Many of them have built the Citadel Spire — virtually — several dozen times."

They watched the robots work on the tower for a while. Zack was shocked at how fast it was rising. Already, most of the first floor of the first tower was framed.

Finally Commander Chase said, "All right guys. Demonstration's over. I gotta get back to work. Sanjay, show Zack and Max more of the ship. I'll be in later when the second shift relieves us."

Zack, Angelina, and Sanjay walked back to the ship. Zack couldn't believe it. Today, he had walked on the Moon, watched a giant robot fly, and seen the grand plan for the Citadel Spire. He was simply elated. He didn't know if it was the low-gravity environment of the Moon or the excitement of the day's events, but he felt like he was floating.

Zack and his friends stepped into the airlock, and, as the exterior doors closed, Zack took a last look outside. He could see a Mech lumbering around the crater carrying beams. He saw another in mid-air. He saw the last Mech standing at the ready, towering over the command platform. A fleet of bulldozers pushed Moon dust around the flattened surface. And at the center of Zack's view was the tiny platform with Commander Chase's orange spacesuit on top. The Commander was surrounded by the glowing images of Mech Command. He was pointing in different directions as he ordered the Mechs and dozers about. He looked like the architect of their future.

Zack smiled to himself as the airlock doors closed and shadowed him in darkness. No, Zack knew who that person was. He was the one who had called Zack's toy robot "juvenile," and — at last — Zack agreed.

CHAPTER 27

Mech Battle

Once inside, Zack, Angelina, and Sanjay removed their spacesuits and embarked on a tour of the ship. First, they stopped by the bulldozer bay at the back of Deck 15. The bay was a hive of activity as dozers flew in and out of their recharging units. Mechanics buzzed about changing broken axles, replacing cracked domes, and oiling stuck wheels. A small team washed down the dusty dozers as they came into the bay for service through a secondary airlock on the side of the ship.

Next, Sanjay took them to an oblong door farther down the hallway of Deck 15. The door looked like an egg that had fallen on its side. As the door whisked open, Zack could see row upon row of Onyx Airstriders wedged into docking cubicles on the sidewalls.

"What are those?" Angelina asked.

CHAPTER 27: MECH BATTLE

"They're Onyx Airstriders," Zack said. "My grandfather had one in his Labradory on Earth."

"His Labradory?"

"Yeah. His lab. It barks."

"Whatever."

"I heard that ship was the prototype," Sanjay said. "It was powered by an Onyx Sun. These are a little different because they are rechargeable like the bulldozers. They run off energy pumped in from the Power Tower."

"Why?" asked Zack.

"Well, the Airstriders don't need that much power and for most pilots the excess speed they get from an Onyx Sun–powered ship is too much to handle," said Sanjay. "We had a few test pilots on Earth that ended up in Argentina before they knew what happened. So, my father had the cubes taken out."

Sanjay took them to the elevator.

"We'll go up and see the rest of the ship," he said. "Deck 14 is just the cargo hold. So, we'll skip that."

"Plus, we've seen it already," Angelina whispered to Zack.

"Deck 13 is cool," Sanjay continued. "It is the Security Team's deck and their command center for all security operations."

The elevator arrived, and they got on board. It whisked them to Deck 13. The doors opened and they stepped out. Deck 13 was dark. Sanjay led them down a dark hallway, to a dark door labeled "Clandestine Room", and they went inside.

Mr. Goodspeed had once taken Zack to the New York Stock Exchange during a family trip. This was Mr. Goodspeed's idea of fun, but Zack had been bored. Seeing the Clandestine Room, however, reminded Zack of the stock exchange, only darker. It had a recessed pit that was open except for several islands of computer monitors. From what Zack could see, these flat screens provided the only source of light in the room. People milled about, but instead of buying and selling stock in loud yells, they moved slowly and talked in hushed whispers. The screens displayed dozens of videos from all areas of the ship. At the front of the room was a large TV screen showing them what was happening outside the ship. There were numerous statistics around the edge of this video, about how many passengers were on board, how many were off the ship, how many were sleeping, and so on. In the bottom right corner was an orange square, which read "Alert Level Orange."

"Come on, let's go," Sanjay said.

"Yeah, these people weird me out," Angelina added.

Next, Sanjay took them to Deck 12, where the Entertainment Troupe hosted the entertainment pavilions. Zack was shocked at the abundance of diversions on the Onyx Pioneer. There was a twenty-four-screen movie theater, baseball and football fields, a dancing ballroom, a skating rink, and an Olympic-sized swimming pool. While they were visiting the swimming pool, a wild crowd of people descended upon the room and leapt into the water. They splashed around, performed swan dives, and ran around the edges of the pool, ignoring the numerous "Do not run" signs.

Sanjay sighed and said, "This is part of the Entertainment Troupe. Well, at least they're not bothering the other teams."

They took a quick glimpse at Deck 11, which was comprised of cook galleys, kitchens, and food storage. Several crew members in white hats and aprons were busy whisking from one part of the deck to the other, leaving a storm of swinging aluminum doors in their wake as they darted in and out of the kitchens.

"We'll skip Decks 8 through 10. Those are just crew quarters," Sanjay said. "If you've seen one, you've seen them all. We'll skip Deck 7 since you've probably seen enough of the Engineering Core for now."

CHAPTER 27: MECH BATTLE

"Totally," Zack said. "I wouldn't mind never seeing that floor again."

Sanjay took them to Deck 6 next, where the SciTechs had their laboratories. They took a quick glimpse through the rooms lined with beakers and Bunsen burners, but only Sanjay wanted to spend more time there.

They also took a quick look at the meditation rooms of the Spiritual Conclave's deck, Deck 5. Zack was impressed by the simple opulence of these rooms. Most of the rooms were wide and flat and covered in a red carpet, edged in gold. Lavish red and gold tapestries flowed down the walls. The rooms smelled of incense.

"Most of the rest of the decks you've either seen or they're not that interesting," Sanjay said. "Deck 1 is — sorry — was the Bridge. Deck 2 holds the offices of the Executive Order. Nothing too interesting there. Just a lot of desks, phones, and meeting rooms."

For some reason, Zack took offense to Sanjay's comments. How could running the entire crew be boring?

"Deck 3 is where the Great Hall is," Sanjay continued. "You've seen that, obviously. And Deck 4 is the education deck. It has the Academy, the Memo File Library, which you've been to, and the Mech Simulators."

"Wait. The what?" Zack asked.

"The Mech Simulators. That's where the pilots learn to drive Mechs."

"And you weren't planning on taking us there?"

"Well, I had assumed you had both had enough of Mechs for one day."

"Are you kidding me?" Zack said.

"Seriously," said Angelina.

"Well, all right. Let's go there."

They took the elevator to Deck 4, strode down the hallway that looked like a white cloister, and arrived at a door labeled, "Mech

Simulator." The doors whisked open for them, then hissed shut behind them. It was pitch black in the room.

Sanjay said, "Computer, spin up the simulator."

A yellow spotlight flickered on. It shone on a line of black pods that stretched around the room like a semicircle of shiny eggs. A slice of a door from one pod slid open as they approached. Sanjay led Zack and Angelina inside. The inside of the pod had a control panel and joystick and looked to Zack just like the Mech controls. Sanjay motioned for Zack to sit down. Zack got comfortable as Sanjay handed him a familiar set of black Velcro strips with white domes on them to strap onto his arms and legs.

Sanjay handed Zack a headset, stepped out with Angelina, and slid the pod door closed. Zack was in darkness except for the faint glow of the controls around him.

"Can you hear me?" said Sanjay over the headset.

"I hear you," said Zack.

"Good," said Sanjay. "I'm going to help Max get into her pod."

"Ok."

Zack waited a few minutes, then heard Sanjay say, "She's all set. I'm getting into my pod now. I'm going to walk you through this. First, both of you look for the power button under the seat on your left."

Zack ran his fingers under the rim of his seat. He felt a small circular button sticking out of the left side and pressed it.

The pod came to life. The buttons on the control panel glowed brightly now in different colors. The joystick slid into Zack's lap. He felt the pod lift and heard the hissing of hydraulics. The seat Zack was on raised a foot off the floor so his legs dangled freely. The main viewscreen flickered on and showed a scene of tree trunks all around him.

"Can you both see me?" said Sanjay.

"I can," Angelina said.

CHAPTER 27: MECH BATTLE

"I can't," said Zack. "What am I supposed to see?"

"My simulated Mech, of course."

Zack looked around. As he did, the pod shifted. The scene of tree trunks moved with him.

"Nope," said Zack. "All I see are more trees."

"Ah," said Sanjay. "You might be lying down. Sometimes when people turn off the simulator, they forget to put the Mech back in its starting position. So, you probably need to stand up."

"Okay. How?"

"First, make sure you are in Motion Mode. Remember the switch Commander Chase showed us?"

Zack saw the switch that said "Movement" on one side and "Motion" on the other. It indicated that the motion function was engaged.

"Ok. I am in Motion Mode," said Zack. "Now what?"

"Now, just stand up, like you normally would," said Sanjay. "Put your arms out, press up, bend your knees, and stand up."

Zack tried this. He saw an orange, robotic arm move into view, mimicking the movement of his own arm. He spun it around to find the ground. As he did so, he accidentally swiped at the trees, splintering a wide grove of them. He felt his arm shudder violently.

"I hit something and felt it!"

"You should," said Sanjay. "You have force-feedback devices embedded in the straps you put on. You should feel everything. Try pushing up from the ground."

Zack reached his arm around until it stopped under him. Even though Zack's arm hung in mid-air in the pod, the force feedback wasn't allowing him to move any farther. He moved his head down. As he did so, the pod and the viewscreen shifted so that he could see a robotic hand pressing into the ground. Zack pushed on his arm and the pod rocked back and forth. He pushed harder. The pod lurched forward.

"Now, push yourself up!" said Sanjay over the headset.

Zack straightened his knees. He felt a little awkward doing this in the command chair, but slowly, he could feel the Mech rise. He pushed harder and the force-feedback pressed him into his seat with simulated g-force. It felt just like Zack thought it might in a real Mech.

Through the viewscreen, Zack could see the trees rocking by, until suddenly, they shot under him. His Mech stretched to its full height, towering over its surroundings.

It was a beautiful day in the simulator. Zack could see he was standing over a lush, green forest on a sunny day. On his left, the forest gave way to a beach and an ocean beyond. To his right, gray mountains rose from the woods. Straight ahead of him, Zack could see the soaring form of another Mech Leviathan a few miles away. He saw another in between them but far to the right, by the foothills of the mountains. Both Mechs lorded over the terrain like titans.

"Is that you, Sanjay?" asked Zack pointing his simulated robot hand at the robot directly in front of him.

In response, that Mech raised its hand and made an unflattering gesture with one of its fingers.

"Guess so," Zack said, as he heard chuckling over the headset.

"All right, now what do we do? I want to move around," Angelina said.

"Ok. Flip the switch over to 'Movement,'" Sanjay said.

Zack did so and the pod lurched a little.

"Good," said Sanjay. "Now, just use your joystick to move."

Zack pressed forward on the joystick suddenly and the pod lurched forward. He could feel all the nuances of the Mech as it took thundering steps forward. It didn't quite feel natural, but Zack thought he was starting to get it. He was having trouble keeping the viewscreen facing forward. He focused on keeping his head straight as he moved and the viewscreen stabilized. The Mech seemed to be

CHAPTER 27: MECH BATTLE

stumbling. So, Zack concentrated on lifting his legs a little higher inside the simulator.

"Good Zack! You're a natural at this," Sanjay said.

Zack saw Angelina's Mech hurrying across the forest, leaving a path of splintered trees behind her. She tripped suddenly and her Mech fell to the earth. As she slammed into the ground, Zack felt a shudder run through the simulator.

"Slowly!" said Sanjay. "You can't rush this. Mechs are very hard to move quickly."

Angelina's Mech stood up slowly. Zack saw a perfect outline of a robot lying in the crushed forest below.

"It's a good thing I turned on the invincibility program," said Sanjay. "Now both of you try again. Slower."

Zack pressed the joystick forward. He could feel the simulated Mech leaning forward as the leg of the robot lifted with a whir. It stomped forward. Then again. Then faster. As the machine crushed forward, Zack could feel the Mech grinding trees into the ground. The feedback devices strapped to his leg vibrated with each step he took. After a few hundred yards, he turned around and saw a trail of broken timber behind him.

"You're doing well," said Sanjay. "Time to show you a few advanced moves."

Zack heard a computer voice say, "Invincibility off."

Zack felt the pod shaking violently, and as he turned back around, he saw Sanjay's Mech sprinting towards him, one shoulder dropped, like a rushing football player. Angelina's Mech also ran into the fray.

"Mech war!" shouted Sanjay over the headset.

Zack shifted his Mech quickly to the left, but Sanjay compensated and rammed into him. Zack felt his Mech soar through the air and slam into the ground. He immediately looked up. Sanjay's Mech sprouted wings and rocketed into the air, leaving a trail of fire behind him that ignited the forest. Zack forced his Mech up. Sanjay flew toward him, one foot extended. Zack dodged as Angelina caught Sanjay mid-air and threw his Mech to the ground. Zack turned just in time to see Sanjay's Mech plow into the ground and slide through the forest. Trees shot off Sanjay's Mech in waves as he slid. Sanjay's Mech cut a trail through the trees and burst onto the beach.

Zack's Mech toppled over as something hit him from the side. He turned to see Angelina's Mech tackling him. She threw him to the ground and lifted a foot to stomp on him. Zack quickly pressed the button that said "blowtorch" and a long pipe emerged from his Mech's forearm. The torch sliced a hydraulic hose on Angelina's other leg. Her Mech wavered then toppled to the ground.

Zack leapt up. He was getting to the point where even more complicated moves were easy. He lurched his Mech forward and made it jump on top of Sanjay's, lying on the beach. The Mech did exactly what Zack intended it to. He realized this accelerated training was teaching him quickly. He picked up Sanjay's Mech head and slammed it into the beach.

"How do you like that?" Zack said laughing.

He heard Sanjay saying "Oof" every time Zack slammed him down. Zack rolled his Mech off Sanjay's. He grabbed the wires around the other Mech's shoulders and dragged him along the beach and into the ocean surf. As he did so, the wires snapped, and he stumbled. Tsunamis of water rose into the air as Zack's Mech fell. Tidal waves crashed into the beach and flooded into the forest.

Sanjay's Mech stood up. Through the viewscreen, Zack could see one of his robotic hands was twisted around Sanjay's shoulder wires.

Sanjay fired his Mech rockets again.

"No!" Zack said, as Sanjay's Mech took flight.

CHAPTER 27: MECH BATTLE

Zack could feel his arm twist as he was dragged into the air. Sanjay flew over the mountains, but Zack could tell his additional weight made things awkward.

Passing over a snowy mountain peak, Zack struggled to free his hand. He balled up his other hand and punched it into Sanjay's back. Sanjay's Mech faltered. Zack ripped one of the rocket cylinders off Sanjay's back.

"Whoa!" Zack heard Sanjay say as they both started to fly in chaotic spirals around the sky. The simulator bumped Zack around in all directions. Sanjay's other rocket engine sputtered to a stop and Zack felt his stomach flip. They plummeted to the earth like two boulders. Zack waved his arms and legs in the air as the intertwined robots dropped from the sky.

They slammed into a mountaintop. Zack's Mech tore loose in a shower of debris. He rolled down the mountain, until finally his Mech stopped. Zack moaned. His body hurt.

"What kind of simulator is this?" asked Zack. "I'm actually sore."

He heard laughing as Angelina's Mech plodded into view. Zack held up his arms in defense, but her Mech made the Peace Sign with two fingers. Angelina helped Zack's Mech stand up, as Sanjay's battered robot lumbered over.

"Pretty realistic, huh?" said Sanjay. "You're a natural Zack. A few more Mech battles like this and you might be able to pilot the real thing."

"Maybe," Zack said, as he surveyed the scene. It was still a nice day, but the simulation zone was a mess. Splintered trees, fire, and flood lay everywhere. Half of the forest was trampled. A towering inferno spread through the rest, sending pillars of black smoke into the sky. The ocean roiled wildly and waves crashed onto the beach. A crushed mountain in the distance now lacked a summit.

"That was fun," Zack said.

"Yeah, it was!" Angelina yelled.

They were still laughing as the pods deactivated and the doors sliced open.

"Not bad for your first time, you two," said Sanjay.

"Yeah, not too bad yourself," said Angelina. "Considering you were missing a rocket engine and most of the wires on one shoulder."

"Ah, well, I was taking it easy on you guys," Sanjay said with a sheepish smile. "Didn't want to beat up on the new kids too much."

"Excuses, excuses," Zack said playfully.

"We better reset the simulator before we leave. We don't want the next cadet trainees to start out in that mess. They might panic," Sanjay said.

Sanjay walked toward the sidewall where a small panel glowed in the darkness. He tapped on the pad while he reset the program. Angelina lingered near the simulators, checking out the controls again.

Zack basked in the adrenaline he felt from the simulated Mech war, but as the excitement wore off, he started to feel bothered. In the thrill of the spacewalk and Mech battle, he had momentarily forgotten about Dr. Machvel. But now images of the man who had betrayed his grandfather came back to him. Zack saw the twisted features of Machvel's face in his mind, and he hated him. Machvel had exploited his grandfather's trusting nature and Zack despised him for it. Zack turned to his friends.

"We have to find Machvel."

"What?" Sanjay looked up from the pad, as if someone had suggested trying to use turnips to fly.

"We have to find Machvel. He's still out there."

"So? He's not bothering us," Angelina said.

"He will," Zack said. "He tried to kill us all and it didn't work. I have a feeling he's just waiting for the right time to try again."

CHAPTER 27: MECH BATTLE

"We have more pressing problems right now, like surviving. Zack, you heard your grandfather. We've got to build the base," Angelina said.

"No, the teams of this ship have to build the base. We're not doing anything. We're moon walking and playing in simulators. Sorry, but we are. We're not really helping and there's a man out there that wants to kill us!"

"What do you suggest we do?" Sanjay said.

"I don't know. Something. What do we know about what happened?"

"That Machvel pretended to be your grandfather's friend but actually was busy corrupting a third of the crew," Angelina said. "We even heard him doing it, Zack. Remember? When we were hiding in the library?"

"Yeah, I remember. Who was that guy he was talking to?"

"I don't know. His name started with a 'v' or something. Vincent. Vince."

"Victor Schultz?" Sanjay asked.

"Yes, that's it," Zack said, snapping his fingers. "That's him. Computer?"

"Online," said the placid voice.

"Computer, find Victor Schultz. Is he still on-board the Onyx Pioneer?"

The computer was quiet for a moment then said, "No, I am sorry. Victor Schultz left the Onyx Pioneer yesterday aboard the supply freighter. He was accompanied by Dr. Ian Machvel, Second Lieutenant Mike Smith of the Security Team, Rakesh Patel, Lindsay —"

"That's enough computer," Zack said.

"End of report."

"You didn't really expect him to still be on-board, did you?" Angelina said.

"No, I guess not."

The gears in Zack's mind started whirring. What would he have done if he were Dr. Machvel? The man had spent years infiltrating Grandfather's teams and corrupting them. He certainly had enough influence to convince a large chunk of the staff to betray Grandfather. If he had enough foresight and willpower to do that, he probably was smart enough to realize the Onyx Pioneer had survived by now.

"Computer, have any new people rejoined the crew in the last twenty-four hours?"

"Zack, how is the computer going to know that?" Angelina said. "In all the commotion of building the base in the last twenty-four hours, there's no way the computer can track —"

"Three voices that I lost after the explosion have been reacquired in the last six hours."

"Who are they?"

"Malik Massur. José Famosa. Visalia Grozny."

"Can't be," Zack said. "Are those —"

"The first guys we met on the ship," Angelina said, nodding. "Two of them are at least. We saw José and Malik right before the meeting in the Great Hall. They were alone too, remember? What were they doing while everyone else was gathered in the Great Hall?"

"I don't know, but we're going to find out," Zack replied. "Computer, where are they now?"

"Malik Massur is working with the Engineering Corps in the bulldozer bay on Deck 15. Visalia Grozny is attending spiritual services in Meditation Room 85 on Deck 5. José Famosa is relaxing in Pool 3 on Deck 12 with the rest of the Entertainment Troupe."

"They're acting like normal team members!" Sanjay said.

"Exactly," Zack said. "They're trying to blend in. Act normal. We have to watch them, though. I have a feeling they're here for a reason."

CHAPTER 28

Spy Games

Over the course of the next several weeks, Zack, Angelina, and Sanjay watched Malik, José, and Visalia as often as they could. Zack followed Malik around the bulldozer bay. It was a challenge for Zack to remain inconspicuous. As he kept his eyes on Malik, Zack ended up bumping into things, which met with the rest of the workers' disapproval. Finally, after Zack knocked a tray of sprocket wrenches into a barrel of oil, one of the workers in the bay put Zack to work. He found himself fixing broken dozer transmissions, realigning some of the wheels, and greasing the hinges that pivoted the bulldozer shovels. Thankfully, given Zack's mechanical skill, he could easily do this while he watched Malik. The other workers in the bay, in fact, grew to respect Zack's work, commenting on how impressive it was he could finish so many tasks while he hardly seemed to pay attention.

Sanjay had a far different job. He volunteered to follow José, which consisted of lying by the pool all day and occasionally following José as he waddled into the steam room or got a massage. The only problem was this made Sanjay significantly more relaxed when they all met at night to report on the day's events. Often, Sanjay had to fight to stay awake while Angelina or Zack recounted the day.

Angelina had the most challenging job though in tailing Visalia. Visalia, a lean, blond woman who had the build of a long twig, sat for hours in the mediation room on Deck 5. She sat cross-legged on the floor and didn't move, eat, or talk from the moment she got there until the end of the work shift eight hours later. Angelina sat behind her each day on the red and gold carpet. She "entertained" herself by counting how long she could sit with her legs crossed before they fell asleep.

Still, when they regrouped at the end of each day in Zack's room, neither Zack, nor Angelina, nor Sanjay had seen anything suspicious.

"It's like she's dead," Angelina said. "She just sits there like a statue for hours, with her eyes closed. She often sits next to another guy, who looks like one of the Mech pilots, but they never talk. Hours pass. Then, she just stands and walks out. She doesn't even talk to any of the other people meditating."

"Same with Malik," Zack said, wiping grease from his cheek, "except he works all day. He doesn't talk to any of the guys in the dozer bay unless they talk to him first. And he moves around really slowly, like he is sleepwalking. What about José?"

Sanjay was asleep on Zack's bed.

"Sanjay!" Angelina said.

Sanjay woke with a start and said, "Oh sorry. What?"

"What's the status with José?" Angelina said.

"Nothing. He just relaxes all day. At first, I thought I was going to go crazy. I had to bring a stack of memo-files to stay busy. But when

CHAPTER 28: SPY GAMES

that drew people's attention in the Entertainment Troupe, I started playing in the pool. He just lies there on one of the recliners by the pool. He doesn't even read. He laughs at some of the other people's jokes sometimes or takes a few pictures with the camera he carries around. But most of the time he's just lying there."

"I don't get it," Zack said.

"Me either," Angelina replied. "Do you think maybe they regret leaving and just want to fit back in? Maybe they realized siding with Machvel was wrong?"

"No way," said Zack. "First off, they did side with Machvel. They were part of his plan for a long time. That's not going to change overnight. Second, how did they get back to the Onyx Pioneer? The crew has looked through the entire ship, and the only craft missing is that freighter. When they came back here, they had to come in that ship. Machvel would have had to give his approval. No, they're here because he wants them to be here."

"Well then, what do you suggest?" Angelina asked.

"We must not be watching them closely enough. After all, we watch them only during the day. Now that I think about it, that's the time they are least likely to do something. Computer?"

"Computer online."

"Have Malik Massur, José Famosa, or Visalia Grozny ever been outside their quarters at night?"

The computer processed this request for a bit, then said, "Yes. All three met in the Mech bay three nights ago."

"See," Zack said to his friends. "Something's going on and they are doing it at night."

"That would explain why they have been so sleepy during the day," Sanjay said.

"That makes sense!" Angelina said. "Visalia never moves. She's probably sleeping. Ok, so what do we do now?"

"Now," Zack said. "We need to program the computer to watch them. The next time they go out at night, it should alert us. Sanjay can you do that?"

"No problem," he said. "I'll work on that tonight from the terminal in my room."

"Hurry," Zack said. "There is no telling what they might do or when they might do it."

Zack, Angelina, and Sanjay did not have to wait long. Three nights later, after Sanjay had reprogrammed the computer, Zack awoke to a siren in his room. Before he could jump out of bed, Sanjay was banging at the door to Grandfather's suite.

"Zack Goodspeed, they're moving!"

Zack threw on some pants and raced out of the suite. He found Sanjay in his bathrobe and Angelina rushing down the hallway in sweatpants.

"Come on you guys!" she said. "We don't have any time to lose!"

Zack raced after her, with Sanjay close behind. They ran to the elevator and took it to Deck 15. Jumping off the moment the doors opened, Angelina led the way as they raced across the long hall to the Mech Bay. They could see long before they got there that the enormous door into the Mech bay was open.

They stopped running and slunk along the sidewall, until they reached the edge of the door.

"Why are the bay doors open?" Angelina asked.

"I dunno. It's way past the time the last shift works," Zack said. "I'm going to take a look inside."

Zack leaned slowly around the doorframe and looked into the Mech bay. Inside, he could see the hulking Mechs and three people in orange spacesuits, huddled at the base of the nearest one. Even in

CHAPTER 28: SPY GAMES

the gloom of Deck 15 at night, Zack could see it was Visalia, José, and Malik. They were talking among themselves. Zack could hear their voices since they hadn't put on their helmets yet.

"So, do you have the airlock code?" Visalia asked Malik.

"Yes. It took me three weeks, but I finally convinced one of the dozer techs to give me the late-night airlock access code."

"Good, and do you have the Citadel Spire plans?" Visalia asked José.

"Yes. Those stupid SciTechs just leave them around the pool area whenever they go swimming. I photographed them without anyone noticing."

"Good. And I have the unlock codes for the Mechs themselves. It's a good thing that idiot Mech pilot talks in his sleep while he meditates."

José and Malik snickered.

Visalia continued, "We have everything we need, then. José and I will drive the first two Mechs out. Malik, you open the airlock for us using the code. Once we're inside the airlock, grab the third Mech and meet us. When we're all outside we can use the plans José took to dismantle the Citadel Spire. In the fragile condition it's in now, we should be able to destroy most of it by just removing a few support beams at the foundation. Then, we'll walk the Mechs back to Machvel's base. We'll see then how long these fools can survive without a base and working Mechs."

The two men nodded. Visalia and José walked over to the first two Mechs in the bay, while Malik ran toward the airlock door in the hallway.

"Lean back!" Zack whispered to Angelina and Sanjay. They did so just in time. Malik ran by but didn't notice them hiding in the shadows.

"What's going on?" Angelina asked.

"They're stealing the Mechs!" Zack said.

"But we'll never be able to finish the base in time if they do that," Sanjay whispered.

"That's their plan," Zack said. "And they're going to try to destroy the base on their way out."

"We have to stop them," Angelina said.

"Yes, but how?" Zack asked.

The squeal of metal on metal vibrated through the deck as Malik opened the airlock door. The first two Mechs stomped out of the bay and marched down the hall. Once they reached the airlock, Malik ran back to the bay. As he approached the shadow Zack and his friends hid in, Zack started to feel desperate. If they stole all three Mechs, the crew of the Onyx Pioneer would be doomed. They would not be able to build a base to live in. They would not have enough fresh air or food to survive. They would be left to die, all of them. Grandfather too, Zack realized.

Suddenly, Zack found himself doing something he did not anticipate. Although Malik was almost twice Zack's height, Zack felt himself dive toward the man as he ran into the Mech bay.

"What the —" Malik exclaimed. "There's a kid on me!"

Malik struggled to peel Zack off, but Angelina and Sanjay dove on top of him too, trying to wrestle him to the ground. Malik tripped and they fell to the deck. Zack landed on top of Malik and felt Angelina and Sanjay plop down beside him. Malik struck his head on the deck and was knocked unconscious.

"Quick! Tie him up!" Zack said. He pointed at some string he noticed in one of the Mech bays. Sanjay raced over to the bay, grabbed the string, and ran back. They quickly bound Malik.

The grinding noise of the airlock closing shuddered across the deck.

"They're leaving with the Mechs!" Zack said. "We have to stop them!"

CHAPTER 28: SPY GAMES

"How?" Angelina asked.

Zack looked around wildly. There was no one nearby. Even if they managed to get help from the living quarters on the higher decks, they would never be able to do so in time to stop Visalia and José. Zack looked up. A towering robot stood over them. It had an enormous "13" written on its chest.

"Into the Mech!"

"Are you crazy?" Sanjay protested, but ran alongside Zack as he and Angelina bounded onto Mech 13's elevator. Sanjay climbed aboard too and Zack pressed the up button. The elevator flew up the side of the Mech's leg, past its waist, and stopped at its chest.

"Sanjay, you have to hack the hand scanner."

"No Zack Goodspeed. I won't."

"Sanjay, this is our only hope! If José and Visalia get away, we're dead. The base will be gone, almost all the Mechs will be gone, and we'll be trapped in a ship that is slowly losing oxygen."

Sanjay looked conflicted. He slowly reached into the pocket of his bathrobe. He pulled a small handheld computer from it and a multitool.

"I don't like this," he said.

"I don't either, but what choice do we have?" Zack said.

Sanjay turned the multitool around in his hands.

"Please Sanjay. We don't have much time!" Zack said.

Sanjay nodded and approached the panel. He used the multitool to open the panel and expose several wires. He then opened the back of the handheld computer and tied wires inside it to the panel's exposed wires. He rapidly punched the keys on the computer.

"Hurry," Zack said.

Sanjay removed the wires, replacing them in the hand scanner panel. He closed the panel quickly.

"Done," Sanjay said. "This Mech is now yours."

Zack put his hand on the scanner. The door into the robot's chest whisked open. Zack ran inside, grabbed a set of black straps with white domes from the supply closet, and put them on. Then, he jumped into the pilot's seat, and strapped in. Angelina and Sanjay followed, closing the door behind them.

"Zack Goodspeed, you can't do this!" Sanjay said. "You have no idea how to pilot a real Mech."

"We don't have any choice," Zack replied. "They have two of the Mechs. They are going to destroy the base. You and Max sit on the sides of the seat. Hurry!"

Zack could see Sanjay open his mouth to protest, but Angelina pressed him onto one side of the seat while she ran around to the other.

"We don't have time for a debate. Zack is right," she said. "I hope you paid attention in the simulator."

"Me too," said Zack, as he pressed the button under the seat. The joystick leapt from the hole in the floor and Zack grabbed it as the control panel swung around. On the control panel was a bright yellow button labeled "Start." Zack pushed it and the Mech rumbled to life. Zack's entire body shook as the robot roared to life. The chair they sat on lifted from the chest and slid into the golden dome above. From here, Zack could see outside the robot in all directions. He could see Mechs standing behind him and to the sides. In front of him, he saw the door to Mech bay.

"Hold on."

Zack flipped the control switch into "Movement" mode and the robot lurched forward, like a car being put in gear. Zack pressed on the stick and the robot responded. It lumbered forward and in two big steps, emerged into the hallway of Deck 15. Although the deck had seemed huge to Zack before, it now felt small. Zack watched all sides of the robot to be careful he didn't hit anything, as he turned to walk toward the airlock door. As they approached the door, a hologram projected onto the dome of the Mech.

CHAPTER 28: SPY GAMES

"Airlock access denied. Late-night override code not entered," it said.

"Do either of you have the late-night code?" Zack said.

Sanjay and Angelina both said "No."

"We have to get it. Those two Mechs will already be outside the ship. We don't have much time."

"Wait!" Sanjay said. "Doesn't Malik have it?"

"You're right," Zack said. He twisted the Mech around so they could see the small shape of Malik on the floor of Deck 15. He still lay there unconscious and bound in the shadows near the edge of the hall.

"I need lights," Zack said. Sanjay pressed a button on the control panel and the hallway flooded with light from the tower-lamps on the Mech's shoulders.

Malik stirred on the floor in the bright light. Then, he jerked to attention as he saw Mech 13 towering over him. He squirmed like a worm to the sidewall.

"I need to talk to him," Zack said.

"Here, take this," Sanjay replied, handing Zack a headset like the one Zack had seen Grandfather wear. Zack put it on and said, "What is the passcode?"

Zack could hear his voice boom throughout the hall. It shook the ground and Malik tried to cover his ears, even though his hands were bound together.

"I won't tell you!"

"What is the passcode?" Zack said again, louder.

Malik cried out.

"What is it?" Zack said again, as loud as he could. The dome shook with the vibrations from his voice. Malik's tiny body bounced along the floor as it quaked with Zack's voice.

"All right!" Malik shouted. "It's 00-A16. Just please don't shout anymore."

Zack turned back to the airlock door. Sanjay was already entering the code into the control panel. As they stepped close to the door, a large "Access granted" hologram illuminated on the Mech's dome, and the airlock door ground open. Zack stomped the Mech into the airlock. The inner doors closed. The outer airlock opened.

Zack could hardly stand the wait. The airlocks seemed to be taking forever to open and close. If they took too long, Zack knew the other Mechs might have enough time to destroy the base. If they did that…Zack forced the thought from his mind.

The outer door ground open and they were immediately met with the bright sight of the Moon. The moon dust radiated the brilliant white of reflected sunlight and contrasted sharply with the black oil of the night sky. Ahead of him, Zack could see the towering metal skeleton of the Citadel Spire and two orange robots lumbering toward it.

"They're too far ahead," Zack said. He forced the Mech forward, but the robot only lumbered at its usual pace.

"We'll never make it," Angelina said.

"Use the boosters," Sanjay said pointing to a red, glowing button on the Mech's control panel.

"Are you sure?" Zack said.

"As you said: what choice do we have?" Sanjay said.

"Ok, hold on."

Sanjay and Angelina leaned in toward Zack. Angelina wrapped her arms around Zack, as Sanjay twisted one hand inside Zack's shoulder harness. Zack reached out a hand and pressed the "Rocket booster" button.

The Mech squatted down and a whirring noise came from its back. Zack looked behind him and saw metal wings and two rocket engines emerge from the Mech's back. A burst of flame shot from the engines,

CHAPTER 28: SPY GAMES

and the Mech blasted off. It blistered forward. Zack tried wildly to keep the robot facing toward the renegade Mechs. The robot twisted and looped around in circles as it rocketed forward. The distance between them and the other Mechs quickly closed. Suddenly, Zack found himself a few hundred feet away from the other Mechs and he shut down the rocket boosters. The wings folded in and the engines sank back, but Mech 13 kept flying forward.

"Things don't stop as fast on the Moon as they do on Earth!" Sanjay said.

Zack tried desperately to slow the Mech, but the best he could do was aim the robot at one of the other Mechs and hope for the best. Mech 13 slammed into one of the other robots and both tumbled to the surface. Vast plumes of moon dust and smoke shot into the air as the leviathan robots hit the ground. Sanjay and Angelina shot out of Zack's seat and slammed against the dome.

Zack lost consciousness.

When Zack came too, he was lying flat. He was in a bed. A hospital bed. Zack opened his eyes. It took a second for his vision to adjust to the white light, but then he saw he was in the Onyx Pioneer's infirmary. The moment he came to, a monitor at the side of his bed started to chatter softly. A SciTech nurse came over, turned off the monitor and smiled at Zack kindly.

"So, how are we this morning?"

"My head hurts," Zack replied. He felt like an elephant had sat on his skull. His neck was tight like a twisted rope.

"Yes, well I suppose that is to be expected after the crash you were in."

"Crash?"

It took a second before he remembered.

"Oh the crash! Where are Sanjay and Max?"

The nurse pointed to the beds next to him, where Sanjay and Max were sleeping peacefully.

"Are they ok?"

"Max has a concussion, and Sanjay had a broken leg. They'll be okay though. You are all very lucky."

A wave of guilt swept over Zack. In the moment of José and Visalia's escape, Zack hadn't considered they could get hurt. Now, looking at his two friends, vulnerable and wounded in the beds next to him, he wondered how he could be so careless.

The door to the infirmary whisked open and Grandfather Goodspeed lurched in, followed by Commander Chase and Dr. Soon.

"Zack, what the heck were you thinking?" Grandfather said as soon as he got to the bed. He inspected Zack. He looked into his eyes and surveyed his arms and legs. "You could have been seriously injured."

"Machvel's agents tried to steal the last Mechs and destroy the base."

"We know," said Commander Chase. "Thanks to your efforts we managed to save two of the three Mechs. The third fled after your crash. The base is fine, but that was a very risky thing you did, Zack."

"Very risky young man," Grandfather agreed. "What would I say to your parents if you died? Oh sorry, your son perished on the Moon? They'd never believe me. Zack you are not to take risks like that again."

"I'm sorry. We just had to stop them. They wanted to leave us here to die."

Grandfather's expression softened. He nodded slowly, then said, "Ok. Fair enough. But you are *not* to do anything like that again. That is not the way you should help us."

CHAPTER 28: SPY GAMES

At this last sentence, Zack saw something strange in his grandfather's face. It was like he was trying to give Zack a hint, but Zack wasn't getting it.

"How did you even learn how to pilot a Mech?" Grandfather said, changing the subject quickly.

Commander Chase blushed a little and opened his mouth to say something, but Zack interrupted, "We learned on the simulators."

"Simulators? Oh I see. Well, the simulators are now officially off limits to all personnel under Senior Cadet level. Dr. Soon, will you be sure to reprogram the computer to accept voice access only from approved personnel?"

"Right away, Fy."

"Good, well, now that is solved. You are to stay out of trouble, young man. The SciTech medical staff tell me you will be in here another week while Sanjay's leg mends and Max is checked on."

A fresh wave of guilt overtook Zack. He had not meant to hurt his friends.

"I only wanted to help."

"Well, from now on, if you want to help, find other ways to do so. You understand me?"

"Yes," Zack said, looking down.

"Good."

"Can I ask one question, though?" Zack said.

Grandfather nodded.

"What happened to the third Mech? And Malik, Visalia, and José?"

"The third Mech fled to the north," Commander Chase said. "Malik we found on Deck 15. We are holding him in one of the cargo rooms for questioning. But Visalia and José? Who do you mean?"

"Visalia Grozny and José Famosa?" Grandfather asked.

"Yes, they were the ones driving the other Mechs," Zack said.

Grandfather stammered, as he said, "But I picked those two for this trip myself. How could they betray us for Machvel?"

"I don't know, Fy," said Commander Chase. "But it seems they have. Computer, give me the last known whereabouts of Visalia Grozny and José Famosa."

"Visalia Grozny and José Famosa were last seen two nights ago leaving Airlock North in Mechs 14 and 15. No new information. End of report."

"It seems they've deserted," Commander Chase said. "But I will have the Security Team scan the ship visually to make sure. We'll also remove them from voice access to the central computer."

"Very good. Thank you, Commander," said Grandfather. He looked at Zack one more time. In all their years together, Zack had never seen Grandfather look at him like this. He was clearly disappointed. This made him feel ashamed. Zack averted his eyes.

"Well then, I think we're all clear about what do to next," Grandfather said and stumbled from the room with Commander Chase and Dr. Soon behind him.

CHAPTER 29

Following the Trail

About a week later, Zack, Angelina, and Sanjay left the infirmary. Zack and Angelina were given clean bills of health, but Sanjay was told to come back in two weeks to have his cast looked at.

"I don't blame you, Zack Goodspeed," Sanjay said, as he hobbled down the hallway on crutches, next to them. "I decided to get in Mech 13 with you and Max, and I'm glad I did."

"Thanks, Sanjay," said Zack, patting him on the back. "I only wish we could find out more about the lost Mech. Like where did it go? Did anyone go look for it?"

"According to my father, when he visited the other day, they have been sending out teams of Airstriders to look for the lost Mech, but haven't found anything."

"Machvel's got to be out there somewhere, though," Angelina said.

"According to my father, they have looked as much as they can. With far fewer people on board to work on the Citadel Spire, they can't divert many to scouting for Machvel."

"Doesn't anyone get it?" Zack said. "This guy is trying to *kill* us and he is still out there somewhere. And he has the Onyx Sun! Who knows what he plans to do with it."

"I agree," Sanjay said. "I am only telling you what my father told me."

"Maybe we should go talk with your dad," Zack said. "To see if we can help find Machvel."

"I don't know. Your Grandfather told us to stay out of trouble."

"We're not going to get into trouble," Angelina said. "We're just going to ask some people some questions. Professor Goodspeed didn't say we couldn't do that."

"Exactly," said Zack. "After all, what else are we going to do? Now we can't even use the simulators."

Sanjay frowned at them but followed as they made their way to the Engineering Core. The core had become a hive of activity over the last few weeks, as all ship functions had been diverted there. It was the new bridge, even though it was a quarter the size. Cadets whizzed in all directions bringing reports from one computer terminal to the next, from one officer to the next, and eventually looping them to either Commander Chase, who stood in the back, or Dr. Soon, who stood near the center hologram island.

When Dr. Soon saw his son come in, he smiled, but his smile faded when he saw Zack and Angelina following him.

"Shouldn't you children be in the library, staying out of the way?" Dr. Soon said.

"We were just wondering if you had found Machvel," Zack said.

CHAPTER 29: FOLLOWING THE TRAIL

"No unfortunately not," Dr. Soon said, turning back to the report he was pondering. "We sent out five scout teams in five different quadrants, but they found nothing."

"Not even Mech tracks?" Angelina asked.

"No, not even that. Apparently, shortly after your crash, the remaining Mech blasted off using its rockets. That makes it impossible for us to track."

"And what happened to the pilot of the Mech we crashed into?" Zack asked.

"That pilot disappeared too. We found some tracks in the moon dust. He must have run from his Mech after the crash. But from there his tracks disappear."

"How could that happen?" Angelina asked.

"The freighter," Zack said. "Someone in the stolen freighter picked him up."

"That is our current theory," Dr. Soon said, "which is disturbing since it means Machvel is in communication with people on this crew. In order to send the freighter, Machvel must have known instantly that you crashed into the other Mech."

"So, if you know he is nearby, why don't you send out more probe teams?" Zack asked.

Dr. Soon sighed and said, "Zack, I know you mean well, but our survival right now is dependent upon building the Citadel Spire. I don't have the resources to both build and explore. Now, if you'll forgive me, I must return to the work at hand."

Dr. Soon gathered his reports and walked off.

"Well, that's about what I expected," said Angelina.

"Come on. Let's go," Zack said. They walked out of the Engineering Core. Angelina and Sanjay followed Zack for some time, until the three of them found themselves outside an oval door on Deck 15 that looked like an egg on its side.

"What are we doing here?" Angelina asked.

Zack looked at them both and smiled. Sanjay immediately understood Zack's idea and began shaking his head.

"No, Zack Goodspeed," he said.

"Come on, Sanjay," Zack said. "You know none of the adults is going to help us. It's up to us to do something about finding Machvel."

Angelina darted glances back and forth from Zack to Sanjay and said, "What? I still don't get it."

Sanjay looked at her then stepped forward. The door whisked open and the Airstrider hangar appeared.

"Oh," Angelina said. At first, she looked confused. Then, a wide smile spread across her face and she said, "Yes. Absolutely. I like this idea."

"No, Max," Sanjay said. "My father would never forgive me if we stole an Airstrider to find Dr. Machvel on our own. Zack Goodspeed, your grandfather would never forgive you."

Zack ignored Sanjay and strode forward. All Zack could think about was that disappointed look on Grandfather's face last week. Zack didn't ever want to see that face again. He was bent on finding Machvel so Grandfather's disappointment would turn to pride. And this time, they would be smarter and safer so no one got hurt.

Zack approached an Airstrider. These ships were different than the one in Grandfather's Labradory on Earth. They were larger, and their cockpits were enclosed in glass. Each ship looked like it could hold eight people. Otherwise, they were the same streamlined, wedge shapes, with large rocket engines running along their sides.

The Airstriders were stacked into columns of three. As Zack approached one column, the bottom Airstrider floated out of its recharging collar and across the floor. It stopped and the glass-domed roof rolled back. Zack climbed inside. Angelina followed.

Even as he protested, Sanjay climbed on board after them.

CHAPTER 29: FOLLOWING THE TRAIL

"We can't do this, Zack Goodspeed."

"Look, Sanjay," Zack said. "I don't want to get you, or Angelina, or myself in trouble. But even more, I don't want Machvel to attack us again."

"I agree, Zack Goodspeed, but what can we do?"

"I don't plan on actually fighting him," Zack said, "but I do think we can find out where his base is and then report back here. Commander Chase can lead an attack when we find Machvel. But the first thing we have to do is actually find him."

"I cannot help you."

"But we need you," Zack said. "We don't know how to fly this thing, but I'll bet you do."

"I have been in a simulated Airstrider, yes, but that is not the point."

"The point," Zack said, "is that none of us will be safe until we find Machvel and do something about him."

Sanjay closed his mouth. Zack could see him processing this information as a storm of emotions played across his face. Finally, Sanjay looked like he had made up his mind.

"I don't like this, but this may be the right answer," Sanjay said.

"Or not," a voice behind them said.

Zack whirled around to see a towering, white-pillar of a person standing in front of the Airstrider. Grandfather looked more disappointed than ever.

"What could you have been thinking, Zack?" Grandfather said as he strode down the hallway, Zack's hand in his. Zack had to run to keep up. They had just dropped Sanjay off at Dr. and Mrs. Soon's quarters and Angelina had been left with Commander Chase. Zack had never seen Sanjay look so dejected, as he hobbled into his parents'

quarters, under his parents' piercing glare. Commander Chase, even though he wasn't Angelina's father, had looked at her disapprovingly too, when Grandfather left her with him.

"After what we just talked about last week, I thought we were clear."

Zack didn't say anything. He didn't think he could. He felt ashamed again to see his grandfather look at him like that, but he also didn't fully regret trying to find Machvel. So, Zack just decided to stay quiet.

They strode to Grandfather's chamber.

"Kalamazoo!" Grandfather said, and the door whisked open.

Zack and Grandfather walked inside. Grandfather let go of Zack's hand, ordered some hot soup for him from the computer, and sat down at the kitchen table. He ran his hand through his tuft of hair.

Zack slid over to the table and sat across from him. Even sitting, Grandfather towered over Zack. Zack dutifully picked up his spoon and began to eat his soup. Puddles of soup lay around the bowl, soaking some of the papers on the table. Zack thought to himself that ordering soup from a computer that dropped things from the ceiling was probably not the best idea.

"What can I do, Zack?" Grandfather said. "It is because of the danger of this mission that I didn't invite you to join me in the first place. You stowed away though. And now, against my wishes, you refuse to stay out of danger."

"I'm not trying to get into trouble," Zack pleaded. "Machvel attacked us. He attacked your ship."

"This is not the way for you to help find Machvel."

Zack felt anger swelling in his stomach, as he continued, "He attacked something you've been working on for years. Years that took you away from other things in your life."

"Yes, Zack, but this is not the way for you to help."

CHAPTER 29: FOLLOWING THE TRAIL

"Years that took you away from me."

"Machvel is dangerous, Zack!" Grandfather yelled, slamming his fist down on the table.

Zack sat back stunned by his grandfather's outburst. Grandfather's pale face was flushed.

"Zack, I had no idea what Machvel was capable of before this, but now that I have seen the depth of his evil, I am concerned for us all. Machvel is clever. He is devious, and he will clearly stop at nothing to have the Onyx Sun and kill us all in the process. We are trying to do something bold, for the betterment of mankind. We are building a colony on the Moon that will help humanity — for the first time — expand into the stars. Zack, once we are out there, settled among all those million points of light, we will be unstoppable as a species. But right now, we are in a very dangerous time. We have only one planet and this little base to call home. If anything ever happens to those habitats — a nuclear war, a global epidemic, an environmental disaster — our race may not survive. Machvel is a great threat to our first steps in space, to our first steps beyond the home world, and to our longevity as a species. But I would never take on this task if I thought for a second that it put you in danger. Piloting Mechs and flying Airstriders is no way for a young boy to help."

"Then, what is?" Zack asked.

Grandfather stood and bumbled to the door.

"I am sorry, but you leave me little choice. You will have to stay in my chamber for the rest of the day. Starting tomorrow, I will have a member of the Security Team escort you and your friends every day to the Cadet Training Academy. You are a little young to enroll, but we're making an exception to keep you out of trouble."

Zack heard what his grandfather was saying but couldn't help but be struck by the *way* he was saying it. Although part of Grandfather's tone indicated that Zack was being punished, part of it almost seemed like Zack was being rewarded. There was a boyish glint in Grandfather's eyes Zack had seen many times before, usually right after his grandfather had invented something new.

"In the Training Academy, you and your friends will be placed into specialties based upon what you are each best at. It is my guess Sanjay will follow his father's footsteps in the Engineering Corps. Max I could see doing quite well among the Security Team."

"And me?"

"You?" Grandfather said that glint in his eyes growing brighter. "I believe you may end up in the Executive Order, my own branch of service aboard the Onyx Pioneer. You'll learn about managing the teams using the processes, reporting structure, and computer systems we have put in place. Pay special attention to how the Executive Order uses the computer systems to manage the teams. There are some functions in there that even I am not able to use."

With that, Grandfather strode from the room, locking the chamber behind him.

CHAPTER 30

The Academy

"You mean you think your grandfather assigned us to the Academy to help find Machvel?" Sanjay asked the following day, as he walked with Zack and Angelina toward the Academy. They were followed by three Security Team members, so they kept their voices down.

"I don't know for sure, but I think so. There was just something in his voice. He kept saying that I couldn't help by driving Mechs or flying Airstriders. But he seemed to be saying I could help in other ways."

"And you think he meant by using the Executive Order's computer systems?" Angelina asked.

"Yes."

"But how? What are we supposed to do?" Angelina said.

"I have no idea. Sanjay, you've been around the ship the longest of the three of us, can you think of any way the computer can help us find Machvel?"

Sanjay scratched his head, then said, "No, I have no idea. The computer can do a lot of useful tasks. Obviously, it runs the entire Onyx Pioneer. It can track people by their voice, but only while they are on the ship. Once they are off it, it is useless."

"Does it remember what people say, even to each other?" Zack asked.

"Computer, replay last thing Zack Goodspeed said on board the ship," Sanjay said.

"Does it remember what people say, even to each other?" Zack heard himself say.

"Ok, I get it," Zack said. "So, can we maybe search the voice files to see if anyone has said anything about Machvel, bombs, or other things that might tip us off to his location."

"Perhaps," Sanjay said. "But there will be a lot of files to go through."

"Not to mention a lot of innocent people mentioning Machvel," Angelina pointed out. "The three of us have said his name probably a hundred times since they stole the Onyx Sun."

"True," Sanjay said. "Plus, we aren't allowed to access the ship's voice files."

"Not even as a cadet?" Zack asked.

"No, not as an Executive Order cadet, you're not."

"Well, who is?" Zack said.

"Only Security Team members with the endorsement of an Executive Order member are allowed access to those files."

Zack and Sanjay turned toward Angelina.

"What?" she said.

"My grandfather said you'd probably join the Security Team."

CHAPTER 30: THE ACADEMY

"But I haven't even chosen which team to join yet."

"That doesn't matter," Sanjay said. "The cadets are trained in the areas they are best at based upon our entrance exams. I could see you being very good at the Security Team sections of the entrance exam."

"What does that part of the test include?" Angelina asked.

"Interrogation, crime and punishment, bomb defusing, among many other areas."

"Sounds fun," Angelina said.

"I hope so. Because you need to get onto the Security Team," Zack said.

"Actually, even if you both are placed into the areas your grandfather predicted, cadets are not full team members and are not given full access," Sanjay said.

"Well, how do we get that?" Zack asked.

"Either you work towards becoming a full member," Sanjay said, "or you find an Engineering Corps member to hack the computer and promote you."

Zack and Angelina turned toward Sanjay. He continued walking forward until he realized what he had said. He slowed down and they came to a stop in the center of the hallway.

"This is not a coincidence," he said.

"No, it's not. I think this is my grandfather's plan," Zack said. "But I still don't know why he can't access the files himself."

"I don't know either," Sanjay said. "But apparently he needs us to do it."

"So, Sanjay's supposed to hack the computer and then you and I give the orders to access the voice files?" Angelina said.

"Yes, basically," Zack replied.

"Wicked!" she said. "When do we start?"

✳ ✳ ✳

The training to become a cadet was not as simple as Zack had hoped. After their conversation, Zack, Sanjay, and Angelina had arrived in a sparsely decorated white room to take their placement test. As Grandfather had predicted, Angelina had been placed into the Security Team, while Sanjay had received advanced placement in the Engineering Corps, and Zack had been admitted as a cadet of the Executive Order.

The following day, they were shepherded — along with a hundred other cadets — into a wide, white room that housed hundreds of glass cubicles. In each cube was a white desk, a white seat, and a pair of memo-file visors.

The cadets were divided by team. Angelina was led to the cubes on the left of the room, while Sanjay was placed with the cadets on the right. The Executive Order cadets, of whom there were the fewest, were ushered to the center cubes. Zack opened the glass door to the glass cube and stepped inside. He heard a soft hiss as the door closed behind him. It was quiet inside the cube. He looked around. He could see some cadets talking in the cubes around him, probably answering a battery of questions after their first memo-file, but he couldn't hear them.

Zack sat down and picked up the visor. He placed it over his eyes and a menu appeared inside the visor showing him the Executive Order reading list.

"Are you ready to begin?" said a soft voice from the visor.

"Yes," Zack said.

The visor highlighted one of the readings titled "A History of Effective Leadership" and before Zack could blink a barrage of images assaulted his eyes. They were accompanied by a bombardment of hyper-accelerated sounds, voiceovers, and audio footnotes. He even thought he smelled things, like the wet grass at Waterloo and the waxed wood of the Appomattox Court House. Zack sat

CHAPTER 30: THE ACADEMY

bolt upright in his chair. The experience felt like sucking soda into his nostrils through two, large straws. His brain tingled like it was popping with knowledge.

The file ended.

Zack was flooded with sudden realizations about what made a good leader and how he should act if he wanted to rise through the ranks of the Executive Order. He saw Franklin Roosevelt's great strength during World War II and Caesar's folly in trusting the Senate.

"Test commencing in five seconds," the visor announced.

A few weeks passed in this manner. Zack learned more about the specific structure of leadership on the Onyx Pioneer, passing most of his tests after only one memo-file viewing. Zack was surprised by how even though Grandfather had invented everything on the Onyx Pioneer he was never listed as a leader of the crew. Other people, like Commander Chase and Dr. Soon, directed the teams. Grandfather seemed to only guide things.

Finally, Zack walked into the Academy one day and on his visor menu was the title, "Using the On-Board Computer Systems to Manage the Crew." Zack watched the file and scored perfectly on the ensuing test.

That night, as he was escorted back to his quarters with Sanjay and Angelina, his mind still tingling with new knowledge, Zack said, "I know how to find the information we need."

"How?" Angelina asked.

"Well, it's not as easy as I'd hoped. Even though the computer is voice activated, we'll have to find a hologram screen to search and sort the information we need."

"But the only hologram screens were on the bridge and that was destroyed," Angelina said.

"Not true," Sanjay said. "There is also one in the Engineering Core."

"But how are we supposed to get in there? It's full all day and at night they lock it," Angelina said.

"I know," Zack said. "I thought of that. We'll have to break in."

"What? How?" Angelina asked.

Zack looked at Sanjay. As if sensing what Zack was about to say, Sanjay looked down at the ground.

"Sanjay, can you get the Engineering Core door open?" Zack asked.

Sanjay sighed then said, "My father would be furious. He has spent over a month fixing the Core, placing the new door, and building the software security to keep it closed at night. He is so paranoid about Machvel's agents disabling the Engineering Core, he spent at least two weeks programming just the security."

"Can you do it?"

"I think so."

"Sanjay, you're at the top of the engineering cadet class. We need to know for sure," Zack said.

"Ok. Yes. But I need a day to prepare."

"Good," Zack said. "Don't forget: you'll also need to hack us out of our rooms. Grandfather locks mine each night."

"So does Commander Chase," Angelina said.

"Ok, that won't be a problem," Sanjay said.

"Great, then tomorrow night we'll finally do this," Zack said.

CHAPTER 31

Unspoken Hints

The following night Zack waited in his grandfather's immense suite for Sanjay to arrive. Grandfather had been gone most nights, as he worked feverishly on the bridge and helped Commander Chase build the Citadel Spire. Even when he did come home, Grandfather must have been in the suite for just a few hours, as Zack fell asleep most nights alone and woke up to find dirty breakfast dishes on the table. Zack had spent much of his time on Earth wanting to be away from his parents. But now, under his Grandfather's care, he realized he missed them, because at least they spent each night and each morning with him.

At last, Zack heard a knock on the door and heard Sanjay's muffled voice.

"Just a second, Zack Goodspeed."

The door whooshed open. Angelina waited outside, while Sanjay crouched by the side of the door. He held a tangle of wires pouring from an access hatch on the wall.

"These are easy," Sanjay said. "The trick will be the Engineering Core."

"Well then, let's go," Zack said.

They quietly ran to the Engineering Core, taking care to avoid the Security Team patrols in the hallways.

"I downloaded the patrol routes yesterday in the Academy," Angelina said, holding up a map of the Onyx Pioneer. "As long as we take the route I have highlighted, we won't run into anyone."

"Nice work," Zack said. "Show us where to go."

Angelina took them up several floors, down long hallways, then down several floors. They were careful not to take any elevators, which might be noticed moving, and were quiet running up and down the stairs. At last, they came to the Engineering Core, and Sanjay told them to slow down. He motioned for Zack to look around the corner in the hallway. Zack did so.

Zack saw now why Sanjay was nervous. In many ways, the new door looked like the old one, only it was reflective silver and had a hundred blue and red beams crisscrossing it. Several cameras also lay around the hall, covering every inch of viewable space.

"The door is titanium alloy," Sanjay said. "So, it will resist most bomb blasts. The blue beams are motion sensors, linked to a ship-wide alarm. The red beams are lasers that can slice through an inch of steel. A heavily armed Security Team, stationed around the corner, watches the cameras constantly. If we are detected at all, it will be like World War III in here."

"Sounds fun," Angelina said sarcastically.

Sanjay wiped his forehead and shook his head. Then, he opened a hatch in the wall they stood by. Dozens of wires of all colors fell out. Sanjay pulled a video camera from his pocket.

CHAPTER 31: UNSPOKEN HINTS

"The first step is to cut the video feed. I took a long video of this corridor while it was empty last night. I'm going to patch the video I have into the wires. That way, when we walk down the hall, the Security Team will see what I recorded last night, not what is happening now."

Sanjay took out a multi-tool and made quick work of the wires. In one motion, he cut several wires and tied them into one that fed into his camcorder.

"There. Hopefully, there was no interruption in the video feed. I tried to do that quickly. Next, I am going to need your help, Zack."

Sanjay led Zack to a ventilation grate in the hallway wall. Using his multi-tool to unscrew the hinges, Sanjay pulled the grate off and reached inside the ventilation shaft. He pulled out a large mirror about seven feet long and three feet wide. Zack helped him remove it. Resting the mirror on the floor, Sanjay reached inside and pulled out four table legs with wheels on them.

"Hold the mirror on its side," Sanjay said to Zack.

Zack did so as Sanjay pulled a tube of glue from his pocket.

"You're starting to remind me of my grandfather," Zack said. "How much stuff do you have jammed into your pants?"

Sanjay handed him the multi-tool and said, "You never know. Here, you can have this one. I have others."

Sanjay glued the table legs to the four corners of the mirror. After a few minutes to let the glue dry, he asked Zack to help him turn the mirror over. Zack did and they rested the mirror on its new legs. Now, the mirror looked like a table with a reflective top.

"This device is for us to slide under the motion sensors and lasers," Sanjay said. "It will reflect the red lasers that would normally slice us in two. But we have to move it slowly through the laser field. Since the blue beams are motions sensors, we can't move it faster than an inch a second. Any faster and the alarm will go off."

Zack nodded, and together they wheeled the mirror-table along the floor until they were within five feet of the door. As they approached the beams, Sanjay held up a hand. Zack stopped. Sanjay got down on the floor and motioned for Zack to do the same.

"We have to move it very slowly," Sanjay whispered.

They edged the table forward.

"Not that fast! Slower," Sanjay said.

Zack gulped. He had no idea how slow one inch per second was. He had never moved that slow in his life. The table inched forward. The mirror was halfway towards the bulkhead when Zack heard a door open in a nearby hallway, followed by voices.

"Stop!" Zack hissed.

Sanjay stopped and looked frantically at Zack.

"Max! Are you expecting any patrols?" Zack whispered down the hall.

Angelina peered around the corner and shook her head.

Zack sat catatonic on the floor, holding the mirror as still as possible. His heart pounded. He could hear the voices coming closer.

"Do we run?" Sanjay asked.

"I don't know. We may not get another chance at this," Zack said.

Zack was on the verge of telling Sanjay to make a break for it, when they heard the voices turn down another corridor and fade into the distance. Zack breathed a sigh of relief.

"All right, let's finish this," he said to Sanjay.

They wheeled the mirror-table the rest of the way until it pinged softly against the door. Zack could see there was now a two-foot-high tunnel under the mirror.

Crouching, Zack and Sanjay walked back to Angelina. Sanjay immediately began working on the wires in the wall. He pulled a handheld computer from his pocket and tied several wires into it. A second later reams of text flowed down the computer screen.

"Ok, now the fun part," he said. "I have to hack the software."

"How long will that take?" Zack asked.

CHAPTER 31: UNSPOKEN HINTS

"I have no idea. Maybe five minutes. Maybe five hours. We'll see."

"Get to work then," Angelina said. "Zack and I will watch for patrols."

Zack and Angelina split up and walked to opposite ends of the hallway to keep watch. Several times they heard voices milling around the adjoining halls, but luckily none of them walked by the Engineering Core. Zack wasn't concerned with patrols, since Angelina had assured him none would be passing the Engineering Core for hours, but he did worry about random people floating around. He looked at his watch. 2 AM. Although it was unlikely many people would be up at this hour, Zack could easily imagine Dr. Soon poking about and running straight into them trying to break into the Engineering Core.

At last, a half-hour later, Zack heard Sanjay whisper down the hall, "I got it."

Zack and Angelina met Sanjay near the door, which was now wide open. Beyond the lasers, he could see the monitors and holograms of the Engineering Core, glowing in the dark room.

"Let's go," Zack said.

Zack went first, sliding on his belly under the mirror and into the Core, then Sanjay, then Angelina. Once inside, Zack led the way to the center console and quickly started tapping on its surface. His memo-file training made this easy, even though he had never done it before. Zack quickly pulled up the master screen for voice recordings, but when he tried to start sorting them, a computer voice said, "Proper authorization required."

"Authorization granted," Angelina said.

"But we only have cadet access," Zack said. Then, he noticed Sanjay under the computer console. Zack watched as Sanjay ripped more wires from the computer and plugged them into his handheld. Zack saw a screen on Sanjay's handheld that said "Downloading new permissions."

A second later, the computer said, "Access granted."

"Nice work," Zack said, slapping Sanjay on the back as he stood up.

Zack wasted no time. He immediately began sorting through the voice data. Each voice conversation had been automatically transcribed into text and was listed on the screen before him. He searched by people who had said "Machvel," "bomb," "Onyx Sun" (there were quite a few entries there), "traitor," "defect," and so on. Angelina and Sanjay stood nearby suggesting other words, as each search turned up conversations that contained no incriminating information. After an hour, they hadn't uncovered a single conversation that seemed abnormal. Sanjay slumped to the floor and Angelina leaned against the wall.

"It's like Machvel's agents are gone," Angelina said.

"I don't see how that could be," Zack replied. "He knows we're here and he knows we're not dead. He has to be planning something and he'll need people on board for that."

"Zack, maybe he's really left us alone," Angelina said. "I mean, who knows what he wanted to begin with. Maybe he stole the Onyx Sun to take it back to Earth. Maybe he's there right now. He hasn't done anything to us in weeks."

"No, I don't believe it," Zack said. "He wouldn't have tried to blow up the ship, steal the Mechs, and destroy the Citadel Spire, if he just wanted to go back to Earth. Sanjay, what do you think?"

Sanjay shifted on the floor then said, "I don't know. Maybe he is gone, maybe he isn't. The only thing we know for sure is no one has said anything about working with him."

Zack snapped his fingers and said, "Wait. That's it!"

The gears started turning in Zack's mind. If Machvel was truly trying to sabotage them, he would have learned from his mistakes. Zack and his friends had used the computer's voice system to find his agents last time. Surely, Machvel wouldn't make the same mistake again.

CHAPTER 31: UNSPOKEN HINTS

"Zack, what's going on?" Angelina asked.

"Here. Look," Zack said. He typed quickly on the console and sorted the voice data by people not talking.

"Zack, that just gives us a list of every person on the ship who's asleep. Most of the ship's not talking right now."

"That's not the point," Zack said. "Watch."

Zack removed the people who were asleep. The list narrowed from a few thousand to a few hundred. Then, Zack eliminated the people currently in their quarters or on security patrols. Three people remained: Edward Lafayette, Greg Hunter, and Claus Schindler.

"See," said Zack. "Machvel must know we caught his last spies by using the computer's voice recognition."

"Yeah, but maybe these three guys are just hanging out," Angelina said.

"Alone and completely quiet in the middle of the night outside their rooms?"

"Yeah, ok, so that's a little strange," Angelina said.

"Computer, where is Edward Lafayette now?" Zack asked.

"There is no current voice data for Edward Lafayette, but his last command was to tell an elevator to take him to Deck 11."

"And what about Greg Hunter and Claus Schindler."

"There is limited voice data for Claus Schindler. His last known location was aboard an elevator heading to Deck 11. There is no information on Greg Hunter."

"Computer," Zack said. "Show us the floor plan for Deck 11."

A floor plan of Deck 11 illuminated on the surface of the console. Zack traced the lines of the walls with his hand.

"Deck 11 is just cook's galleys and food supply cabinets," he said. "What could they be doing there?"

"Maybe they're hungry," Angelina said.

"Maybe Machvel wants to poison our food," Sanjay suggested.

"No," said Zack leaning close to the floor plan. "I doubt it. The crew eats in shifts. So, people would start getting sick before the entire crew had eaten. It's got to be something that will affect all of us."

Zack looked at the map. What could Machvel want there? It had to be something. Machvel was a master of exploiting the ship's weaknesses. He had co-designed most of it with Grandfather and was now using that knowledge to cripple the ship and kill the remaining crew. Suddenly, the answer hit Zack. He jabbed a finger at blueprint showing the sides of the ship.

"The atomic emitters?" asked Angelina, reading the blueprint.

"Of course!" exclaimed Sanjay. "There are atomic emitters all along the hull of the ship. They are what keep us in the air when we fly. An explosion while the atom emitters are on would destroy the entire ship."

"I know," Zack said. "One of my memo-files last week gave me an overview of the Onyx Pioneer. It included some information on the ship's weaknesses. It told me that a conventional explosion near one of the atomic emitters, while it was on, would cause a chain reaction and incinerate the entire ship. This time, the explosion wouldn't take down just the bridge."

"But someone would have to turn on the atomic emitters first. The only place that can be accomplished is here in the Engineering Core and in the Power Tower."

All three of them turned around at the same time. They peered through the wall-window in the back of the Engineering Core. The Power Tower room was bathed in its usual undulating blue-purple glow. The dark silhouettes of the catwalks crisscrossed the chamber. A dark outline of a man walked across one of them toward the Onyx Sun.

"There!" Zack said, pointing at the figure. "That must be Greg Hunter. He's trying to manually start the atomic emitters. We have to stop him!"

CHAPTER 31: UNSPOKEN HINTS

Zack, Angelina, and Sanjay darted for the door simultaneously. After shimmying under the mirror-table, they bolted down the hall.

As they reached the nearest elevator bank, Zack said, "We have to split up. Sanjay, go find your father and Commander Chase and get to the Power Tower. Stop Greg Hunter. Max and I will go to Deck 11 to try to stop Edward and Claus."

Sanjay and Angelina nodded. When the elevator arrived, Zack and Angelina took it to Deck 11, while Sanjay tore off down the hall to get his father.

For the first time, Zack thought the rapidly descending elevator couldn't go fast enough. Although they were only four decks away, the levels seemed to tick by slowly. Finally, the elevator dinged and the number eleven displayed on the floor indicator. The doors slid open and Zack and Angelina leapt out.

Deck 11 was utilitarian. It had white, curved walls split on the left every hundred yards by aluminum doors. On the right were a series of smaller doors labeled "Food Supplies." The hallway curved away in both directions.

"Why do you think they are on this deck? They could have put a bomb anywhere near the edge of the ship on any floor," Angelina said.

"I don't know," Zack said. "But if I were them, I'd do it here because at night, no one's around."

"Good point," Angelina said.

Zack pointed to the hallway on the right, and they slipped down it toward the stern. Zack tried to walk as quietly as possible, but he felt rushed since the hallway seemed to go on for miles. Zack's heart was thundering in his chest. Thoughts raced through his head. What would he say when they found Machvel's agents? What would he do?

Zack did not have long to consider this, as two figures appeared at the end of the hallway. Zack sprinted towards them suddenly, as did Angelina. He had little time to think. As they approached Edward and Claus, Zack did the first thing that came to his mind. He leapt at them.

The two men turned around at the exact moment Zack took flight. They did not have time to react, as Zack crashed into Edward and Angelina crashed into Claus.

They all tumbled to the floor. Zack saw Angelina land firmly on top of Claus, but Edward twisted away as Zack fell. Edward leapt up and ran down the corridor. Zack pushed himself off the floor and sprinted after Edward until he saw Claus viciously throw Angelina off him and into the wall. Zack spun and leapt on the man's back. This knocked Claus off balance and he crashed to the floor again, this time hitting his head on the ground. Angelina picked herself up and dove on top of Claus as well.

"We know you plan to blow up the ship. Where is the bomb?" Zack shouted.

Claus thrashed about violently, but Zack managed to keep him pinned down.

"I'm not telling you anything!" he said. "You'll get what's coming to you very soon."

"If the ship blows up now, you'll die too!" Angelina shouted.

"That's a sacrifice I am willing to make," Claus shouted back.

"You'll kill seven thousand people," Zack said, slamming Claus's struggling arms down.

"Those who serve with your grandfather deserve to die," Claus said, grunting while he tried to struggle away. He suddenly stopped struggling. "They all failed to recognize the true power of the Onyx Sun."

Claus's eyes drifted briefly to the kitchen door nearby. Zack shot a glance at the door. He saw Angelina nodding. They leapt off Claus and ran into the kitchen.

"It is too late! It's over," Claus shouted, as he staggered to his feet and ran away, following Edward's path.

CHAPTER 31: UNSPOKEN HINTS

Zack and Angelina slammed the swinging doors aside as they plunged into the kitchen. The kitchen looked like any other: covered in stainless steel tables, packed with pots and pans, and full of lots of great places to hide a bomb. Zack whirled around. He looked frantically at Angelina, who calmly said, "Just look everywhere."

They darted off in different directions. Zack threw open cupboards, looked in pots, threw empty drawers on the floor. He pushed aside stacks of cooking books. He climbed on top of the grill in the center of the room and peered into the wide vent that sucked smoke off the stove. Nothing. The kitchen lay in ruin around them. Every pot had been searched, every crevice of the kitchen covered.

"Did we make a mistake?" Zack said. "Is it somewhere else?"

"It can't be," Angelina said, trying to catch her breath. "Or maybe I should say it better not be. We don't have enough time to search the whole deck."

"I know," Zack said scanning the kitchen again. He saw it. It was a very subtle hint, but there it was. A grate attached to the vent that ran through the room was slightly off its hinges. Zack pushed a steel table under the vent and climbed up. Angelina joined him. Together, they gently slid the vent cover off.

Inside the dark shaft of the vent was a flat, square device, with exposed wires, blinking lights, and a lot of C-4. Even though he had never seen a bomb, it looked much like Zack had expected. He reached out to touch it.

"Careful, Zack!" Angelina said holding his hand back. "You could set it off."

"Well, what are we supposed to do?" Zack said. "It is going to go off if we don't do something. We have to try."

"Try what? Randomly pulling out wires?" Angelina said. "I don't know too much about bombs, but I am pretty sure most blow up if you do that."

"We have to do something!"

Angelina looked pensive and said, "Maybe we can move it. Throw it outside or something."

"Good idea," Zack said. He reached inside the vent slowly.

"Careful!" Angelina whispered.

"I am being careful," Zack hissed back. He pulled gently on the base of the bomb. It didn't budge. He pulled a little harder. Nothing. "I can't move it. It seems to be attached to the bottom of the vent. Maybe we can cut the vent with a welding torch and take the whole thing outside."

"That'll take too long," said Angelina. She looked at Zack with a worried expression. "You have to go find help, Zack."

"What? And leave you here? No way."

"You have to, Zack," she replied, grabbing his arm and forcing him to look at her. "I will stay here with the bomb. If it starts to tick, or beep, or look like it is going to go off, I'll try to pull some wires. What choice do we have at that point?"

"No, Max. I'm not leaving you."

"You have to, Zack. I'll be all right. Go. Go find your grandfather. He'll know what to do."

Zack stood there.

"Go!" Angelina said, pushing him off the table. He stumbled to the floor and ran to the door. He paused briefly, one hand on the door, looking back at her on the table. She had wisps of black hair in her mouth and her eyes sparkled with intensity.

"Go!" she shouted and he dodged out the door.

Zack sprinted to the elevators. He slammed the elevator call button.

"Come on, come on!" he shouted, stomping his foot and pounding the button some more.

The elevator door slid open and Zack jumped inside.

CHAPTER 31: UNSPOKEN HINTS

"Fyodor Goodspeed's quarters on Deck 8!"

"Compliance," the computer said.

Zack hoped his grandfather was in his suite. Otherwise, he would never find him. The elevator doors closed. The elevator shot up quickly, but zoomed past Deck 8.

"Oh, come on! Computer, take me to Deck 8!" Zack shouted. What was this, another Entertainment Troupe prank, he thought.

The elevator ground to a halt at Deck 4. The doors opened. Zack pressed the button for Deck 8, but the elevator refused to budge. Zack stepped out of the elevator.

"Computer, where is Fyodor Goodspeed?"

"Fyodor Confucius Goodspeed's location is currently unknown," the computer reported.

Zack huffed. He would have to find someone to help him on this deck or he would never get back to Angelina in time.

"Somebody! Anybody!" Zack screamed, frantically running down the corridor. Despite his calls, no one came. "Is anybody here? I need help. Someone!"

Zack ran and shouted. He slammed his hand on the doors around the corridor, trying to rouse anyone who might be inside.

"Hello? Can somebody help me?" Zack said, running farther. He had no idea how much time he had, and that uncertainty made him even more nervous. He couldn't let Machvel's agents destroy Grandfather's ship.

At that moment, Zack's heart stopped as he heard the atom engines warming up. The ship shuddered as the rumbling whine of the engines reverberated through the hall.

He had to do something quickly. Zack sprinted down the corridor, calling for help, and banging frantically on doors. Suddenly, he found himself in front of a slightly larger door labeled "MF Library." It didn't even register in his mind where he was until he turned to bang on the door and it whisked open. The warm library with its glowing blue books stood in front of him as in a dream. Zack stepped over the threshold, like a zombie. It was like his prayers had been answered.

Zack ran into the library and started frantically searching the titles of the memo-files. He scanned file after file, but there were too many.

He whirled around and faced the center of the room. "Computer!" he shouted. "Highlight memo-file titles having to do with bombs!"

"Acknowledged," said the lilting computer voice. Several scattered memo-files turned from glowing blue to a bright white. They looked like stars sprinkled across the thousands of other memo-files. Zack raced to each one, reading the spines.

"Notable Bombs of Pre-atomic Earth," one read.

"Bombs and You: How to Avoid One," said another.

"Underappreciated Principles of Bomb Manufacture," the next one read.

There were still too many files, Zack realized.

"Computer, narrow files to those dealing with bomb defusing."

A single file lit up on the top floor of the library. Zack flew up the stairs and read the spine, "Advanced Principles of Bomb Defusing."

That's it, he thought.

He bolted down to the center of the library, shouting as he did, "Computer. Load 'Advanced Principles of Bomb Defusing.'"

"Compliance," the computer said, as Zack threw a visor on.

The world became dark as the visor snuffed Zack's senses. His eyes, ears, nose and mouth were almost completely covered.

Then, a pinprick of light far in the distance appeared on the visor screen. It shot at him like a freight train until Zack's entire vision was covered in a blistering montage of images, sounds, tastes, sensations, and smells. Bomb schematics whipped by in nano-seconds, followed by bomb-making ingredients, common bomb development and defusing

CHAPTER 31: UNSPOKEN HINTS

techniques, famous bomb makers, the evolution of bombs, specialized bomb methods, religious misuses of bombs, and the best places not to be when a bomb goes off.

Then, the visor went black again. Zack ripped it from his head. His spine was rigid and his body swayed as if he had just been thrust into a fifteen-second rock concert and placed right by the loudest speaker.

At first he thought he was no wiser than before. Then, suddenly, thoughts occurred to him.

"An explosive device is comprised of six main elements: the charge, the detonator, the wiring, the timer (optional), the LED indicator (optional) and the battery to fire the detonator," Zack said to himself, half in a daze. He shook his head, but the knowledge stuck.

"The best ways to defuse a bomb are either to defuse the charge or to separate the detonator from the wiring," Zack said. He smiled. He felt like he could teach bomb defusing. He only hoped enough knowledge stuck from this one memo-file for him to defuse the bomb.

Zack shot up from the bench and ran to the door, just as he heard the visor say, "Testing on this memo-file will commence in five seconds."

"This test I have to pass," Zack said to himself as he sprinted through the door.

He shot down the hall and, this time, opted for the stairs over the elevator. He ran down to the kitchen corridor, aware in the back of his mind the engine warm-up was growing louder.

Zack shot into the kitchen. Angelina stood on the table, her hand inside the vent, wrapped around one of the bomb's wires.

"Wait!" Zack said jumping on the table. Angelina withdrew her hand as if she had been shocked.

"What?" she said.

"If you had pulled the secondary lead wire, this thing would have gone off for sure!" Zack said.

"Since when did you know anything about bombs?" she asked.

"Memo-file," said Zack.

Angelina searched his face as if looking for his new knowledge, then said, "Well, let's hope you paid attention."

Zack closed his eyes and took several slow breaths to relax. This was the first thing the memo-file had recommended before defusing a bomb. Zack knew now shaky hands or nervous decisions killed thirty-three percent of bomb technicians. For a brief second, doubt crept into his mind. What if he didn't retain the important facts? What if he had chosen the wrong memo-file? What if he messed up? He had never defused a bomb before. What made him think he could do so now? Zack pushed these thoughts aside. He had to focus. Zack pressed his hands together as if praying, and then slowly opened his eyes.

The bomb looked entirely different to him. Before, it had been a mess of wires and strange blinking lights. Now, it made logical sense. Zack could see the lead wire connecting the main charge to the detonator. He understood which wires powered the detonator by connecting to a set of batteries. He also saw a unique variation seldom used to back these up by linking the batteries directly to the charge.

Instead of being scared of the bomb, he was now unimpressed with it. By all estimations in his extensive fifteen seconds of experience, this was a fairly common device.

The atom engines on the other side of he wall spun up to full speed. The room shook with a violent fury. At the same time, the bomb began to beep rapidly.

"Hurry, Zack," Angelina said, leaning away from the bomb, her eyes squinting.

The bomb began to beep faster. The lights on it flickered wildly. A whining noise sounded from the detonator.

CHAPTER 31: UNSPOKEN HINTS

Zack reached out and calmly pulled a red wire from the timer. He then removed a green wire from the batteries. He twisted these together.

The bomb fired.

Angelina gasped.

There was a soft click.

A thin wisp of smoke rose lazily from the bomb. The device whined as it short-circuited itself.

Zack looked at Angelina, who was leaning as far off the table as she could without falling. Her eyes were squeezed shut. She opened one eye and squinted at him.

"I guess I passed," he said.

CHAPTER 32

Machvel's Pyramid

"You defused it?" shouted a voice at Zack and Angelina. They spun around to see Claus and Edward in the doorway.

"Yes, I did," Zack said. "It actually was quite easy. I just short-circuited the two-stage ignition device. Even if you wanted to blow up the ship now, you couldn't."

Claus and Edward stormed toward Zack and Angelina, catching them off guard. Claus swiped at Angelina's legs. She plummeted to the ground, knocking herself unconscious as her head hit the floor. Edward lunged at Zack. Zack tried to dive over him, but Edward wrapped his arms around his legs and brought him to the ground. Zack kicked Edward in the jaw and slipped away.

Claus tripped Zack as he ran, and Edward clambered on top of him. Edward put a thick arm around Zack's throat and held him like a vise.

CHAPTER 32: MACHVEL'S PYRAMID

"The girl?" he asked Claus.

"Leave her. Machvel wants only him," he said.

Zack struggled with the arm around his throat. He glanced wildly at Angelina on the floor. He kicked at the table near him. He struggled for air as everything went black.

Zack woke with a start. His head throbbed and his body felt woozy. A bright light blinded him, but he couldn't determine its source since his vision was still blurry. He tried to move his arms and legs, but they were strapped to the metal platform he leaned against. As his vision cleared, the light became less bright and he could see again.

Zack gasped. He was inside a large, pyramid-shaped room. The walls were made of black glass, but Zack could faintly see the undulations of the Moon's surface beyond them. A skeleton of scaffolding supported the walls throughout the chamber. Bright spotlights shone from the scaffolding. The floor of the pyramid was a series of stages. Zack was positioned on the highest stage that edged the walls at about ground level. The stages below him held computer banks, like Zack had seen on TV when newscasters visited NASA's Mission Control. The computer banks had a number of monitors, with attendants at each station. Some of the people Zack recognized. He saw Visalia chatting with Claus, as they leaned over a monitor on the near side of the room. Edward and a man Zack didn't recognize stood on the far side of the room, staring at Zack and laughing like hyenas. José was also there, sitting at a computer monitor with his feet on the desk.

In the center of the floor, on the lowest level, stood the twisted shape of Dr. Ian Machvel. He was facing away from Zack so all Zack could see was his jet black hair and the olive skin of one arthritic hand clutching a walking cane. It seemed to be the only thing holding him up. Machvel's bulging knuckles accentuated the misshapen form of his hands. The bones between the thick joints were skinny and fragile-looking. Machvel wore a black flight suit with a collar that pointed up. The suit hugged his narrow form.

"Ah, so our visitor is awake," Dr. Machvel's viperlike voice hissed through the chamber. Machvel turned around, and Zack saw the black coals of his eyes hidden in the dark pools of his eye sockets. Machvel smiled and exposed a row of yellow teeth. He limped up the stairs toward Zack, using his cane to hold him up as he mounted each step. The cane clicked on the floor as he moved, sounding throughout the hollow room.

Dr. Machvel at last reached Zack's level and limped so close to him Zack could smell and feel the hot stench of his breath.

"Why am I here?" Zack said, turning away.

Dr. Machvel paused for a moment and smiled, clearly enjoying Zack's reaction.

"Let's just say you are an insurance policy until we complete our plan."

"I don't understand," Zack said.

"No, you don't," Dr. Machvel said. "You don't understand a great many things. But you will."

Dr. Machvel motioned to Visalia, who pressed a button on the computer panel she stood near. Through the pyramid's glass walls, Zack saw a hole open in the Moon's surface. A long tower rose from the hole with a black rocket attached to it.

"What is that?" Zack asked.

"The beginning of your understanding," Machvel said, a creaky laugh rising in spasms from his throat. He put on a pair of dark laboratory glasses, as the crew inside the pyramid did the same. Machvel placed a pair over Zack's eyes, as well. Visalia pressed another button on her panel and the fuselage of the rocket split open.

A flood of purple-blue light poured from inside the rocket. Even with the sunglasses on, Zack had to squint. As his eyes adjusted,

CHAPTER 32: MACHVEL'S PYRAMID

however, he could just barely see — through the storm inside — the shape of the Onyx Sun. Wild wisps of blue energy poured from the rocket and streamed over the outside of the glass pyramid, as the cube violently whirled around.

"What is it?" Zack asked slowly.

Machvel turned toward him, smiling. In the bright storm of purple-blue light, Machvel looked like a twisted, black demon as he hissed, "A symbol — an icon — for the end and beginning of all life on Earth."

"What?" Zack said.

Machvel motioned for Visalia to close the rocket, and as she did so, he took off his sunglasses and removed Zack's. Machvel limped back down the steps into the center of the chamber.

"Your grandfather is a fool," he said. "He invented the single greatest source of power in the history of man and what does he do with it? Nothing. Fy Goodspeed is obsessed with an ideal vision. He wants to uncover the mysteries of the universe and establish humanity in the stars. He looks beyond our world for answers to humanity's problems when he possessed the real solution the whole time."

Machvel gestured at the rocket and said, "The solution is the Onyx Sun itself. There is a cataclysmic weapon concealed in its simple shape. It is what mankind has needed all along: extinction and rebirth."

Machvel cackled.

"Why try to solve something that can't be fixed? Mankind today is not a race that deserves to populate the heavens. Look at what we have done to our own planet. We have a history of spreading war, poverty, and oppression. We are masters at ruining ourselves."

Machvel spun around and pointed at the stars beyond the glass, and said, "What good would it be for us to spread our disease further? We'll make the same mistakes. No, our mistakes will be even larger, because there will be more of us."

Dr. Machvel let his arm fall and limped up the side of the pyramid that faced the rocket, "Wipe the slate clean and start afresh, I say."

Machvel spun on his heels and looked at Zack. "With this rocket, I have built a weapon capable of wiping out every human on Earth, while not destroying most buildings, plants, and other animal life. Fy was correct when he said the Onyx Sun had unique properties. If he had only taken the time to understand all of them, as I have. I have figured out how to configure the Onyx Sun to eliminate mankind while preserving the rest of the planet. Your grandfather has given me the very methods to end man's madness in one shot. This rocket is a symbol indeed — of man's second chance. At last, we will be able to restart, to build a more perfect society of people. After the Onyx Sun obliterates mankind on Earth, the colony of man in this compound will resettle a more perfect world!"

"You're dreaming," Zack said, surprised at the note of courage in his voice.

Machvel cackled again. He pointed at the crew assembled in the pyramid. "It is not a dream I have alone. In this base, there are thousands who share the same vision. They left your grandfather's idealistic voyage to join me. They realized as I did that we are not colonists of space but founders of a new Earth."

Dr. Machvel turned back toward the glass wall and folded his hands behind his back. "Your grandfather's greatest invention may have been the Onyx Sun, but mine will be far more profound — the rebirth of our species."

A thousand questions pressed against Zack's mind and spilled out of his mouth at once, "How could you possibly do this? How could you betray my grandfather, who trusted you? You can't hold mankind hostage like this!"

Machvel shook his head slowly and said, "So young. So idealistic."

CHAPTER 32: MACHVEL'S PYRAMID

Machvel hobbled down the stairs. "I do not hold anyone hostage, little Goodspeed. I have made no demands of Earth. I don't expect them to do anything. I only expect them to die."

Machvel met Visalia in the center of the chamber. He kept his eyes on Zack, as he told his compatriots, "Start the countdown."

"No!" Zack shouted, twisting against his restraints.

"Don't worry, young one," said Machvel, again limping up the stairs toward him. "You won't live long enough to concern yourself about this. Once life on Earth is obliterated, I'll have you tossed from an airlock and then I'll finish off your pathetic friends. Not one of you has a place in our new world. I don't want your grandfather's tainted ideas infecting our dream. Plus, I owe you one for the injury your friend, Commander Chase, gave me." Machvel tapping his cane against his leg. "His bullet will be a reminder to me of some people's misguided loyalty to that old man."

The platform Zack was strapped to spun around so he could see through the opposite window-wall. Zack was stunned to see the shining sapphire of the Earth in the distance. Machvel stepped next to him.

"Beautiful, isn't it?" Machvel hissed. "The perfect new home world for the perfect new race."

A voice sounded throughout the chamber, "Commence final countdown. Engage booster engines. Onyx Sun set to 100 percent."

The rocket beyond the window started to shake as a pillar of blue fire shot from the tail. Moon dust kicked up like a storm in its wake. The rocket bucked against the restraints as hard as Zack did against his.

Dr. Machvel made a small hand gesture to Visalia, she pressed a button, and the rocket launched. It shot from the tower in a flash, spreading a plume of dust and blue fire in its wake. It arced into the black sky, and leaned toward Earth.

Zack strained against his straps, as Machvel whispered to him, "Relax, child. Enjoy the fireworks."

Zack stared terrified at the rocket streaking into the distance. He thought of his mother and father back on Earth. Today, like any other day, Mr. Goodspeed would be going to work at McKinley Bank & Trust and his mother would probably be substitute teaching. They would have breakfast like always. They would have dinner. They would have no idea what was about to happen until it was all over.

Suddenly, their daily routine didn't seem boring to Zack, but special. He thought how nice their kitchen was on sunny mornings. He remembered how funny it was that his father grunted as he read his paper. He thought about his mother's delicious blueberry pancakes. He thought about the way his parents smiled at him, in that proud, loving way only parents can.

All that was about to end, and it was only now when Zack appreciated it all. A normal life, in normal times, in a normal family was better than this. Zack realized he would happily trade his experiences on the Onyx Pioneer and return to his previous boredom to save his family. He would give anything to rescue them and the other innocent people on Earth.

Tears welled in his eyes, as he twisted and screamed in his restraints. Machvel looked indifferent, as he watched Zack struggle.

Zack stretched his body out, until his arms and legs screamed from pain, and yelled, "No!"

At that moment, the incredible happened. A thundering noise roared over the pyramid shaking the very ground. Machvel tipped back and fell down the stairs. Several of the glass window panes cracked. A colossal shape flew over them, like a dragon's shadow. It blocked out the light of the stars in the sky and the sphere of the Earth as it rocketed by. At the speed it was moving, Zack thought it would be beyond the pyramid at any moment, but its dark shape continued

CHAPTER 32: MACHVEL'S PYRAMID

to race by overhead. The yells of Machvel's crew inside the pyramid were blocked out by the rumbling of the surface and the scream of the engines.

Finally, the object whipped past, and Zack could get a clear view of it.

Mech 13.

"Hold on, Zack," said Angelina's voice over the pyramid's speakers.

Mech 13 thundered into the sky after the rocket. Entire mountains in the Moon flattened as it blew past them. Craters collapsed into themselves, and yet Mech 13 pressed on, building speed. Zack had never seen anything move so quickly. The Mech had to be going much faster than it was possibly built for.

The orange robot stretched into the sky, chasing the thin trail of rocket smoke. Zack could see the Mech shake as it stretched out its arms and extended its fingers toward the rocket. The rocket raced forward, just out of reach. Mech 13 pressed on harder. The frame of the robot was vibrating violently. The fingers of the Mech just touched the tail of the rocket, but the rocket slipped out of reach. The Mech managed to tip the rocket to the side, but it righted itself and thundered on.

The Mech crouched and stretched forward in a violent, last-ditch effort to grab the rocket. Its fingers reached around the tail. The rocket started to tip out of its grasp again, but Mech 13 twisted around just in time to wrap its hand around the tailfins. The Mech grabbed the missile firmly, and it slowed even though the rocket continued to spit flames.

The Mech spun toward the pyramid, grabbed the rocket in both hands, and snapped the fuselage like a twig.

The spinning Onyx Sun inside exploded from the broken fuselage like a blue bullet. It arced through the black sky, leaving a trail of blue flame in its path. It sailed over the pyramid, just past the walls of glass, and plummeted to the ground, shaking the surface like an earthquake. A geyser of Moon dust shot into the air and settled over the glass of the pyramid, blocking out the view on that side.

"Dr. Machvel!" Claus said from the monitor banks. "We have multiple targets moving toward us at high speed."

Machvel spun around. He fell against a computer panel, as he steadied himself with his other hand.

Earthquakes shuddered through the pyramid. Zack saw Mech 13 race back, land on the ground, and run toward Machvel's base. A squadron of thirty Airstriders roared by overhead. They flew in long arcs past Mech 13 then swooped around to fly in before it. Five of them darted into the launch silo left empty by the rocket.

An explosion shook the pyramid, as someone shouted, "The complex has been breached!"

Machvel looked around wildly. He glanced at Visalia and José. Visalia nodded to him silently, as José pressed a button on the console. A passageway appeared on the ground level of the complex and the three of them leapt toward it.

Before he escaped from sight, Machvel turned back to Zack and said, "This is not over, Goodspeed. Tell your grandfather that this war has just begun."

Then, he fled. The crew, sensing their leader's flight, escaped after him.

Moments later, Zack saw oval escape pods bursting from the soil of the Moon. It was like watching raindrops upside down.

Just then, a cadre of Security Team members, led by Grandfather Goodspeed, poured into the room. Grandfather leapt up the stairs toward Zack, lurching erratically into several computer banks as he did so.

"Oh thank goodness!" he said. "Thank the heavens you are alive."

CHAPTER 32: MACHVEL'S PYRAMID

He simultaneously hugged Zack and helped him out of his restraints. Then, casting a look around the pyramid, he said, "This is not good. Let's get out of here. This pyramid is about to collapse."

Zack looked at the ceiling. The fissures in the glass from Mech 13's flyover were widening, and Zack now noticed the sharp tinkling sound of cracking glass.

Zack and Grandfather raced from the top level of the pyramid, down to the center and out the hallway. The team followed them. The passageway twisted around several times as they ran. Grandfather led them to a wide airlock that separated the base from the missile silo. Five white-and-gold Airstriders sat there, side by side. Zack couldn't even comment on the excellent parking job before Grandfather pulled him inside one of the ships. The moment they closed the dome of their Airstrider, a sharp crack sounded from the hallway and the air rushed from the room. It pulled the ships forward firmly.

Grandfather tried to turn the ship around, but the rush of air from the depressurizing pyramid was too powerful.

"Follow me!" he shouted over his headset. "We're going to have to go this way!"

Grandfather raced the Airstrider forward into the hallway through which they had just run. He ricocheted off several walls, but managed to keep the craft hurtling onward. They took a hard right turn at one bend, and an Airstrider following them crashed into the wall in a fireball. The other three aircraft made the turn and flew through the flames.

Suddenly, Zack and Grandfather's ship shot into the central pyramid chamber, like a bullet sucked through the barrel of a gun. Grandfather struggled to lift the nose of the Airstrider. Zack could see a hole on the far wall venting air.

"Grandfather, you are going to miss the hole!" Zack called.

"I can't turn the ship," Fyodor grunted. "I don't think we're going through *that* hole. Kalamazoo!"

Zack pressed himself into his seat, turned his head, and squinted. The Airstrider raced toward the wall and a tiny square of glass between thick metal scaffolding.

✳ ✳ ✳

From the outside, Angelina sat next to Commander Chase in the hulking form of Mech 13. She stared attentively at the tiny, black pyramid. A hole in it was venting a thin trail of air. She wondered where the Airstriders were. They had gone in a long time ago. She began to worry that in their hurry to catch the rocket, Commander Chase had flown too close to the pyramid and caused this catastrophe. She fretted about how she would feel if anyone died, especially Zack or his grandfather.

Angelina looked at the flight suit she wore. Her helmet sat nearby. Then, she looked at Commander Chase, who just sat in the pilot's seat watching the pyramid like a chiseled statue.

She thought about asking him if she could go outside to help, but as she opened her mouth to do so, an Airstrider suddenly punched through the pyramid's glass wall and shot over Mech 13's shoulder. Seconds later, another punched through a different part of the wall and raced between the Mech's knees. Two more, following each other, made a third hole, and Commander Chase just managed to lurch the Mech aside as they raced past.

Angelina heard the exhilarated scream of Zack over her headset, "Wa-hooooo!" as Mech 13 spun and fell to its knees. Tears streamed down her face as she watched the sparkling atom fires of four Onyx Airstriders racing into the distance.

CHAPTER 33

Goodbyes

Back on the Onyx Pioneer, Grandfather landed the Airstrider on the wide expanse of Deck 15. As Zack climbed out of the ship, he was leapt upon by a large crowd. Sanjay pressed through the crowd and threw his arms around Zack, his head planted firmly on Zack's shoulder.

"Oh, thank goodness you are alive, Zack Goodspeed," said Sanjay, squeezing him tighter. "I thought I might never see you again."

"I wasn't sure I'd see anyone again either, but I'm ok," Zack said, squirming out of Sanjay's grasp. Holding Sanjay back at a safe distance, Zack gave him an appreciative pat on the shoulder.

"What do you mean?" asked Sanjay.

Grandfather stepped up to them and said, "Machvel invented a bomb to wipe out all life on Earth."

The crowd fell silent. Zack looked at his grandfather, and Fy nodded back.

"I saw what flew out of the rocket when it split open. I should have known. In my excitement the last few years, I let myself forget all great powers can be exploited. A weaponized Onyx Sun should have been obvious to me. How could I have been so careless?"

Zack put one arm around Grandfather's back and said, "You couldn't have imagined what Machvel was planning. It wasn't your fault."

"No, maybe it wasn't my fault, but it was my responsibility," said Grandfather. "Things are going to be different around here. Security will be tightened. Machvel will never get his hands on the Onyx Sun again."

"Speaking of, where is Dr. Machvel?" Sanjay asked.

"Who knows?" Grandfather said. "Gone. For now. But he'll return. And when he does we will be ready, this time. You were right, Zack. From the start, you were right. Machvel is our greatest concern."

Grandfather was interrupted as the blaring siren of the airlock sounded and the yellow alert lights spun to life. The inner airlock roared open and Mech 13 lumbered into the corridor. The room shook and even the Airstriders skidded along the floor as the Mech stomped to a stop in front of the crowd. It opened one massive hand. In it was the original Onyx Sun. Mech 13 placed it on the ground before the crowd. People cheered. Zack's fingers and toes tingled as he felt the energy sparking from the cube.

The Mech whirred down, as Angelina jumped out of the robot with Commander Chase behind her. They rode the elevator down the side of the robot. The crowd erupted into cheers again and Commander Chase and Angelina were also leapt upon as they reached the deck.

Zack and Sanjay ran to her. She pressed through the crowd and met Zack in the middle of the corridor. She jumped into Zack's arms and they spun around, hugging. Sanjay danced around them, clapping them both on the back.

CHAPTER 33: GOODBYES

"I was so worried you wouldn't make it," she said.

"How did you find me?" Zack asked.

"When you disappeared, your grandfather flipped out," she said. "He deployed the entire Airstrider fleet to find you."

"He did?" Zack asked. He looked back at the crowd and saw Grandfather shaking hands and laughing with droves of team members.

"Yeah. He did," Angelina said. "But it wasn't until we captured Greg Hunter that we knew roughly where to search. Your grandfather interrogated him personally. It was only a matter of time then until we found Machvel's pyramid on the front side of the Moon. Zack, I'm not sure that old man could live without you."

Zack just smiled back. He let himself soak in her words. He let go of his anger toward his grandfather and just took in the moment. Here he was on the Moon, in a spaceship powered by an infinite energy source his grandfather had invented. And suddenly, it was ok his grandfather had gone missing so many times in the past. Zack realized now he had always brought back more than he had taken.

Several weeks later, Grandfather's suite buzzed with activity. The chamber looked like an art gallery opening. People, dressed in freshly pressed uniforms, milled around Grandfather's onyx-colored suite, laughing and patting each other on the back. Grandfather wandered about, towering over his guests, leaning on people a little more than usual with one hand while he held a cocktail glass in the other. People roared in laughter at the things he said as he awkwardly mimed stories of Machvel's escape.

Zack, Angelina, and Sanjay sat on the floating couches on the top floor, overlooking the party. They watched the partygoers while eying a closet on the far side of the room.

"Think it will hold?" Zack asked.

"Don't worry," Angelina said, but they both heard the door moaning with the weight of the papers stashed behind it.

"Well, we had to put them somewhere," Sanjay said.

They all laughed. Zack leaned back on the couch. The cushions sank toward the floor then rose as they adjusted to the shift in his weight.

"So, now what?" Sanjay asked.

Angelina looked at Zack with a half-smile and glistening eyes. It seemed that Sanjay had said what they had been thinking all evening.

"Well, Grandfather will be taking Max and me back to Earth tomorrow," Zack said.

"Just in time for school. Lucky you," said Sanjay with a wink.

"I thought you liked school?" Zack said.

"I did. But now I prefer memo-files," Sanjay said. "Especially after you saved us all with that lesson on bomb defusing."

"Yeah, me too. Except every time I walk into the library now, the visor threatens to flunk me if I don't sit down and take the test," Zack said.

They both laughed, but Zack noticed Angelina didn't.

"Max? What the matter?" he asked.

"Zack, I'm not going back."

"What?" he said. "How can you not be coming back? What about your foster parents?"

Angelina looked down at the floor again and said, "Zack, I have bounced around from foster home to foster home for years. I've never found a place where I really feel at home — except here."

Zack caught a glimpse of Commander Chase in the crowd peering at them. He watched Angelina with fatherly concern. He waved to Zack.

"I think I understand," said Zack. "Commander Chase is a good man and will take good care of you. He misses his own family on Earth. So, I guess you two can keep each other company."

CHAPTER 33: GOODBYES

"He's a good person, but that is only part of it," Angelina said. "I belong up here. I want to spend everyday here, for the rest of my life, learning more about life *off* Earth. Our planet is only a tiny piece of a much, much larger mystery. There is so much out there we've never seen or done. Stars we've never visited. Planets we've never stepped on. Maybe even other cultures we've never met."

Zack nodded and said, "I get it. If you want to stay, then stay. Just email me. And attach a memo-file once in a while so I can spend more time outside playing baseball."

Angelina and Sanjay laughed. Zack nudged Sanjay and said with a smile, "Take care of her, huh?"

"I think she'll be fine on her own, Zack Goodspeed. She might be taking care of me," said Sanjay.

"Everyone! May I have your attention please?" Grandfather's voice boomed throughout the suite. He stood at the prow of the chamber, surrounded by the tall windows of his room that had been ceremoniously covered in red velvet. Holograms of the crowds assembled in the rest of the ship surrounded him. Even the Entertainment Troupe's hologram seemed to settle down a little as he spoke. Grandfather waved his arms in the air as he tried to get everyone's attention. Behind him stood the golden statue of the angel taking flight. For a brief moment, Zack remarked how similar the statue and his grandfather looked. Zack caught Grandfather giving him the briefest of winks.

Then, Grandfather stepped forward and lowered his arms. He slowly looked at each and every guest. At last, he ended by quietly greeting and shaking the hands of the two men at his sides: Commander Chase and Dr. Soon.

"Everyone. Wow! What a ride we have been on," Grandfather said. A wave of appreciative laughter flowed from the crowd.

"All right," Grandfather said with a smile. "Maybe that was an understatement. But with all we've been through, it's hard for me to say things simply. We have flown to the Moon! We have faced a mortal enemy and conquered traitors in our own ranks. We have overcome near disaster. Yet, we're still here."

Grandfather spread his arms wide as if he was trying to hug the crowd around him.

"We started as ten thousand and lost a third of our crew. But I would rather stand here with you people, who are committed to our vision, than stand with a million who aren't. It is your dedication that has helped us survive. It is your optimism, patience, and perseverance that has helped us rebuild the ship, rid us of our enemy, and assemble humanity's first, permanent, extraterrestrial habitat."

A buzz of excitement raced through the chamber. People whispered to each other. Several people in the back of the crowd stood on tiptoe so they could see.

Grandfather pulled a remote from his pocket with a big red button on it. Zack was sure the button was labeled "Kalamazoo!". Grandfather said, as he pointed the remote into the air, "There is nothing that gives me greater pleasure than to present to you a monument — a symbol — of our next great step. Ladies and gentlemen, I give you — The Citadel Spire."

Grandfather thrust his hand into the air and pressed the button. Nothing happened.

Grandfather's arms went limp. He clicked the button several more times. He looked up at the crowd and shrugged.

Commander Chase leaned in and, extending a hand, patted the side of Grandfather's suit. He pulled another remote from Grandfather's jacket pocket.

"Perhaps this one?" Commander Chase said.

"Ah, yes. Why, of course," Grandfather mumbled as he put one remote back into his pocket and took the other from the Commander. Grandfather shot his arm into the air again and shouted, "The Citadel Spire!"

CHAPTER 33: GOODBYES

The red velvet curtains scrolled back from the prow of the chamber. As they pulled wide, Zack gasped at the sight beyond the windows. Where once only a dusty plain had existed, there now stood a gleaming white structure stretching miles in every direction. Five bladed towers rose from the surface, attached to wide hallways that met at the center, where a single larger tower shot towards the heavens. The entire base glimmered as its interior lights sparkled through a hundred thousand windows. Each of the five towers was capped with a golden spire. A squadron of thirty automated Airstriders, which Zack had heard Grandfather had developed especially for the occasion, buzzed by, flying in wide arcs between the towers. They looked like a flock of pigeons, dwarfed by the skyscraping towers around them.

Grandfather's chamber erupted into applause. Grandfather beamed back at the crowd and almost stumbled as he stepped aside to let people stand near the windows.

Everyone hugged and patted each other on the back. Commander Chase and Dr. Soon shook the hands of members from each of the six teams and introduced the leaders responsible for the success of the base. Sanjay stood and walked downstairs to join his father.

Zack looked at the scene of milling and cheering people standing before the largest structure he had ever known. He gazed at the horizon of the crater and the symphony of stars twinkling in the night sky. They too seemed to applaud the Citadel Spire. Zack turned to Angelina and said, "I understand why you want to stay, Max."

She squeezed his hand and said, "Maybe your grandfather will let you come back someday."

Zack just nodded and stared at the scene below them. Even if he couldn't come back, he thought, he was incredibly happy he had been able to see this. For now, he knew the people that called Grandfather a fake were wrong. Fyodor Confucius Goodspeed was the most incredible person Zack had ever known. He was brilliant and caring. He was a benefactor of all of humanity. He would lead them all into mankind's next great adventure.

Suddenly, as if a light bulb turned on, Zack Goodspeed realized he was actually quite proud to have an abnormal life.

✳ ✳ ✳

The next morning, after breakfast and some hurried goodbyes, Zack and Grandfather stepped onto the bridge of the Onyx Pioneer. The entire room had been perfectly reassembled. They stood in a crowd of a few hundred seats near the back of the room. Halfway toward the front, the room dipped down some stairs just like before the blast. The command center was a perfect replica with Commander Chase's captain's chair at the center, flanked by two smaller chairs at either side. In front of the chairs stood a bank of control panels. Behind them waited several banks of computer monitors for the rest of the crew. The ceiling was a wide dome of glass.

From this vantage point, Zack could see the Citadel in front of them and the last Airstriders ferrying passengers and supplies from the Onyx Pioneer to their new, permanent home on the Moon. He also saw a pack of thirty Mech Leviathans plodding around the base already updating the station. After Commander Chase had recovered the original cube from the ruins of Machvel's base, Grandfather had managed to separate the smaller Onyx Suns and reinstall them in the robots.

"I'm going to miss this place," Zack said as they walked toward the front of the bridge.

"Well, you know, you may be able to come back someday," Grandfather said.

Zack shot him an excited smile and grabbed his arm. "Really?" he said.

CHAPTER 33: GOODBYES

"Well, yes, I think maybe," said Grandfather. "It is a nice coincidence your adventure fit almost perfectly into your summer vacation. Maybe next summer you can come back."

"Really? How?" Zack asked.

Grandfather smiled down at him, his eyes gleaming behind his cracked spectacles. "Well, I don't know for certain. But I'm sure I'll figure something out. Rumor has it I'm some kind of smart guy."

Grandfather winked at him as they took their seats in front of the control panels. Zack looked around at the complex, glowing controls, then back at the empty bridge.

"Grandfather, are you sure you can fly this alone?" Zack asked.

Grandfather smiled down at him again, "You know, I did invent this thing, Zack. Plus, with all those heavy Mechs finally off my ship, it will be like piloting an Airstrider."

Grandfather put on a wireless headset and handed one to Zack.

"Citadel Spire, this is the Onyx Pioneer awaiting launch clearance," Grandfather said into the headset.

A tinny voice came from the headset, "Roger, Onyx Pioneer you are cleared for take-off. Please enter launch code."

Grandfather pulled a small envelope from his suit and tore it open. Now that he was nearby, Zack could see a series of numbers printed on the slip of paper inside. A blue holo-panel appeared in front of Grandfather, and he quickly tapped the numbers on the paper onto the hologram. Zack heard the exterior airlocks sealing. The engines whirred to life and a shudder vibrated through the ship.

"Roger, launch code accepted," said the voice on the headset. "Good luck and Godspeed."

The hum grew in intensity as the Onyx Pioneer lifted from the surface. A plume of dust rolled from under the ship as the atomic repulsion engines titled the ship skywards. The Onyx Pioneer turned.

The Citadel Spire rolled out of sight as the edge of the Aitken Crater appeared. Grandfather lifted the ship over the ridgeline and accelerated. The Onyx Pioneer shot upward. Zack was pressed back into his seat and the familiar feeling of heaviness returned. The ship whisked over the waves of the lunar surface, as they flew toward the side of the Moon always facing the Earth.

Zack saw the faint outline of a broken, black pyramid coming into view, and as they whipped by, just above it, Zack saw fractured glass shatter more and fall into the structure.

Grandfather gave Zack a devilish grin and said, "Whoops. I guess that was too close."

Zack laughed. Grandfather pointed forward and Zack looked just in time to see the Earth appear over the horizon. From this distance, it looked like a blue marble in a sea of oil. Had he been born on the Moon, Zack would have thought the Earth was several times smaller than the Moon, but he knew it was only really far away.

The Onyx Pioneer accelerated and tore away from the Moon's gravity. Once in space, Zack was again amazed by the brightness of the trillions of stars crowding the sky.

Grandfather caught him staring out the ceiling window and said, "Lots of new adventures out there."

Zack looked back at his grandfather and said, "You will wait for when I come back, won't you?"

Grandfather chuckled and ruffled Zack's blond hair. "My boy," he said, "there will be plenty of new adventures out there for every person on Earth. We'll leave something for you. Plus, I doubt we'll get much beyond finishing the inside of the Citadel Spire in the next year. Even with the construction bots I am bringing online, we still have to build most of the interior. It is just a hollow shell right now."

"Construction bots?" Zack inquired.

CHAPTER 33: GOODBYES

"Yes! A new toy I started developing in my spare time," Grandfather said.

"When was that, exactly?" Zack asked surprised.

Grandfather reared back and let out a belly laugh, "Yeah, I guess I've been busy in the last few years, huh? Well, I had a few spare moments here and there to build the bots. Basically, they are mini-Mechs. You'll see sometime. Maybe next summer."

"Wicked," Zack said, borrowing Angelina's word.

The Earth grew larger in the viewscreen. Zack let a few hours pass in silence as he stared into space. Then, he turned to his grandfather, who looked lost in thought.

"Grandfather, there's one thing I don't get."

"Yes?"

"If all we had to do to find Machvel's agents was access the voice files, why didn't you just do it?"

"I was wondering when you would ask that," Grandfather said. He tapped the control panels, and a soft voice said, "Auto pilot engaged." Fyodor turned toward Zack. Zack was surprised to see him furrow his brow as a shadow fell over his face.

"Zack, I am being followed."

"What?"

"Yes, I am afraid so. I fear Machvel's agents have not all been removed from my crew. I am quite certain my every move is being followed."

"Why don't you just have Commander Chase arrest them?"

"I would, only I can't. I don't know who they are. I turn around and I catch shadows disappearing down side hallways. I see cameras in the ship following my every move. I found a monitor in the Clandestine Room dedicated to watching my suite."

"But I thought we uncovered all of Machvel's agents," Zack said.

"I had hoped so, too," Grandfather said, looking down. He rubbed a thumb on the inside of his palm. "I think your efforts helped, but we are far from knowing the extent of his treachery. We'll be dealing with Dr. Machvel for some time after you leave, I'm afraid."

Zack was shocked. He felt like his efforts had been in vain. He wanted to tell his grandfather to not go back to the Citadel Spire, but he knew it would be useless. He knew Fyodor would never abandon his crew who were still loyal to him.

"Be safe, please," Zack said. "I want to see you again."

Grandfather smiled. He put a hand on Zack's cheek and said, "I will, my boy. I would never let anyone take me from you."

There was something in the way Grandfather said this that Zack didn't believe. It was like Grandfather was…unsure, Zack thought. Zack remembered Machvel mentioning in the library that Grandfather had indebted himself to the government. Machvel hadn't said which government or what they wanted from him. For a second, Zack considered asking him, but he couldn't bring himself to do it. He didn't feel ready for the truth behind all of Grandfather's secrets.

A control panel beeped. Grandfather turned to it.

"Hold on," he said. "Re-entry."

The Earth lay in front of them now like a wide dish. Zack could see nothing but the vast expanse of blue oceans, rocky coastlines, and white, swirling clouds. Suddenly, it hit him that his months on the Moon — with its black skies and gray surface — would soon to be replaced by blue skies and grassy fields. His stomach flipped in excitement, even though he yearned to be back on the Citadel Spire. He looked behind him and saw a thin black slice of starry sky in the bridge dome. The Onyx Pioneer dipped into re-entry, and the slice slipped out of view, replaced entirely by the blue planet they were rushing toward.

The ship quaked as it plummeted toward the Earth. Fire shot up around them as they broke through the atmosphere, but the Onyx

CHAPTER 33: GOODBYES

Pioneer's streamlined shape quickly slipped through the barrier. The shaking stopped and the ship floated down like a silent missile. The Earth rose up at them quickly and just as Zack thought they were going to plummet into the ocean, Grandfather tapped a button and the ship leveled out. They whipped across the wavy surface of the blue seas, only feet above the highest crests. This sent squalls of sea mist into the air as they passed. They flew over a small fishing vessel and Zack waved. He didn't have enough time to see Reginald Flank diving into his cabin and hiding his head under some life jackets.

The thin line of a golden brown coast came into view on the horizon. The Onyx Pioneer lifted a little and shot over the cliffs. Sea lions barked at them as they whipped over in a silent rush of wind.

"Isn't anyone going to see us?" Zack asked.

"We're moving too fast for anyone to see what we are," said Grandfather. "Plus, most normal people wouldn't believe it even if they did see us."

Zack smiled at this and said, "How true."

Houses began to dot the hills they flew over. They crested a ridgeline, and a valley of suburbs appeared beyond. Grandfather pressed some buttons on the panel and the ship dipped toward Zack's neighborhood.

Zack looked around him, as if he were on another planet. It had been so long since he had been on Earth that the bright sun, crowded neighborhoods, and congested highways all seemed new to him. He admired cars sitting in driveways as if they were alien visitors.

The Onyx Pioneer approached a wide park. Grandfather found a field in the center and lowered the ship. It cast a shadow over the entire park.

"The field's not big enough for me to land," Grandfather said. "You're going to have to jump out the airlock."

"What?" Zack asked in surprise.

"I'm kidding," Grandfather said. "Actually, I'll lower you using the air-a-vator."

"What's that?"

Grandfather looked at him, his eyes wide, "Well, it seems I still have some inventions you haven't seen, mmm? It is a shaft of air that I can control to slowly lower you to the surface. It uses atoms charged by the Onyx Sun. Kind of like an elevator."

Zack's face whitened at the mention of an elevator. Grandfather noticed this and looked concerned. Then, Zack remembered the things he had been through — and survived — the last three months. He swallowed his fear, and said, in a weak voice, "Wicked."

"Zack, I'm sorry. I forgot," Grandfather said. "If there was any other way —"

Zack just looked at his grandfather levelly and said, "No. Don't be sorry. It is all right. I'm…looking forward to it."

Grandfather smiled proudly and hugged Zack. As they let go, Grandfather rummaged in his pocket and produced a black remote, with a big, red "Kalamazoo" button on it. He gave it to Zack.

"If you ever need me, call me," Grandfather said. "I'll come anytime, night or day."

Zack looked at the remote doubtfully. "Are you sure this is the right one?" he asked.

"Scout's honor, it is," said Grandfather holding one hand over his heart and another in the air. "Commander Chase helped me test it and then I removed all the other objects from my suit before I put that one in."

"That must have made quite a mess," Zack said.

"Yes," said Grandfather. "Dr. Soon was still cursing it when I left the Engineering Core."

They both laughed and hugged again. Then, Grandfather led Zack to a small room on Deck 15. The room was fairly featureless. It

CHAPTER 33: GOODBYES

had only a podium on one side and a circular indentation in the floor near the center. Grandfather walked toward the podium and pressed some buttons. The indentation slid open and Zack could see the grass of the field far below.

"All right. Step in the hole, my boy," Grandfather said.

"What?" Zack exclaimed. "I thought you said it was an elevator. That is just a hole!"

Grandfather leaned toward the hole, from behind the podium and looked at it. "No. That's an air-a-vator," he said. "The charged air will hold you up. It kinda feels like being in a big hairdryer."

Zack hesitated. He looked at the hole. The grass had to be at least a few hundred feet below them. Zack doubted he could fall from this distance and escape with less than two broken legs and a seriously shortened stature. His heart began to race. His palms sweated. He began to feel dizzy.

Then, a sudden calm came over him. He thought about all the harrowing moments he had been through and how he had not only survived them, but once he was over the fear, he had been proud of his accomplishment. The Spinning Shaft. The Burning Beams. The Dastardly Death. Sneaking onboard the Onyx Pioneer. Traveling to the Moon. Falling through the vents. Piloting a Mech. Defusing the bomb. Saving the Earth. Escaping Dr. Machvel. Seeing the completed Citadel Spire.

Zack looked down at the hole, again. This was just another challenge he would face, but this time, he would do it unafraid. He took a deep breath, closed his eyes, lifted one leg into the air, and stepped into the hole.

He had expected to fall. Even with Grandfather's reassurances, he had been certain he would slip right through the hole and end up with a grassy mouthful of earth. But he didn't fall. In fact, he felt like he was standing on solid ground.

Zack opened his eyes. He was standing right in the center of the hole. All he could see under him were his legs in open space above the field far below. Wind whipped up at him. His wavy, blond hair flew around his head and licked at his face. The wind flapped his shirt wildly and his pants puffed out.

He was standing on nothing but a pillar of fast moving air. He looked at his grandfather. Fyodor Confucius Goodspeed just beamed back at Zack. A wide smile lit up his face, and Zack could again see the little boy inside his grandfather.

"Some people say there is no fear, but fear itself," Grandfather said. "Now you have learned that's not true. There is no fear, if you choose no fear."

Grandfather pressed a button on the panel and the shaft of air began to rush up at Zack slightly less wildly. Zack could feel himself slowly descending. He slipped through the hole and as he came to be eye-level with the deck, he saw Grandfather slowly raise a single hand and wave at him. In his white suit, Grandfather looked like a marble statue of some hero saying goodbye.

Zack floated through the hole. He stood in the open air under the ship but felt completely steady. Above him he could see the massive, gold underside of the Onyx Pioneer. The gold hull reflected the trees and field below it. On all sides, Zack could see the neighborhood surrounding the park. And below him, he saw the ground slowly approaching.

He touched down gently on the grass. The pillar of air stopped whipping around him and dissipated in the light breeze of the park. Zack looked up. He hoped to see Grandfather's friendly face appear and smile at him one last time, but the hole unceremoniously closed without any sign from Grandfather. The ship hovered there for a minute. Then, the engines of the Onyx Pioneer hummed more loudly. The ship

CHAPTER 33: GOODBYES

lifted into the air. Zack felt the sunshine hit his face as the ship drifted away. Then, as it edged upwards, the engines whirred to life, and the Onyx Pioneer blasted out of sight. It left in a rush of wind that swayed the treetops and rustled the leaves, as if they were cheering.

CHAPTER 34

Homecoming

Zack had a decent walk in front of him before he got home, but he waited to see if he could spy the Onyx Pioneer racing skyward. He saw nothing beyond the sun, grass, and blue skies of a perfect day. He heard only the chirping of birds. No whirring of engines. No crash of thunder as the ship broke into the upper atmosphere.

Zack turned and started his walk. He walked under the trees and through the fields. He marveled at the greenness of everything. As much as he had enjoyed his trip, it was here that he felt truly at home. Earth, he now realized, really was a jewel planet. The Moon, while exciting, had none of Earth's gentle winds, warm sun, and gorgeous skies. The Moon was largely gray, and even though it was covered with the spotlights of billions of stars, Earth was home.

CHAPTER 34: HOMECOMING

He walked through a small forest and came across a baseball field. Three boys were playing ball, and Zack walked by them to watch. It was only when he was within ten feet of the boys Zack realized his mistake.

"Hey! Badspeed!" Tom Riley called, from his position on home plate.

Zack didn't stop. Jeff and Peter Otis snickered, as they caught up to Zack and pushed him back toward Riley. Tom Riley poked Zack in the chest with the baseball bat he was holding.

"Where have you been all summer, Badspeed?" Riley asked.

Zack looked up at the boy he had once feared so much.

"What difference does it make to you?" he said. He straightened his back and tried to seem as tall as the bigger boy.

The Otis brothers whistled. Tom stepped close to Zack, while he beat the bat against the palm of his hand.

"Will you check this out," Riley said to the other boys. "Badspeed went and got himself an attitude this summer."

Tom Riley walked so close to him, Zack could smell his bad breath. Riley said, "You'd better pray you were at kickboxing camp all summer, because I am going to mess you up."

"Go ahead," said Zack with more confidence than he really felt. "Try it."

Tom Riley pushed Zack. Zack tumbled backward. The Otis brothers split apart so Zack fell right between them. Zack hit the ground hard. The dirt of the baseball field shot into the air around him and landed in his mouth and eyes. Zack fumbled in his pocket, as he coughed and rubbed his eyes with his other hand.

Tom Riley stepped forward with Jeff and Peter flanking him. Tom Riley held the baseball bat limply in one hand as he pointed down at Zack and said, "You need an attitude adjustment Badspeed, and — as it happens — we are offering a special on those today."

The Otis brothers snickered and said stupidly, "Yeah, attitude adjustments. We offer those."

"Shut up, you two," Riley said, pressing them both back with his baseball bat. "I am going to knock his attitude out of the park."

Tom Riley grabbed the baseball bat with both hands and wound it back. He stepped toward Zack. Zack tried to scramble away, but Tom stepped on one of his legs. Zack yelled in pain. Tom Riley wound back, as he stepped over him.

Just then, a large shadow overtook them. Zack saw Jeff Otis tap Riley on the shoulder and say timidly, "Uh, Tom."

"What?" Riley shot back, but the Otis brothers were just pointing and staring at something behind Zack.

Tom Riley looked up and his face went white. The baseball bat fell from his hands and he stumbled back. Zack jumped to his feet and whirled around.

The hulking wedge of the Onyx Pioneer dominated the landscape behind him. It floated just above the grass and sent massive plumes of wind into the air from its engines. The trees around the park waved like an angry mob. The bullies stumbled backward, but the ship edged forward aggressively. Tom Riley tripped and fell.

Jeff and Peter Otis took off. Tom Riley scrambled to his feet, running after them, and screamed, "Wait for me, guys!"

"That'll show you, Riley!" shouted Zack after them. "And don't forget you still owe me a baseball!"

Without turning around or slowing his sprint, Jeff Otis threw the baseball they were using over his shoulder. The ball rolled to Zack's feet. He bent over and picked it up. On the side of the ball, written in black marker, was the word "Goodspeed." Zack immediately recognized it as the ball they had stolen from him.

Zack spun around. The gigantic ship moved back enough and slid to the side so Zack could see the small figure of Grandfather on

CHAPTER 34: HOMECOMING

the bridge. Zack held up the ball in one hand and the remote he had used to signal the Onyx Pioneer in the other. Grandfather laughed and gave him the thumbs up.

Then, the Onyx Pioneer turned for a second time and sped away. Even after it was gone, Zack could see the three bullies running through the park in the opposite direction and could hear Tom Riley screaming, "Wait for me! Wait for me!"

Zack arrived at his house around dinnertime. He lingered outside for a moment to look at the strange shape of his grandfather's empty house next door. Without Grandfather there, the house looked empty and cold. Zack wondered for a second how long it would be until he saw the lights of Grandfather's house on again and his warm voice calling Zack to join him in the Labradory.

Then, Zack opened the front door of his house and stepped inside.

Mr. and Mrs. Goodspeed sat at the kitchen table when he walked in. They had never looked so abnormal. They both seemed to have aged twenty years. Mr. Goodspeed stared at the folded newspaper on the table in front of him but was not reading it. His hair was askew, and he looked like he hadn't showered in weeks. Mrs. Goodspeed stood, her hands on the countertop, as if she needed the support. When Zack walked in, it took her a moment to turn and face him. Mr. Goodspeed looked up as well. They both just stared at him, as if they were zombies who could not register what was occurring.

Then, Mrs. Goodspeed's hands shot into the air and she screamed. She rushed over to Zack and fell to her knees, as she hugged him. She sobbed onto his shirt and hugged him so tightly Zack thought his eyeballs might pop out. Mr. Goodspeed bolted from the table as well and crossed the kitchen in two steps. He wrapped his arms around

Zack, while he repeated, "My boy! My boy!" He grunted repeatedly, but Zack saw this time it was in a vain attempt to hold back the tears already streaming down his face.

Finally, after Zack felt like a wet rag, they released him enough so Mrs. Goodspeed could ask, "Where have you been?"

Zack looked into her puffy face. He smiled and as gently as possible said, "Mom, you'd better sit down."

Zack's parents both looked like zombies again as they sat around the kitchen table. But this time, they stared at Zack like they could believe he was here, but they could not believe what he had just said.

Finally, Mr. Goodspeed cleared his throat, grunted, and said, "You expect us to believe that?"

Zack nodded.

Mr. Goodspeed pushed himself back from the table and looked at the ceiling. "Zack that is the most incredible story I have ever heard. It is impossible. What really happened? Were you kidnapped? Were you brainwashed?"

"No, dad," Zack said calmly. "I was on the Moon. I know it sounds ridiculous, but that is where I was."

Mr. Goodspeed's fist slammed into the table. The newspaper slid off and hit the floor. "I refuse to hear that, Zachary Atticus Goodspeed! There is no such thing as space travel, bases on the far side of the Moon, or this Onyx Star you keep talking about."

"Onyx Sun, Dad."

"Whatever!" Mr. Goodspeed said slamming his fist down again. He looked at his wife. Mrs. Goodspeed just held a single hand to her mouth and stared at Zack. She looked like she was debating something in her mind.

CHAPTER 34: HOMECOMING

"This is what we get for letting you hang out with your grandfather," Mr. Goodspeed said. "Jen, do you have *anything* to say to this?"

Mrs. Goodspeed just stared at Zack, so Mr. Goodspeed repeated, "Jen?"

She shook herself from her thoughts. She blinked several times as if emerging from a dream.

"Huh? Uh, oh. No. I don't have anything to say."

"Do you believe this *ridiculous* story?" Mr. Goodspeed said.

Mrs. Goodspeed stared at Zack with eyes that looked like glass, then said in a faraway voice, "I'm not sure."

"I don't believe this!" Mr. Goodspeed said. He turned and stood. He paced back and forth across the kitchen. "Well, one thing is for sure: we're sending you to a psychologist to have your head checked out. No story this crazy could come from a Goodspeed!" His eyes darted out the window toward Grandfather's house. "Well, no Goodspeed under this roof at least!" he added.

"Jack," Mrs. Goodspeed said in a voice so faint it was almost a whisper, her eyes still on her son. "I'm not sure a psychologist is what Zack needs."

"What?" Mr. Goodspeed said, whirling toward his wife. "That's the only thing he needs right now. He needs some straightening out!"

"No," Mrs. Goodspeed said. "No, I am not sure that is the solution here. I think there is a story behind Zack's disappearance. Maybe not one he wants to tell us, yet, but a story nonetheless."

Mr. Goodspeed looked thunderstruck. Grunts emerged from his throat in rapid succession, until he finally said, "Well, one thing is for sure, you're grounded, young man. Go to you room right now. When you do finally tell us the truth, you'll be lucky if we ever let you out!"

Zack nodded slowly and stood up. He shuffled upstairs to his room but not before he heard the hushed voices of his parents debating his future.

Walking into his room was like an adventure. It felt like a strange land to him. As he closed his door behind him, he turned on some lights and looked around. He saw baseballs, posters, and a bed with fresh sheets on it. His room was ridiculously clean. The last thing Zack noticed, though, was the model of the Onyx Pioneer Grandfather had given him.

Zack walked over to it. It looked just like the real thing only infinitely smaller. Zack remembered all the times before his trip that he had looked at the model and marveled at it. It had always seemed to be a grand idea to Zack. Only now, the model looked small.

There came a quiet knock at his door. Mrs. Goodspeed poked her head in and asked, "Can I come in?"

"Sure," said Zack. He sat on the side of his bed, as Mrs. Goodspeed walked in and closed the door behind her. She walked over to Zack and smiled down at him. She brushed a wisp of blond hair out of his eyes. Mrs. Goodspeed was quiet and seemed far away.

Finally, she sat down next to Zack. "You know, your father used to be a lot more understanding when he was younger," she said. She looked absently at the far wall of Zack's room and laughed to herself. "I remember he used to do these crazy things. One time he actually rode a cow from Mr. Riley's farm into town. He was a nut. That was actually one of the reasons I fell in love with him."

Zack looked at his mother as she told him this. He could never imagine his father riding anything but his midsize SUV. Her eyes looked far away, but her face glowed. She smiled to herself. She looked young and pretty to Zack.

Mrs. Goodspeed saw Zack admiring her and put her arm around him. She hugged him as she rocked him back and forth. "I think it was only years later that your father lost that. I don't remember when it was exactly, but I remember he became more serious as we got older.

CHAPTER 34: HOMECOMING

He lost some of that boyishness. I think it had to do with the things people said about your grandfather."

Mrs. Goodspeed released Zack and looked at him, as she said, "People have always said mean things about your grandfather. I think people who do new things often get criticized by those who don't. Your dad used to not care, but as he started to look for jobs to pay for our new house and our new baby, he changed. Suddenly, he did care. I think he decided even though he loved his father, he would rather provide for us than deal with Grandfather's eccentric ways. It was a difficult choice, but he made it. For us. Do you understand that?"

Zack nodded and said, "Yes Mom."

Mrs. Goodspeed smiled and hugged him again, "Your grandfather — although strange — is a very smart and inventive man. I've had a lot of time to think about how important that is too. And I hope you don't ever make the decision your father did."

"I wouldn't," Zack said. "People are wrong. They have no idea what Grandfather is capable of."

"Is that why you invented this story?" Mrs. Goodspeed asked. "To prove to others how smart your grandfather is?"

"I didn't invent it, Mom. It's true."

"All right, honey," Mrs. Goodspeed said soothingly, rubbing his arm. "I'm just glad you're home safe."

"Me too," said Zack. "It feels good to be home."

Mrs. Goodspeed kissed him on the forehead and stood up. She walked towards the door but paused after opening it.

"I don't know where you have been this summer, Zachary Goodspeed," she said. "But if you really believe this story you told us, I would rather you grow up a wild dreamer, than just grow up."

"Thanks, Mom," Zack said.

Mrs. Goodspeed turned off Zack's lights and closed the door behind her. Zack climbed under his bed sheets. He pulled his comforter around his head and peeked out just enough to look through his bedroom window, where a full moon was rising over the horizon.

EPILOGUE

The Dawn of War

Angelina Maximillian still didn't feel comfortable inside the Citadel Spire. It had been almost nine months since Zack had left, but something about being on the lunar surface still felt strange.

"Maybe I'm just not used to the Moon yet," she laughed to herself, as she strode down a curved, white hallway interspersed with doors.

Her feet felt weird when they touched the floor. It wasn't like walking on the Earth. The Moon had one-sixth Earth's gravity. Even with the belt she wore that used small bursts of air to hold her down, walking here felt different. She was more bouncy than she should be. Each step lifted her higher in the air than it should. She felt like if she jumped suddenly, she might be able to touch the ceiling eight feet above.

"Maybe my gravity belt's broken," she thought. She knew one person who would know for sure: Sanjay.

Angelina turned around and walked to a bank of human-sized, glass shafts a few yards away. She pressed a button on the wall. She heard a rush of wind in the glass tube the furthest to the right.

The air-a-vators were Angelina's favorite part of the lunar colony. Although many people found them scary, Angelina loved that Professor Goodspeed had designed the Citadel Spire without normal elevators. Each time she rode in the shafts of wind controlled by ionic repulsion, she felt like she was on a rollercoaster on Earth. The only downside, she thought, was that they left her a little deaf and wind-blown afterwards. Still, it was worth it.

The wind in the right tube grew louder. Angelina stepped up to it. A couple of women from the Spiritual Conclave popped into the shaft. The glass door slid aside and they stepped onto Angelina's floor. Their blond hair covered their faces, and their robes wrapped around them like party streamers.

"Honestly, I don't know how Fy Goodspeed expects us to live like this," one of the women said, as she straightened her robes and pulled hair out of her mouth and eyes.

"I know," the other said. "Can't that man do anything *normally?*"

Angelina scoffed loud enough for the women to hear. One of the women shot her a poisonous look. Angelina returned the gesture. The women both looked taken aback and shuffled off down the hallway.

Angelina heard one of them say, "Wasn't that one of the cretins who helped that old fool defeat Dr. Machvel?"

Something about the way the woman said this bothered Angelina. The woman's tone wasn't like she was making small talk. It seemed accusatory, like Angelina had done something wrong. The way she said "Dr. Machvel" sounded like the woman respected him.

EPILOGUE: THE DAWN OF WAR

"Hey, you two! Who are you? What are your names?" Angelina called after them.

The women glanced back then took off running. Angelina chased after them. The women scurried into a nearby room, shutting the door behind them. Angelina pounded on the door, but it refused to open.

"Come back!" Angelina yelled.

"Computer, who were those women?" Angelina called into the air. There was no response.

"Computer?"

Angelina suddenly realized the voice-activated computer program, which helped the crew on the Onyx Pioneer, wasn't installed yet inside the Citadel Spire. Until this moment, Angelina hadn't really cared. She found the computer annoying since it listened to everything everyone said on the ship. However, she realized now how valuable it was. Without the computer, there was no way for Angelina to find out who those two women had been, nor could she open the door with the enhanced level of security access Commander Chase had given her.

Angelina pounded on the door once more. Then, she huffed and walked back to the air-a-vators, glancing behind her occasionally to see if the door opened. It didn't.

The shaft on the far right was still open and Angelina stepped into it. The now familiar sensation of weightlessness overtook her. For a second, she floated erratically in the empty shaft. Then, she felt herself straighten. It wasn't like standing on the solid floor of an elevator, but it was close.

The air-a-vator had six buttons on its inside, one for each team in the base. Angelina pressed the "Engineering Corps" button. The elevator shot up and Angelina felt her heart skip a beat in excitement. The shaft turned sharply and the air-a-vator flung Angelina sideways. Unlike the elevators on Earth, an air-a-vator could move in any direction. This was important because each of the six teams of the Citadel Spire were housed in different spires. The Citadel had five bladed towers on the outside for the Engineering Corps, Spiritual Conclave, Entertainment Troupe, SciTechs, and Security Team. The center and largest tower held the offices and residences of the Executive Order. This distributed organization required the air-a-vators to go in all directions so people could slide between towers quickly.

The shaft twisted her around, shot her left, then right, then up and down a bit. Finally, the wind slowed and a glass door popped into view. It slid aside, and Angelina stumbled out.

The Engineering Corps lobby she stepped into was massive. The room was easily a few hundred feet high and a few hundred feet wide. It was box-shaped and adorned on the far end with a large, golden gate. The gate looked like it was cut from pure gold. Around the edges were carvings of tools: hammers, axes, wrenches, and computers. In the center of the gate, high above the floor, a cube jutted out of the wall. On the front of the cube was the icon of a hand grabbing a lightening bolt.

Angelina walked across the wide lobby and through the gate. On the opposite side was a tall atrium of glass bounded by the bladed shape of the tower walls. Beyond the glass, Angelina could see the serene environment of the Moon's white surface, the distant rim of the Aitken Basin, and the black sky above.

Angelina walked across the atrium and came to a circle painted in the floor near the atrium window. There was a panel with hundreds of buttons just outside the circle. She pressed a button labeled "136". Wind began to whip around her in the circle. Her feet lifted off the floor, and she shot into the air. Windows streamed by in front of her, as floors did on her left. She arrived at a platform that had "136" painted on the end, and the wind slowed. She stepped off.

Angelina walked down the platform and through a doorway exiting the atrium. Floor 136 was a laboratory floor. It was covered in

EPILOGUE: THE DAWN OF WAR

white lab tables with engineers hunched over each. They fiddled with Bunsen Burners, built small devices, and rewired computers.

On the far end, Angelina saw Dr. Soon gliding between stations, inspecting each engineer's work. She picked her way among the tables, nearly having her arm set on fire more than once.

"Ah, Max!" Dr. Soon said. "How go things? How is your Security Team training these days?"

"Good, Dr. Soon. We're learning how to handle riot situations right now."

"A useful skill. You'd be surprised how necessary it is even in civilized cultures. What brings you up here?"

"I'm looking for Sanjay. Is he around?"

A small explosion rocked the lab. An engineer fell back from a table a few yards away as smoke rose from the Mech arm he had been fixing. The arm suddenly leapt up and tried to grab the people around it. When they scurried away, the arm hurled itself off the table and started pulling itself along the floor toward the nearest engineers.

"He's on lunch break," Dr. Soon yelled to Angelina as he ran off to help the other engineers. "I think he goes to the Rutan Café on Floor 2."

Dr. Soon leapt into the fray, grabbing a broom handle from a nearby table. He and the other engineers kicked and prodded the rogue robot arm until it was corralled against the wall. Angelina tried to help, but several engineers pushed her back. Unable to assist, she left to the crash of a lab table being overturned.

Angelina took the air-a-vator to Floor 2. Most of Floor 2 was restaurants, cafés, and social clubs. The Rutan Café was pressed against the far wall of the Engineering Corps tower. As she walked in, Angelina noticed few people were having lunch at this hour. It was easy to pick out Sanjay, sitting alone at a table near the window.

"You're just Mr. Popularity, aren't you?" Angelina said, walking up to Sanjay.

Sanjay put down the handheld computer he was using and smiled at her weakly. She'd expected him to laugh more at her joke, like he usually did. But something about Sanjay looked different. He looked exhausted.

"Hey, Max," he said slowly. "Yeah, I like to work on stuff over my lunch break. It's easier when other people aren't around. What are you doing here?"

"I've been feeling a little weird this morning, like something's off. I was thinking maybe my gravity belt isn't working because when I move around I feel strange."

"Hmm," Sanjay said. He held a hand to his mouth and suppressed a yawn. Then, he motioned for her to take off the belt. She did so and handed it to him. While Sanjay looked the belt over, she sat down since she now felt much too light to be standing up.

"I don't see anything wrong with it," he said. "But let's take it up to the lab and run some tests."

"Uh, I don't think you want to go up there right now. Minor emergency."

"What now?" Sanjay said while yawning again.

"Mech arm on the loose."

"Oh. That happens. All right. Let's see what I can do here."

Sanjay took several wires out of his handheld computer and plugged them into the gravity belt. Then, he pulled a multitool from his flight suit and unscrewed a panel on the side of the belt.

Angelina watched him as he worked. Usually when Sanjay worked on fixing things, he got a sparkle in his eyes and a small smile on his lips like he was enjoying himself. Now though, he just looked run-down.

"Not sleeping much these days?"

EPILOGUE: THE DAWN OF WAR

"I'm sleeping fine."

"They giving you too much work?"

"No more than usual."

"You look kinda tired," Angelina said.

"Yeah, I am. But you look a little out of it too."

"Yeah, I am," Angelina said. A thought occurred to her. "Maybe we just miss Zack."

"If we do, that's not going to be a problem for long," Sanjay said. "Professor Goodspeed told me yesterday he's bringing Zack Goodspeed back this summer."

"Are you serious?" Angelina said.

She hopped in her chair. In the Moon's gravity, this made her float higher than she'd expected. She grabbed onto the table, which was bolted to the floor, and held herself down. Angelina felt more excited than she had for months. As much as she enjoyed Sanjay's company, it wasn't the same without Zack. Zack and she had started this adventure together. It didn't seem right here without him.

"Yep. Professor Goodspeed said he is going to get Zack to join us in a week."

"Is he going to pick him up in the Onyx Pioneer? Do you think I can go?"

"I don't know. He didn't say much."

"Who is going to get him? Is Commander Chase going?"

"He didn't say," Sanjay said between yawns.

"Does Zack know?"

"I don't think so," Sanjay said. "We just got the inter-space communication relay working yesterday."

"Wicked. Let's go tell Zack!"

Angelina grabbed her belt from Sanjay, threw it on, grabbed his hand, and pulled him from the table. She knew each tower had a communication center in its atrium. So, she led him down to Floor

1 and across the chamber to the computer terminals on the far side. Sanjay showed her how to load the text messaging application and contact Zack. For a few minutes, Angelina didn't think it was going to work. Sanjay had to fiddle with some wires under the terminal. She tried typing messages to Zack several times. Then suddenly, a message appeared on her screen from "Zack G".

"Who is this?"

"I'm going to make him guess," she said to Sanjay. "Get on the other terminal so you can chat too."

Sanjay loaded up the terminal next to her. Just as his computer bleeped on, Angelina found herself giggling.

"He's guessed it's me. Say 'hello'."

Angelina saw a line from Sanjay in the text chat. She wanted to say so much to Zack. She wanted to tell him what the Citadel Tower was like, how the crew had changed, and what she had learned from Commander Chase about Mechs. She also knew he would want to know how his grandfather was doing, but since Angelina hadn't seen the Professor much, she didn't know what to report.

Mechs are the most fun, she thought. I'll tell him about that.

She only managed to get a few lines of conversation in with him though before gibberish started appearing on her screen. Sanjay crawled under the terminals again.

"I've lost the signal," he said.

"Really?" Angelina said. She felt like a friend had just left town. She hadn't realized how much she had missed Zack. It had felt so natural talking with him, and suddenly her all-day funk seemed a little more bearable.

"Yeah, sorry Max," Sanjay said. "This stuff is still really finicky. I have to get back to the lab now."

"I know," Angelina said. "I should get back too. Thanks for trying."

EPILOGUE: THE DAWN OF WAR

Sanjay walked to the air-a-vator, as Angelina walked back through the main gate. She kept wondering if she really did feel better. She was excited she had gotten to talk with Zack, but something was still tugging at her. She felt a little dizzy and her stomach was gurgling. She looked at the belt. In her hurry to get to the terminals, she had pulled the belt from Sanjay before he'd finished working on it. Two panels lay open and wires dangled from the inside.

Great, it's probably even more broken now, she thought.

She took the main air-a-vators back to the Security Team tower. Like the Engineering Corps, her team had a gilded gate, only the Security Team's was plain. She walked under the gate to the atrium, then rode the air-a-vator to the Ness Restaurant on Floor 2. Being in the Rutan Café had made her hungry.

Most of the Security Team ate a little later since no one wanted to leave the security monitors until the last possible moment. So, maybe there would be someone in the restaurant to talk to about the way she was feeling.

Walking in, she grabbed a tray, lost in her own thoughts. She turned the corner to where the food servers were and stopped. Her heart leapt into her throat. She dropped her tray. How was this possible? All around the restaurant people lay on the floor. Hundreds of Security Team members sprawled around the room, not moving. People, who must have been in line waiting for their food, were piled on top of each other as if they had fallen where they stood. Angelina ran to where the servers gave people their food. She vaulted the countertop so she could see into the kitchen. Even the chefs were passed out on the floor. A bowl lay next to one of them, lettuce spilling from its side.

Angelina rolled over the counter and ran up to one of the servers. He wasn't dead, but he looked like he was in a deep sleep. She shook him. Nothing. She patted his face lightly. Nothing. She smacked him. The chef didn't even blink. He seemed like he was in a coma.

Angelina was terrified. She jumped back over the counter, ran to the air-a-vator, and took it to the top: Floor 200. The pinnacle of each tower was the command center for that team. For the Security Team, the top floor housed the new Clandestine Room where the most senior members of the group could monitor the entire base. Angelina didn't normally have access to this room, but she had to try to warn someone.

The air-a-vator whirred to a stop, and she leapt off it. She ran to the black door at the end of the platform and banged on it.

"Open up!" she screamed. "Something's going on! I need help."

She pounded on the door. Surely, they had to open up. She whirled around until she found the camera by the door. She jumped up and down, waving her hands in the air and yelling.

"Let me in! It's an emergency!"

Someone must have heard her, she thought, as she heard the main door hiss. Someone was opening it.

The door split open and a young man stumbled out. He didn't look right. His eyes were half-open, and he was stumbling around like he was drunk. He saw Angelina and lurched toward her. She ran to help him. Once she got to him, his legs gave out, and he slumped on top of her. He was too heavy for her to hold up. He fell to the floor taking Angelina with him.

"What is going on?" she said to him.

The man moaned and rolled around slowly on the floor, his eyes fluttering. Angelina smacked him. His eyelids opened for a second then fell shut again.

"What is going on? Tell me!"

She smacked him again, but all he did was moan. He was saying something. She leaned into him.

"It's all ruined," he whispered.

"What?" Angelina yelled, shaking him. "What does that mean?"

EPILOGUE: THE DAWN OF WAR

The young man's eyes opened, and he looked up. He was looking over her shoulder, as if gazing into empty space.

"What did you say?" Angelina yelled.

His eyes flicked to her and he whispered a single word:

"War."

His eyes shut, and his head lolled to the side. Angelina jumped up as if he had stung her. War? Was it Machvel again?

The door into the Clandestine Room hissed and started closing. Angelina sprinted for it and dove through as it sealed shut behind her.

The Clandestine Room, just like the one on the Onyx Pioneer, was a dark room covered in desks and computer monitors. Angelina looked around the room. At every monitor was a Security Team member hunched over. Most of the monitors showed scenes of the barren Moon or where the Onyx Pioneer parked outside the Citadel Tower. Strangely, she noted in her frantic glances at the monitors, the Onyx Pioneer wasn't there.

One monitor caught her attention the most though. She walked up to it, afraid to believe what she was seeing. She pressed the "Main Screen" button. The image transferred to the massive monitor at the front of the room.

Angelina gasped. How could he be back already? How could he have assembled his own ships? She had to tell the Professor. They were defenseless.

Angelina lurched for the door. She pressed the exit button and the door slid aside. She ran down the platform toward the air-a-vator, but suddenly she stumbled and fell. She tried to pick herself up, but her arms and legs felt like thousand pound weights. She yawned. She was so tired all the sudden. She felt like the world was pressing down on top of her.

Then, it hit her. They were all drugged! Her mind told her to get up and find Professor Goodspeed, but her body was shutting down.

Even keeping her eyes open seemed an impossible task.

She heard wind from the air-a-vator and the two women from earlier popped onto Floor 200. They moseyed up to her, wry smiles on their lips. Others appeared on the platform behind them.

"Now, my dear," said one of the women. "We'll see if that old fool can stop Dr. Machvel this time."

The two women cackled.

Must stay awake, Angelina thought. Must warn the Professor.

Must stay awake.

She realized something suddenly that sent a fresh bolt of fear through her.

Machvel was coming for them again, and Zack had no idea.

Like this book? Don't like it? Change it!

Visit *www.onyxsun.com,* where you can access and rewrite the entire text of this book.

Add characters, change plots, create new environments for Zack to explore! Then, share your writing with your friends or review the work of other people just like you.

The highest-rated work is reviewed and commented on each month by Christopher Mahoney.

To get started, just open the envelope below and use the enclosed launch code to access the growing universe of the Onyx Sun…

Acknowledgments

Many people made this book possible. To my family, thank you for your many forms of support. You helped me literally (and literarily) at every stage. Your generosity touched me very much! To Pat, thanks for being such a great friend through all the years and for being a gracious host when I first moved to California. To Kim, your love and encouragement are my bedrock. You support me in everything I do, and it means the world to me. To Rudy, you are truly gifted. I am honored to have your artwork in my book. To my favorite independent cafes and bookstores, like Coupa Café in Palo Alto, CA, the Tattered Cover in Denver, CO, Café Algiers in Cambridge, MA, and Gallery Café in San Francisco, CA. Keep the coffee strong, Internet high-speed, and power free! To JJ, Amanda, Krista, and Dan at Rogue, thanks for hosting me the many long hours I hogged a table while editing. To Katie, Colin, Deanna, Alex, Aidan, and all my early reviewers and critics, your feedback was invaluable! To Richard and Elon, for commercializing spaceflight. Your businesses are making the dream of the Onyx Sun series a reality! And most of all, to my readers, thanks for reading! Kalamazoo!

Join Zack, Max, and Sanjay as the adventure continues in:

The Wicked Adversaries of the Onyx Sun

Machvel returns stronger and more devious than before and threatens the survival of the fledgling space colony with a force far more massive than ever assembled.

Visit *www.onyxsun.com* for more information.

Coming soon!

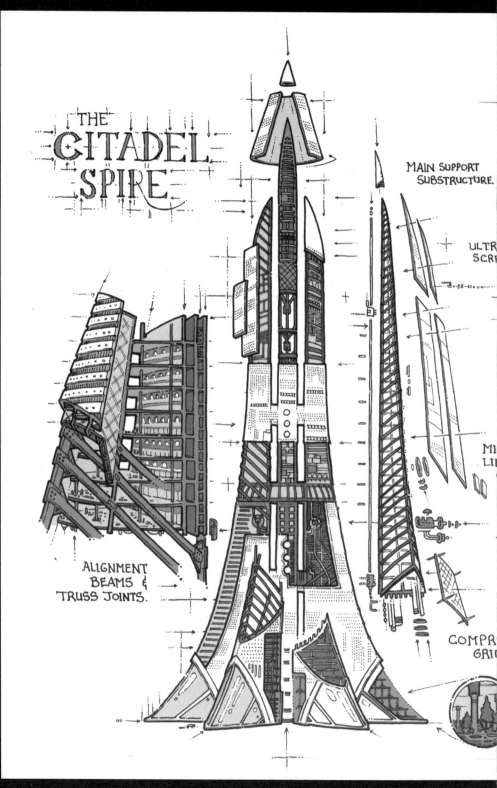